Dear Carrie —
Thank you for your continued
support. It means the world to
me, and I SWEAR I won't forget to
send you the next one as my
gift to you! Dan

Isle of a Thousand

Worlds

Book 2 of The Weirdwater

Confluence Dualogy

By Dan Fitzgerald

ISLE OF A THOUSAND WORLDS

First edition. January 15th, 2022.

Copyright © 2022 Dan Fitzgerald.

Written by Dan Fitzgerald.

Cover Art by Karkki

Cover Design by Jessica Moon

Editing by Jessica Moon & Mandy Russell

Formatting by Mandy Russell

This book contains explicit, consensual sex scenes
and is intended for adult readers only.
Keep this book away from children.
Give it to their grandparents instead.

Table of Contents

One

Patia checked the stoppers one last time, then laid out the slender vials on a rag. She rolled the cloth over the first vial twice before adding the second, repeating the process until all four were snug and secure. She wound a ribbon around the bundle to hold it tightly, then tied it off and put it in the waterproof case. Four vials of meditation tincture, though not her best, should net her sufficient coin from Endulai to make her way downriver to Rontaia, with enough left over to feed her until she could find Paoro. Whether or not she could convince him to share his secret was another matter, but she had other means to persuade him if her alchemical skills alone were not compelling enough.

If the rumors were true, Paoro, a second-rate alchemist with his head in the clouds, had somehow produced the Universal Tincture, the key to unlocking the Thousand Worlds of the mind. She'd spent the past thirty years struggling to survive by making meditation tinctures for the Endulians, with such paltry recompense she could hardly afford the time and materials to pursue the Great Work on her own. Over that time, she had developed the knowledge and skills she was sure would allow her to solve this ancient puzzle if she only had the time and money to focus on it, but Endulai's stranglehold on the market forced her to accept too little coin for far too much work. And though alchemists were secretive about the prices they'd received, Patia was convinced Endulai paid her less for her tinctures than her male colleagues.

She often daydreamed of walking into Endulai with a vial of Universal Tincture, seeing the taster's wide eyes and shocked expression as he realized what she had made. She would listen to his offer, so low as to be laughable, and politely tell him to stuff it up his metaphysical ass. If she alone held the formula, she would become rich beyond her wildest imagining, and the old boys club of Guluch alchemists would mutter in grudging recognition of her talent.

Anyone who bought her tincture could travel across the continent in their minds, connecting with whomever they wished at any time, with no need for the phony meditation training or magical tech the Endulians guarded so closely. Every city, bank, mining company, and family of painted faces would have to deal with her. Endulai would no longer hold the monopoly on the Thousand Worlds, and their precious Caravan would be relegated to a sideshow. She might even give away her formula once she'd cemented her nest egg and her legacy, just for the pleasure of watching their little fiefdom crumble.

She tucked the case into her bag, casting a last wistful glance around her shop. Filimin had agreed to look after her things, no doubt eager to test out Patia's custom-made aludel from the Silver Docks workshop. Though it pained her to leave her most prized possession behind, she had a long, uncertain journey ahead of her, and she had to travel light.

She booked passage on a boat called the *Dashi*, run by an all-female crew. It wasn't the cheapest boat at the docks, but it was the least sketchy, and the smell of cooking fish and pungent spices wafted up from the galley. It was a monthlong trip down to Rontaia, and a decent cook would make a world of difference.

A dark-skinned woman with a pink scar running down across her nose squared up to Patia and took her hand with a firm grip.

"Captain Olin, nice to meet you."

"Patia. Pleasure." She looked at Captain Olin's brawny shoulders, then up into her eyes, which were hard, but with a twinkle beneath. "You do stop off at Endulai, correct?"

"Two hours, not a minute more." Olin released Patia's hand and relaxed her posture, crossing her thick arms over her chest as she leaned against the cabin wall. "You got business at Endulai?"

"I do."

"Well, hopefully, you can get it squared away in two hours. In the meantime, let me or my crew know if you need anything, and welcome aboard the Dashi."

The passengers were a mix of tradespeople like herself and middle-ringers from Tralum and Anari. Some of them spoke the Rontai dialect among themselves, which brought a smile to Patia's lips. She hadn't been to Rontaia in decades, and she missed the exuberance and the flights of verbal fancy inherent its speech. She had once been fluent, and she still understood it well enough if someone was speaking directly to her, but she caught less than half of what they were saying to each other with all the noise of the boat. It would make a nice backdrop for her trip, and help her find the tongue more quickly, which would make finding Paoro much easier.

They reached Endulai by early afternoon. The docks were festooned with faded flowers and tattered ribbons from one of their seemingly endless ceremonial days. Patia had seldom seen the docks without some sort of decoration. The herb and flower market was in full swing, and a half-dozen alchemists waited outside the tincture tent holding bags and boxes close to their bodies.

"I'll ring this bell twice when you've got fifteen minutes left," Olin said to the passengers assembled for the stop. "If you miss the boat, you just paid thirty *lep* for a one-way trip to Endulai."

Patia wove through the children hawking sweets and charms to the flower market, where she cast a quick eye on the stalls to see if anything exotic was on offer. She didn't have the money to buy, but she liked to keep a mental inventory of what was available in case she ever needed something for one of her tinctures.

She took her place in line behind the other alchemists outside the tincture tent. They were all men, and she recognized several of them from Guluch, but only one of them, an apprentice in Thea's workshop, met her eye. He flashed a shy smile at her greeting, and she contemplated his lithe stature, the soft skin on the back of his neck, and imagined what it would be like to place just the tiniest kiss behind his

3

ear. She shook her head to clear it as the line shuffled forward. An alchemist exited the tent, his face drawn as he clutched his hand to his chest, where he had no doubt stored the coin he'd received for his wares, less than he'd expected if his frown was any indication.

Patia made it inside the tent within half an hour, moving forward as Jeno summoned her with a gentle wave. Jeno's table was flanked by two Endulian guards, who stood with fingers tented together, their faces eerily blank. Though they carried no weapons, Patia knew their hands and feet were as deadly as any blade, and their minds doubly so. The counter, a beardless little man who looked like a twelve-year-old boy, sat at a smaller table behind Jeno with his hands on a lacquered wooden box. Jeno dipped his head in a slight bow, and Patia returned the gesture.

"Patia, so nice to see you. Have the days been kind?"

"They have, but the nights have been lonely. And yourself?"

"I find my peace when I can, and embrace the chaos when I cannot." She rather liked Jeno, despite the role he played in keeping her in poverty. He looked her up and down, and his face took on a questioning look as he eyed the small case in her hands. "You have brought something?"

Patia nodded, opened the case, and laid the bundle on the table under the watchful eye of the guards.

Jeno rubbed his hands together as he untied the ribbon, his eyes alight with anticipation. "Such a small amount, I assume it must be something...special?"

"I'm sorry to disappoint you, Jeno, but I've had a bit of a setback with my quicksilver supply. I'm headed down to Rontaia for a bit, to look into some things that have caught my attention."

"I'm truly sorry to hear that," he said, unstoppering one of the vials and inserting the tiny testing spoon. "We have been quite pleased with your output of late." Patia's stomach roiled at the thought of the precious few coins they'd given her to show their alleged appreciation. He lifted the spoon beneath his nose, which wrinkled slightly. He slid the spoon into his mouth, closed his eyes for a moment, then laid the spoon in a bowl of greenish-tinted water. "Six," he said, twisting his mouth sideways. "You repurposed the quicksilver from something else?"

"A batch of antiseptic salts, and some vermilion ink." She smiled ruefully at the ease with which he'd detected her clever workaround.

4

Jeno raised his eyebrows and shook his head with a smile. "With your talent, you could come work at the Annex. The equipment we have there—"

"Yeah, I've heard all about it. How they have you watched every second, so you can't concentrate, and certainly can't come up with anything new." In truth, she would have killed to get access to the equipment in their fabled Annex, but not on their terms. "I prefer the life of a freelancer, thank you."

He held up his hands as if in self-defense. "As you wish. Fifty." He waved five fingers over his shoulder, and the little man fiddled with something on the box's lid, opened it, and laid out five stacks of coins on his table. Patia had expected forty, but she took the money without comment.

"The extra is for your troubles, which I am sorry to hear of. I hope you will come visit me on your return and show me whatever it was that drew you all the way down to Rontaia."

"Count on it. If I find what I hope to find, you're going to be seeing a whole lot more of me."

"I certainly hope so. The offer still stands, regardless. About the Annex, that is. If you were ever to change your mind."

"Never going to happen, but I appreciate it all the same." Patia bowed to him, and he inclined his head slightly in response.

A waft of grilled nut twists hit Patia as soon as she walked out of the tent, and she held her coin purse tight to her chest as she forced herself past the food stalls and made her way back to the dock. Olin stood on the deck, leaning against the cabin and smoking a cheroot. She glanced up at the water clock, then smiled at Patia through a cloud of blue-gray smoke.

"Get your business all squared away?"

Patia nodded. She didn't get the sense Olin was prying, but the look in her eyes showed she had guessed Patia practiced the Good Works.

"You been sitting on this ship the whole time?"

"The Dashi is a boat, not a ship." She pointed to one mast, then the other. "Takes three masts to be a ship. And yes, I don't leave her alone for a second. Not even at Endulai." She must have noticed Patia eyeing her cheroot, and she pulled another from a little leather case and offered it to Patia, who nodded, salivating. Olin handed it to her, along with her own cheroot, and Patia lit it, sucking the harsh, earthy

5

smoke into her cheeks and blowing it out in a thin stream. She held it up in thanks, and Olin blinked in response.

"You been to Rontaia before?" Olin asked after a long silence.

"Went to school down there for a while, then worked in one of the big workshops." Besides its arts and shipbuilding industries, Rontaia was known for its alchemical workshops, which produced good-enough tinctures at affordable prices. Patia had met Paoro in Helo's workshop there, and they'd shared a room for a time, and occasionally a bed, when Patia needed a release. He'd been the most respectful of the crew she'd spent those long, sweaty days with, and he exuded a kind of quiet magnetism. Paoro had been too timid to make any advances, but he'd never turned her down either. She wondered if that would still be true. He'd always had a cute smile, and was fun to be around when he wasn't on one of his little mystical kicks.

Patia was stirred from her reverie by the sound of the bell ringing two times. Olin tossed her cheroot stub into the water and ran her hands over her face.

"You ready to head downriver?"

Patia stubbed out her half-smoked cheroot and tucked it into her belt pouch.

"How long til we reach Rontaia?"

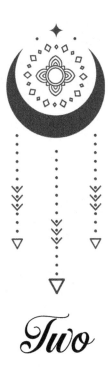

Two

Gilea burst through the coppery light and found herself standing in the central courtyard of Endulai with soft sunlight pouring through the open dome. She swayed and might have fallen, but Amini's gentle hands propped her up. The fountains burbled, the little birds chirped in the upper eaves, and a few acolytes flashed serene smiles. Gilea blinked several times, thinking the illusion would dissipate, but she was here, in the courtyard, which looked the same as it always did. The scent of jasmine reached her nose, and she closed her eyes and breathed it in. It was as rich and delicate as ever, and she turned to Amini, whose wrinkled face showed understanding.

"*It feels so real,*" Gilea said, and the acolytes nearest her looked at her with indulgent smiles.

"*You don't have to broadcast your thoughts to everyone. Let your words flow, mind to mind, as you have trained for.*"

"*Sorry, I…*" Gilea touched the leaves of a rosebush, fingered the thorns, which were as sharp as needles. "*I guess I thought I'd be able to tell the difference.*"

"*I'm not sure there is a difference.*" Amini gestured toward the nearest pool and knelt, and Gilea joined her. Two thinkfins circled the edges of the pool, turning to meet in the center, then shimmied away after barely touching, just as they did in a dozen other pools in Endulai. *"To these fish, the water is one world and the air another. Who is to say which world is more real? There are a thousand worlds, a thousand realities, but they are all connected. They are all one."* She lowered her fingers into the water, and the thinkfins swam over and brushed against them. *"You will come to see this too, given time and experience."*

"I thought the Thousand Worlds was just a metaphor."

"Just?" Amini lifted her fingers from the water, and the thinkfins resumed circling the pool, meeting in the center, touching for a moment, then repeating the cycle. *"A metaphor is as real as a stone, just as our thoughts and our souls are as real as the leaves on a tree, or the wind that moves them."*

Gilea watched the fish for a time, losing herself in their rhythm as Amini's words sank in. A breeze tickled the back of her neck, and she closed her eyes and felt it caress the fine hairs there. She heard the sound of bees humming in the nearby flowers, felt the sting of little rocks under her knees. She had often tried to picture what the Caravan would look like, how it would feel, but she had never imagined it could be so physical, so real. She opened her eyes again and focused on the pool, on the space between the thinkfins' movements, the ripples they left on the surface as they circled, touched, swirled, and circled again. She sank into the movement, letting her eyes lose their focus, and her mind soon followed. There was no pool, no fish, no dome, no courtyard, no Amini, no Gilea, only an infinite sea of interconnected currents, mixing and flowing without end.

Gilea's attention returned slowly as Amini's gentle presence surrounded her like a cloak.

"It's time we return, for now."

"So soon? It feels like we just got here."

Amini smiled, cupping Gilea's cheek with her warm, wrinkled hand.

"Most people tire after a short while on their first trip. Even for you, it's best to take one step at a time. Close your eyes and follow me."

Gilea closed her eyes, and in the darkness behind her lids, she saw the copper tunnel stretching out before her. She flowed into it, but it felt like she was leaving a part of herself behind.

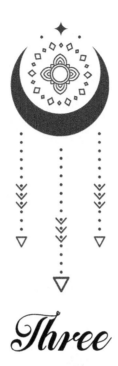

Three

Patia eyed the passengers as they returned to the Dashi, some carrying flowers, bags, and assorted goods, others empty-handed. Most of the passengers were paired up in some way or another, either couples or families or friends. There was even a group of three painted faces, though why they would be traveling on a boat such as this was a mystery. Perhaps they weren't all as rich as the rumors told. There were a few solo passengers, but one, in particular, caught her eye and stirred the itch she so badly needed to scratch. He was in his fifties, she thought, cleanish if not well-groomed, and his worn coat could not hide the sturdy build of someone used to manual labor. His fingers were those of a craftsman, strong but subtle, and his bushy beard did not entirely hide the hint of a smile he flashed her as he passed. He had noticed her attentions, but whether he was just being polite was impossible to guess.

It took Patia only three days to bed the man, a glazier named Iski returning from a big job in Anari. He was a bit more traditional than she preferred at first, but within a few days he came out of his shell a bit, and they passed many a pleasant evening together until they reached Rontaia. They got in a good hour's workout most nights

while Patia's bunkmate visited with her parents, and they mostly ignored each other during the daytime, as if by some unspoken agreement. He spent his days playing Seven Rings and cracking wise with
a group of older gentlemen who formed a quaint little cadre between
meals on the dining deck.

Patia split her time between watching the passengers on deck and
leafing through her Works book by the weak light of the porthole in
her bunk. There was nothing new to see in either case, but above as below, she discovered hidden facets to already familiar figures. The painted faces were headed to a funeral in Rontaia; one couple was on their
honeymoon; another couple had recently broken up but hovered near
each other for the entire trip, never touching, as if bound by a tether
but kept apart by repelling magnetic fields. Below deck, as she scanned
the pages of her book, her eyes lingered on the shapes and orientation
of symbols in the mystical diagrams, some of which were words, others more esoteric.

Patia had copied eight pages from a book in the workshop in
Rontaia where she'd done her apprenticeship decades before, sneaking
into Master Helo's study while he slept off his drink. It had been a risk
since everyone knew what Helo did with young women he cornered in
his study, but Patia knew the stages of his drunkenness like the most
basic alchemical formula, and he had not stirred from his stupor. She
would have felt guilty for stealing his secrets, but he was a lazy, lech-
erous slob who surely didn't deserve whatever ancient knowledge was
in that book.

She'd had no idea what most of the symbols meant, and she had
never studied ancient languages, so her copy was bound to be imperfect. Occasionally, if she stared at them long enough, she would puzzle
out the connection to a symbol she knew; she'd figured out the symbols for quicksilver, water, and fire, and a handful of others, but the
majority of them remained a mystery. She was convinced that somewhere in those eight pages, among the seemingly random arrangements of symbols and seaweed-like mystography surrounded by lines
of tiny notes, she could find something related to the Universal Tincture, if she kept coming back to look at it with an open mind.

The principle was simple enough in theory: separate the gaseous
essences of the four elements, maintaining them in incorruptible vessels, each at the appropriate temperature, then unite them in a bath of
living water under pressure. She had commissioned her alembic from

the Silver Dock workshop to accommodate just such a feat, but there were so many possible permutations for each step, each of which took time and money to try. In the last few years, she'd largely given up on the decades-long project, focusing her efforts on producing concentrated meditation tinctures for Endulai, which paid the bills with little left over to save up for the main work. There were always hitches with the supply of quicksilver or other precious ingredients, not to mention thieves, accidents, and one long bout with Ulver's cough that had put her out of commission for several months.

When the swirls had wiped out her entire supply of quicksilver, she'd raged for a few days, but once she'd recovered, she'd chosen to see it as an opportunity. She'd never achieve great Works if she kept being underpaid for her work by Endulai and scrabbling to make ends meet. If she could find Paoro and wheedle his secret from him, she had a chance to disrupt the system entirely.

Patia had taken to sitting with Olin and the crew as they drank whiskey at night under the stars, or under the roof of the dining deck when it rained. They played skip-stone, wagering mop and cleanup duty in high-stakes tournaments, or engaged in games of word play. The word games were fascinating, as they used words from many dialects of Southish, and even a few words from the languages of the southern seas. Patia never joined in the games, as they moved too fast for her, but she enjoyed the back and forth, and when the games were over, they would sit and talk until they were too drunk or sleepy to continue.

One night when the rest of the crew had gone to their bunks, Patia sat with Olin, who drank a steady stream of whiskey that would have laid low a lesser being. Olin put down her cup and looked to Patia with bright, glassy eyes.

"How's it going with your glazier friend?"

"I've had worse," Patia said with a wink. "Anyway, it's good to keep the body in shape."

Olin raised her cup and took a sip. "Think you'll keep up with him once you get to Rontaia?"

Patia waved her off, taking a larger sip than she intended, as she was fairly drunk already. "He's got a wife down there, who will be in for a few surprises when he gets back."

Olin's laugh echoed off the roof of the dining deck, and she covered her mouth with a guilty look. "I expect you'll have business to attend to anyway." She was fishing, and Patia was feeling unusually loose with the whiskey in her system.

"I do at that. I'm looking for a man I knew long ago, who I'm hoping has need of my skills."

Olin raised her eyebrows a little, but she said nothing. Patia could tell Olin knew she was an alchemist, or had some idea anyway, and she didn't figure there was any harm in sharing a little with this boat captain.

"He's in the same business as me, you know, and rumor has it he's made some kind of breakthrough with one of his tinctures, but he never had the precision to pull off much by himself. So, I figured I'd see if he could use a pair of skilled hands."

Olin poured another two fingers in her cup and one finger in Patia's. She leaned back in her chair so far Patia was sure she would tip over, drunk as she was, but she did not, and when her chair landed flat again, she put down her cup and looked up at Patia, her face twisted with something like mischief.

"You said he lacked the...precision to pull it off by himself. So, how'd he make this breakthrough then, do you think?"

Patia looked down in her cup with blurry eyes, wondering if she was drinking the same whiskey as Olin. "That's exactly what I'm going down there to find out, and I won't take no for an answer." She smushed her index finger into a puddle of water on the table. "You know, that's just why I got on this...beautiful boat. You should be really proud by the way. This is a nice sh—boat."

"She is." Olin raised her glass and took a sip, and Patia followed suit, slapping the table as the whiskey burned down to her stomach and most of the way back up. "But you were saying?"

"Yes, well, Paoro, that's this guy's name, I probably shouldn't tell you but who the hell cares? He's a really sweet guy, funny as hell in his odd little way, and he knows his theory, but he never could get the little things right, you know? The...the tiny details that make all the difference. Idiot!" Patia drained the last few drops from her cup, waving the proffered bottle away as she choked down a belch. It turned her stomach to think about someone like Paoro succeeding where she and so many others far more talented than he had failed.

"So, what, you think he had help?"

12

"Could be, but he's hard to work with because he's suuuch a flake, you wouldn't believe. No, I think," Patia said, steadying herself with both palms on the table, "he discovered it by accident, which is highly unlikely, or he got the tincture from somebody else." Patia winced as her stomach gave a little heave, but she breathed out slowly and held it together.

"Well, I hope you find him, and I hope he's not completely useless."

The river widened to over two miles as they approached the outskirts of Rontaia, becoming tidal, and the briny breeze lifted Patia's spirits. Even the most squalid corners of Rontaia benefitted from the salty air, which scoured away the city's many pungent odors, unlike Guluch, where the stench of chemicals and decay hung over everything like a filthy shawl. They followed the shipping flags between the islands, moving on oar power alone. The rhythmic grunts of the crew and the oars squealing in their locks formed a chaotic harmony with the squawks of seagulls and the crash of waves against the boat's sides. Patia marveled at the unbelievable sprawl of waterside shanties spread for miles along both sides of the river, seeming to have doubled since she was last here. Patia had once worked a delivery boat for alchemical supplies, and she smiled as she saw the thin plumes of smoke from the alchemists' forges. She could almost see the sweaty old men working their bellows, one eye on the fire and another on some concoction bubbling on an oil burner. For an instant, she even thought she caught a whiff of red sulfur carried by the breeze across the water.

Olin's crew maneuvered the boat into a tight spot on a crowded dock, where an inspector with the signature red and yellow striped hat stood with a ledger and pencil, squinting to see the boat's name, then waving at Olin with his pencil hand. Patia and Iski exchanged a nod from across the mob of passengers crushing against each other by the gangplank as Captain Olin stood by, exchanging words and sometimes handshakes with them as they left the boat. Patia was last in line, and Olin gave her a firm handshake, putting her other hand on Patia's shoulder.

"It's been a pleasure. I'm on a three-month rotation, so if you're looking for a ride back up to Guluch, you can find me in three, or six.

Just check with the harbormaster."

"I'll do that. Thanks for a safe trip."

Patia waved and walked across the gangplank, which rose and fell gently with the waves. She clutched her bag to her chest and kept her eyes mostly down as she waded through the throngs. The smell of fresh tri-fries weakened her knees and her resolve, and she dropped a couple of *nomi* in the vendor's hand in exchange for a golden-brown triangle so hot she had to keep moving it from hand to hand. She cracked off a corner in her teeth, keeping her mouth open for a moment so she wouldn't burn her tongue, then closed her eyes as her mouth exploded with hot, eggy, honey-and-cinnamon goodness.

It was good to be back in Rontaia.

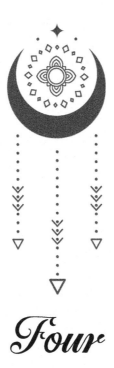

Four

Gilea's throat twitched at a drop of the tincture that hadn't quite made its way down, but she steeled herself against the burn as she lay back in the cradle and pulled the circlet over her head. She closed her eyes as the acolyte lay the heavy blanket over her, and she felt Amini's reassuring presence guiding her through the darkness and into the tunnel of light. She drifted through the coppery portal with a little more control this time, stumbling just a bit as her feet touched the sandy stone floor of the warmly lit chamber. Two men lay in parallel reed hammocks hung from carved wooden poles, swaying gently, their fingers locked together. They turned their heads lazily toward Gilea and blinked a vague greeting. Another man approached, wearing an orange cloth draped over his shoulder and wrapped around his waist. His olive tan skin glowed in the light of the stained-glass lanterns that dotted the walls. His smile grew wide as he held out his arms toward Amini, who did the same, both of them squeezing the air but reacting as if the hug had been physical. He turned to Gilea, bowing with hands at heart center, and she bowed back at him.

"Gilea, so good to finally meet you. I am Tiru. Welcome to Guluch!" He spread his arms wide as if displaying a great treasure, though all Gilea

could see was a round room with hammocks and couches around the edges and a small terra cotta furnace in the center. Muskwood incense burned in a brazier atop the furnace, whose warmth relaxed Gilea's face into a comfortable smile.

"*It's a pleasure to be here*," Gilea said, and the two men in the hammocks glanced over with bemused and slightly disapproving looks. "*Sorry,*" she said, narrowing her focus to Tiru and Amini, and the men returned to their staring contest.

"*No sorries or worries here. Come, relax here on the couch, or would you rather sit on the veranda?*"

"*The veranda, I should think.*" Amini flashed a tight smile, and Tiru turned, stretching his arm toward an arched doorway.

Gilea followed him, her feet feeling every grain of sand on the stone as she walked through the doorway onto a spacious terrace. She looked over the wooden railing, and far below saw a wide blue river lined with dense forest on either side, broken up by creeks and wetlands like fingers spreading through the green. Tiru slung himself onto a couch next to a long table, and Gilea sat in a deep cane chair with cushions that snuggled her body. Amini sat in a plain chair, leaning her elbows on the table and looking Tiru in the eyes.

"*So are we here on business or pleasure?*" Tiru smiled, looking from Amini to Gilea, then back to Amini. Gilea knew the Caravan was used to arrange business deals, but she wondered about the pleasure part.

"*Instruction.*" Amini tilted her head toward Gilea. "*But a little pleasure surely wouldn't do her any harm. Gilea is learning how to travel the Caravan and trying to build up her stamina. She's a quick study, as you can see; she's already more comfortable here than some of our more seasoned travelers. Given a bit more practice, she'll be going solo before we know it.*"

Amini's words warmed Gilea to the core. She did feel comfortable in the Caravan, perhaps more so than in the almost sterile calm of Endulai.

"*And what is your pleasure, Gilea?*" Tiru's wide eyes and open expression put Gilea fully at ease, and she sank back into the chair's cushions.

"*I've never been to Guluch before, but you know what they say about it. I was thinking maybe you could show me the other side?*" The texture of the crossroad was so real, down to the subtlest scents and sounds, and she found herself desperate to explore, to experience more and more of this magical world the Endulians in Guluch had somehow created with the power of their minds.

16

Tiru rubbed his hands together, his eyes sparkling with excitement. "*Now that would be my pleasure.*" He turned and motioned with his chin to someone across the veranda and held up three fingers. "*But first, you've got to try the newest dockside cooler.*" A young woman no older than twenty arrived with a tray and set three copper-rimmed glasses on the table, filled with a slushy purple concoction, with slices of green citrus impaled in the rims.

Tiru raised his glass, and Gilea and Amini followed suit.

"*To the confluence of worlds,*" he murmured.

"*To the confluence of worlds,*" she found herself saying in time with Amini.

"*This is a recreation of what the Agra would have looked like before humans settled it.*" Tiru's hand swept slowly across the horizon as he leaned against the boat's railing, and Gilea felt a spark of wistfulness in his thoughts.

Gilea watched a pair of huge coppertails cruising side by side along the edge of a field of water lilies. "*The water's so clear.*"

"*Yes. We don't know if it was as clear as this, but it surely wasn't as muddy as it is today. And I find this clarity soothing.*"

"*And you can just...make it any way you want?*"

"*Pretty much.*" He shrugged, flashing a melancholy smile. "*It takes a bit of work to make structural changes, but you can design a crossroad however you like. We tried to capture the essence of Guluch, what it must have once been like, what it could be again. What it is now, deep down, if you know how to look.*"

"*Well, it's beautiful. Reminds me a bit of a place I once visited.*" Gilea felt Tiru's curiosity, but she did not share. She had promised to keep the Living Waters in her heart and out of her mouth, or in this case, the part of her mind she used to communicate in the Caravan.

The boat moved with gentle splashes of twin waterwheels, though the wheels were turning too slowly to account for the movement of the boat.

"*It's an homage to the designs of our greatest inventor, the late Dirié, who dreamed up all sorts of mechanical contraptions, inspired by the legends of the great automatons of old.*" Tiru's eyes grew distant, his smile tinged with sadness. "*She would have powered it with burning coal, but no one was ever able to figure out how to make the pressurized furnace required. No doubt many of our tinkerers and scientists are working on it as we speak; it's a perennial training ex-*

ercise in our universities and academies."

"And all I knew of Guluch was the brick and tin factories and the soma dens."

"We have those too, of course. The economy has to run on something."

"I suppose it does." Gilea paused, thinking of Endulai, its great ease, which could only come from great wealth. What was the basis for its economy? How did it acquire the sunstones, the tinctures, the building materials, the food? She had only ever seen money change hands in the markets outside the walls. Inside the holy city, there was no commerce of any kind, yet no one seemed to want for anything.

Gilea felt Amini's pulse in her head, summoning her. She wanted to protest; she felt fine, not fatigued in the slightest, and the thought of leaving this place left her feeling suddenly deflated.

Amini nodded to Tiru. *"I think it's time we took our leave."*

"So soon? It's a pity. I was going to show you the alchemical laboratory. It's still under construction, but I love what the designers have done with it. I could get lost staring at the charts, the pictures, and the elaborate glass and copper devices. Perhaps another time?"

"Another time." Gilea felt Amini's mind wrap around hers, and she closed her eyes and drifted away from Tiru, the boat, and the river. Darkness surrounded her, and she glided through it, following a faint coppery trail, which expanded into a wide ribbon twisting through space. The ribbon curled into a tube, and she flowed through it, losing her sense of place and self. At last, she burst out the other end, crashing into her body, which convulsed and sat bolt upright. She heaved for breath as she tore the circlet from her head. The acolyte took the circlet and offered her a cup of water, which she drank. It was fragrant with orange blossoms and fortified with a dose of some sweet liqueur. She downed the cup, and her breath slowly fell into a normal rhythm.

"You need to work on your landing," Amini remarked, leaning on the edge of the bronze latticework of Gilea's cradle. "It will come with time. You just have to imagine yourself falling, light as a feather, as you feel the suction at the end of the tunnel."

Gilea nodded. She could almost see what Amini meant; there had been a change in pressure just before she'd been dumped back into her body.

When can we do it again? The thought appeared in her head, but she kept it inside, hoping Amini had not noticed.

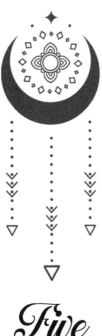

Five

Patia wandered along the docks, away from the vendors and beggars and the swelling crowds of travelers. Seagulls patrolled the barrier between the busy passenger docks and the cargo docks, where mule-drawn carts lined up waiting for their loads to be removed before moving to another line to be filled again. Inspectors with brown and yellow striped hats moved between the two lines, scribbling on clipboards and checking documents. Patia paused to watch the dockers load and unload the carts, their muscles glistening in the bright sun. She used to hang out at one of the dockside bars when she was in school and short on coin, and the dockers were usually happy enough to buy her a drink. They were a lively crowd, and she enjoyed their shouting over table games and occasional singing of direful sea ballads when they were too far in their cups. And once in a while, she'd go home with one, which was a nice change of pace from the oh-so-polite young men in the natural philosophy crowd.

She walked past the mile-wide swath of cargo docks, continuing along the worn boardwalk leading toward the artisanal docks, where hundreds of small-time smiths, brewers, tanners, and alchemists plied their crafts in rickety waterside shacks not too different from her own setup in Guluch. She counted the coin in her pocket with her fingers; she had a little over thirty *lep*, enough for maybe a month in a boarding-house, if her estimate of Rontaian prices was correct. If she couldn't find Paoro right away, she would need to find work. She hoped one of the alchemists on the artisanal docks would take her on as an assistant, though finding one who'd respect her craft might be a challenge.

She rejected the first three boardinghouses she found, settling on one set back in the warren of streets in the Lowers, which had a sign reading "Women only." She'd been through enough close calls in her days in Rontaia that it was a relief to have one less thing to worry about. Though it was shabby and smelled of sewage, the floor had been swept and there was fresh straw on the bunk. She slipped the matron an extra *nomi* to keep watch over her things and set out to look for Paoro.

She spent several days with aching feet and an increasingly weary soul wearing out the boards of the artisan docks and the cobbles of the Lowers, and another in the dusty Chemist Market, asking anyone she could get up the courage to approach if they knew of Paoro. Most steered clear of her, and she didn't blame them, as her dirty clothes and the odor of her unwashed body no doubt made her seem like a beggar. The minority who took the time to answer just shook their heads, and only a few wished her good luck. She got the familiar impression of being an outsider at an old boys' club; even if they knew Paoro, they weren't likely to give her any information.

As she trudged across the artisan docks one evening, the smell of sulfur and sage hit her from a dockside shack wedged in between a blacksmith and a tanner. She approached the doorway, blocked only by a tattered curtain made of scraps of sails stitched together. She heard the huff of a bellows, the sound of a fire being poked, and some cursing. She smiled and pulled the curtain aside.

"Close the damned curtain! The light will ruin my infusion!" grumbled a crooked little man pumping a bellows with one hand and arranging coals with a hearth shovel in the other.

"The light won't make a damned bit of difference," she said, letting the curtain fall behind her, "but if you don't spread out those coals evenly, you'll burn the bottom and have to start all over."

"Well grab a spoon and start stirring if you know so much." His grumble warmed and he gestured toward a wooden stand on a nearby table. Patia picked a flat-bottomed spoon and moved to the man's side, finding the bottom of the kettle and scraping the light film that had already formed.

"It's a good thing I got here when I did. The bottom's started to stick. But I've got it scraped now."

"I was getting to it," he said, spreading the coals a bit wider and letting the bellows deflate.

She paused, sniffing the concoction, which was grayish-yellow in color, with clumps of sage floating amid foaming bubbles. There was something unusual, beyond the sage and sulfur, that she couldn't quite place. The man watched her intently as he stood up, keeping one hand on his lower back and bracing himself on the table with the other.

"This is some kind of tincture for digestive problems?"

He grinned, showing a mouth surprisingly full of teeth. "You're not far off, except it's something else entirely." All traces of irritation were gone from his demeanor. "But I don't even know your name, so why would I tell you anything?"

"It's Patia, and you'd only tell me if you thought I could help."

He looked her up and down, his eyes lingering on her bag. "I don't suppose you've got an aludel in there? My middle tube is cracked, and I haven't had time to take it apart and fix it."

"I don't, but I'm pretty good with ceramics. I'll have a look if you like, and see what I can do."

He nodded, studying her face, squinting, as if trying to discern her intentions. "Gero," he said, extending his hand. "And what would you be looking for in return?"

Patia woke with a stiff neck and aching hips from sleeping on a thin mat on the floor with a rolled-up shirt for a pillow, but there was only one bed and she hadn't sensed any inclination on Gero's part to share his space or whatever might be left of his libido. She did catch him peeking as she struggled into the one change of clothes she had brought, and she didn't let on that she'd noticed. Though he wasn't really her type, who knew if their arrangement might take on a more intimate turn, one in which she might actually sleep in a bed instead of on the

21

floor? Gero slept with one pillow under his head and his arms wrapped around another; maybe if she played her cards right, she could at least get a pillow out of him.

She walked to squat in the corner where a hole in the floor sat over the river's edge, though it was low tide and there was nothing but wet sand and rock to catch her waste. Gero averted his eyes, then turned back around once she'd finished, sitting up and stretching his wrinkled arms at a crooked angle. His back curved slightly to the left, and he stretched his torso this way and that until at last Patia heard a gruesome pop, and he let out a noisy sigh and stood up.

"I've got some of yesterday's bread in the box, assuming the mice haven't found their way into it again." He gestured to a battered tin box on a table, and Patia opened it to find a meager half-loaf of bread that was limp in the middle and the wrong kind of crusty on the outside. She tore the loaf and handed the larger half to him, keeping the smaller portion for herself. She nodded as her jaws worked the bread into something she could eventually swallow.

"If you can fix the aludel while I distill, you can stay another night and I'll help you find your friend. What did you say his name was again?"

"Paoro."

Gero's bushy eyebrows raised slightly, but he said nothing.

She had the aludel patched up and drying above the furnace by noon, while Gero worked the alembic with a gentle flame to distill the yellow liquid to a dark, cloudy syrup like urine left in the sun too long. He collected the purified water into a copper jar and screwed the lid tight, then poured the syrupy liquid into a small pot, which he placed over the same flame and began adding various ingredients. He worked with his back to her at all times, no matter where she moved. He clearly didn't entirely trust her, not that she could blame him. A strange woman showing up unexpectedly to help with his Works must have seemed rather suspicious. It took a while for her to puzzle together what he was doing. He added some kind of oil, as well as a modest amount of white powder, possibly white lead, stirring the concoction with care. Every so often he would lift the copper spoon from the pot and watch the creamy mixture ooze off the spoon until at last he scraped it against the edge of the pot and moved it off the flame.

"Skin cream?" Patia asked. Gero's eyes twinkled, but he kept his mouth closed. "For the painted faces?"

Gero nodded, at last, shaking a finger at her. "You are far too good to have traveled across the continent for no reason. Be a dear and bring me that ceramic jar, the one with the lead lid."

Patia brought him the jar, letting her fingers brush against his as she handed it off. His eyes blazed with amusement for a moment, then he set to work transferring the creamy mixture into the jar. He wiped the jar with a rag, then inked a stamp and pressed it onto the lid, leaving a mark like a circle with a line through the middle, surrounded by an elaborate G.

"Salt, for purity, and G for your name," Patia said. Gero showed all his strong teeth in a smile.

"Precisely. I have four more like this to make. If you want to help, I'll cut you in." He held up a stern finger. "Ten percent, after expenses. I could do this myself, you know."

Patia smiled and extended her hand. "Deal." She could hardly believe her luck.

Gero held her hand for a moment after shaking, and his grip showed a strength that belied his age and appearance. His eyes stayed with hers as he let go, then shook his head and gestured toward the pot.

"If you don't mind, wash this and we'll get started on the next batch. I'll tend to the fire."

Patia picked up the pot and various utensils, brushing against him with her hip as she walked to the end of the dock, where the water was just high enough that she could rinse the pot if she leaned all the way over the edge.

They walked several miles, past the passenger docks, where Patia bought some tri-fries for them both, despite Gero's protest that she save her coin. They cut through the narrow streets toward the Chemist Market, seated at the base of Brachys Hill, where the city's elite lived in luxurious dwellings overlooking the city and the ocean. The market was set to open within the hour, and vendors were setting up at long tables, some in the already hot sun, others under tents. Gero gave a *lep* to one of the market admins and received a wooden placard with the number two hundred sixty-three on it. Patia's mind was flooded with memories of her days as an apprentice, hauling and setting up Master Helo's wares, then delivering his coin to him, which he counted with malicious deliberateness.

They wove their way through the tents until they found the number on a table in the sun, next to a young man with a ridiculous curling mustache laying out vials of tincture on a square of black velvet. He wore the green robes of a newly minted premier apprentice, though apparently, no one had told him the robes were for the ceremony only. He returned their greeting with a stiff smile he probably thought made him seem aloof and mysterious. Patia was ready to dislike him, but the color and consistency of his tinctures looked right, so she granted him a silent pardon for his foolishness.

"Three of these are earmarked for the Deiyarrhs, one of the oldest families of painted faces in the city." Gero took three jars out of his bag and set them on the table. "With any luck, we can sell them the other two, or perhaps get a reference." He set to work laying a dozen wooden tubes on the table, painted crimson with fine black lines in the shape of flames.

Patia picked up one of the tubes, pulled the cork, and sniffed. It smelled like alcohol, cinnamon, mint, and soma.

"An aphrodisiac?" she asked with a smirk.

"Don't laugh. They work, and most importantly, they *sell*."

"Maybe with any luck we won't sell them all."

Gero took the tube from her hand, corked it, and laid it back on the table. He looked up at her, his brown eyes squinting against the sun, his face twisted into an odd smile.

"If you want to sleep with me, no aphrodisiac will be required. I find you desirable, and if you can tolerate me, I see no reason why we can't have a bit of fun. There's no need for suggestion or subterfuge."

"So you prefer the direct approach, then?" Patia moved to lean against him, running her hand around his neck and down his shirt, until he took her wrist and removed it, gently but firmly.

"I prefer the private approach, particularly when my clients are headed this way." He held onto her arm to stand up, bumping her playfully with his hip as he did so.

"Here comes Mrs. Deiyarrh, with her wife and daughter, and her fiancé." He licked his lips, straightening up the jars on the table. Patia watched the four painted faces drift out of the tented area, putting up their hands against the sun, despite their wide-brimmed hats and gauzy veils. The two women were not quite Patia's age, and their daughter held the arm of a thin man who walked with a fragile gait. Their faces were painted in complementary shades of blue and purple, and Patia wondered if they coordinated their colors. The crowds parted at their approach, perhaps less out of deference than disdain.

"Stand back behind me and don't say anything. These are long-standing clients and they don't like surprises."

Patia sighed audibly, moving a few steps back as the painted faces approached the table.

"Punctual as always, Master Gero," said one of the women, whose face was painted sky blue.

"I wouldn't want to keep you waiting in this sun." He gestured toward the sky. "It's going to be a hot one."

"Isn't it always?" the woman commented, snapping open her purse and laying a neat stack of ten-*lep* coins on the table.

Gero slid the three jars toward her, and she passed them to her daughter, who put them in her bag. "I have two more, in case you'd like to stock up."

"Not today," she said, half turning away, "but I'll put a good word in."

"Thank you, and may the winds blow cool upon your face."

"And on yours, Master Gero." Her gray eyes flashed to Patia for a moment, then she turned and led her charges back toward the tents.

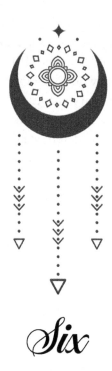

Six

Gilea studied the tincture in the vial, which glowed pale pink in the reflected light of the wall lamps. It was thinner than the meditation tinctures, and smelled faintly of rosehips, though its taste was as bitter as bile.

"You won't need to be fully immersed," Amini said, laying the weighted blanket over Gilea's body as she lay back in the cradle. "You can switch your attention between the Inkwell and this room, though it takes a bit of practice. Once you get the hang of it, you can write the messages yourself, but for the first time, you'll have to dictate it. Hopefully, you'll get a patient operator."

"And how long do I have before the tincture wears off?"

"About ten minutes, which is all the time they'll give you anyway. You'll be able to send your message, but unless she's right there, you won't get your response until later."

Gilea swallowed to clear the last bit of the foul tincture that lined her throat, took a deep breath, and nodded. Amini laid the circlet on her head and lowered her hand over Gilea's forehead.

"Just relax, and set your destination firmly in your mind. The cradle should do the rest."

Gilea closed her eyes and pictured herself on the boat with Temi, their hands touching as they approached the twisting spires of Anari. Her heart warmed, and her mind followed as she felt the pressure of Temi's forehead on her own. The spot of wet chill when she pulled away, the residue of Temi's paint on her skin. The ache in her heart as she watched Temi climb into the carriage, their eyes holding tight to each other's until the carriage turned and was swallowed up in traffic.

Gilea felt lost and alone as the city bustled around her, but a warm light glowing from the top of one of the spires drew her attention, and she floated up, moved by a steady, unseen force. She braced as she approached the light, and felt the change of pressure, but it was gentler this time. She emerged with only the faintest jolt and found herself sitting on a comfortable leather chair facing a bald person behind a desk. The contours of the space around them were hazy and out of focus, but she got the impression there were other chairs and other desks with persons sitting behind them. The operator looked up from a ledger, flashing a curt smile.

"*Welcome to the Anari Inkwell. Could you please tell me your name and crossroad?*"

"*Gilea Harkoven, from Endulai. I have a message for Temithea Fluellin.*" She felt Amini's reassuring hand on her shoulder, and could almost see her out of the corner of her mind, but she returned her focus as the operator wrote in the ledger.

"*I'm all ears.*" They smiled pleasantly, and Gilea could sense they knew it was her first time, but she tried not to let it bother her.

"*Tell her...*" Gilea faltered, her throat catching as the words she had so carefully prepared flew from her mind like released butterflies. Amini's hand pressed gently into her shoulder, and she brought her mind back into focus. "*Tell her things are well in Endulai and I...I think of her often.*"

The operator smiled as their quill scratched on the ledger. They looked up with arched eyebrows and a bemused expression on their face.

"*Anything else?*"

Gilea squeezed her eyes tight to stop the tears from forming. "*I would like to speak with her if she's available, in one week's time, at sundown.*"

The operator scribbled for a moment, then turned to another ledger, flipping the pages and scanning. They nodded, writing something in the second ledger.

"*Very good.*" They laid their quill in a tray and folded their hands on the desk. "*If there's nothing else...*"

Gilea shook her head, and the operator began to fade. Gilea was drawn away from the room, briefly glimpsing Anari's many rings from on high before they too dimmed, and her awareness returned to the cradle. She opened her eyes and saw Amini's benevolent face beaming down at her.

"Your attachment to this Temi is quite strong. Does she practice too?"

Gilea sat up, feeling only slightly lightheaded. "No, but she has..." She struggled to find the words. "We have shared minds."

Amini's brow furrowed, though her smile did not fade. "In the Living Waters?"

Gilea nodded, looking down for a moment. She had promised not to share about the *sitri* and the *ipsis*, but she sensed Amini already knew. "She showed remarkable aptitude."

"Perhaps she will be drawn to practice. The temple in Anari is quite welcoming, despite the prejudices common in that city."

Gilea pushed herself to stand, feeling surprisingly stable. The effects of the Inkwell tincture were much less intense than the Caravan tinctures.

"Tea in the garden?" Amini said with arched eyebrows. "Though the Inkwell does not take it out of you the same way as the Caravan, I find I need a few moments of contemplation afterward to re-seat myself, so to speak."

"That sounds like perfection."

Gilea followed as Amini retrieved her copper key and fitted it into the hole in the floor. The bronze door swung open, and they passed through the entry room, out into the curving hallways of the interior dome, the light from above growing brighter as they wound their way toward the center garden.

"In a week, if she joins me—"

"She will join you. With the bond you have, she will not miss the chance."

Gilea's heart fluttered at Amini's words. "When she joins me, will I...will I see her?"

Amini stopped in the arched doorway that led into the round space of the center garden, where the afternoon sun poured a rich, warm light across the white stone. Several dozen people sat or lay around its many pools, and the only sounds were the burbling of fountains and the chirping of birds echoing off the walls. Amini leaned in with her forehead, and Gilea joined her.

"You may see her, or you may not. It depends on the strength of her aptitude. Do not be disappointed if you can't see her the first time. But with practice, you may be able to see and hear each other as if you were in the same room. In some cases, even touch is possible."

Gilea felt lightheaded as their foreheads pulled apart, but not from the mindshare. She had grown accustomed to that. Her forehead tingled, in the irregular spot where Temi's paint had been, and she channeled the sensation into her heart, willing herself to accept it, as it was. The feeling stayed with her throughout her meditation, but as the tea and the tinkling water and the twittering of the birds wove a cocoon of tranquility around her, she settled around the space Temi occupied inside her and found a measure of peace.

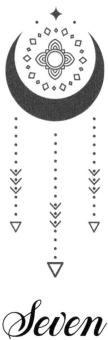

Seven

Patia listened to Gero snore for a while as he napped, his mouth half-open in a faint smile. She shook her head gently as a twinge of affection for this ridiculous little man sparked in her heart. She slipped through the curtain and headed toward the Lowers, her feet leading her unerringly through the sprawling shantytowns between the docks and the brick-lined streets of the city. She gripped her wicked little knife just inside her sleeve, her index finger in the grip hole and her thumb atop the blunt edge of the blade. She didn't know if crime in Rontaia had gotten better or worse since she was last here, but she didn't intend to take any chances.

The city seemed to ignore her, and her heart felt light with the freedom of wandering alone in a city at once strange and familiar. She slowed as she reached the zigzagging stairs leading up over the mounded wall that was supposed to protect the Lowers from storm surges. Almost every year they found their way through, leaving the inhabitants drenched in water thick with sewage and debris, the smell of which would linger long after the floodwater drained away.

"Donation for the people, ma'am?" The young Endulian acolyte bowed with palms pressed together, staying a respectful ten feet away.

Patia ignored him, but that didn't stop him from wishing her "a day filled with peace and harmony." The Endulian sect in Rontaia was a far cry from the hermetic practices of Endulai, but at least they kept their distance. She glanced over at the yellowed dome of the Endulian temple at the center of the Lowers, and a smile grew on her face.

The tinctures of the Rontaian alchemists were often of lower purity than those of Guluch and Tralum. Gero didn't seem to meddle in meditation tinctures, but he had the setup and enough money to fund the first batch if he were willing. She was sure her tinctures were far superior to what was commonly produced here, though the Rontaian temple was known to be even stingier with its coin than Endulai. But some of the ingredients were more plentiful here, and living was cheap enough, so she was sure she could make a go of it if it came to that.

Patia found the building housing Paoro's family apartment easily enough, crammed in among newer structures in the apparently now chic Lees Quarter. A tailor's shop next door sported elaborate ball gowns in its windows in the traditional black and pink colors of the *Noxi* month, with the requisite skulls and poisoned daggers peppered throughout. An inn across the street had a dining room open to the street and a beer garden that overflowed onto the sidewalk and the narrow spaces between buildings. A vendor hawking "piping hot, sweet and spicy" tri-fries served a line of university students taking their leisure between classes.

Patia's heart twinged at the sight; forty years ago, she would have been standing in that line, though there were never any sweet and spicy tri-fries back in those days. She watched the body language of the students, their unsubtle flirtation, wistful tears surging in her eyes. When the money had run out and Patia had been forced to look for work instead of finishing her degree, she'd missed the studies, but more than that she'd missed the camaraderie, the late nights drinking, the easy hookups. The alchemy sweatshops were dull and dreary places with precious few prospects, which was how she'd gotten mixed up with Paoro in the first place.

The door to the foyer was locked, so she rang the weathered bell that hung from a dried-out leather strap above the door. A girl of about eight poked her head out of a window above, turning to look behind her as someone inside called out "Who the hell is it?"

"I don't know, mum. It's some old lady."

"Is she a beggar?"

31

"I...I don't think so..." the girl cocked her head to study Patia. "You're not a beggar, are you?"

"Idiot," Patia muttered under her breath, then forced her best smile, which probably wasn't very convincing.

"Of course not, dear. I'm just looking for an old friend. A colleague, name of Paoro."

The girl scrunched her eyebrows, then shook her head almost imperceptibly before turning halfway around and shouting: "Mum, do you know anyone named Paoro?"

A laugh echoed out, quickly becoming a cough before turning back into a laugh. A woman peered out of the window, her hair pinned up like a crazed flame atop her head.

"Paoro hasn't lived here for about five years," she said, looking Patia up and down. "Came into some money or something, bought a place in the Bluffs I think. Least that's what he said, but he was never known for being overly truthful."

"That he wasn't," Patia agreed. "You wouldn't happen to know anyone else who might still be in touch?"

"Why, is he your long-lost boyfriend or something?" The woman bumped the girl with her shoulder, and they shared a giggle.

"For a mercifully short time, but that's not what I'm here about."

The woman took in a sharp breath and held up a finger, which she moved slowly toward the girl's face. "She must be one of those alchemists," she said, touching the girl's nose as she finished her sentence. "Isn't that right, Ms...what's your name anyway?"

"Patia, and yes, that's right." Rontaians were rather blasé about those who practiced the Good Works, unlike those in Guluch, who tended to take a more superstitious view of the profession. "I need to find him for some super-secret alchemist stuff," she said, winking at the girl.

"Well, I don't have the slightest clue where he's got to, and he always kept to himself. You might try poking around at the Chemist Market, or on the artisanal docks. Name's Genipi, by the way, and this is little Lot."

"Well, thanks all the same, Genipi, and of course Miss Lot."

The woman turned suddenly and let out a sigh as she disappeared from the window. "My eggs are burning. Best of luck!" she called. Lot took another long look at Patia, then turned away from the window, watching her mother with serious eyes.

Patia heard Gero humming as she approached the curtain, and she peeked through before entering. His head was bobbing as he lifted tiny fish out of a bucket one at a time and laid them in what must have been hot oil, from the way he pulled his fingers away each time. The tune he was humming was familiar, but it took her a minute to realize where she knew it from. It was the lamentation from the Seven Sins of Balthus, though his humming wove in a few major keys, making it surprisingly uplifting. The oil sizzled and spattered as he laid another of the little fish in the pot, and the smell hit her right in the gut. She realized she hadn't had a bite to eat since the crust of bread this morning.

"Come, come, they're almost done," he said, dropping two more fish into the oil and wiping his hands on a rag, then stirring the pot with a wire fry-spoon. "I don't suppose you picked up any bread?"

"No, I didn't. Idiot!" Patia cursed herself.

"There's a baker's cart just up the dock. I heard him pass by a few minutes ago. You'll find five *lep* in that basket there."

"I can cover the bread," Patia said, her fingers clutching her meager purse. Except for the tri-fries, she'd hardly spent any money, but her margin for error was tissue-thin.

"Yes, you can, with your cut from the skin cream. Ten percent, after expenses, just like we agreed." He gestured toward the basket, and her fingers slid over the coins, scooping them into her purse, which suddenly felt less desperately light.

"Thank you," she said, feeling a genuine smile bloom on her face, despite her best efforts to twist it into a smirk. Something about Gero's matter-of-factness had cracked her façade.

"Thank me by getting some bread before these fish get cold."

When she returned with the bread, the table was set with a tattered scarf as a tablecloth, a bowl of the little fried fish, a crusty bottle of yayay pepper sauce, and a stubby candle. The pots, jars, and vials had been moved onto a crowded shelf to make room.

"Well aren't you the charmer," she said, sliding onto the bench opposite Gero, whose smile beamed from the depths of his beard.

"I am a simple man, but I like to think I do simple well. Lavender wine?" He unstoppered a bottle and poured two glass distillation vials full of the wine, which had the faintest purplish tint in the light reflected off the river. He handed one to her and raised his, clinking her vial. "To our fortuitous encounter."

Patia's foot found his under the table as she drank, trying not to down the whole vial in one gulp.

By the time they'd finished the fish, the bottle, and most of the bread, Patia's head felt warm and fuzzy, and the warmth spread down her body. She'd spent the meal touching Gero with her hands and feet as often as she could, and he neither shied away from her touch nor reciprocated, but the hint of a smile and a glimmer in his eye gave him away. He was hers for the taking, and though he wasn't her usual type, she found she wanted him in a way she had not felt in a long time. She took his hand in hers. It was soft and warm, and his fingernails were well trimmed and clean. He gripped her fingers, then raised them to his lips and kissed them, though Patia felt more beard than flesh. She slid her fingers up his wrist, and he breathed out a long sigh as his eyes fluttered closed. She grasped his forearms and pulled him toward her, leaning over the table and finding his lips with hers among the underbrush. He hovered for a moment, then sat back, flipping his hands over and laying them over the back of hers.

"I'm seriously considering whether this may be some kind of dream or hallucination." His eyes fixed on hers with tenderness and wonder, but there was a catch of hesitation in his voice.

"This is real. I'm real." She slid her foot up his calf, ran her toes over his knee, and was stretching her leg to slide her foot between his thighs when he trapped it with his knees.

"Of that, there can be no doubt," he said, releasing her hands. She let her foot slide down his calves and across his feet before bringing it back under her bench.

"But?" she asked, her heart thumping in her chest at the tone in his voice.

"When you get to my age, you want to slow things down sometimes, to make them last."

"We can go as slow as you want. I'm sure my patience will be rewarded."

"Of course, and it will be, trust me. I intend to take my time with you." His eyes ran down Patia's neck, down to her hands, then back up to her face, which suddenly flushed with desire. "Let's give it a couple of days first, to get to know each other better. I find it...adds to the effect."

"Idiot," Patia said softly, running her fingers over his, swallowing her frustration. "But okay. What's the hurry, right?"

"Exactly. And it will give you time to tell me about what really brought you down to Rontaia. If you're looking for this Paoro, you must think he has something you desperately need." Gero's eyes flashed with mystery for a moment. He struggled back off his bench and shuffled over to pull a smaller bottle off the shelf, then poured them each a slug of something golden-brown.

"Chestnut whiskey. From Tralum, as it happens. A gift from the Deiyarrh family last solstice."

They clinked vials, and Patia took a sip, hesitated, then downed the rest. Gero refilled hers right away, and she raised it and took a smaller sip. Her head was warm from the whiskey and the curious confidence of this strange little man. If anyone could keep her secret, it would be him.

"I know Paoro from the old days. Worked with him in an alchemy workshop, and even shared a room with him, for a while." Gero listened, his eyes inscrutable. "The thing is...I heard a reliable source say he discovered the Universal Tincture."

Gero's eyes stayed with hers as he raised his vial and downed the rest of his whiskey, setting the vial down with care. "A reliable source, you say?"

"Yes, but here's the thing. Paoro was never really that good, not when I knew him. He had his head in the clouds, and in a lot of books, but his technique was sloppy. There's something wrong with the story, and I intend to find out what it is."

Gero stared intently at his vial as he refilled it, then topped hers off and clinked glasses with her.

"Your source was correct." He took a sip, licked his lips, and blew out as if in pain. "And so were you."

35

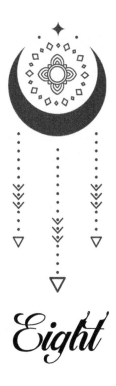

Eight

Gilea sat in the group meditation room, along with Amini and a dozen others, in a semicircle around Affito, one of the more reclusive masters at Endulai. His silent lectures were a rare occurrence, and to be invited to them was considered a great honor, which Gilea was sure she did not deserve. A thin plume of smoke rose from a single stick of incense in a small brazier in front of Affito, who sat cross-legged with eyes closed, palms together at his forehead. Gilea glanced around at the others to see if their eyes were open; some looked up at Affito, while others, including Amini, kept their eyes closed. Gilea was about to close her eyes when she noticed Affito's fingers form a circle on his forehead, with his thumbs on the tip of his nose. Everyone repeated his gesture, and all eyes closed. Gilea followed suit, and as she held her fingers in this peculiar position, she felt a channel open from Affito's mind to hers. His energy poured into her, like the morning sun reflecting off a lake. Her thoughts receded as the stillness subsumed her, and Affito's words rang in her mind like a bell echoing in a great chamber.

"In Cloti's treatise, we read: To find the Thousand Worlds, we must seek within as without, and in so doing we will see the universe reflected inside us, and ourselves shining down from the heavens."

A deep silence followed, and the words reverberated in that silence, filling it, becoming it.

"Within as without, those were her words, and much ink has been spilled, many breaths expended, in discussion of their meaning. But even the words themselves are a translation, or a translation of a translation, as there are none alive who can read her words as she wrote them in the Time Before. There are those who would say it is hopeless to divine their true meaning, that the gulf between our language and hers is too great to bridge, and we can only access a shadow, a reflection, an echo. But in studying a shadow, we can learn much about the figure that cast it. A reflection, though the wind may ripple the surface of the water, can show us the colors and shape of the original object. An echo can hint at the sound of the voice, its timbre, the emotions that drove it. They are not the thing itself, but they are a part of the thing, and our collective experience can help us fill in the gaps between our perception and the underlying reality."

Another silence followed, and Gilea's mind filled with images of the coppery tunnels of the Caravan, and the darkness it traveled through. Was the darkness pure nothingness, or was it a substance, a world of its own?

"Within as without. The universe is in us, and we are in the universe. These are not separate things. We are not separate things. The mind is thought to originate in the body, but the body cannot contain the mind. When we move through the Caravan, are we traveling within, or without? The tinctures, the cradles, the meditation, do they transport us outside of ourselves, or allow us to access parts of ourselves we cannot otherwise perceive?"

"The Thousand Worlds are inside us, as we are in them. Within is without, and without, within."

Gilea grasped at the words as Affito's energy drained from her, and their connection dissolved. She became aware of breathing, the faint rustle of clothing, the heady smell of the incense. A hand touched her shoulder, and she reached up to take Amini's soft hand in hers. She opened her eyes, which met Amini's, and in that moment she felt more connected, and more alone, than she ever had in her life.

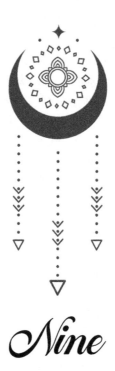

Nine

Patia bought tri-fries and brought them back for breakfast, nibbling on the corners of one as she ambled along the docks. It was an extravagance, but Gero had taken her in, and she wanted to feel like she was contributing something. Proper tri-fries were the thing she had missed the most while living in Guluch; there were a couple of tri-fry carts at the docks, but they inevitably over- or under-fried them, and there was never enough cinnamon. She found Gero straining tea into a pot, and his eyes lit up as he saw her walk through the curtain.

"Those things'll kill you, you know." He poured two cups of tea and set down the pot, plucking one of the still-steaming triangles out of the handkerchief she'd carried them in, which was now spotted with grease. "Mmm." He closed his eyes as he sat down on the bench, showing a big smile through his beard. "I don't get these often enough." He dunked his tri-fry in his tea, cupping his hand to catch the drippings as he raised it to his mouth, then licked the tea off his hand, looking up with a guilty smile. Patia did the same, and Gero watched intently as she licked her hand more slowly than was strictly necessary.

"So, what's on the docket for today? More skin cream?" Patia picked up another tri-fry and bit the corners off one by one, then dunked the exposed surfaces and sucked the soggy bits off the edges.

Gero shook his head, sipping his tea and watching her eat. "I don't have another order due for a week and a half, so I plan to putter around a bit, sort through a few things, maybe work on a side project." His eyes stayed with the tri-fries and his tea, but he wore a little self-satisfied grin.

"What kind of side project?" She tried to sound casual, but it came out a little hopeful. *Idiot*, she thought.

"Well I have a couple things in the works, but I heard there's this young hotshot from Guluch in town who makes a mean meditation tincture. I thought I might see if I could go in with her." His eyes met hers, and they showed amusement, but also the kind of earnestness that only comes from the promise of a big payoff. She hesitated for about five seconds.

"We split fifty-fifty, after expenses," she said, pointing her tri-fry at him. "And that's generous, considering my tinctures always rate at least seven, and sometimes eight. And that's at Endulai, mind you." She glanced around at his equipment and his supply shelves. His setup was a little better than hers back in Guluch; if she could find the right materials, she could do quality work here.

"All right, no need for a hard bargain. I accept." He raised his teacup, and they clinked and sipped in unison. "When we're done with breakfast, you can give me a list of what you'll need, and we'll see about acquiring the necessary ingredients."

Patia paused, chewing on her last bite and washing it down with her now lukewarm tea. "I need to try to track down Paoro first. Last I heard, he'd moved to a place on the Bluffs."

"The Bluffs? He'd be the first alchemist to have ever gotten that rich, and from what I heard he was never able to recreate the feat, so I doubt he would have been able to stay long. I'll be curious to hear what you find out. You go off on your little manhunt while I visit the Chemist Market for supplies, and we can reconvene for dinner." He gazed out the open back door at the water. "When the tide goes down, I should be able to get some blue stars off the rocks, and I have a bag of red rice I can cook up."

Patia had only ever eaten starfish once, and she remembered a lot of work for not much meat, but she was charmed by Gero's enthusiasm.

"Sounds delightful."

"With a little butter and garlic sauce, fresh out of the water, they're a lot better than people give them credit for." He slid a ledger and quill across the table toward her. "I've got quicksilver, so no need to worry about that. Just write down whatever else you'll need, along with any possible substitutions if I can't get exactly what you want, and I'll see what can be done."

Gero puttered around the hut while she wrote her list, straining her brain to recall which ingredients might be less common here, and what the workarounds would be. Would the slimy secretions of brackish water catfish work the same as fresh? Would the soma be of lower purity? There were so many unknowns, but as she puzzled over the permutations, Patia found herself humming along with Gero. She hadn't been this energized in a very long time.

Once they'd gone over her list and crossed off the things Gero already had, he did some calculations, writing them in a separate ledger in small, remarkably precise mystographic symbols. Patia smiled at the excess of caution; anyone interested in the recipe would almost certainly know mystography, but Gero's old-fashioned meticulousness warmed her heart. He was not one of those given to flights of philosophical fancy, like Paoro, whose mind was so engrossed in the mystical that he neglected the physical. Gero's movements were slow and measured; he clearly favored precision over speed. It occurred to her to wonder how that might play out in the bedroom. A man with a mind like his might well understand the secrets of more than mere chemical reactions.

"Go to the Bluffs and see if you can find anything, but I wouldn't hold out hope. I'll ask around at the Chemist Market. Someone's bound to have heard something."

"Go easy," Patia said, taking hold of his forearm and pulling him a little closer. "Don't let on why you want to know." She lessened her grip but moved closer still, leaning her mouth toward his ear. If other alchemists knew why she was looking for Paoro, they might think there had been new developments, and she didn't need any competition for his attention if she ever found him. "I don't need everyone knowing my secrets." She breathed hotly into his ear, then ran her tongue around the outside of his earlobe.

Gero closed his eyes, exhaling in a tight stream. "Of course. Best to keep certain things just between us."

The city's crowds thinned out as Patia made her way up the zigzagging cobbled streets toward the Bluffs, moving to the side as carriages barreled downhill or lumbered up. She noticed several of them carried painted faces, which surprised her a little; she mostly associated them with Brachys Hill. By the time she reached the top, the only people she saw on foot were the maids, cooks, gardeners, and other working people who tended to the neighborhood's rows of blackstone houses and immaculate terraced gardens. Patia was acutely aware of how much she stood out here; even the workers looked at her sideways. She approached one of them, a woman older than she with chalky brown skin, walking with the limp of a bad hip. She carried a cloth bag over her shoulder and wore a silk scarf around her head.

"Good morning," Patia said, feeling hopelessly awkward as the woman turned dull eyes to meet hers.

"Good morning to you too," she replied, her eyes sharpening as they scanned Patia from face to sandals and back up again.

"I'm sorry to bother you." Patia turned and paused a little in front of the woman, who stopped, shifting her bag on her shoulder. "Sorry, my name is Patia, and I'm looking for an old friend who used to live here. His name is Paoro."

The woman studied her face for some time, her mouth drawn tight as she adjusted her scarf, retying it under her chin. "Don't know any Paoro," she said in a gravelly voice. "And you might not want to go around asking too many questions. Folks who live up here like their privacy." She stepped forward, and Patia backed away, her heart sinking.

"Thank you for the advice, and nice to meet you."

The woman waved her hand lazily over her shoulder. "Name's Sovi," she said, pausing, then turning back to face Patia. Sovi looked around, licking her lips a bit. "I can ask around for you. Catch me a little after sundown at the oyster bar at the bottom of the hill. I'll be heading back home then. Maybe you can buy me a drink."

"I'll buy you two, and a dozen oysters, if you can find out anything." Patia hoped the risk was worth the reward, but she hadn't found a trace of Paoro, and she was starting to get desperate. She crossed her arms over her chest and bowed slightly in thanks. Sovi waved her off with what might have been a smile.

Patia wandered through the neighborhood until she came to a gate that blocked off access to the largest of the cliffside estates. Two stone-faced guards manned the gate, and their bearing kept Patia from getting a closer look, but she could almost smell the money behind the gold-painted bars. As she made her way back through the neighborhood and down the cobbled hill, she wondered if Paoro had made that kind of money off his tinctures. It was hard to imagine a limit to the price a vial of Universal Tincture would demand, and if Paoro had made one, he had surely made many more. It might well have been enough to set him up in one of the big houses behind the gate. Though how a man of his nature and talents had been able to achieve the dream that eluded every alchemist on the continent defied the imagination. It was possible his craft had improved in the thirty years since she'd known him, but it was much more likely he'd stumbled upon the secret somehow, and would need help to recreate it.

Patia's feet were swollen and her hips sore from walking up and back down the hill, so she collapsed onto a stool at the oyster bar and took a glass of dreadful white wine and a half-dozen fresh oysters. It was several miles to Gero's hut, then several miles back, and she wasn't sure she had that much walking in her. She considered whether it would be better to just hang around here and wait, though poor Gero would be terribly disappointed. She had another glass of wine, thinking of Gero arranging his purchases on his worktable, humming his little tune, and climbing down the rickety wooden ladder to collect blue stars from the rocks laid bare by the low tide. These thoughts and the wine brought a flush to her face and renewed energy to her body, and she paid up and trudged back across the Lowers and through the shantytown, her legs heavy as she reached the docks and made her way to Gero's hut.

Gero was fast asleep on his bed, irregular snorts and snores punctuating the silence. Patia glanced out the open back door at the river, where she could make out blue shapes amidst the clumps of seaweed decorating the wet rocks. She found a basket and tongs hanging from the wall. She hooked the basket under her arm and climbed down the ladder, wishing she had something sturdier on her feet than a pair of flimsy sandals. She crept gingerly across the rocks, feeling every sharp point and slippery side, nearly twisting her ankles several times, until she reached the water's edge, where blue stars sagged among the rocks and seaweed. Patia used the tongs to collect two dozen of the thorny creatures, which waved their points faintly as she lifted them and dropped them in the basket. She made her way back over the rocks as the tide began to creep up, and she climbed the ladder with wet feet and a sore shoulder from carrying the now-heavy basket.

"I see you've gone and fetched dinner," Gero said, leaning over the basket to inspect its contents. "I can't say I'm terribly displeased. How did it go up on the Bluffs?"

Patia rolled over onto her back, aching from her neck to her toes, but Gero's gentle smile eased her pain a little.

"It's not the most welcoming place, I have to say, but I might have a small lead." She pushed up on her elbows, and Gero held out his arm and helped her to stand, straining with the effort.

"Well, a small lead is surely better than none. I asked around a bit, being careful like you said, and I heard nothing more than what you already know. It seems this Paoro has become a ghost. But on the bright side, I found everything you needed for the tincture, more or less. I couldn't find any devil's trumpet, so I got some maiden's bells instead, but I think it will have the same effect."

Patia sat with raw fingers and a pile of starfish husks scattered across the table in front of her, the taste of butter and garlic and the almost-too-pungent starfish coating her mouth. Gero picked the meat out with a small pincer, moving with practiced ease, stuffing bits into his mouth every few seconds, though a few shreds got lost in his beard along the way. The light coming in from the river had softened, and Patia knew she needed to get moving to make it back in time to meet Sovi. She downed the last of her wine, then poured a half cup of water and swished it around her mouth.

"I have to go," she said, wiping her fingers on the rough napkin, which was none too clean to begin with.

Gero's eyes softened with concern. "Be careful out there after dark. Folks can sense when you're out of your element."

"I'm right in my element." She reached her hand across the table, and he wiped his fingers and took her hand in his. "Plus, I have a wicked little knife, and I haven't forgotten how to use it."

He squeezed her hand, flashing a smile before his face went serious again. "Wake me when you return, just so I know."

Patia leaned across the table and found his lips buried in his beard, which was much softer than it looked. She kept her lips pressed against his for a long moment, then pulled back, releasing his hands and standing up.

"I will."

Patia was on her second glass of the dreadful wine when Sovi shuffled across the terrace of the oyster bar and sat down heavily on the stool opposite her. A waiter brought her a glass of wine and a half-dozen oysters without being asked, and Sovi touched him on the arm.

"Thanks, Armin." She lifted her glass and clinked Patia's, then took a long sip and exhaled through her nose.

"Long day?"

Sovi waved her glass in the air. "No longer or shorter than the others." She ate two of the oysters in rapid succession, slurping the brine from the half-shells and setting them upside down on her tin plate. "How about you?" She leaned back, seeming to shrink by several inches as she drooped over her stool.

Patia felt embarrassed at how she'd spent her day, walking the streets and enjoying a leisurely dinner with Gero.

"My feet are tired from all the walking, but it's good to be back."

Sovi raised her glass and downed the rest, then raised it a bit higher to get the waiter's attention. Patia fidgeted in her seat, desperate to ask about Paoro, but Sovi's expression said she would not be hurried. It might have been the most interesting thing that had happened to her in a long time. Patia played along, asking about the house where Sovi worked (enormous), the family she worked for (diabolical), and her co-workers (unbearably lazy). If Sovi noticed her discomfort making small talk, she showed no sign of it and proceeded to give a full accounting of her four children and seven grandchildren, soon to be eight. Sovi ate an astonishing number of oysters and drank an equally impressive amount of wine, and Patia hoped Sovi hadn't misinterpreted her offer. She couldn't afford such a feast unless it led her to actionable information about Paoro. Just when Patia was about to give up hope, Sovi set her half-full glass on the table, let out a loud belch, and lit a cheroot. Patia fished out the stub she'd saved from the boat trip and lit it with the oil lamp on the table, her fingers trembling with anticipation.

"So this Paoro you were asking about, is he an old boyfriend or something?" Sovi grinned, bumping Patia with her knee.

"Something like that," Patia admitted, hoping that was enough. "I've been away a long time and wanted to see what he was up to."

"Thought you could get in on some of that Bluffs money, eh?" Sovi grunted a laugh, waving Patia's frown away. "I'm just playing. It's not my business anyway. And from what I heard, his money ran out, or at least most of it. One girl, who you can be sure was sleeping with him, in case you were wondering. Anyway, she said he got into all that Endulian shit, started going to the temple, every day from the sound of it."

Patia nodded, adjusting her grip on the cheroot, which was down to a bitter nub. She took one last hit and dropped it on the ground, crushing it with her sandal. Paoro had always been into the mystical side of alchemy, so it wasn't much of a leap.

"Not surprising. He always did have his head in the clouds."

"Well, gods know what they do in there, but apparently one day he went down there and never came back. Left all kinds of alchemical equipment and books and everything, which they sold at auction, though I bet that girl squirreled a few things away."

Patia studied Sovi's face, trying to figure out if she was hiding anything. She had never been very good at reading people, but there was nothing in Sovi's expression suggesting deception.

"And how long ago would this have been?"

Sovi delicately stubbed out her half-smoked cheroot on her plate and tucked it into her purse. "A couple of months ago, from what she said." She covered her glass when the waiter hovered. "The first two glasses and a dozen oysters are on her. Put the rest on my tab." The waiter nodded, and Patia paid the bill, more than she wanted to spend, but if the information was accurate, it was worth it.

Sovi shifted in her seat before pushing up to stand. "I'm going to hit the latrine and then head on home. Which way you headed?"

"Toward the docks."

Sovi shook her head. "I'm in the Lowers, south end, so the opposite direction."

"Well thank you for your help."

Sovi smiled and leaned into Patia's shoulder as she shuffled past. "Best of luck. I hope you find whatever it is you're looking for."

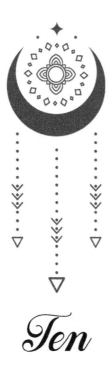

Ten

"Something troubling you, Gilea?" Amini asked from the doorway to Gilea's chamber. It still took some getting used to, how she always seemed to sense what Gilea was feeling.

"Not exactly. I was thinking about the silent lecture. About the Thousand Worlds."

"Affito's words have a way of lingering in the mind." Amini sat on the chair facing Gilea, an expectant expression on her face. They sat in silence for a time, until Gilea felt the gentle nudge of Amini's mind, and she opened up the shared space between them, which she could now do without touching foreheads.

"What part of the lecture were you thinking about?"

"If the Thousand Worlds is already inside us, why do we need the tinctures and the cradles? Why can't we just travel within to go without?"

Amini's smile deepened her wrinkles, and Gilea felt her approval lapping like tiny waves on the shore of her mind.

"It might interest you to know that Affito no longer uses tinctures or cradles. He seldom visits the Caravan, not in any way I have seen, but he sometimes sits in his room for days at a time, and he is surely doing more than simply meditating."

"Is he visiting the Thousand Worlds, then? Simply with the power of his

mind?"

"*He has never spoken to me directly of it, but in his lectures, one gets the sense he has firsthand knowledge of them. The tinctures help break down the mind's barriers, and the cradles channel our energy, but in theory, with enough practice, one has no need of anything but the mind itself. Within, as without, and without, within. Those were Cloti's words.*"

"*Within, as without,*" Gilea repeated, but something tugged at the corner of her consciousness, something Amini was not sharing.

"*You are very perceptive, and I shall keep no secrets from you. Cloti's poems contain many mysteries, but she writes of a universal elixir that would allow anyone to access the Thousand Worlds, with no cradle and no training. Most see this passage as metaphor, but Cloti is considered by some to be the first great alchemist, so her words may refer to some kind of alchemical tincture, and alchemists are forever parsing her words for clues to the process for making it.*"

"*So the Thousand Worlds might be accessible through training and practice alone, or through this universal elixir?*"

"*Within as without.*" Amini pulled back, and Gilea felt their shared mindspace dissipating. Amini studied her for a moment, a smile growing on her face.

"I am glad you came, Gilea. Pleone will want to use your talents to further the business side, brokering trade deals and the like, but anyone with training can do that. Things have gotten too comfortable here of late. We have need of someone with your…curiosity."

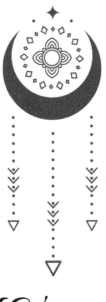

Eleven

Patia laid out the bowls in a neat line on the table, in the order she would need the ingredients to make the tincture. She glanced over at Gero, who had separated the fire on the hearth into three neat piles, bobbing up and down a little as he touched up the coals with his shovel.

"Go ahead and load the furnace," Patia said, and Gero scooped up the biggest pile and slid it into the furnace door with slow, sure motions. He pushed the metal door closed with the shovel, which he lay on the hearth, looking up at her with bright eyes. She wanted to grab his scruffy beard and plant a big kiss on his mouth, but she needed to stay focused, so she turned back to her chart, scanning the ratios for the tenth time. They were going to do a trial batch of ten vials, more than she would have done at home, but with an extra set of hands, she could double her output. Since she was going to have to split the profits with Gero, and the price to be had in Rontaia might be lower, making a larger batch seemed the right business decision.

She combined the liquid ingredients in a steel pot and removed the furnace top, setting the pot into the round opening so its bottom sat above the coals. She poured the powders into the first condensation vessel with a funnel, then pushed the tube into the gummed hole in the top of the steel pot so the steam would travel into the vessel. She measured the quicksilver one dram at a time, spooning it into the finishing vessel, which sat inches above a charred metal bowl set in a square of stone. She nodded to Gero, who shoveled the smallest pile of coals into the metal bowl, testing the heat beneath the vessel with his hand. He shook his hand, wincing, and moved back to the hearth, awaiting her command.

"Be a dear and mix those catfish secretions with the corn spirits in the bain-marie and set it over a low flame," she said, lifting the lid on the pot over the furnace to stir it with a steel spoon. The bottom had begun to thicken a bit faster than anticipated, and she splashed a bit of the burning mixture onto her hand as she stirred. She shook her hand and replaced the lid, making sure the tube was properly attached, and stared at the unfamiliar vents and knobs of Gero's furnace.

"The triangular one, two turns to the right," Gero commented, making a delicate gesture with his hand. "Assuming you're trying to lower the temperature by 10 percent."

Patia flashed him a warm smile and turned the knob, watching as one of the vents opened wider.

"You can slide the top one over a notch or two if that doesn't do it," he added.

"We make a good team." She brushed her fingers over the back of his hand. "Now check and see if that bain-marie is up to temp."

The afternoon's heat had passed when Patia stoppered the last vial and handed it to Gero, who dipped it in the warm purple wax. He applied his stamp, tracing a little P in the wax with a fine metal pick next to his insignia.

"We've got to let them know who made it, in case they like it and want more," he said with a smile as he stood the vial in the wooden stand next to the others and sat down hard on the bench, wiping the sweat from his brow. It had never occurred to Patia to sign her work before, but she liked the little touch and the gesture.

"Oh, they will," she assured him, putting her hand on his shoulder and leaning her body into his. "I think this one's going to be a solid seven, or maybe higher, if what they say about the standards at the

Rontaian temple are true." She paused, picturing Paoro sitting with legs crossed, staring at a flame, or a wall, in the temple. She wondered if he was still doing alchemy there, or if he had abandoned the chemical for the metaphysical. He had always been into the spiritual aspects of alchemy, and she had seen him meditate on a few occasions in the old days, but she had never thought much of it.

"Meditation tinctures are not my specialty, but I know the reputation of Guluch's alchemists in this domain is high. I think we should do quite well."

"Well, the tincture has to settle for a few days, so we have time to figure that out." Patia straddled the bench next to Gero, sliding her hands up his back to massage his shoulders and neck. He sighed, angling to straighten his back as she applied pressure to one side of his neck, then the other.

"Gently on the left side," he murmured, and she softened her grip, sliding her thumbs up the thin muscles in his neck.

She massaged the base of his skull, and he let out a low groan of pleasure. She continued rubbing with one hand and let the other roam over his shoulder, down his arm, and slid it between his arm and torso. She formed her fingers into a claw shape and raked gently between his legs, feeling him stir beneath his robes. He grew harder as she tightened her hand around his cock through the fabric, squeezing and releasing several times, smiling as his breath grew short. He whimpered as she let go and slipped her hands inside his robe, her fingers threading through the coarse hair on his chest, her fingertips brushing against his nipples, circling the wrinkled skin of his chest. She gave his nipples a gentle twist, then ran her hands down his stomach through the increasingly thick hair around his privates, and his hands caught her wrists, bringing them in to wrap around his chest.

"You've got me under your spell," he murmured.

"I aim to work such sorcery with your body you'll see stars," she whispered in his ear.

He twisted his neck around to lock his eyes with hers.

"We will practice some Great Works together," he said, kissing her gently on the chin. "But I would not inflict my filthy body on you in this state."

"I don't mind," Patia said, gripping the back of his head and finding his lips, slipping her tongue between them and giving him a playful bite. He had a point, though; neither of them had had more than

51

a rough spongebath with a bucket of soapy river water since she'd arrived.

"Well I do," he said, pulling his head back a bit. "Living as a bachelor, hygiene has not always been my highest concern. Let me be clear: tonight, I will take you to bed, and we will find our pleasure together. But I have an errand to run first, and then I think a trip to the baths is in order."

Patia stared at her Works book while Gero was out on whatever mysterious errand had gotten his eyes twinkling extra hard. Since hearing about Paoro's visits to the Endulian temple, Patia had started to think further about the Universal Tincture he had supposedly discovered, and what it might actually be. The foundational texts often spoke of a mystical uniting of male and female elements to make a greater whole, a potion that would grant whoever imbibed it infinite life and knowledge. A lot of the iconography fit this depiction, but other works, including the well-worn pages she'd copied from Master Helo's book, suggested a less binary approach. Though artwork had never been her strong point, the image of a swirling wheel she had copied from the original text suggested an infinite number of composite elements, not just two, unified into one. But whatever its composition, a few practitioners theorized that the Universal Tincture was not the assemblage of two things, or all things, into one, but a single compound that could grant access to the Thousand Worlds they said surrounded and intersected with this one. It was this compound she was after. The Paoros of the world could philosophize as much as they wanted, but Patia had always been convinced that the greatest secrets were physical and chemical in nature and could be discovered through careful study and experimentation.

Another image she had copied showed an infinity sign in bold ink, with repeated ovals of lighter ink spreading out away from the original to form a perfect circle filled with overlapping curves. It was just this kind of image that Paoro would set next to his recipes as he worked, sometimes becoming so lost in contemplation he forgot to stir, or mixed imprecise amounts of his ingredients. Patia had long dismissed his alchemical abilities, but she wondered if there weren't a dram of truth in his method. Perhaps he had discovered something in the texts and symbols beyond mere alchemy, something closer to the Endulian way. It could explain why he was continuing his work in their temple here in Rontaia.

Patia heard Gero's humming and his uneven footsteps, and she stashed her Works book in her bag as she turned toward the curtain. The man who slipped through the doorway looked nothing like the bushy-headed old alchemist she had come to know. His beard had been trimmed to less than half its length, and his hair had been cut as well, not to mention cleaned and groomed. His smile radiated from the clearing in his now neat beard, and he struck an adorably self-possessed pose as she stood and walked to him. She ran her fingers through his hair and down over his soft beard, then gave him a kiss, which he returned with some fervor before pushing her back to arm's length.

"Well, what do you think of the new me?"

"You look a little less wise, but even more handsome, if such a thing is possible."

"I doubt that very much, but I accept the compliment regardless."

"Doesn't it feel strange, though?" She took his face in her hands, running her fingers through his beard again, which was redolent with the tang of barber's powder.

"The air does feel a bit cool on my chin, but I didn't want all that hair getting in the way tonight." Gero's eyes ran from her face down her neck and along her body, which warmed as his knowing gaze lingered around her hips before rising to meet her eyes again. Something in his expression told her he would not be so stolid as the glazier she'd met on the boat. "But if you're up for it, I thought a trip to the baths might be just the thing."

Patia smiled so wide it almost hurt. This rickety little man with his twisted back and hunched gait was making his play like a young peacock flashing his colors. It had been quite some time since anyone had looked at her this way, without calculation or hesitation, and she had half a mind to throw him down on the bed there and then, stench and weeks-old dirt be damned.

"It sounds perfectly delightful," she said with as much delicacy as she could muster.

She had never been to the riverside baths before, as there were several baths near the university she'd used with the other students all those years ago. It was nicer than she had expected, and more private too; the central pool had numerous branches, each with small circular pods big enough for no more than three or four people. A few dozen men and women, mostly older craftspeople, were scattered here and there among the pods, talking quietly or sitting with their eyes closed. Gero dropped his clothes in a cubicle without the slightest hesitation, perfectly comfortable in his wrinkled brown skin. His movements were more assured, and he seemed to walk with less of a limp as he made his way along the pool's edge, the scrawny muscles in his legs and ass flexing with each step. Patia shed her robe and followed Gero, who looked over his shoulder at her with hungry eyes.

She followed him along the alveolar branches off the main pool to an unoccupied niche far enough from the other bathers to give them some privacy. He dipped his toe in, his balls dangling awkwardly between his legs, then descended a wooden ladder into the pool. His eyes closed for a moment and his smile showed wide in his now trim beard.

"Come on in," he said, his eyes scanning her body, then locking on her eyes. "The water's delightful."

The water was warm but not hot, perfect for the fall weather, which in Rontaia was a lot closer to summer than winter. Patia waded over to sit next to Gero on one of the low stone benches underwater.

"How do they warm the water?" She scanned the baths but could see nothing that looked like a furnace.

Gero lifted his arm out of the water, pointing toward a channel where steaming water poured out of one of the walls of the mandmade grotto. "The water runs through stone tubes just under the furnaces of the bigger alchemical workshops in the East Middle. That's why this bath is only open while the furnaces are active. The construction is said to be ancient, just like the baths themselves."

Patia ran her fingers over the edges of the pool, which were made of smooth, curved marble, yellowed and cracked with time.

"These ancients really knew what they were doing," she said, sliding her body sideways to put her feet in his lap.

"As an alchemist, that should not surprise you."

Patia's slid one foot between his legs and began toying with his cock, getting an immediate physical reaction, though his face showed only its usual mysterious smile. He lifted her other foot to the surface of the water, running his fingers along her arches, over her bunions, then sliding them between each of her toes. He rubbed her skin thoroughly, massaging every pad and crevice, and she closed her eyes and braced her arms against the edge of the pool to keep her balance. Her other foot continued to stroke his cock half-heartedly, but she was so absorbed in the pleasure of his fingers on her skin that she soon let her other foot float to the surface. He set to work on it, rubbing it from one end to the other and back again, then moving his hands up to massage her calves, which sorely needed it after all the walking and standing she'd been doing.

"You have beautiful feet," he said, holding one of them out of the water for inspection. Though it was cleaner than it had probably ever been, with its crooked big toe and raised veins, it did not strike her as particularly attractive. "Working feet, strong, but sensitive too." He ran his fingers along her sole, and she squirmed and clenched her jaw until he increased the pressure, pushing his thumbs into the flesh of her feet and straight into her heart. She let him play with her feet and calves for a little while longer, then pulled them away, scooting closer to him as she turned around, pressing her ass into him and running one hand in circles around his knee.

"Get my back?" she said, craning her neck around to smile at him.

"For starters," he said, laying his hands on her shoulders.

"There's no hurry." She leaned back into him, closing her eyes and nearly purring with contentment.

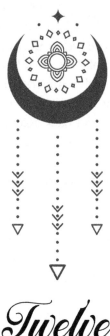

Twelve

Gilea clutched the edges of the cradle's cushion, her heart thumping irregularly and her mind racing. Though Temi had sent her a message saying she'd be waiting, it didn't feel real, and her mind nagged her with visions of sitting alone in a chair, waiting, while the operator stared at their nails. She pressed her eyes shut and stretched every muscle, down to her fingers and toes, and felt the tension in her mind dissipating, spreading into an even layer throughout her body that was low enough to keep under control.

Temi would be there. But would Gilea see her? Hear her? Surely, touch was out of the question on their first meeting, but if she could feel Temi's presence, even for a moment, it would be enough. The spot on her forehead warmed at the thought, and she felt the cradle's suction as the tincture took full effect.

This time she arrived in the Inkwell almost immediately, so fast it was a little disconcerting. The operator smiled at her.

"*Name and crossroad please?*"

"*Gilea Harkoven, from Endulai.*"

They checked their ledger and nodded. "*Your party is waiting for you. One moment, I'm transferring you to a private nook. The light will begin to fade* when your time is almost up."

"*Thank you*," Gilea said. They wrote something in their ledger, then faded as her field of vision went white.

When her vision returned, she was in a small round room with a couch and a low table, on which lay an inkwell with a quill sticking out and a book bound in rich brown leather. The words *Temithea Fluellin* were embossed on the cover in gold letters. She picked up the book, sat back on the couch, and fingered the red ribbon bookmark. She slid the ribbon to the edge of the book and opened it to a blank page.

Gilea

Her name appeared on the left page as if written with a quick, precise hand. Gilea's hand flew to her mouth as she recognized Temi's handwriting. She picked up the quill, whose tip was perfectly wet but did not drip.

Temi, I'm here, she wrote on the right page. *How are you?*

Gilea watched as Temi's words appeared in response, and she smiled, picturing Temi's serious face and her delicate fingers holding the quill. *Busy with the new pottery line. Breathfins, mostly, and swirls. Mother plans to get it on a few key tables this fall to make a trend for the winter equinox. We've had a lot of interest.*

Gilea's heart leapt at the words, which she could almost hear in Temi's voice. She held the pen near the book, but she had so much to say, and none of it would translate through mere written words. Amini had not explained how communication beyond script might be possible, but she had to try. She stared at the page, pushing past the blankness, through it, as if sticking her head underwater. The whiteness dissipated like mist, and she saw Temi's face, painted yellow, with green on her lips and eyebrows, though her outline was a little fuzzy. Temi gasped, but Gilea could only hear it faintly.

"*Gilea, gods, is it really you?*" Temi's words came as if through a heavy layer of gauze, and her aura was weak, faded.

"*It's me, but I can barely hear you. Can you lean in a bit and push with your mind, see if we can make a stronger connection?*"

Temi's brow furrowed, and her pale hazel eyes burned into Gilea's. The lines of her face sharpened, and Gilea could see a swath where the paint on her left cheek was thin, and a smudge on the outer edge of the green on her eyebrow. Temi's eyes grew wide, and her aura radiated through. Gilea's heart swelled with the joy passing from Temi into her.

"*Temi*," Gilea began, but her words stuck in her throat as emotion swept over her. She had spent the past few months in Endulai cultivating a dispassionate clarity, and the sight of Temi's face, the soft gleam in her eyes, the way her mouth curved up ever so slightly at the edges—it was overwhelming. Gilea felt her control faltering, and she feared she would fall out of the Inkwell and into her body. She steeled her mind, focusing on Temi's eyes, which were bright and wet with almost-tears.

"*You're yellow*," Gilea managed.

Temi let out a tiny laugh, sniffing and dabbing her eyes with a handkerchief. "*It's the color I wore when we first met, so I thought...*"

"*It's perfect.*" Gilea's mind flashed with the picture of Temi's face without her paint, as it often did when her mind wandered, the moment when she'd walked in on Temi cleaning her face. The shocking whiteness, the panicked look in Temi's eyes, her own pang of guilt. She hoped to see Temi's face without her paint again, in calmer circumstances.

"*So what about you?*" Temi's face grew larger as if she were leaning in. "*You look amazing, like there's this peaceful sparkle floating around you. Everything good in Endulai?*"

Gilea's heart ached at hearing Temi's voice, and she nodded, fighting back tears. "*I've been busy, learning some new things. Deeper mindsharing, for one, and...it's hard to explain, but I've been to some new places, in my mind.*" She wasn't supposed to talk about the Caravan, though everyone knew about it, or knew the rumors anyway. "*I've learned a lot.*"

"*That's so good to hear. I know what it meant to you.*" Temi paused, looking down for a moment. "*And this mindsharing, is it like what we—I mean, not that I don't want you to, of course, it's just—*" Temi's voice quavered a bit, and when she raised her eyes, they were a little unsteady.

"*No, no, no,*" Gilea said softly, reaching out her arm instinctually, wanting to touch Temi's cheek, but the connection was airy and insubstantial. "*Nothing is like what we had, what we have.*" Gilea's heart lurched at the pain she felt flowing from Temi, wishing she could conjure magical words like medic's balm to heal her distant wounds.

Temi took a deep breath, blinked hard, and her expression stiffened. "*I want you to feel free to explore whatever there is to find in Endulai, in your own mind, and the minds of others. I would never want you to feel like you couldn't...*"

58

"*The only thing I couldn't do is forget you, or what we've shared. I share minds at Endulai, every day, but there's a part of me that no one has the key to unlock except you. And the thought of seeing you again, of sharing with you again, is what gives me strength when I'm too tired or too overwhelmed to go on.*"

Temi sniffed, dabbing her nose and eyes with her handkerchief and shaking her head. "*Gods, how can I be so strong with my mother and so weak with you?*"

"*It was your strength that saved me in the Living Waters, you know.*"

Temi laughed into her handkerchief. "*Well, you saved me too, so we're even I guess.*"

"*I might need you to save me again. I don't think I could stay here forever. I want...*"

Gilea closed her eyes and tamped down the edges of her mind. She focused on the image of Temi's face and imagined pressing foreheads with her, like in the Living Waters. The sticky warmth of her paint, the sweat on the nape of her neck, the drum of her heartbeat beneath Gilea's hand. She opened her eyes, fixed them on Temi, and pushed out harder with her mind. She felt herself drawn closer to Temi, and she reached out again with her hand, which she now saw in ghostly transparency, raising to Temi's cheek. Temi's eyes closed as Gilea's fingers moved through the ether where her face would have been. She could not touch Temi, but her fingers tingled as her mind conjured the warmth of Temi's skin, her hot breath on Gilea's wrist, the wisps of Temi's hair tickling the back of her hand.

"*I wish I could...*" Temi looked down, as if at her hands, and her face fell.

"*No, it's fine, I'm just glad to see you.*" She made a move as if to brush Temi's lips with her thumb, then withdrew her hand as she remembered she couldn't touch her here.

"*Have you heard from Leo?*" Temi said, shaking her head a bit as if to clear it. "*He said he was going to...*"

"*Rontaia, yes. I've been thinking about it too.*" Gilea paused, contemplating her upcoming trip to the Rontaian crossroad, the delicate balancing act she was being asked to perform. "*But Leo, no, I haven't heard from him yet. He's supposed to be scouting for some kind of island adventure he's cooking up for a winter roughabout. I sent him a message, but I haven't heard back. He's probably too cheap to send one through the Inkwell, so maybe I'll get his letter in a month.*"

Temi laughed, then grew quiet. "*I was thinking...once we finish pro-*

duction of this new line, I told my mother I was taking a trip down to Rontaia, to scout for workshops that might be interested in taking on a commission. She thinks we have to move fast, strike with the hot iron."

"She probably knew you were going whether she wanted you to or not. You looking for company?" Gilea's smile grew as Temi gave a shy blink.

"I'm not going down there without you."

The words sent a jolt of warmth through Gilea's mind. "Of course, just say when, and I'll be in Anari in three days."

"I thought I might pick you up on the way. Maybe you can show me around Endulai a bit?" Temi cocked her head as the light began to dim, and Gilea could feel their connection straining.

"Anything. Everything. Just send me a message." The light dimmed further, and Temi's image receded into the mist.

"I will," came her whispered reply, and Gilea stared again at the open book, which was beginning to appear fuzzy around the edges.

I love you Temi, she wrote, then dropped the pen into the inkwell as the darkness closed around her, dumping her back into her body, into the cradle. Gilea rubbed her hands together quickly, then cupped them over her eyes, creating a little pocket of calm warmth in which to hide her tears.

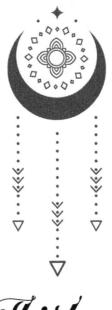

Thirteen

Patia sipped her lavender wine as she studied the jars arranged in a neat line on the table before her. She heard splashing as Gero rinsed the plates in the river, humming all the while. She smiled, picking up a small jar labeled *Eternity*, which contained a pale gray creamy mixture. That one would be for Gero, she thought. The next one was larger, labeled *Rapture,* full of a red oil, an enhanced lubricant, perhaps. Though in her youth she had eschewed the use of lubricants almost as a point of pride, as she got older, she had accepted she often needed something to smooth things along. The third held a yellowish-orange powder and was labeled *Empathy*. This piqued her curiosity, as she had never heard of any such powder used in this context. She unscrewed the lid and wafted the smell with her hand. Fenugreek, she thought, for desire, and soma, which was good for just about everything, and perhaps lemon mint, to relax. But there was something a little musky she couldn't quite place. *Gola*, perhaps? It had been a long time, but she recalled some students using it before big examinations, as it boosted their mental acuity.

"I see you've discovered my private collection." Gero eased down onto the bench opposite her. His pained wince turned into a smile as his eyes fell on the jar in her hand.

"Yes, even though you so cleverly hid it in the middle of the table." Patia's foot found his, and he did not resist as she ran it up his leg, parting his cloak and reaching his knees, but the distance did not allow her to go any further.

"Well, I thought you should know what I have available, should you desire anything extra."

"I have everything I need right here." She reached across the table and ran her fingers over the soft veins running across the top of Gero's hand. "But I like having options, and I must admit to being curious about this one." She set the jar on the table. "What's in it?"

Gero flipped his hand and traced his fingers under her palm. "And here I thought you were going to ask me what it does."

"Well, I figure if you tell me what's in it, I can puzzle that out."

Gero sat up straight, slipping his hand out from under hers to pick up the jar and hold it up to the light. "You tell me what you think is in there, and I'll tell you if you're right. I have to keep some of my secrets, you know." He opened the jar and set it in front of her.

"Of course." Patia lowered her face near the jar and wafted again with her hand. "Fenugreek, I'm sure of that, and soma."

"Both correct," he said as if it were obvious.

"And lemon mint, I think?"

Gero nodded, his smile growing. "Go on."

"Well, I was going to say *gola*, but now I'm not so sure."

"You're right not to be sure." Gero fidgeted in his seat, resting his chin on bridged fingers. His eyes blazed bright up into hers, and she felt a smile well up from deep in her chest. These were the eyes of a man who wanted her for what was in her brain, not her body, and it was as intoxicating as any philter she had ever consumed. She gazed down into the powder and wafted again, and it hit her.

"Seahops?" She'd heard of their use in certain obscure meditation tinctures, but they were not readily available in Guluch, so she had never experimented with them.

Gero sat bolt upright and pointed a finger at her chest, his face beaming with delight. "Very good indeed."

She took his finger, put it to her lips, and flicked her tongue against his fingertip several times. Gero shifted in his seat, emitting an almost inaudible moan. She let his finger drop as her eyes fell on the lid.

"Empathy. I like the name. But it's not your handwriting."

Gero shook his head, picking up the carafe and filling both their vials with lavender wine. "I stick with what I'm good at." He picked up a half-dram spoon and dropped three even spoonfuls into each glass, then stirred until the powder disappeared into the wine, which grew cloudy. "I got these from a colleague at the Chemist Market for a jar of cadmia powder, which I had from a time when I was experimenting with philosophical medicine tinctures. It never was my forte."

He raised his vial, and Patia clinked and took a sip of the wine, which had taken on a heady mint flavor, with an aftertaste of bitter grass. She took a longer sip, wincing as the bitterness built up. Gero downed the rest of his vial, coughed, and pounded the table, his eyes wet and his face scrunched into a pained smile. Patia finished hers and blew out a long, slow breath as her stomach roiled. Gero poured them each a half vial of wine, which Patia swished around in her mouth a bit to clear the bitter taste.

"You never asked me what it does," he said with a wry smile, holding his vial at an angle, then taking another sip.

"I figure there's only one way to find out." Patia felt a pleasant lift from the soma, a small enough dose it wouldn't impair her, but just enough to make the edges of her world grow soft. Whoever made this powder knew what they were doing.

Gero set his vial down on the table and reached out his hands, palms up. Patia laid her fingers on top of his so they were barely touching. The warmth of his palms and his fingertips flowed into hers, and she looked into his deep brown eyes, whose sparkle had softened into something more earnest. His fingers curled up to grasp hers, and she lifted them a little higher, maintaining the light touch. The dusky light from the riverside door dimmed as the orange stripe of sunset on the cluster of buildings across the river vanished. The lone candle on the table cast warm light across Gero's brown skin, and he leaned forward, taking her wrists in his hands. His eyes stayed open as their lips met, and she closed hers, letting the gentle pressure of their kiss build without moving for a long moment. The warmth in her lips radiated through her head, which grew heavy and light at the same time. As their lips moved together, heat flowed down to her chest, which filled with a tingling sensation. Her heart thumped slow and strong, pushing the building warmth throughout her body, which tensed as she half-stood and leaned over the table.

Her hands grabbed the hair on the back of his head and pulled his face tight to hers, and they kissed, slow and soft, until at last, he pulled back, holding her hands up to his lips, kissing the tender undersides of her wrists, as if he knew exactly what she liked. She held his hands as she moved around the end of the table to stand next to him, feeling his body heat from a foot away. She let go and ran her fingers up his arms, across his shoulders, and down his chest, her hands slipping inside his robe and clawing him gently.

"I'll be taking off your clothes now," she said, sliding her hands down to undo his belt as she pushed her thigh between his legs.

"I aim to return the favor." He leaned in to kiss her as she dropped the freed ends of the belt and slid his robe off. He fumbled with the strings to her robe for a moment, but soon they stood flesh to flesh, her heart pressed against his, their hands roaming over each other's bodies. She worked him over with her hands, and his body leapt at her touch, but not enough. She could tell by his breathing that he was aroused, and she could feel his desire filtering into her mind through the effects of the powder, but the flesh was weak.

"The...jar," he stammered, pointing at the table. "The gray cream."

Patia held onto his cock with one hand, pulling him toward the table, and she wrestled the lid from the jar with the other, never lightening her grip on him. He let out a little whimper as she rubbed the cream over him, massaging every inch as her lips explored his chest, lingering to suck on each nipple, which elicited further whimpers. When he was just about hard enough, she maneuvered him toward the bed and was about to push him down onto it, but she stopped as his eyes twinkled again, as if with some deeper mischief. She could suddenly feel his intent, and her body melted as his desire poured into her mind.

"If I may," he said, turning her toward the bed and pushing her shoulders down. Patia's heart throbbed and her mind crackled as he ran his soft hands down her body, squeezing her breasts for a moment before easing onto the bed atop her. His soft beard tickled her skin as he kissed her nipples, between her breasts, and down her stomach, his fingers raking through her pubic hair. She could almost taste his hunger for her as his lips followed, and she ran her fingers through his hair as he kissed and licked his way down her thighs, the bristles of his beard sending little electric shocks through her. After a torturous eternity, his tongue finally swiped across her cunt and began flicking up and down, and she angled up into him, grabbing his head and pushing herself against his mouth.

As he buried his face in her and her pleasure rose, she felt his desire buzzing up through her, almost as if it were her own, the giddy joy he felt working her up to her limit, then pulling back, bringing her closer and closer each time. Her body hummed with the building tension, and she dug her heels into his sides for purchase as she pressed against his face with all her strength. Her breath caught as his fingers joined the play, gently and expertly finding her sweet spots and massaging them just right, just as she would have done had she been alone. His lips and tongue continued their work as if he knew just what she wanted. Was it the empathy powder? she wondered for a moment until her rising orgasm banished all coherent thoughts. Her hips rose and she clutched him roughly by the hair as she pulsed against his touch, each wave of pleasure cresting over the pain streaking down her back at the unaccustomed position, until at last, she collapsed, squeezing her knees together as she pushed his forehead back with sweaty fingers.

Gero flopped onto his back, breathing heavily, and wriggled his way up beside her on the narrow bed. They lay in silence for a while, their fingers barely touching, in the shrinking pocket of warmth from their lovemaking. She took his face in her hands and kissed him full, his breath heady with the taste of wine and her cunt. Her hands ran along his ribs, down over his hip, and between his legs. He was as hard as a stone *olli*, and she squeezed him tight as she kissed him, feeling his need and desperation radiating out like heat from a furnace. Her body responded, suddenly hungry for more, a rare occurrence in recent years. She kissed him once more, then lay a finger across his lips as she squeezed him tighter.

"Don't fucking move, idiot." She released him and moved to the table, her hips creaking, and fumbled to unscrew the lid of the jar labeled Rapture. She spread some of the red oil over her cunt, which warmed and tingled, and she hurried back to the bed, where he lay on his side, watching her with bedazzled eyes.

She rolled him onto his back, moving to the side as he scooted over to avoid falling off the narrow bed, both of them giggling for a moment. She moved to straddle his legs, running her hands over his chest, scratching, kneading, and pinching. His eyes glittered in the dim light from the candle, and she smiled as she slid forward, feeling him throb beneath her, relishing his feeble gasps, the little whispers of his desire that skittered across her consciousness like wind-blown leaves. She raised her hips, which groaned with the effort, held his cock firm, and lowered herself onto him. He ran his hands over her legs and gripped her hips as she began rocking back and forth. Every movement triggered new sensations, not just her own, but his too, the feeling of bathing in her warmth, the ineffable connectedness they now shared. The oil gave her freedom of movement, and her pleasure rose with delicious languor, building and building as if there were no possible limit.

The sound of waves lapping against the dock merged with the slow creak of the bed, and she took her time, slowing down when his breath grew too short and she could feel he was getting close, then bearing down again, squeezing him inside her as she ground against him. Tiny shivers ran through her, and with each tremor she bore down harder, closing her eyes as she felt him teetering on the brink. Her body moved of its own accord, and her eyes shot wide open as she clenched, quivering, wave after wave of ecstasy shooting up to her head and back down again. Gero's little moans rose to a desperate shout as his body tensed and his fingernails dug into her skin. They locked eyes in the darkness, their bodies bonded in a moment of infinite tension, then she collapsed onto his chest. Little aftershocks of pleasure hit, one heartbeat at a time, until at last, they lay in stillness, locked together, their hearts beating at different cadences mere inches apart.

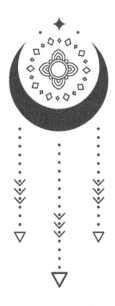

Fourteen

Gilea knelt next to Amini in the central courtyard, staring into the still pool, whose surface wrinkled with the faint breeze swirling in from the open roof of the dome. Nervous ripples arose in her mind as she thought of the task ahead. She willed them flat, one at a time, and the pool before her seemed to calm in response. She felt Amini's aura gently pressing against hers in reassurance, and she leaned into it, taking comfort in Amini's gentle strength.

"Pleone will be joining us today." Amini's mindvoice was calm as always, but there was a note of caution beneath. Gilea had never met Pleone or even seen her, but every mention or thought of the Overmother from anyone in Endulai was tinged with awe. Her power was such that she was said to be able to read the thoughts of anyone in the holy city, despite never leaving the bed where her body had lain immobile for decades. Gilea lost her center as she imagined Pleone studying her mind, her technique, and finding her lacking.

"It is an honor I do not deserve," she managed.

"It shows both the progress you have made and the scrutiny your rising position brings. The mountain crossroad may hold the key to our future, and Pleone watches every interaction there with great interest. Take what time you need to re-fo-

cus before we go to the cradle room."

Gilea closed her eyes, moving her arms upward as slowly as possible until they formed a circle above her head. Though few in Endulai used this type of movement in their meditation, it was the path she had chosen, or the one her mind and body had chosen for her. She held her fingertips barely touching for a time, until she could feel the energy cycling around her arms, through her heart, and back again, with her mind in delicate balance in the center. She let her fingers press together, one digit at a time, until at last her thumbs and palms closed the circle completely, bringing strength and stability to her mind. She held the pose until she lost all awareness of her hands, her arms, and even her body; her mind expanded to fill the space, then beyond, rising along the curving walls of the dome, opening to the sky, which flowed into her as she poured into it.

"It is time." Amini's mindvoice brought Gilea's awareness back to her body, and her mind shrank down until it slipped back into her head with a slight jolt. They arose together, without words, and Gilea followed Amini through the curving hallways to the bronze door. Amini pulled the bronze key from the pocket of her robe and handed it to Gilea, who felt tears rising behind her eyes at the gesture. Amini blinked gently, and Gilea knelt, removed the stone key, and shielded her eyes from the light as she inserted the bronze shape into the hole in the floor. The shining door swung open, then shut behind them as they passed into the cradle room.

As Gilea lay back in the cradle and the acolyte placed the heavy blanket over her, she leaned on Amini's stability, which she could feel from across the room as if they were standing side by side. Their connection had grown so strong she sometimes heard whispers of Amini's thoughts while she slept, and in her waking hours she had only to think of Amini and their minds would link. Gilea closed her eyes as the acolyte lowered the ring onto her head, and she slipped into the coppery stream like a swimmer pushing off into a lake.

"I should warn you, the Maer present very strangely," Amini mindspoke as they moved through the copper tunnel. *"I'm not sure if that's how they really look or if it is just a projection, but it may take you a moment to get used to."*

Gilea's mind spun visions of islanders she had met, one group with ridged tattoos from their fingers up their forearms, another with faces painted in elaborate floral patterns. But perhaps it was something else entirely, more like what she had seen in the Living Waters.

She passed through the shining doorway, emerging onto a rough stone platform with freshly rebuilt battlements overlooking a wide valley with forests, farmland, and a river sparkling in the distance. The scenery below was a little hazy, unlike the finely crafted vistas of the other crossroads she had visited, but the platform itself felt real; every detail convinced her senses she was on a mountaintop tower, standing near a large pigeon cage filled with cooing birds. An older woman arose from her seat next to the cage, and as she approached, Gilea could see her face, hands, and feet were covered in fine hair, like a beard over her entire body. She wore a flowing orange silk robe that moved over her plump frame too smoothly to be real. Her eyes were kind and soft, but when they fell on Gilea's they seemed to see deep inside her.

"*Welcome back to Castle Maer, Amini,*" the hairy woman said in an unusual accent. "*And Pleone was just telling me about you, Gilea. I am Ujenn.*" Her mouth curved into a smile as she looked again at Gilea, but her gaze was softer this time. "*It is a pleasure to meet you.*" She pressed her hands together and bowed, and Gilea repeated the gesture.

"*The honor is mine.*"

"*We come, as you know, to present Gilea as our new liaison,*" Amini said. Ujenn nodded, gesturing toward Gilea, who found herself staring at the grayish-brown hair on Ujenn's outstretched hand.

"*Provided she comes with open mind and heart, we accept.*"

"*Of course.*" Gilea pressed her palms together at her forehead and bowed. "*My mind and heart are open to you.*"

"*I should tell you from the start, we appear as we truly are, which I know may come as a surprise if you have never met a Maer.*" She paused, displaying her hairy arms and feet. "*Though the dress, as you might have guessed, is just a bit of whimsy.*"

"*I love the color.*" After seeing the *sitri* and the *ipsis*, a woman covered in hair did not bother Gilea as much as she might have expected.

Ujenn twisted her body so the dress flared a little, then blinked a smile. "*Thank you. This orange is traditional for the summer solstice, but I wear it year-round here, to remind me of warmer days.*"

"*Is it cold where you are?*"

"*The first snow has come and gone. Winter comes early in the mountains. And often.*"

Gilea was about to ask more when she felt a nudge in her mind from Amini, whose thoughts came creeping in.

"*I have business to attend to at Endulai. If you accept Gilea as liaison, I will*

69

leave you two to get acquainted."

Gilea felt faint for a moment as Amini's presence faded, but a wave of warmth from Ujenn grounded her again. She could sense the hairy woman's power, very different from Amini's, less refined, perhaps, but equally strong.

"No doubt she hopes your freshness will disarm me and help her gain advantage in negotiations for the brightstone," Ujenn said. She smiled without malice as she sat down, gesturing toward a stool next to the pigeon cage. Gilea sat, nervous at the hairy woman's words, but an aura of calm and contentment surrounded her. She somehow felt she could trust this woman, though the notion flashed through her mind that Pleone could still be lurking about, spying on their conversation, and even her very thoughts.

"I hardly know anything about it. I...I thought I was here to establish cultural relations."

Ujenn barked a small laugh, reaching into her pocket and tossing a handful of seeds into the cage. The pigeons scrambled and pecked and boxed each other out for the choicest bits, and Ujenn dusted off her hands and turned to face Gilea.

"I find cultural relations work best in the context of concrete mutual benefit. We will get to know each other as we work together."

"Of course." Amini had not prepared Gilea for detailed trade negotiations, but she had tasked Gilea with laying the groundwork for a deal on sunstone. *"Have you visited the crossroad at Endulai or the others?"*

Ujenn shook her head, poking her finger through the cage as a large pigeon with a black head strutted over and gave her finger a couple of pecks. *"I am too old and set in my ways to travel for now, even through... this."* Her fingers fluttered through the air around her head. *"I am training a few of my more promising students, who may one day have the skills to venture out beyond our refuge. But for now, I welcome, we welcome, the opportunity to meet and work with visitors from the other crossroads."*

"Amini said this is the first new crossroad in her lifetime. I am sure they will all want to meet you too."

"Perhaps. But not all would come with as open a mind as you or Amini. Some humans are put off by..." Ujenn stroked her beard, which flowed down to her chest, with numerous braids framing its wavy length. *"But it doesn't seem to bother you. Much."*

"Oh, well in truth I've never seen..." Gilea paused, and Ujenn's smile spurred her on. *"You said some humans. Meaning you're not..."*

"*We are called the Maer. We're no different than you, except for the hair, but it does tend to throw people off.*"

"*Well, I'm sure once they get to know you, they'll—*"

"*They'll swallow their bigotry and deal with us because we have something they want. Brightstone.*" It was the second time she'd used that word, instead of sunstone.

"*So it's true then?*"

"*We have a source. And we'll cut a deal with Endulai before anyone else, not to worry. Pleone can sleep well knowing that.*" She reached into a pocket of her dress and pulled out a black cloth bag. She opened the bag, shielding her eyes, and held out an object that shone so brightly Gilea had to look away, though she knew it was an illusion. The light dimmed somewhat, and she turned back to see the glowing shape floating inside a smoked glass sphere. It still took her eyes a moment to adjust, and when they did, Gilea saw a worked crystal the size of an apricot. Ujenn handed the globe to Gilea, who took it, studying it from all angles. The globe was cool to the touch; the sunstone did not seem to give off any heat, though there was no saying for sure if there actually was a sunstone, or a tower, or a pigeon cage. It all felt perfectly real, but so did the crossroad at Guluch.

"*Fix it in your mind, as you've no doubt been trained to do. Show this image to Pleone, and tell her to return when the quarter moon is directly above us. Hopefully, she'll bring you with—*" Ujenn stopped suddenly, and Gilea felt a strange shift in the air. She wondered if it was Pleone, who she'd thought was already here. Perhaps she'd left? Ujenn scooped the globe from her hand and dropped it back in the pouch, which she pocketed. She looked around, wrinkling her nose slightly.

"*Did you feel something?*" Gilea asked. She could still sense it, whatever it was, but she looked around and saw nothing.

"*It's probably just a ghost,*" Ujenn said. "*These rings are thousands of years old, and I sometimes feel like I can sense those who wore them before.*" Her face fell for a moment, and she bit her lip, then smiled, her eyes a little glassy. "*I've got to go. It's been a pleasure meeting you, Gilea, and I look forward to seeing you again in another quarter cycle.*"

Ujenn put her hands to her forehead, a slightly awkward imitation of the Endulian gesture, and bowed to her. Gilea bowed back, and the tower began to fade, the cooing of the pigeons becoming fainter as the coppery light surrounded her, rushing her along its sinuous curves back toward Endulai.

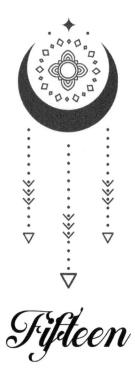

Fifteen

Patia lay on her side, struggling to roll safely onto her back because her arm was asleep and a hot streak of pain ran from her left shoulder down to her ass. Her neck was sore and her hips raged from sharing the tiny bed with Gero, who slept on his back and snored like an ox. He groaned as he rolled toward the other edge of the bed and took some time sitting up and stretching. Patia reached over and let her fingertips graze his lower back, and his groan turned softer for a moment. He turned with some difficulty, staring down at the parts of her body revealed by the tangled sheet before bringing his eyes to meet hers.

"Good morning," he said softly, taking her fingers in his and bringing them to his lips.

"Mmm," she managed, closing her eyes for a moment.

"Darkroot tea?"

"Sounds delightful." She tried to roll over to get closer, but the pain shot through her again and she fell onto her back. "And some liniment, if you have any."

Gero chuckled, rubbing his neck. "I have seven different kinds to choose from, and I'll be putting two on my neck." He winced as he rotated it partway forward and back again. "Show me where it hurts."

Patia steeled herself and pushed onto her side, letting out a small cry at the pain. She wound her arm behind her and pointed.

"From my shoulder all the way down. I must have pulled something last night."

His soft fingers traced a line from her shoulder down to her ass, where they rested for a moment.

"I think some icewort cream will do the trick," he said, leaning over to kiss her shoulder. "Let me just get the water on and we'll tend to our various infirmities."

Patia's back was feeling better after ointments, tea, and sea biscuits, which Gero apparently ate for breakfast most of the time when he didn't have company.

"They don't go bad, or at least not worse, and they do the job well enough," he said, dunking one in the cinnamon-laced darkroot tea. Though she would have loved some frothy milk mixed in, the tea stirred up fond memories, of breakfast in the great hall with the other students, the chatter and flirting before classes, the scholarly exuberance of the natural philosophy crowd. She knew many of them had gone on to have distinguished careers in science or medicine, and part of her wished she had been able to follow that path. The straightforward pursuit of science had such appeal, and though she brought much of her training to her alchemical endeavors, she missed the certainty of it all.

She thought of the painted face scientist who'd come up to her dock after the swirls had taken her quicksilver, his pampered curiosity about the Good Works. She'd puzzled it out that he was on one of those roughabouts she'd heard of, where the painted faces took a few weeks to "see the real world" before going back to their walled compounds. He was no doubt sitting comfortably in some lecture hall or well-equipped laboratory in Anari, leaning against a desk and speaking with a faraway look in his eye.

That could have been her life, but for a few more *lep* forty years ago. But then she never would have discovered the Good Works, never felt the thrill of chasing the impossible. She never would have stumbled across Gero's riverside shop, seen his bemused little smile, felt the sparkle in his eyes lift the weariness from her heart.

73

"Thinking about Paoro?" Gero asked, brushing the crumbs from his hands onto the plate, smushing his index finger onto each one, and sticking it in his mouth.

"I was thinking of you, actually. *Idiot*," she murmured, touching him under the table with her foot. "Why, are you jealous?"

Gero's face crinkled with mirth as he waved her off. "I'm supposed to be jealous of someone you were with decades ago? I don't care who you were with, who you *are* with, when you're not with me. And when you're with me, you may think of whomever you like. I lay no claim of any kind to you."

"You laid your claim pretty clearly last night."

"As I recall it was you who laid the claim. I merely played the role you wished me to play." Patia pushed out a pout, and Gero lay his hand on hers. "Which, as it happens, was precisely the role I would have cast myself into, and gladly would again, if it came to that."

"It might just." She squeezed his hand, looking from his bright eyes to the sun shining off the river, barely slowed by the bead curtain hanging over the dock doorway. She could get used to this light, this workshop, this feeling. "But I didn't come all the way down here just to fuck you, not that it wasn't exquisite." She raised his hand and kissed it, surprised at the way her heart leapt when his smile widened a crack at the gesture. "I have to try to find Paoro, and those tinctures need to sit another day at least, if not two, before we can take them to the Endulian temple."

"Actually, they buy in the Chemist Market on the weekend. They have two stalls, side by side, in the big tent." He pulled his hand back and poured them each another cup of tea. "I know one of the buyers, a little. And they know me by reputation, though they will be skeptical, as I'm not known for dealing in meditation tinctures."

"You could introduce me," Patia said, trying to hide her eagerness. If she couldn't find Paoro, or if he had nothing of use left to offer, she would need to earn a living, which meant starting her reputation afresh.

"Your initial is on the seal. I'll tell them who you are, but they only deal with one person at a time, and that must be me, the first time at least."

Patia nodded, taking a long, hot sip of tea. "Well, I'll be off to the temple, to see if Paoro's been around."

Gero sat back, stroking his now short beard. "It's a big place, and

74

while they welcome visitors, they might want to protect the privacy of those who live and work there. It's not like they'll let you wander through the complex, calling out his name."

"Ye of little faith." She picked up another biscuit, sighed, and dunked it in her tea. Even soggy, they were rock-hard in the middle and a challenge for her to chew, but she needed the energy for the day ahead. "I can be very persuasive, and persistent. I'll bring a note, and a bribe, just in case."

"Now you've got the right idea." He downed the last of his tea and struggled to his feet. "I, on the other hand, have got some ingredients to procure for my next batch of skin cream. We start work in three days. That is, if you..."

"Count me in, partner." She stood and held out her hand, straight as a board, and Gero shook it firmly as if he were closing a business deal. Which, in fact, he was.

"Well, good luck. Will I..." Gero shook his head with a wistful little smile.

"I'll be back in time for dinner. How about I bring us a chicken?"

Gero seized her by the shoulders and gave her a rough kiss. "See you tonight."

Patia smoked a cheroot as she studied the temple entrance. The building was ancient, its marble walls and columns yellowed and rounded with time, but the hundreds of colorful dyed fabric squares tied to every available structure made it seem almost alive as the breeze circled the wide plaza before it. Endulian acolytes walked in pairs, their robes aggressively drab against the rainbow of fluttering cloths. A figure sat cross-legged in the middle of the plaza, with three rows of seated pilgrims facing her with eyes closed and palms held to foreheads. The crowds broke around them as they sat, still and silent, under the warm autumn sun. Some stopped to watch the ritual, which as far as Patia could see consisted of moving the hands from forehead to chest, then down to the ground, and finally back again, with several minutes of stillness between each slow movement. Her eyes weren't what they used to be, but she did not see anyone among those seated, or the roving pairs of acolytes, who matched what she imagined would be Paoro's profile.

She stubbed out her half-smoked cheroot, tucked it away in her bag, and entered the plaza, moving close enough to the circle to be sure Paoro was not among the fifty or so participants. The figure in the center was a woman with a shaved head and a tattoo on the back of her neck that looked like the Mirrored Sun, a circle with a square inside it, with several decreasing repetitions of the design until it came to a black dot in the center. In alchemy, the Mirrored Sun represented the magnification of the sun's power through a series of convex mirrors to heat without flame, but the philosophical interpretation was the power of the soul amplified by self-awareness and introspection. It was the kind of thing Paoro had been into, which had distracted him from the attention to physical detail necessary for any kind of advanced tincture.

An empty basket sat before the seated woman, and when at last she stood, using only her legs to rise from her seat, the crowd rose with her, and each person tossed a coin in or near the basket before giving her a slight bow and turning away from the circle. The woman picked up the coins and the basket, and her eyes met Patia's and stayed with them as she glided toward the temple. Patia felt a slight warmth in her chest and an unexpected smile on her face. When the woman's head swiveled away, Patia let out a hard breath, shaking her head to clear the strange feeling. It was as if her mind had been shushed and her heart filled the open spaces inside her, which quickly shrank as the woman disappeared between the festooned marble columns of the entrance. She clutched at her heart, which beat soft but strong, and closed her eyes until the feeling passed.

She knew Endulians possessed great powers of the mind, but she had never seen or felt it while doing her business at Endulai. Mental discipline and meditation were one thing, but what she had just felt was another level entirely. She wondered what kind of tincture the woman had taken to call up such power. Most meditation tinctures Patia was familiar with were soma-based, with various stimulants and focus-enhancers mixed in careful proportions. She had never had the means to experiment with the more specialized tinctures, but she could feel the little wheels turning in her mind. Some combination of chemical and herbal elements had made this feat possible, but she doubted the tincture alone would suffice. It would take years of training to use the tincture in this way. Patia sampled each batch of her meditation tinctures before selling them, and though they made her feel a bit sharper and

76

more relaxed, and occasionally high as a kite, they never made her feel like she could project her thoughts or emotions onto someone else.

She watched the acolytes for a time and noticed two of them standing on either side of the temple entrance, with baskets at their feet. Visitors would stop and bow, drop a few coins into the baskets, then enter. She fingered the note and the coins in her pocket, took a deep breath, and crossed the plaza toward the entrance.

"Peace be upon you," one of the acolytes flanking the door said, and they both put their hands to their foreheads and bowed.

Patia bowed back, though she did not put her hands to her forehead. "And on you."

"Have you come for the stand-in?" asked the other one, a young woman with close-cropped hair and a shy smile.

"No, nothing like that. I've come...looking for a friend."

"Here you will find nothing but friends," said the first acolyte.

"I've no doubt," Patia said, choking back the *Idiot!* that rose in her throat. "I'm looking for someone in particular, who I heard might be in residence here."

The acolyte tented his fingers together, his beatific smile tensing a little as his eyebrows raised.

"Those who seek the Temple Way do so in full expectation of the privacy and isolation required for such study."

"Of course, I understand completely. I just wondered," she continued, pulling out the note and several coins, "if there might be a way you can get him a note?" She held the folded paper out, making sure the coins in her palm were visible.

The acolyte looked at the note, at the coins, then to his colleague before turning his eyes back to Patia.

"If you will offer a donation to the poor, I will take your note, and if such a person is in residence, you can be assured they will receive it. Whether they choose to respond would be up to them."

Patia nodded, letting the coins slide into the basket, where they jingled among the others. "The note says where he can find me, and there's a *nomi* wrapped up inside for the post if he wants to respond."

The acolyte took the note in both hands, feeling for the coin, then slipped it into his pocket and bowed.

"I will see to it myself. In the meantime, the stand-in will begin in just a few minutes. Are you sure you won't join us? It does wonders for one's peace of mind." Through the entrance, she could see a crowd assembling in a wide circle inside an open area lit with candles, and the silence from within was more striking than the din from the streets outside.

"Perhaps another time." Patia bowed, and the acolytes put their hands to their foreheads and bowed back.

She made her way slowly back to Gero's shack, lingering in the maze of narrow market streets in the Lowers. Impromptu stalls with colorful cloth curtains lined both sides of the street, leaving no room for horses and little enough for pedestrians. She kept one hand on her knife and the other on her purse, keeping a sharp eye out for pick-pockets, as she had learned in her days living in Rontaia. She eyed the chickens in their wicker cages at several stalls, pretending not to hear the prices called out by the barkers until she heard the lowest num-ber. She haggled for the customary five minutes before leaving with a trussed and squawking chicken, which she held clutched against her chest, next to her purse.

She was about to exit onto Docks Road when a flash of brilliant colors caught her eyes, and she swiveled to see a stall adorned with scores of bright silk scarves in every imaginable hue. The sharp-eyed barker pulled down two of the scarves, one yellow and the other blue, and waved them in opposing circles, so they briefly appeared green where they crossed over each other.

"Ten *nomi* for two," he said with the smile of someone who knows they've already made a sale. Patia stood staring at the scarves, espe-cially the yellow, which she thought would complement her skin tone. She pictured Gero's eyes when he saw her wearing the frivolous thing, and her heart fluttered annoyingly at the thought. She smiled as she thought of the ragged gray scarf he always wore replaced with a bright blue one, and she sighed and crossed the street. A few minutes and six *nomi* later, she found herself walking down Docks Road with a chicken under her arm and a bright yellow scarf billowing around her smiling face.

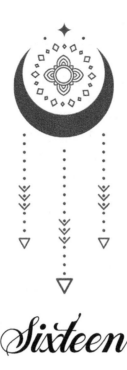

Sixteen

Gilea sat on the wicker chair outside Pleone's chamber, trying not to stare at the guards who stood, motionless and blank-faced, outside the door. She sat up straight as a thought rang through her mind as suddenly and clearly as a bell.

"You may enter."

Gilea stood up, and one of the guards opened the door and ushered her through with a sweep of their hand. The room was smaller than she expected, with only a wardrobe, a bookshelf, and a bed by the open window. Gilea drifted toward the bed, where the thin outline of a human form lay under a thick comforter. Pleone's head lay on the pillow like a shriveled apple, her scalp showing beneath her wispy white hair, which was tucked underneath a shining copper circlet like the ones in the cradles.

"Take my hand." Gilea found Pleone's hand under the cover, and she took it gently, feeling the fragile bones beneath a thin layer of skin. Gilea's head grew light and her vision dimmed as she felt herself falling backward into a void. A golden light flashed in her mind, and the light, airy room was replaced by a shadowy chamber lit by a small lamp.

"I'm glad to finally meet you in person." Pleone sat in an upholstered

red chair, holding a teacup in one hand while the fingers of her other hand rested on a book in her lap. Her voice sounded much richer and fuller than voices in the Caravan.

"I...how..." Gilea's breath came in shallow huffs as she looked down to see herself seated on a leather chair across a table from Pleone. The room was smaller than Pleone's bedroom, with no windows, and the furniture was totally different. "*Is this some kind of crossroad?*"

"*Not exactly. More like my private den, open only to those I choose to invite.*"

"*And you...*" Gilea shook her head, resolving not to ask too many questions, lest she seem even more clueless than she was. "*Sorry, I mean, thank you, for meeting with me.*"

"*It has been some time since we had someone with your raw talent join our ranks. The Lonely Way seldom yields such impressive results. I saw your work with Ujenn in the Maer crossroad. I can see Amini was not wrong about you.*"

"*Thank you,*" Gilea said, trying to suppress all the thoughts and questions swirling around her mind. So Pleone had been with her, watching her, as she met with Ujenn. But why had she not made her presence known? "*It seems she is agreeable to your wishes. About the bright— the sunstone.*"

"*Yes, though she has yet to name her price. It may be she hopes to use us as a way into the Caravan, to the wider market. It's what I would do, in her shoes. As long as we make the first deal, we will have the best deal. If she truly has the source she claims, of course. Show it to me again.*"

Gilea cocked her head, unsure if she could summon the image in this strange place, but she cupped her hands facing each other, and the smoked glass globe materialized between her fingers. The stone inside was so bright she had to look away for a moment, and when she did, she noticed Pleone too was squinting against the light.

Gilea's fingers relaxed of their own accord, and the globe floated over to Pleone, hovering above her outstretched fingers, which looked stronger and more substantial than the hand Gilea had grasped under the covers. She briefly wondered if the body Pleone had chosen to create was what she had been like before she'd fallen into a coma, or whatever state her body was in on that bed in her quiet bedroom.

"*It's quite impressive.*" The globe rotated above Pleone's fingers, which moved as if she were holding it in her hand and spinning it around. "*The size and quality of the stone itself are beyond anything we've seen from the Timon, though the workmanship is somewhat unrefined. I'm inclined to believe this is based on a real sunstone; if it were fake, they would have made it more perfect.*"

"*Unless they wanted us to interpret it just as you have.*" Gilea's face grew hot as Pleone's sharp eyes met hers, then softened as a smile deepened her wrinkles.

"*You are right to be skeptical, but if you look closely enough, you can feel the authenticity in the stone itself. Whoever made this simulacrum used a real stone as the model; of that, there can be no doubt.*"

Gilea nodded, unsure what to make of the statement. She was new to the mysteries of the Caravan, and while some of the things she saw there seemed more real than others, she couldn't tell anything about the sunstone, other than the fact that she had never seen anything like it, and she longed to hold it in her hands again, even if it was just an illusion. The globe floated back and hovered between her hands just as she was thinking this, and when her eyes met Pleone's, she could tell it was no coincidence. It made her feel a bit dizzy, knowing the woman could read her mind without her being aware of it, but there was nothing to be done about it. She stared at the stone inside the globe, trying to see or feel whatever it was Pleone was talking about. Her eyes and her head ached from the effort, and when she finally released her concentration, the globe blinked out of existence. Gilea slumped in her chair for a moment, suddenly exhausted, then straightened up when she felt Pleone's gaze fall upon her again.

"*Have a cup of tea.*" Pleone set down her own cup on the table, picked up a steaming teapot, and poured a cup for Gilea. "*Hibiscus and fenugreek, with a touch of honey. It was always my favorite.*"

Gilea's spirits lifted as she sipped the tea, and her mind grew sharper.

"*There's something you want to ask me.*" Pleone folded her hands across her lap, her eyes soft and bright, but not probing. She was holding back, inviting Gilea to share, which was bewildering, since only moments ago Pleone had been reading her every thought. Gilea took another sip and closed her eyes, willing herself to relax, to put herself entirely in Pleone's hands. There was no use worrying or resisting; only the truth would do.

"*When I was in the Maer crossroad, near the end, I...I felt something, a presence. I thought it might have been you, but it seems Ujenn felt it too. She said it was...a ghost or a spirit of one who had worn the circlet long ago?*"

Pleone closed her eyes for a moment, her face pained. "*This is why I have called you here.*" When she opened her eyes, they had a hard glint

81

to them. *"That presence is no ghost. I don't know who it is yet, but I believe it is someone who is accessing the Caravan outside the usual channels, and I have not yet been able to figure out how."* She paused, picking up her teacup and taking a sip, staring off into the shadows. The hair on Gilea's arms stood up as she thought about what that meant. Pleone was without a doubt the most powerful person in Endulai, and her ability to travel the Caravan, to read minds and realities, was unparalleled. Gilea shivered to think of what someone more powerful than Pleone could do, and the Caravan suddenly became a much scarier place.

"You've felt them before?" Gilea said, struggling to relax her mind, which was spinning with the possibilities.

"I have, and it's part of the reason I shadowed you in the Maer crossroad. They seem to show up most often on the moon's quarter cycles, which the Maer also follow. I don't know if there's any connection, but it behooves us to investigate further. Their aura is masked, or perhaps slightly out of sync with the Caravan, so it is difficult to see, but from what I have glimpsed, they are human, not Maer. And I believe they may be based in Rontaia."

A chill ran up the back of Gilea's neck. She was scheduled to travel to the Rontaian crossroad in a few days' time.

"You don't need to worry." Pleone leaned over the table, and the distance between them shrank as if the space they occupied had been drawn tighter. Pleone took Gilea's hand in hers. *"They have never seemed to do more than observe; in fact, I believe it may be all they are capable of, given the shifted way they seem to exist in the Caravan. But I do want you to be aware when you visit the Rontaian crossroad. I want you to focus all your energy on any hint of hidden motives, of unusual reactions, when you offer to introduce them to the Maer crossroad."*

"You won't be joining me?"

Pleone shook her head almost imperceptibly. *"The Rontaians will not meet with me, due to some disagreement on the principles of the Caravan."* She paused, and Gilea knew she could not ask. *"You must do this alone."*

Gilea's breath grew short, but Pleone's hand held hers tight, and a comforting warmth flowed through her arm and into her chest.

"I will do my best." She wasn't sure how she could manage such a mission by herself, but Pleone's aura wrapped around her like a warm blanket, and she knew it would be all right.

"You will do more than your best. Though I cannot join you, I can lend you some of my awareness, if you will allow it."

"It will be my honor."

"Come to me just before you go. I will show you the way."

The light from the lamp next to Pleone grew brighter and brighter until it filled the room, swallowing the shadows, illuminating Pleone like a glass statue refracting the sun's rays, blinding Gilea and forcing her eyes shut. When she opened them, she was sitting next to Pleone's motionless form in the quiet bedroom, with her hand in her lap. A cool breeze blew in through the open window, and Gilea wrapped her robe tight around her neck.

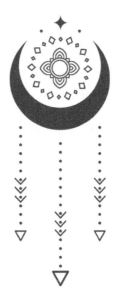

Seventeen

Patia smiled as she watched Gero bleed the chicken into a glass bowl set on the crowded table among the various bags and jars from his day's shopping trip. He closed his eyes and his lips murmured silent words as he held the chicken's body above its head, letting the blood spurt, then trickle, then drip into the bowl. It wasn't much more than a cup, as the bird was on the scrawny side, but he poured it carefully into a jar, using his finger to wipe every drop from the bowl into the jar. He closed the jar and licked his finger, giving a sheepish smile as he looked up and noticed Patia watching him.

"It's supposed to be good for the digestion, and I know an herbalist who uses it in some of her medicine. I'll see if she wants it tomorrow."

"Want some help plucking that bird?"

They sat with the parboiled carcass between them, shucking feathers and tossing them into the river, creating a flotilla of brown and white curls on the water. When they were all finished except a few stray feathers, Gero groaned his way up to standing and went inside to tend the fire in the cracked furnace he used for cooking. As Patia sat plucking the stubborn holdouts, an otter surfaced amid the feathers, seeming to study her as it approached the dock.

"It's okay, Vera," Gero cooed, and the otter swam over to the ladder and clawed its way up. It kept its distance, head bobbing up and down, little black eyes focused on the chicken. Gero pulled the knife from his belt, cut off a wing tip, and tossed it to the creature, which picked it up in its paws and lay down on the dock, tearing at the skin with its teeth.

"You never said you had a pet."

"Vera's no pet. More of a beggar, and an aggressive one at that. Though she does sometimes curl up at my feet at night when the weather gets a little cooler. *No*, greedy one, no more chicken for you!" Vera lay her head flat on the dock, looking up at him with wide eyes. "Oh, all right, I'll give you a piece of seabiscuit, but just one, and that's final." He shuffled into the hut, and Vera's eyes stayed locked on him until he returned. Vera sat up and scooched a little closer, eyeing Patia warily. Gero crouched a few steps away from her, and she crept over, rising up to take the corner of seabiscuit in her teeth with great gentleness.

"Now shoo," he said, standing up slowly and waving her away with his hands, and Vera scampered over to the edge of the dock, gnawing her prize. Gero returned to stand with his legs against Patia's back. She leaned into him, closing her eyes and letting the sounds and smells of the river flow over her.

"I don't think she likes me," Patia said.

"She just needs to get to know you a bit. It's been a very long time since I had a visitor."

"You think she'll warm up to me in time?"

"I am certain of it. Here, let me help you finish up." He leaned on her shoulder rather heavily as he lowered himself back down, letting his legs dangle over the edge of the dock. She scooched over so their thighs touched, and he bumped her gently with his shoulder, setting her heart aflutter. She couldn't believe that this silly little man with his crooked back and his twinkling eyes had captured her heart so entirely.

After a few minutes of silent plucking, he said, "I got everything we need for the skin cream, except for white lead powder. My usual supplier was out, and the only other purveyor I could find wanted twice the usual price and wasn't in the mood to bargain. I'll have to check back in a couple of days when we go in to sell our tincture."

"Isn't white lead toxic?"

"It can be unless you soft-bind it with bone powder and calcite, which keeps its whitening properties but limits absorption. That's why I keep the same customers year after year; they know my product is safe, which I certainly can't say for everyone peddling skin creams for the painted faces."

"It wouldn't surprise me if some of them were doing it on purpose."

Gero turned to her, his eyes sad behind their twinkle. "You're probably right, but it bothers me. The painted faces live such a pathetic existence when you stop and think about it. Living in their little cloisters, hiding away from the sun, especially here, where it's damned hard to escape. And they've never been anything but kind to me."

"I guess." Patia plucked the last few stray feathers and rinsed her hands in the bucket, then shook them over the river and dried them on her robe. "It just galls me, you know? We're down here fighting for scraps while they're being waited on, drinking the best wine, and spending their great-grandparents' wealth on fine robes and face cream."

Gero washed his hands and shifted to one knee. Patia held out her hand and they stood up together, their foreheads bonking slightly as they straightened up.

Gero rubbed his head with a pained smile. "I for one would rather be living off scraps with you down here by the river than shut up in some house on the Bluffs any day."

"Idiot," Patia murmured, leaning in to give him the softest kiss she could manage, which sent a tingle down to her heart and back up to fill her head.

"Come, let's get this bird in the stove and sit down to schedule our work week. We have a lot of tasks to juggle, now that we have our fingers in two pies, and I like to have everything buttoned up long before I start mixing."

They licked the grease from their fingers, sitting in contented silence as the waves lapped gently against the dock. Gero drank the last of his wine, then picked up the tin platter with the chicken carcass and hobbled toward the doorway. Patia had noticed it always took him a few steps to straighten his gait, which she understood all too well.

"Are you going to feed the crabs?" she called, following him.

"Yes, and then they're going to feed us." He pulled a wire cage down from a hook on the wall, undid a latch on the cage, and stuffed the carcass in. "They crawl in here, but they usually get stuck on the way out, because of this tangle of wires." He tied the cage to a rope, then heaved it into the water, where it sank in a sizzle of tiny bubbles, barely visible in the rising moonlight.

"Mmm, I love crabs." It had been decades since she had eaten them, but crabbing parties were one of the natural philosophy students' favorite pastimes, and she had spent many nights picking crabs around small fires on the rough public beach just upstream from the docks.

"With any luck, our dinner will be in the cage by morning." Gero rinsed his hands in the bucket, then dumped it out and lowered it on its rope into the river. He struggled to pull it back up, and Patia moved to help him, but he waved her off. "I've got it," he said, his face pained with the effort as he hauled the bucket up, sloshing half its contents onto the dock as his chest heaved and he gasped for breath.

"Well, wash your hands extra carefully. I have a surprise for you," Patia said.

She felt Gero's wide smile more than she saw it. "I surely will, but I should warn you, I'm not sure if I'm up for another bout of love-making so soon. I'm not as young as I used to be. This old body needs a day or two to recharge."

"We'll see about that, but that's not what I was talking about." Patia squatted next to him, scrubbing her hands with the brick of harsh soap and rinsing them in the brackish water, which never really felt like it got them all the way clean. "Finish up and come on inside."

While Gero was washing up, Patia pulled out the scarves, attaching the yellow one around her neck and folding the blue one into a neat triangle, which she lay on the table across from her. When Gero returned, wiping his face and beard on a cloth, he stopped a few feet from the table, staring at Patia's scarf, then the blue triangle, an expression of joyous wonder on his face. He stepped to the table, shaking out the scarf and running it through his fingers.

"For me?" His eyes grew soft as he untied the filthy gray rag he wore around his neck and replaced it with the blue scarf, arranging and

87

fluffing it. He stood up straight and turned his eyes up to meet Patia's.

"You look like a regular dandy," she said, leaning over the table to straighten the scarf, and sneaking a quick peck on his lips while she was there.

"And you look like..." He paused, looking from her scarf to her body to her hands, then back up to her eyes. "You look like a dream distilled, the sublimated quintessence of a dream." They held hands across the table, breathing, smiling, their fingers lightly tensing and releasing, until at last Gero blinked and pulled gently from her grasp. "Speaking of sublimated quintessence, I just remembered I'm a little short on coal dust as it turns out, and I'll need to get some more at the Chemist Market tomorrow."

"Oh Gero, I love it when you talk dirty."

He grinned as he dipped his quill and wrote on his list in the tiny, controlled mystographic symbols he favored. "Anything else you want to try on your next batch?"

Patia shook her head gently, then stopped, slowly raising a finger. "Seahops. That's what was in that empathy powder, right?" The powder had helped them become attuned to each other's feelings, which could have been due to its effect on the *parthi*, theoretical organisms too small for the eye to see that were thought to make up all living beings. Perhaps it somehow allowed the *parthi* to communicate between bodies through the invisible fields they were thought to emit.

"Seahops," he said, nodding his head as he scribbled it down. "And how were you planning on incorporating it, if you don't mind my asking?"

"Does it come in powder?"

"Dried leaves, but I have a mortar and pestle."

"I think we grind it, soak it in lemon oil, and mix it with the soma and the catfish secretions in the bain-marie."

"Very good. Lemon oil, and..." He slid the pen into its holder, blew on the paper a couple of times, then blotted it and slid it into the leather case where he kept his important papers. Patia scooted forward on the bench, sliding her feet up his legs and past his knees. He let out a hoarse breath, his hands frozen with the clasp to his briefcase half-closed.

"Now let's see about coaxing a little life out of that weary, aging body of yours."

Gero's fingers affixed the clasp, then gripped the edge of the table as her feet found their way between his thighs and began squeezing his cock gently from both sides. He stiffened a little; it would take a bit more time and some extra ministrations, but they could make this work. She slid down, fixing his surprised eyes with a mischievous expression as she ducked under the table. She spread his knees wide, ran her hands up his legs, and flipped the bottom half of his cloak aside as he whimpered with anticipation.

As they lay spent upon the bed, squeezed into the too-small space, Patia found herself eyeing her reed mat. Though it was not quite a bed, at least she could stretch out there. She rolled toward Gero and put a hand on his chest.

"Gero, you don't mind if I—" She stopped when she heard his raspy sleeping breath, the first hint of a snore. She removed her hand slowly and slid to the edge of the bed, pausing when he stirred in his sleep. In the dim light of the low candle, he looked every bit his age, if not more so, but there was something childlike about his face, the corners of his mouth turned up into a faint smile, even in sleep.

She poured another half-vial of wine, blew out the candle stub, and drank in silence. Flickers of pale light danced in from the moon on the water, and she thought about what tomorrow would hold, and the day after that, and the weeks and months that followed. How long could she live here in this riverside shack with Gero, making love between batches of tinctures and skin cream and eating of the river's bounty? It was comfy here with him, and she hadn't felt this way about anyone in a very long time. There was a lot to like here, but she had torn herself away from her life, her routine, her little shop, to go looking for something bigger, a chance to really make her mark, and show the Endulians and all the dismissive male alchemists what she was capable of. The Universal Tincture.

If she could find Paoro, she was sure she could get the information out of him, but what if she couldn't find him? What if he didn't want to share his secrets, or if he truly was just a fraud who had somehow stumbled onto something beyond his ability? If he turned out to be a dead end, would she stay in Rontaia with Gero, for however many years he had left? And then, what, take over his shop in her own dwindling years, until every step became harder and harder, and she diminished into someone who would be found dead a week after no one noticed she had passed on?

She drained her vial and took a long pull from the bottle, pushing the cork back in with her thumb and easing the bottle onto the table so it wouldn't make a sound. The wine in her system helped ease the discomfort of the thin mat, and sleep soon found her, flowing over the intrusive thoughts of her own demise to bury her in a blanket of oblivion.

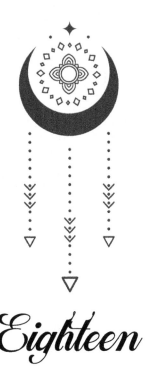

Eighteen

Gilea followed Amini down a side hallway and through a door she had never noticed before. Beyond the door was another short hallway, and a circular chamber with a bronze door and runes in the floor, just like the entry to the cradle room. Amini swapped out the stone key with her bronze one and the door swung open to reveal a large rectangular room filled with bookcases. A half-dozen people, most of them older, sat at tables scattered among the stacks, studying scrolls and books by the light of glass-encased lamps. Amini led her to a table where an acolyte Gilea recognized from some of her meditation sessions sat poring over a thick book that looked to be ancient. She looked up, her face softening when she saw them.

"Gilea, I've been wondering when you would join us! Amini, a pleasure, as always."

"It's past time," Amini said, laying a gentle hand on Gilea's shoulder. "We're here to introduce Gilea to some of Cloti's texts."

"Excellent," the acolyte said, sliding the book to the side and opening a ledger. "Would that be in translation?"

"For now," Amini said, turning to Gilea. "Though I do hope you'll study Cloti's script someday."

Gilea had heard of Cloti's script, a form of mystography from the Time Before, which was said to be completely unrelated to the ancient languages known to be common from that period. The acolyte made a note in the ledger, blotted it, then closed it and slid the large book back in front of her.

"Let me know if you need any assistance," she said, her eyes turning back to the book as Amini nodded. Gilea glanced at the pages as Amini took her elbow and led her around the desk; they were not written in Southish, or not modern Southish at any rate. Following the Lonely Way, Gilea had a poor foundation in textual studies, and she had begun to see the advantages of the Temple Way, despite its limitations. She followed Amini to a bookcase filled with scores of books, as well as some scroll cases, and a small number of odd bronze cylinders covered in tiny raised points.

"Cylinder scrolls," Amini said, gesturing toward the cylinders. "Originals, we think, from the Time Before, collected from far and wide over the centuries. We have only a fraction of Cloti's writing in this form, but they are the basis for most modern scholarship, and they match the earliest written texts perfectly. You roll them across paper, or more likely some form of animal skin, then ink the indentations to form letters, or in this case mystographic figures. Perhaps someday you will take up the study of original sources, but for today, I think we will start with…" Her fingers traced across the spines of some of the books until she stopped and pulled one out, a thin volume, well-worn but not ancient from the look of the leather binding. "Fergle's abridged primer is a good place to start. It's the first version I ever read, many years ago, and though some more accurate translations have been made since then, Fergle had a sense for the rhythm and feel of language that has yet to be equaled."

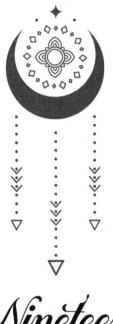

Nineteen

Patia stood in line with Gero at the Endulian stalls in the Chemist Market, along with a dozen or so other alchemists with bags, boxes, and small carts loaded with vials and bottles. Two serious-faced guards with quarterstaffs kept a wide space between the line and the stalls. At each of the tables sat a taster, both of them women, and a neatly dressed man with an abacus and a metal chest sat at another table behind them, with two more guards flanking him. Patia felt a smile creep onto her lips as she recalled the martial demonstrations the temple put on at solstice, which she used to attend along with her fellow students. Monks in brightly colored tunics would square off with staffs, and onlookers would place bets on their favorite color, with half the take going to the temple's charity fund, or so they claimed. Though the guards at Endulai were no less fearsome, she had never seen them carry weapons of any kind; their mental powers were thought to obviate such base means of defense. The difference between the practices in the two cities was so great it was hard to believe they shared the same belief system. Perhaps they were more different than she had realized.

"Wait here," Gero said as he raised his arms so the guard could pat him down. He winked at Patia and advanced to the table. He held out a vial to the taster and pointed to the seal, then back to Patia. The taster showed no signs of being impressed, but as she held the vial up to inspect it, her eyebrows raised a bit. She cracked the seal and used the tiny spoon to place a small dab on her tongue. She closed her eyes for a moment, then opened them, glancing at Patia with a glimmer of respect, though her face remained impassive. She turned and spoke to the man at the table behind them, who used a key around his neck to open the metal box and take out several stacks of coins. Gero laid the rest of the vials on the table, and the taster wrote something on a slip of paper and handed it to him. They bowed to each other, and Gero moved to the side, where one of the guards took the money from the accountant and brought it to Gero on a little tray. The guard in front of Patia gestured with his staff, and she moved along the rope barrier to meet Gero, whose eyes blazed with pride.

"Eight, you beautiful sorceress!" He held out his cupped hands, which were full of bright silver ten-*lep* coins. He leaned in and gave her a rough kiss, then scurried out of the way to an empty table to count the coins, checking against the receipt. Patia kept her eyes on the crowd, standing between Gero and the throng of pedestrians as if her presence would stop anyone. A smile bloomed on her face as she thought of the rating, which was a full point higher than it would have been at Endulai. And that was only their first try. They should be able to hit nine, maybe even ten with time, on the Rontaian scale, with a little more practice. She glanced back at the line of alchemists, who eyed her and Gero with bitter looks. There was no real competition here. She and Gero could make a fortune. The sound of coins jingling into a pouch caught her attention, and she turned to see Gero patting his chest, grinning like a little kid.

"What do you say we celebrate with a bucket of clams and some iced beer? I know a place just past the shipping docks. With this weather, the breeze..." He gestured toward the cloudless sky, his fingers fluttering in the air as they descended to land lightly on her arm. "It's on me, partner." His hand slid down to take hers, and they walked through the Chemist Market arm in arm. They stopped so Gero could get some white lead powder, which fortunately was back in stock, then made their way along the waterside. They walked at Gero's slow, steady pace, talking shop for a bit, then falling into a lull as they picked their way through the noisy passenger docks.

Patia eyed the dockers hauling cargo at the shipping docks, their arms bulging as they hefted barrels and huge sacks on and off the ships. No doubt they took her and Gero for an elderly couple, making their way back from the market with their provisions. They weren't entirely wrong, of course, and she did feel a twinge of desire at the sight of their straining muscles, but then she remembered the expression on Gero's face as he had kissed her knee, then continued down her inner thigh with maddening slowness. She had known a few dockers in her day, and as bracing as it was to be kneaded and bent and pounded without remorse, they seldom showed the patience or concern to truly fulfill her.

The clam shack was better than she had imagined, with a set of high tables and tall stools facing the river and a sturdy canvas awning to block the bright autumn sun. The clams were fresh and the beer was indeed iced, via a tiered salting dome next to the shack. It cost five *nomi* for a thick glass mug, but the cold beer and the briny clams with garlic vinegar brought a fuzzy peace to Patia's head and heart.

"We could make a batch twice as big next time if we wanted," Patia said, swirling the last swig of her beer around the mug.

"Or we could make the same amount, but refine the technique, see if we can score a nine next time." Gero cocked his head, and Patia leaned over to bump shoulders with him.

"Why not shoot for a ten?" She raised her mug and clinked with his, which was still more than half full.

"To the pursuit of perfection."

As the last cool sip fizzed down Patia's throat, she found herself wondering if there were any greater perfection possible than this very moment.

"You've got mail," Patia said as she approached the shack, her legs weary from the day's walk.

Gero shuffled up, his bright blue scarf puffing in the breeze from the river. He pulled a wax-sealed square from the mailbox, broke the seal, and scanned it with his eyes, which narrowed with puzzlement as he studied it, turning it sideways, then back again.

"It's for you," he said, holding out a piece of paper with what looked like a page from an accounting ledger on one side and an elaborate drawing on the other. Above and below the drawing were a few lines in some form of mystography Patia did not recognize.

"That's Enduli script," Gero said, shaking a crooked finger at the paper. "Written on the back of an old receipt, to conserve paper."

"Yes, I—" she thought she recognized a word, sulfur, written with inverted and rearranged letters in an elaborate script that confused her eyes. "Can you read it?"

Gero held out his hand, wobbling it a bit as he winced. "I can make it out, more or less, with time. But I'm pretty sure this is your name." He pointed to a word at the top of the paper, which she could now see was a version of her name. "And these symbols you recognize." He pointed to a dot inside a circle, set between two equal triangles.

"The Sun Resplendent," she murmured. It had been some time since she'd seen it, but it represented pure, unrestrained power.

"Yes, but I believe it may be a play on words, or symbols, in this case." He laid an arm on Patia's shoulder and shepherded her through the doorway, scanning the surroundings as if for spies. "Let's come inside and study this with a bit more privacy," he said in a low voice as he straightened the curtain behind him.

"This must be from Paoro," Patia murmured as she spread the paper on the table and studied it further. In addition to the Sun Resplendent, there were a dozen or so other symbols, some of which she recognized from the pages in her Works book she'd copied from Master Helo. There was an X with three vertical lines through it, surrounded by a circle, which she believed was the symbol for copper, though the circle was not typical in works she'd studied. There were the usual variations on interlocking geometric shapes, but what caught her eye were some more organic forms that vaguely resembled seaweed. She had copied similar forms in her Works book, but she'd never been able to make heads or tails of them. Gero sat down with a pitcher of water and poured them each a vial. He arched his eyebrows and gestured at the paper, and Patia turned it around and slid it to him.

"I recognize some of these symbols, but these here have always mystified me. Are they letters?" She pointed at the organic shapes, and Gero nodded, furrowing his brow.

"More like words," he said, running his fingers over them. "I can't read them, and there surely aren't many who can, but I've seen them before, in a copy of an ancient scroll said to be from the Time Before. It's called Cloti's script, and it's thought to be a form of proto-mystography."

"So we have Enduli and ancient mystography, along with alchemical symbols from several different sources. Is this some kind of test?"

"Either that or a sign of madness or deep paranoia. Give me a minute with the Enduli script." He picked up a reading lens, holding it a few inches above the paper and moving it slowly along the text. He repeated the process several times, his lips moving slightly. Patia fidgeted in her seat as she watched, and she had a sudden urge to pull out her Works book and compare the symbols to what was in there. She had never shared it with anyone, but if she was ever going to open it up to anyone, it would be Gero.

"I think he's asking you to meet him, at noon, which is the Sun Resplendent, but I can't figure out what day. I think these symbols may represent some astrological timeline." He tapped the paper, put down his reading lens, and stood up, wincing as he swung his leg over the bench. He hobbled over to the shelf next to his bed and returned with a thick book with a worn diagram of the sun, moon, and planets on the cover. "We should be able to puzzle it out easily enough." He set the book on the table, found the bookmark, and eased it open. The pages were full of columns of numbers and symbols, and as she leaned over the table to get a better look, she could see it was a list of dates and astrological cycles. Gero flipped a couple of pages forward, scanning the text with his reading lens, until he stopped, resting his index finger on the page.

"This is today, and we're four days from the first quarter moon, with Mars ascendant." He turned back to Paoro's note, his fingers hovering over the symbols, then touched a symbol that looked like an off-centered cross sitting in a bowl. He emitted a loud "Ha!" and Patia's heart leapt at the sound, his pure delight at his discovery, whatever it was.

"I believe this is the Enduli symbol for Mars, which is not far from our own, but the curve is inverted, see?"

Patia nodded. "And this one before it, can you make it out?"

Gero studied it, shaking his head slowly, then rubbed his face with both hands. He looked suddenly drained, and the spark in his eyes had dimmed.

"I think he might be saying noon tomorrow, but my eyes are swimming. I'm afraid I'm too tired to proceed at the moment. I'll have another look once I've had my nap."

Patia followed him to the bed and pulled the sheet over him. He smiled as she took his hand, soft and warm, and held it. Gero wrapped his other hand over hers, a faint spark returning as he looked into her eyes.

"Not to worry," she said. We'll figure it out. We have time yet."

Gero smiled faintly and his eyelids fluttered closed, his fingers slipping from hers to fall limp on the pillow.

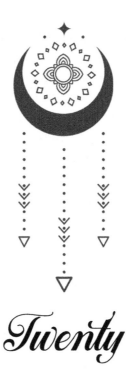

Twenty

Gilea cupped her hands, leaving a slim crack between her pinkies and positioning them so she could see the candle's flame filling the space. She slitted her eyes, staring through the filter of her eyelashes at the unwavering flame, until the edges of her vision dimmed and the pure yellow-orange of the flame filled her mind. Once she had fixed its shape in stillness, she summoned the image of the page of Cloti's script from the book she had studied. She spread the symbols across her mind; some of them resembled seaweed, while others looked a bit like the alchemical symbols she had seen in some of the books in Wulif's library. She couldn't recognize any of them, but she felt a kind of power emanating from them, a deeper meaning than the symbols themselves. She widened her focus, trying to see them as a whole, rather than individual symbols, and she grew dizzy for a moment as if she were on the edge of a great abyss, and the slightest wind would blow her over the edge. Her blood thrummed in her ears as the symbols began flowing together and rearranging themselves, then they scattered as her mind lost focus. The candle flickered and she dropped her hands and sat back, heaving for breath.

Tears of frustration welled in her eyes, and she worked to steady her breath, inhaling for a five-count, then exhaling for seven. She knew she must not be greedy, that understanding would come with time and practice, but being in Endulai felt like starting over every single day. There was so much to know, an infinity of knowledge beyond her grasp, so great it seemed insurmountable. She cupped her hands again and studied the candle through the gap between her fingers, letting all thoughts drain from her mind, sending them into the flame to be transformed into invisible smoke.

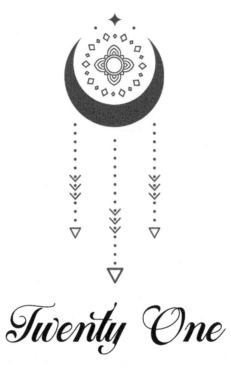

Twenty One

Patia shaded her eyes as she studied the sun angle. There were no bells in Rontaia, but it would be about noon, and if she and Gero had read Paoro's note correctly, he would be expecting her. She crossed the busy plaza, waving away a pair of Endulian acolytes begging with obnoxious politeness. She fingered the coin and the note in her pocket as she approached the temple, whose colorful little flags rippled in the faint breeze. It was still damnably hot in Rontaia, despite the advancing season, and she wished she had brought a waterskin to ease her parched throat. She bowed to the acolytes flanking the entrance, and they bowed in response, then again when she tossed a coin into the basket. She recognized the one to whom she'd given the note, and she spoke directly to him.

"I'm here to see Paoro. He is expecting me."

The acolyte nodded, closing his eyes for a moment. "Follow me, Patia."

She followed him through the doorway into a large domed room with round windows set high in the walls. The air was cooler here from the weight of the stone, and the din of the street was replaced by an eerie, echoey silence. A handful of acolytes and people in street clothes sat cross-legged on the floor in the wide-open space, facing the center of the room, which was dominated by an oddly shaped stone sculpture. Its surface was composed of irregular geometric forms as if several polyhedral shapes had been fused to form an abstract impression of a human heart. Its edges were worn smooth and shiny, and Patia had the urge to stop and study it more closely, to run her fingers along its glossy surface, but she followed the acolyte around the edge of the room and through an arched doorway on the opposite side.

They emerged into a large, airy courtyard garden lush with tomatoes, beans, and other vegetables. A worn stone path led through and around the garden in a labyrinthine pattern, and narrow channels of water crisscrossed the courtyard. Acolytes tended the plants or sat cross-legged or on their knees, eyes closed and faces serene. At the other end of the courtyard was an open space with a dozen or so cots, all of them occupied by people who appeared sick or injured. Several acolytes tended to them, and a woman in a green robe knelt by an older man, pressing her hands into his chest. His face showed pain, but also relief, and his eyes fell on Patia for a moment as they closed. She had heard that the Endulian temple offered healing services to the poor, but she had never seen it up close. She had to hurry to follow the acolyte through another doorway into a large rectangular two-story building.

"This is the dormitory," the acolyte said in an exaggerated hiss. "Please speak only in a low voice."

Patia mouthed "Okay," though neither she nor anyone else had spoken above a whisper since she'd entered the complex.

She followed the acolyte down a long, dark hallway lined with featureless doors, then up a set of stairs and down another dark hallway, which ended in a door that seemed more substantial than the rest. The acolyte took a deep breath, then knocked on the door so gently it hardly made any sound. His face was tense as he stood back, and they waited for a minute with no sound or sign of life from within. Patia watched him for any sign that he might knock again, but he stood still, eyes cast down, until at last, the door swung open silently, revealing a dark room lit by the purplish light of a Chemist lamp. A figure stood in the doorway, tall and gaunt, with long braids trailing down around his shoulders.

"Patia," said a voice she recognized instantly. "I knew you would come." The acolyte bowed and scurried away as Paoro stepped to the side and gestured her into the room.

His powerful body odor was rivaled by the metallic tang of the Chemist lamp and the lingering funk of something fishy and rotten. The lamp sat on a table next to a large glass tank half-filled with rocks and murky water. A desk and a large table overflowed with books, papers, dirty dishes, jars, bottles, and various pieces of alchemical equipment, none of which showed signs of being in use. The shades were drawn tight against the sun outside; Patia figured the windows would overlook the garden. A rather large bed sat in the corner of the room, and a sheet was stretched across the ceiling above the bed, with an array of symbols and lettering that looked strangely familiar.

"I know what you're thinking," Paoro said, moving a plate, a cup, and some papers off a small couch and gesturing Patia to sit. "I've gone mad." His voice was soft and oddly musical, and his eyes had a faraway look, like someone on a heavy dose of soma.

Patia inspected the surface of the couch, then sat. "I wouldn't rule it out, but no, this just seems like the logical conclusion of the man I knew thirty years ago."

Paoro sniffed a laugh. "I can't fault your assumption, but I assure you it's something quite other." He lifted the desk chair, brought it over next to the couch, and sat facing Patia, his knees mere inches away from hers. She found herself tensing, and she felt for the knife in the pocket of her robe, which helped her relax. The Paoro she'd known before had never had much of a temper, but he had clearly changed quite a bit, and she didn't want to take any chances.

"Do you want some wine, soma, anything?" He gestured around at the debris littering the various surfaces.

"Some water, if you've got any."

Paoro closed his eyes, and she could see his lids twitching as if his eyeballs were moving back and forth while dreaming. His eyes flew open and he snapped his fingers, then sprang up, returning moments later with a pitcher and a wooden cup, which he filled, spilling a few drops on his robe.

Patia sniffed the water, then drank. It wasn't the freshest, but it was clean well water, and it did the job.

"They gave you the master suite," she said, gazing around the room. She noticed a round carpet with a pattern of ever smaller and interlocking circles, spiraling to a black circle in the center. It reminded her of the Mirrored Sun, if woven by someone using a hallucinogen.

Next to the carpet stood a row of candles in jars, none of them lit.

"I needed space, for my Works." He gestured around at the cluttered room, then turned his eyes slowly to hers. "I thought you were in Guluch."

Patia shook her head to clear the chill that ran across her skin. How could Paoro have any idea where she'd been? They hadn't seen each other or communicated in over thirty years.

"I was. I am. I just..." She hid behind her cup and took a sip. "I needed a change."

"You came looking for me." He crossed his hands across his chest. "I'm touched."

"Well, I had a bit of a setback as it turns out, lost all my quicksilver, and I had no easy means to recover it. I heard about..." Patia lowered her cup and steeled herself to look into his haunting, rheumy eyes. "They say you achieved what so many have sought, and failed."

"The Universal Tincture." Paoro closed his eyes, his face pulling into a spacey smile. "The key to the Thousand Worlds." He opened his eyes, his hands floating in the air at his sides. "Is that what you heard?" His sugary tone and beatific smile needled her like an ingrown toenail.

"Idiot!" she spat, her face flushed with the airless heat. "I didn't come all this way to play games, Paoro, and looking around, I don't see evidence of any works at all! What the hell are you up to?"

Paoro sat back, brushing his braids off his shoulders and craning his head to stare at the ceiling. He remained still and silent for long enough Patia started to wonder if he wasn't just incredibly high on soma and had forgotten she was there. He let out a raspy sigh as he turned to face her. His expression had turned more serious, though he still wore a hint of a smile.

"There's no reason in any of the Thousand Worlds I should tell you a thing." He paused, taking a deep breath in through his nose, then let it out with a low hiss. His mouth opened as if he were about to continue, then clamped shut.

"Oh, of course not, because you've got this all under control here." Patia gestured to the empty alembic and the furnace, which had a thin layer of dust and a teacup sitting on top of it. The teacup, in particular, pissed her off, though she couldn't have said why. "You don't need anyone's help to recreate the Universal Tincture, right?" Her voice rose, then quieted when she realized where she was, and Paoro received her words in silence. After a moment he raised his head, with an odd, sad gleam in his eyes.

"Have you ever noticed," he said, leaning forward and resting his elbows on his knees, "how as soon as you find something really special, something that means something to you, something you worked so hard for..." He stood up, turning to pace toward the door and back again. His shoulders slumped and he held out his right hand in a vague gesture. "Someone always tries to take it away from you?"

Patia closed her eyes as a wave of something akin to guilt welled up inside her. She recalled the glint of silver flashing in the sun as the swirls had carried her quicksilver away, felt again the hollow pit in her stomach when she'd realized what she'd lost, what they had taken from her. The expression on Paoro's face, the quaver in his voice, moved Patia, and her heart warmed with pity for the gaunt creature who stood before her. Paoro stepped past Patia to the glass tank, tracing his fingers along the lines from the moss growing on the inside.

"I came here to help," Patia said, lowering her voice as she rose to face Paoro. "I'm not going to lie, I'd expect fair recompense, but if I can help you get back on track, wouldn't it be worth it?" She took a half-step toward Paoro until she could feel his body heat radiating off him.

Paoro shook his head, stepping behind the couch to the round carpet and lowering himself to a cross-legged seat next to the candles. "You can't help me." He lit the candles, one by one, and the muskwood scent filled the room. "I'm too far in. I have to keep trying, keep probing the void until I find the answer or time runs out." He scooted back to the center of the carpet, formed circles with his thumbs and index fingers, and held them out wide. His face relaxed, his wrinkles softening in the warm light of the candles. "You may go now," he whispered, then closed his eyes.

Patia stood watching him for a moment as he sat with his arms straight out to the sides, his body still, almost seeming not to breathe. She scanned the papers scattered across the surfaces of the furniture, trying to set the various symbols and writing in a half-dozen different languages into her mind, for later study. As she moved toward the door, she noticed a worn book open on the table, and she paused at the constellation of symbols on the pages. She recognized it instantly: It was from the pages she had copied from Master Helo, which she so often pored over in her Works book, complete with the seaweed mystography. As she stared at it, she noticed a few things that were different; she had copied it in a hurry, so there were bound to be mistakes. She could set this in her mind and recall it later, she was thinking, when a voice like a rusty knife shot across the room.

"You may go now." Paoro's eyes remained closed, and his pose had not changed, but the lines around his eyes seemed to have sharpened a bit.

Patia gripped her knife in her pocket as she hurried out the door.

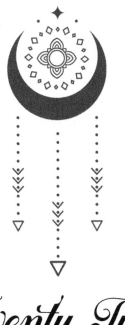

Twenty Two

Gilea felt Pleone's welcome as she crossed the bedroom, now dark due to the angry clouds billowing in the sky. She approached the motionless figure on the bed, such a small hump in the covers, with wrinkled skin drooping off her thin face. The low hiss of Pleone's breath was swallowed by the rumble of distant thunder as Gilea sat and found Pleone's hand under the comforter.

"You are nervous." Pleone's voice rang clear like the bell that ended the evening meditation sessions in the dome. *"It's your first time solo. I'd be worried if you weren't."* Pleone's words settled over Gilea like a warm shawl. *"You will do fine."*

"I will do my best." Gilea's mind felt heavy, grounded, with Pleone's presence.

"It is all we can ask. But you will not be entirely on your own. I will lend you a bit of my awareness if you will accept it. Think of it as a lens, to help you see more clearly."

"Of course." Gilea tried to push down the doubts that had been nagging her, but they stubbornly remained on the surface.

"I will not see what you see, or have any knowledge or sway over what you do or say. I know you are worried. It is so hard for you to give up control, and I would

not ask that of you, even if I could."

Gilea brought her awareness back to her body for a moment, long enough to even out her breath.

"I am ready."

"Open your eyes and look out at the clouds, but let your mind stay with me." Gilea opened her eyes but kept a distance between her vision and her thoughts. *"Very good. Now study the clouds. Watch for dark spots. Watch for lightning."*

Gilea focused in on a darker patch of cloud visible just above the white rim of the dome. The edges of her vision grew hazy as the contours of the cloud came into focus as if she were seeing it through a field glass. Her awareness was pulled toward the dark mass, much like the feeling of suction when she entered the Caravan, and she could feel the static charge of the clouds jostling together, the myriad sparks arcing just beneath the surface. She felt the pressure building inside her head as the energy in the cloud collapsed into itself, then exploded downward in a jagged bolt of lightning, which forked several times on its way down to earth. The cloud began filling again as the charged masses of the other clouds pressed in on all sides, merging with it and sending another booming jolt down to earth.

The pressure in her head lessened, and she allowed her vision to pull back as she let out a slow breath, counting to five on the exhale, then inhaling for another five. She went through two more cycles of breath before Pleone's words came to her, less crisp than before, almost weary sounding.

"It will be there when you call upon it."

Gilea felt a strange impatience as the copper tunnel stretched ahead of her, and she leaned in with her mind to see if she could move faster, but the Caravan moved at its own pace. When at last the golden archway approached, she settled her mind, feeling Pleone's awareness just beneath the surface, ready to be called.

She emerged into a space so familiar it almost brought tears to her eyes. She gazed up at the curving ivory walls, the circular windows releasing round shafts of sunlight into the temple where she had first come into contact with Endulian practice. She remembered the odd feeling she'd had as a child in Rontaia when she had wandered past the smiling acolytes outside the outer doorway, into the cool darkness of a large domed room, where dozens of people sat cross-legged on the floor, motionless as statues. Some had eyes closed, their fingers looped together like puzzles, their faces smooth and blank. Others watched and imitated a robed figure who moved their arms with almost unbearable slowness, curving one arm over their head while the other wound behind their back. They repeated the motion in the opposite direction, and Gilea had sat down in an empty space on the floor and followed along. Her tiny arms had ached with the strain of the unfamiliar movements, but her heart had found peace in the silent languor of the temple.

The temple before her was exactly as she remembered, including the large sculpture of the Soulshape, which she had spent countless hours contemplating. Several dozen figures sat meditating here, just as in the real temple she recalled from her childhood, and she wondered what transcendent state might be achieved through meditation in the Caravan. A man in a brown robe moved toward her, stopping ten feet away to bow with arms crossed. She smiled, repeating the familiar gesture, and suddenly felt more at home, more welcome, than she ever had at Endulai.

"Gilea," he said, pronouncing her name with the throaty Rontaian 'G' as he stepped toward her. *"I am Sali, and I welcome you home."*

"It is an honor," she said, studying his dark tan face and deep brown eyes and seeing nothing but openness and friendship.

"Honor connotes a difference in stature, which I assure you does not exist here." He spoke like a true believer, with no trace of doubt or apology in his voice or expression. *"Come, sit with me."* He gestured toward the statue, and she followed him, lowering herself to sit as he did, no more than ten feet away from the Soulshape. She heard him inhale through his nose, and she joined in the familiar breathing ritual, a short breath in and a long breath out, repeated three times, followed by several minutes of silent, steady breathing with eyes closed.

She opened her eyes, glancing at Sali, whose eyes were still closed, then turned her gaze toward the Soulshape. The Rontaian practitioners believed if they stared at it long enough, they could achieve a level of enlightenment that would allow them to perceive the adjacent realities thought to shadow their own, the Thousand Worlds, and the alternate selves that hovered around the periphery of the conscious mind. Through knowledge of these proximal realities, a master would be able to extend their understanding and influence into other times and places. A few months before, the idea had seemed like pure mythology, but now it seemed as natural as rain or the tides. The Caravan had shown her that all things were connected, however secret and circuitous the connections might be.

"*You have studied here before,*" Sali said. "*I can see it in the way you look at the Soulshape.*"

"*When I was a kid,*" she murmured. "*I used to come here, while my mom was working. It was always so quiet, and peaceful. The exact opposite of the city outside.*"

"*Rontaia has its charms, to be sure, but it can be a bit chaotic. And you, it would seem, have not been back for a while. You've almost lost your accent.*"

"*And don't even try speaking Rontai with me. I'd only embarrass myself.*" Gilea's mother had always insisted on speaking proper Southish with her, and though Gilea had spoken Rontai with her friends, it had been twenty years since she'd been around it. She shook her head, smiling, as she realized how easily Sali had put her at her ease. She cracked her neck and refocused, and Sali's smile seemed to flicker for a moment.

"*We take in people from all over, so we do everything in Southish anyway.* Bit of a shame,*" he added in Rontai. "*At any rate, it is good to welcome a native Rontaian back home. It must seem a bit different from what you're used to in Endulai.*" His tone was pleasant, his face almost blank. Gilea did not know whether he was really that earnest or if he was hiding something. She closed her eyes for a moment, summoning Pleone's awareness, which unfurled inside her mind, giving a crispness to her vision. She sensed no deceit from Sali, but there was something unsettling in the atmosphere that she couldn't quite place.

"*It's a lot less formal here. It's so different from Endulai.*"

"*Every crossroad has its traditions.*" He paused, pursing his lips, and Gilea felt a momentary whiff of resentment in his aura before his cheerful disposition returned. "*But tell me, how many crossroads have you visited? Amini tells me you are a novice, yet you conduct yourself like a veteran. Your entry was seamless.*"

Gilea's heart warmed with the compliment, which she brushed aside to concentrate on the strange feeling hovering around the edges of her consciousness. She closed her eyes and brought all of Pleone's awareness to the fore of her mind, and for an instant, she could sense the source, a single mind, just out of reach. The feeling faded, and Sali's voice brought her back.

110

"Is something wrong?" he said with genuine concern in his voice.

"No, it's just...in the spirit of the openness you have shown me, is there someone else here who is...not entirely here?"

Sali smiled, and this time Gilea could sense his hesitation, something hidden behind his smile.

"Your awareness is sharp indeed. In the presence of the Soulshape, we often feel those who have been here before." Ujenn had told her much the same thing, but Sali's tone was ever so slightly off. *"Or those who are here, and not entirely here, in the limbic spaces between worlds."* That part rang true at least. *"Most people cannot sense it. You have learned much at Endulai."*

"And elsewhere. I've come to learn the world, or worlds, have more depth than I ever imagined."

"Indeed. I hope you can join us someday, to explore these worlds further. I can't speak to the practices at Endulai, but we favor exploration without limit. Even in a thousand lifetimes, one could always find new worlds to discover." He paused, staring at the Soulshape, and his aura took a more serious tone. *"I gather you have been to the new mountain crossroad?"* Down to business, at last, she thought.

"I have, and I found it a most welcoming place. More like here than Endulai, I think. You would like it there."

"My heart leaps at the opportunity to meet new people and share knowledge with them. It has been a long time since a new crossroad opened."

"They are eager to meet you, and representatives from the other crossroads as well. They do not travel the Caravan yet, and their crossroad only seems to be open at certain mooncycles."

"That would explain," Sali said, closing his eyes for a moment. *"We have sensed it, and were waiting for the right moment. It is not connected in the same way as the others, and we did not wish to intrude by forcing our way in."*

"We hope to introduce you to Ujenn at the next quarter-moon."

"Ujenn," he said as if his mouth were tasting the unfamiliar name. *"I look forward to meeting them."*

"And she, you."

They sat in silence for a moment, Gilea wondering if she was doing this right. Though she had grown comfortable with the feeling of being in the Caravan, of negotiating the mental space, she struggled with the social and political complexities of this strange new reality.

"But tell me," Sali said, turning his body to face her, *"in the spirit of openness, what interest does Endulai have in connecting us with the mountain crossroad? We have not always seen eye to eye of late."* Gilea felt the strain of

111

judgment beneath his polite tone, and she wondered how much of her uncertainty he could sense. As much as she'd learned from her time in Endulai, there was something hermetic about their philosophy, a resistance to engage with the outside world except on their own terms, that had begun to rankle her. She steeled her mind to focus on the task at hand.

"*Your openness is appreciated, and I will return it in kind. It seems the Maer—that's the name of the mountain tribe—have a source of sunstone, which they call brightstone, and are willing to trade for it.*"

Sali's eyebrows raised, then his face fell into a grimace. "*I suspected there was an economic motive behind it. I suppose the...Maer, is it? offered Endulai some kind of deal in exchange for linking them up with other potential markets, like us?*"

Gilea flushed with uncertainty. She was out of her depth, and she did not want to betray Endulai, but Sali would no doubt suss out any deception on her part.

"*I am not privy to all of the details of the arrangement, but I believe that is in the works. Do you not...you do use sunstone here, don't you?*"

He nodded, his frown deepening. "*As long as we have it, but our source has nearly dried up, and we will soon be forced to resort to burning falin oil or coal to keep the crossroad running. I shouldn't tell you that, but I expect Pleone already knows.*" He shook his head, frustration clouding his aura. "*It shouldn't be like this. People should be able to communicate, to share their knowledge and culture, without having to worry about hoarded minerals or exclusive trade deals. The Caravan exists to free us from such limitations, not bind us further to them!*" His voice rose as he spoke, and a few of those seated on the floor opened their eyes and glanced disapprovingly in his direction.

Gilea took advantage of the moment to return Pleone's awareness to the front of her mind, and as she did so, she felt the presence again, more clearly this time, as if it were hovering just behind Sali, or perhaps even coming from within him.

"*I hope, with time, we can move the Caravan back in that direction,*" Gilea said.

Sali inhaled deeply, and his smile returned on the exhale. "*Then you are welcome here any time, Gilea.*"

112

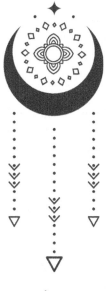

Twenty Three

Patia studied her Works book on a chair by the dock doorway, where the light of the setting sun reflecting off the river was just enough to read by. Gero was busy sorting, weighing, and re-weighing his ingredients for the next day's big batch of skin cream. His method was even more meticulous than Patia's, which was a good thing; she had noticed he sometimes forgot little things that had happened only a few minutes before. He had failsafes built into every step of the process to protect against just this tendency, which he acknowledged with wistful good humor whenever it happened.

It felt strange reading her Works book in view of another person. Every alchemist had one, and they were almost never shared, or even talked about, as if the mere mention of them would somehow endanger their secrets. She knew that Gero kept his on a shelf behind several used-up ledgers, as she had seen him retrieve it and return it, but as curious as she was, it never occurred to her to take a peek while he was out or asleep. Not only would it be a gross invasion of his privacy, but it would also feel like admitting her own skills and knowledge were insufficient. As it was, the contents of her own Works book contained mysteries she had yet to unlock.

She opened to the copied page of symbols that was the same as the one she had seen in Paoro's book, closing her eyes to recall the differences between the two copies. It was common for scholars to make changes, either on purpose or by oversight, when transcribing such texts, thus it was possible that even if she had copied it perfectly it might not quite match up with Paoro's version. As she studied her pages, she saw that several of the symbols had been switched or inverted, and there had been an additional line of the seaweed mystography in Paoro's, which she had committed to memory as best she could. She took her pencil and wrote the best version of the line she could manage, though she had to continue it in the margins, as there was not enough space between the symbols on her copy. She traced faint circles around the other discrepancies, adding arrows to indicate Paoro's version.

She pocketed her pencil and stared hard at her book. Something nagged at her as she studied the symbols; they were too uniform in size, compared to the symbols in Paoro's copy. Some had been rather small, and others large, which looked odd, but as she returned again and again to her memory, she was certain it was true and equally sure that the size differences were no accident. The script was too neat, the symbols too meticulously perfect. Whoever had made that copy had done so with great care, and the original they were copied from surely had the same variation. Patia must have made them all the same size in her hurry years ago, but she could see now that there was something unusual going on.

Another thing that bothered her were the different systems of symbols. All of them were ancient, and some she recognized, while others looked like the seaweed-shaped letters on the message Paoro had sent her. This had to be some kind of code, but her knowledge of ancient mystography was woefully inadequate to this task. Even Gero would be of limited help; he'd been able to help her puzzle out Paoro's message, more or less, but she could tell this was not his forte either.

Gero cleared his throat as he approached, and Patia instinctively moved to close her Works book, but something in his timidly curious eyes stopped her. She pushed the pages wide and turned the book toward him, lifting it up when he stooped down for a closer look.

"Are you sure you..."

"I insist. I copied this from Master Helo's Works book decades ago, and I've been puzzling over it ever since." She tried to keep an even tone, despite her mind spinning with the implications of sharing this with him. They had shared a bed and their bodies, but this felt more intimate, somehow.

"Copied it without his consent?" Gero's tone showed mild but genuine admonishment.

"He was a pig and a hack who deserved worse, but that's not the point. I saw this exact same drawing in a book in Paoro's room."

Gero gave a tiny, muffled harumph, then raised his finger, running it along the line of mystography she'd copied from memory.

"This doesn't look quite right, but I'm not an expert. You recognize this script?"

"It's the same as on Paoro's invitation. Part of it, anyway. He mixed it all up, just like this drawing does."

"I assure you it's no mix-up, but I'll be damned if I can tell you what it all means. This line, however, which I'm sure you recognize from Paoro's note, I am pretty sure is Cloti's script. It comes from one of the old cylinder scrolls, don't you know." He glanced up at her, and she cocked her head, digging through her memory. She recalled some references to cylinder scrolls in a few of the texts she'd studied, as yet another set of indecipherable clues of the sort alchemists never seemed to tire of, but she'd never heard much about them.

Gero straightened himself up, waving his finger at the line. "I can't read it, and I bet you could count the number of those with this knowledge on one hand. Either Paoro can, or he has a copy of one of the scrolls. He might have copied it onto your invitation, despite not knowing what it meant, which admittedly doesn't make much sense."

"Why is it called Cloti's script?" The name was familiar somehow; it had nagged at her mind since he'd first said it when they'd seen Paoro's note.

"Cloti was known as a great alchemist, as well as a healer, among the mountain tribes, according to Gourni's history." He paused, eyeing her briefly as if to be sure she knew what he was talking about. She'd heard of Gourni's encyclopedia of early alchemy but had never read any of it. There had been a copy in the university library when she was in study, but only students of chemistry and history were allowed supervised access to it.

"Okay, and she, what, invented her own form of mystography?"

"Possibly, but most likely it was just the form common to her people. There are as many versions as there are languages, and there were many more languages in the Time Before than we even know how to count, let alone translate. Most of the cylinder scrolls are written in the ancient Mountain tongue, or tongues, I should say, for scholars believe there may have been scores of different languages. Forgive me, I do go on. It was a passion of mine, once."

"Well, enough about your bygone passions," Patia snapped, feeling guilty about it but unable to stop her rising agitation. "How does this help us figure out what Paoro is up to? Because he sure isn't doing any kind of alchemy I ever saw. His furnace had dust on it if you can imagine. Dust!" Patia waved her hands in the air as she spoke, suddenly exasperated by the whole thing. She could manipulate materials to extract their essence and find ways to maximize its potency, but this talk of ancient languages and mystography was making her head spin.

"Quite right. Quite right." Gero shuffled over to his shelf and pulled out his own Works book from behind the old ledgers. "Cloti is said to have discovered the secret to the Thousand Worlds and to have hidden it in one of her many treatises. This line in Paoro's book may tell us that this drawing, of which you have an imperfect copy, if I may say so without causing offense, was one of Cloti's." His voice rose as he spoke, becoming almost melodic. "And I believe I have seen that very line before, or the line you attempted to copy here, again, with no offense intended."

"None taken. *Idiot,*" she added softly. "Show me."

Gero set his book on the edge of the table, then moved the bowls and jars he had so painstakingly laid out to the side, one at a time, in the same orientation. He opened his book and began thumbing through it, his lips moving as his wrinkled hands lifted the edges and turned the pages with reverence. The book was much thicker than Patia's, with long written passages in several different languages and scripts, most of which she could not read.

"Aha!" He beamed as his hands displayed a page of dense writing, with a single line of the seaweed mystography in the center of a circle. She lay her book next to his, and though she had copied half of it wrong, it was clearly the same script, the same sentence.

"Well, what does it say?" Patia asked, her breath held tight inside her tense chest.

"This entire page is devoted to a deconstruction of the sentence," he said, "which I won't bore you with. The best translation the scholar could come up with was this:

"To find the Thousand Worlds, one must seek without as within."
He cocked his head. "Though to be fair I've heard it the other way around too, *"Within as without."* He shook his head, raising his eyebrows in uncertainty.

Patia's rattling sigh broke the silence following his words. "Well, that's just about as useless as teats on a billygoat. Let me guess, your scholar has a bunch of contradictory theories about what that means, too." Gero's sheepish blink told her she was not wrong. "I was hoping this was a recipe or a process description or something, not some of that quasi-philosophical mumbo-jumbo Paoro is obsessed with. I shouldn't be surprised though."

"Well, it *could* be a recipe, I suppose, but..." Gero cocked his head this way and that, tracing his finger in the air above the symbols, nodding briefly, then shaking his head. "I honestly don't know. It doesn't make any sense. Some of these symbols are for the same thing in several different systems. This one, for instance, lead, in standard ancient mystography, then in one of the Islish versions, and again in this Mountain pictograph. If it were a recipe or a process description, why would they need to repeat the same ingredient in different scripts like that?" His eyebrows furrowed disapprovingly, and he shook his head again, turning away from the book to stare off at the river. "I'm sorry, I'll have another look in the morning, but this has me completely befuddled."

Patia stared at the pages again, and the shapes began to blur and merge together in her fatigue. She blinked hard a few times, then closed the book, fitting the stretched-out hole in the strap over the little brass nub. She stood and walked over behind Gero, who leaned back into her as she grew close.

"We'll figure it out tomorrow," she murmured in his ear, "or we'll busy ourselves with things we know can make us money now." Her fingers crept up his back, finding the tense, stringy muscles of his shoulders, then inching their way up his neck. He let out a low moan as her fingers massaged the strands of muscle running up into his scalp, and she leaned into his back and ass, feeling the heat grow inside her as her fingers found their way to his earlobes. She rubbed them gently between her fingers, smiling at the tufts of soft hair sticking out of his ears. She folded his lobes over, then formed little rakes with her fingertips, which she ran down his neck, standing on her tiptoes to reach his chest as he leaned back harder against her. She ran her hands back over his shoulders, down his sides, and around, finding him rising beneath his robe. He gasped as she slid one hand inside his robe and grabbed his balls, squeezing a little as she breathed hotly into his ear.

"Let's see if we can't jog your memory a little about those obscure, ancient letters in that book of mysteries from the Time Before. Take off your robe."

"I—" he began, stopping as she squeezed him a little tighter, then released him and spun him around, holding onto him so he wouldn't fall. His eyes met hers, hot and surprised and more than a little curious.

"You'll do what I say when I say it," she said, giving a little growl to her voice, her heart warming as he shed his robe with eyes sparkling. "Now find that gray cream and get to work."

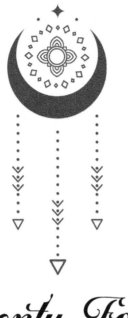

Twenty Four

Gilea sat in the library, staring at a scroll of Cloti's script held flat with four smooth black stones on the corners, letting the mysterious letters and symbols fill her mind. She did not try to analyze them or puzzle out their meanings; she took them in as a whole, like the rock gardens in the central courtyard. She shifted her focus to the spaces between the symbols, where she could glimpse a hint of an infinity beyond imagining. She bathed in this space, feeling herself stretching, spreading through it, until she was the space, and the symbols floated in her like lily pads seen from below the surface. Their roots and tendrils glowed in the coppery sunlight refracted through the water, dangling, reaching toward the primordial darkness below. She followed their trail down into the shadowy depths, pressure mounting inside her, her focus threatening to buckle at any moment. She pressed on, sensing a glow beneath the darkness, a source of infinite energy connecting the glowing threads from below. Her vision dimmed as she felt herself pulled back up toward the surface, feet first, her hands stretching to hold onto the roots, now slippery and ethereal beneath her fingers.

She gasped as she rose back into her body, her heart racing, and held up her palms toward the other scholars in the library, who looked up to see what the disturbance was. She closed her eyes. It took her some time to steady her breath, and when she opened her eyes, she had to quickly remove the stones and flip the scroll over so she wouldn't be drawn back in. There was power in Cloti's script, and she was not ready to face it again, not sure if she'd ever be ready.

A warmth spread through her, the comforting peace of Amini's energy, which always seemed to find her when she needed it most.

"Little by little," Amini's mindvoice whispered. *"With time, you will come to see."*

"Within as without," Gilea responded, and Amini's presence squeezed her like a gentle hug.

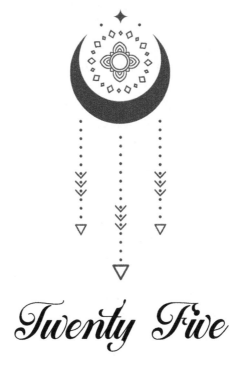

Twenty Five

Patia heard the knock at the door as she was squatting over the waste hole, but Gero was sound asleep and snoring, so she called out "Just a minute!" as she quickly finished up and hurried to the door, adjusting her robe.

A messenger girl no more than twelve years old stood, one hand on her hip and the other holding up a wax-sealed message.

"Is this Gero's residence?" The messenger cast a dismissive eye through the doorway, and Patia had the urge to smack her several times across the face.

"It is."

"Are you Patia?"

"I am." She reached for the message, but the girl swung it up out of reach.

"My fee? Ma'am?" The girl wielded the last word like a cudgel.

"Idiot," Patia grumbled as she stomped across the room, softening her footfalls as she noticed Gero rolling halfway over in his sleep. She fished a *nomi* out of her purse, hesitated, then got another one.

"Wouldn't kill you to be a little nicer." Patia dropped the coins in the girl's hand, eliciting a sudden bright smile.

"Sorry, ma'am, and thank you." The girl handed her the message with an almost sheepish look. "Have a nice day."

Patia waved her off, unsealing the wax, which was stamped with the Soulshape. The message was written in hasty mystography, and it said only: *Come today at noon.*

"It's from him, isn't it?" Gero sat on the edge of the bed, grimacing as he stretched his back this way and that. Patia smiled, and Gero's grimace reversed. "I expect he wants to see you again."

"Today, at noon." She glanced through the curtain at the sun, which had already burned away most of the morning's cool. Though it was technically fall, it still felt every bit like summer in Rontaia. "I wish he didn't have to ask me over during the hottest part of the day."

"He needs something from you." Gero stood up, twisting side to side, then walked to squat above the waste hole. Patia turned away, though Gero showed no modesty, not that it would have done any good in such a small space. Still, a curtain would have been nice.

"Like what?" she asked when he had finished and begun lighting the fire for their tea.

"Well, you said he's not so good with the technical side. Maybe he needs your...precise touch."

"Gero, he wasn't even practicing, as far as I could tell. There was no evidence of...anything, except this mossy glass tank, with a Chemist lamp next to it." She paused, suddenly wondering what was in the tank, and what the Chemist lamp was for. In all her excitement about the book and its drawings, she had pushed it to the back of her mind.

"Maybe he's looking for crystalline elements in a suspension or traces of hot lead, but..." Gero shook his head. "It doesn't track with everything else you've said. Frankly, I've seldom heard of Chemist lamps being used in alchemy, but Paoro has the distinction of being the only person known to have produced the Universal Tincture, so I suppose he must have his reasons."

"Well, I aim to find them out. Whatever it takes."

Gero blew on his tea, shooting her a worried glance.

"Not like that," she said, sliding her hands across the table and clasping his. "You've nothing to be jealous of. He's filthy, not to mention touched."

Gero squeezed her hands, a wry smile on his face. "I'm not jealous in the slightest. As I told you before, what you do when you're not with me is your own business. I'm just thinking about that batch of skin cream, which needs to be made today, and the preparations for the tincture. I'll manage, but..." He raised her hands to his lips, kissing one, then the other. "Try not to be gone too long."

"Oh gods, of course, how stupid of me! Let me just have a bit of breakfast and I'll get a head start on prepping materials to make the tincture." They weren't planning to start production until the next day, but Gero liked to have everything measured and organized ahead of time.

"I can do the skin cream by myself, obviously—I've been doing that for years. And we have no firm deadline on the tincture, so it doesn't matter much. I can adjust my schedule." He glanced over at his ledger, where he kept a calendar of his work plans, as well as lists of materials needed for upcoming projects and the days each market was open. "If I'm being candid, I find that I..." he paused, running his fingers between each of hers, then over the veiny backs of her hands. "I prefer working with you over working alone. After all these years, I thought I had achieved what I'd always wanted, a stable setup, a workable routine, where I could finish out my days quietly making creams and tinctures by the river. Then you came wandering through that doorway, and now just a few weeks later I can hardly imagine setting a fire beneath the aludel without you at my side." He looked away, as if embarrassed, and Patia swallowed the growing lump in her throat. She did miss her solitude at times, but Gero knew when to give her space and when to draw closer, and the thought of endless quiet days mixing, distilling, and making love with him filled a part of her she hadn't realized was empty.

She stood and rounded the table, leaning into his back and head, running her hands down his arms and crossing them across his chest to hold him tight. She had never wanted anything more than the freedom to practice her works and perfect her technique, and though she'd had more than her share of sexual partners, she had never wished for any intimacy beyond the occasional moment of sweaty pleasure. As enticing as the prospect of the Universal Tincture was, the idea of spending more time with Gero here in this little riverside shack was almost more appealing.

"I promise," she whispered in his ear. "I will be here with you tonight, and for as many nights after as you will have me."

The acolyte at the temple entrance bowed in recognition as she approached, then turned and gestured her to follow him.

"Paoro's expecting you, and we're glad you've come," he said in a low voice as they crossed the circular meditation room and stepped into the garden-filled courtyard. He stopped, looking around to make sure no one was within earshot, and leaned in close. "He's become very agitated since your last visit," he whispered. "He's been acting strangely, even for him." His tone matched the pleading look in his eyes. "I hope you can help him find what he's looking for."

"He hasn't been able to recreate it since he first came here, has he?" Patia asked. It was a gamble, but she sensed weakness and decided to press her advantage.

The acolyte closed his eyes and shook his head. "He's always cryptic when asked, but he has not produced any new tincture. We were hoping..." He tented his fingers together, his eyes wide.

"I'm not a miracle worker, but I'll see what I can do." She followed him through the garden and into the dormitory, where he stopped.

"It might be better if..."

Patia blinked him away, then strode down the long, dim corridor, up the stairs, and back again to Paoro's door. She raised her hand, hesitating on whether to do a soft tap or a hard knock, and decided on three modest taps. After a long moment, she heard footsteps, and the door opened partway.

"Come in, quickly," Paoro hissed, holding the door open just enough so she could slip through. The room was dark, as before, lit only by the purplish light of the Chemist lamp and the sunlight peeking through the cracks around the edges of the curtains. The chaos of the room's furnishings was even greater than at her last visit; a mess of bowls, vials, and jars showed evidence of some alchemical attempts, as did the smell of sulfur, though the mess of yellow powder around the work table did not bode well for any results. A pot with a conical vented lid sat on a low burner, pouring steam and heat into the fetid air, like a sauna that had never been cleaned. Dishes and papers had been heaped even higher on the few remaining surfaces, and Paoro did not even gesture for her to sit.

"I don't know if I can trust you, but I definitely can't trust them," he said as if continuing a long-running monologue. "Time is running out, which leaves me no choice." He stalked over to the table, returning with his Works book, which had an uneven dusting of yellow powder on its opened pages. Patia winced at the sight; an alchemist never brought their book near their food, their drink, or their Works.

"You saw this, the last time. You saw it, and you recognized something." He held the open book out toward her, blowing the powder off the pages so it swirled up in her face. She waved it away, confirming her suspicion it was sulfur, then stared down at the book, whose details she could make out now that her eyes had adjusted to the darkness. She compared it in her mind to the drawing in her own book and the additions she had made, hoping she hadn't missed anything important. She pointed to the line in the seaweed script.

"To find the Thousand Worlds, one must look without as within," she said.

Paoro's face fell, but his eyes gleamed with hope.

"You can read Cloti's script?"

"Not a word. But I know people who can. What does it mean?"

He pushed the book toward her, and she took it from him. It was heavy, and she had to reposition her hands to hold it without straining. Paoro turned away, moving to the side table where the glass tank and the Chemist lamp sat, and he stood staring into the tank for a long moment. When he turned around, half his face was lit by the faint purplish light from the lamp, while the other half was dark with shadow.

"You must tell no one," he said in a hoarse voice.

"Your secret's safe with me," she replied, though she didn't see how she could keep it from Gero.

"Promise me!" he hissed, the shadows highlighting the anguish and desperation on his face. "Not a soul."

Patia looked down at the book, angling it to see better in the dim light from the Chemist lamp. She wondered what the other pages contained, how many secrets he had compiled before he finally came upon the detail he needed.

She took a deep breath. "I swear upon my own Works, I will keep your secret." Knowing she would regret it. Not sure if she could keep her word, but she had never gone back on such a promise before.

Paoro's expression eased somewhat, and he stepped toward her, his face looking suddenly old as he left the purple shadows. But not like Gero, whose wrinkles were accumulations of years of wisdom and

125

wry smiles. Paoro's face was like the gaunt mask of a soma addict, one who had glimpsed the eternal and was forever haunted by its absence.

"To find the Thousand Worlds, you must look without as within." He spoke in slow, hollow tones, his eyes moving up from the book to meet hers. They were bloodshot and wild, but with an iron certainty in the center. "This is not a recipe, Patia. It is not a technical guide, or a process description, or even a philosophical text." He moved closer, and she could smell the alcohol from his breath, the rank odor of old sweat in older, unwashed clothes. A trembling smile grew on his lips, and he pointed his index finger down to the book.

"It is a map."

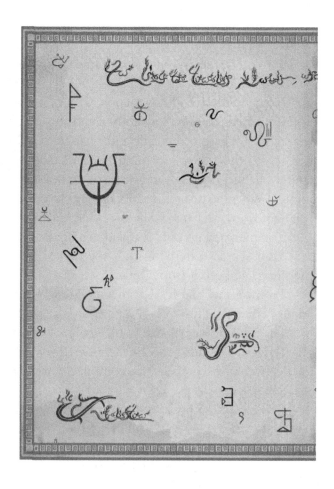

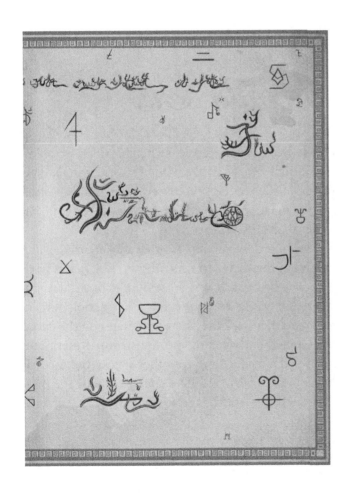

127

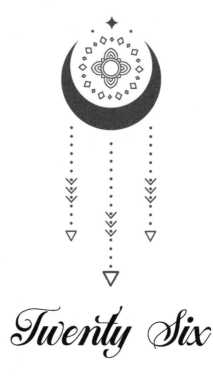

Twenty Six

Gilea paddled from the back of the canoe, switching sides frequently to compensate for Amini's weak stroke. Amini was fit for her age, but Gilea tended to forget she was close to ninety years old. In Gilea's mind, she remained the ageless figure who had helped her find her center after her mother died and she drifted from Rontaia.

The Annex was a mile downstream from Endulai proper, and there was no path through the dense forests on this side of the river, so the only way to go was by boat. It was so seldom spoken of Gilea couldn't decide if everyone was keeping it secret or had simply forgotten it existed. It was where they took the tinctures bought on the cheap off alchemists from Guluch and Tralum and transformed them into whatever was needed for the cradles, and for other specialized meditations Gilea was not yet privy to. As far as she could tell, only the masters and tasters ever visited the Annex, and they never spoke of what they did there.

Amini pointed a crooked finger toward a small creek, and Gilea steered the canoe into it and around a corner, where it opened into an almost perfectly circular lake. Fields of fading water lilies dominated one side, across from a low building of gray stone whose exact dimensions were obscured by the forest it was ensconced in. Two Endulian guards stood on the dock, fixing intense gazes on the canoe, on Amini, and especially on Gilea, who suddenly felt as if they could see through her clothes and her body to her naked core. A wall rose instinctively within her, and she willed it back down, letting them scan her aura. It was an uncomfortable but brief experience, and she and Amini were soon being helped onto the dock by the guards and led toward a large stone door with a neat crack between two slabs but no visible handles or opening mechanism. The two guards moved to either side of the door and pressed their foreheads against circles of what appeared to be tarnished bronze. The slabs slid apart silently, and Gilea followed Amini inside, turning to stare at the doors, trying to see how they worked. The doors closed behind them as quickly as they had opened, leaving Gilea and Amini in a semicircular room.

A wide desk with two scribes behind it occupied the wall in front of them, with archways on either side of the desk. Benches lined the other walls of the room, and a half-dozen people were scattered across the benches, talking, studying various papers, securing well-worn crates with heavy straps. Jars half-filled with a glowing liquid were lined up next to each of the doorways. Amini stepped to one of the desks, and the scribe bowed so his forehead touched the desk. Amini bowed deeply in response.

"Amini, it is a rare pleasure." The scribe spoke with such earnest warmth Gilea could not help but be charmed. "You are unexpected," he continued, scanning the ledger in front of him, then looking up with a smile, "but always welcome."

"Oliss, it is good to see you. I'm here to show Gilea, our new ambassador, around." She gestured, and Gilea stepped forward, exchanging bows with Oliss.

"Anything you need, Gilea," Oliss said, making a note in his ledger.

Amini picked up one of the glowing jars, gripped Gilea's arm, and guided her through the archway to the right. Whereas Endulai was redolent of flowers and candle wax, the air in the Annex was sharp with metallic and chemical smells. The stone of the hallway was old, perhaps even older than most of Endulai, with shiny depressions running the length of the hall from centuries of heavy foot traffic. The hallway was lit by the glowing jars, which were placed every ten feet or so on the floor, creating pools of eerie orange light with deep shadows between them. An acolyte pushed a cart toward them, struggling to keep the wheels on either side of the indentations. The smell of burning things seeped out of several doors as they passed, and a powerful vinegary tang emanating from a hallway to the right cleared Gilea's sinuses.

"It can be a little intense sometimes, especially when we get to the kitchen," Amini said, releasing Gilea and breathing in deeply. "But I've always loved the smell. Reminds me of home." Gilea smiled, thinking of her days as a child roaming the artisanal docks in Rontaia, peeking in the crooked doorways and windows at the tanners and the alchemists as they stirred, measured, and poured, always tending several fires.

"I've always wondered what it must be like. I mean, I've seen the little shops, but the big workshops have always fascinated me."

"It's good to know where your tincture comes from." They reached a large wooden door flanked by two guards, who pulled the door open without a word. They passed into a circular room that was immediately familiar, with bronze runes laid in the floor in front of an ornate bronze door, just like the one outside the cradle room. Gilea paused, studying the runes; they had a familiar look, not unlike parts of Cloti's script. Amini stooped to remove the key, replacing it with her own knob to stop the light pouring up toward the ceiling, and the door swung open.

The room beyond was long and spacious, with rows of open windows set high in the walls. A dozen or so figures worked bellows and little furnaces, pots, alembics, and other strange vessels made of glass or metal. The air was heady with the smell of burning coal, sulfur, vinegar, and other potent aromas that commingled to form an intoxicating fog. Gilea saw an older woman scraping something clear and slimy from a bowl into a bain-marie, immediately stirring it as she wiped the sweat from her brow onto the sleeve of her robe. She wondered if this same woman had been involved in mixing the tinctures she had used to access the Caravan, or perhaps the Inkwell. She wanted to stop and watch, to ask what the woman was making, but she felt Amini's mental pull, and she hurried to catch up with her. The woman was ninety years old, but Gilea kept finding herself falling behind.

Amini approached a large door of dim gray metal set into the wall and pulled down an enormous latch. The door popped open and Amini ushered Gilea inside with a sweep of her arm. Gilea walked past Amini into an oppressively small space, perfectly spherical, with just enough room for the two of them to stand without hitting their heads. Amini closed the door and pulled up the lever on the inside, straining until it emitted a loud *thunk*, and the heavy silence of the room enveloped them.

"What is this place?" Gilea stared around at the smooth, dull metal walls, which seemed to swallow the orange light from the jar.

"It's the absorption chamber. Some rare metals, like hotsilver, are dangerous to be around, and they're stored here until they are needed. The walls are lined with lead, which absorbs their energy. Don't worry, it's safe to be in here for a few minutes." Amini took Gilea's hands, and her droopy eyes had a deep, worried look.

"What's wrong?" Gilea asked, feeling suddenly faint. Amini squeezed her hands, and Gilea felt a reassuring warmth flow over her.

"I brought you here because it's the only place Pleone cannot see or hear." Panic rose inside Gilea's mind, and even Amini's calming vibes were not enough to snuff it out completely. "We need to talk about something, then I will teach you how to hide what we've discussed."

"Hide? I don't see how, if Pleone's reach is as far as you say. I can't wall myself against her; she's too powerful."

"Not everything is about walls. There are subtler ways, which I will show you. But first, we need to talk about Rontaia."

Gilea closed her eyes and took in a deep breath, struggling to calm her nerves as released it in a steady stream. She had worried that her sympathy for the Rontaians had seeped through, and if Amini was asking, that must have been the case. She took another deep breath in, let it out slowly, then opened her eyes.

"Okay. What do you want to know?"

"You are sympathetic to their philosophy, to their cause, as I am. As many of us are." She released Gilea's hands and folded her own together. "They say they wish to share everything freely with the world, the peace of their practice, their knowledge, their works. The good they do, working with the poor, the sick, the lost..." Amini's eyes crinkled with a soft smile. "I wish we did more work like that here."

"But why don't we?"

"There is a delicate balance, which not everyone perceives the same way. If we opened Endulai to the masses, it would be overwhelmed, and the peace and deep meditations we practice would be impossible. Even in Rontaia, only part of their complex is open to the

131

public. They, too, have hidden places like this, secrets they guard jealously. Surely you sensed something hidden while you were there."

"I did. I..." Gilea paused, calling to mind the figure she had sensed in the Rontaian crossroad. "I was speaking with Sali. Do you know him?" Amini blinked yes. "Anyway, I kept getting the sense there was someone else there, hidden, just out of reach of my awareness. Like a ghost."

"You felt it in the Maer crossroad too."

"Yes, and Ujenn did as well. Do you know what it was?"

"*Who* it was, and no, we don't know exactly, but someone is accessing the Caravan without a cradle." Amini and Pleone had both mentioned the possibility, but the certainty in Amini's voice sent chills over Gilea's skin

"How do you think they are doing it?"

"We don't know for sure, but it sounds like the Universal Tincture."

Gilea swallowed. She knew the stories, that in the Time Before there was a tincture so powerful it could allow access to the Thousand Worlds from anywhere, and Amini had mentioned it before. She wasn't entirely sure if the Thousand Worlds from the ancient texts were the same thing as the Caravan, but she couldn't see what else it might mean.

"Do we think they have it, then? The Universal Tincture?"

Amini frowned, casting troubled eyes down at her feet. "It seems someone does, but if the Rontaian temple had it, they would not be so desperate for sunstone. And they are, no matter how much they pretend otherwise. They may resent Endulai, but they need sunstone like any crossroad to run at full power. Otherwise, they'd have to use *falin* oil or some other fuel source, which is even more expensive in the long run and does not allow for the same stable connection."

"So, whoever has the tincture is not in the temple?"

"This is what we don't know, what is most puzzling. The presence is most often felt at the Rontaian crossroad, and the reason for Pleone's rift with them is because she pressed them too hard on the subject, and they abruptly shut down her access. As powerful as she is, she cannot force uninvited entry across the continent."

"Why bring me here to talk about this?"

"If Rontaia gets the Universal Tincture, if they can reproduce it at will, they will no longer need sunstone or any other power source.

Their travelers will be able to access the Caravan with little training and without a cradle. Rontaia will become the *de facto* center of the Caravan and all commerce in the South. They might even bypass the Caravan entirely if this tincture can allow direct communication between minds over distance. Endulai's influence would diminish, and Pleone will go to any lengths to prevent that from happening."

Gilea paused, trying to imagine what lengths Pleone could really go to if she felt Endulai's control slipping. "I still don't see—"

Amini took her hands again, bringing them to her chest. "Pleone may not be able to act directly against Rontaia, but her influence is wider and more potent than anyone else. I fear..." she pressed Gilea's hands together inside hers. "I fear that Pleone's desire for control will bring the whole system down, and Endulai with it."

"What do you want me to do?"

"I will tell you, but first I need to show you how to hide this conversation." She leaned to press foreheads with Gilea, who slipped into their shared mindspace as if she were entering a perfectly warm bath. *"Summon the reflex you have when you need to pee but have to hold it. This will be your defense against Pleone's prying. She will not read your thoughts when you are using the bathroom. If you can reproduce this technique at will, without reflection, your thoughts will be protected. Follow my thoughts, then return to your own mind and repeat the process."*

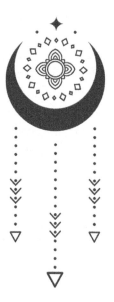

Twenty Seven

Patia's heart thudded in her chest as she studied the page with fresh eyes. If the text was a map, it would explain why the symbols were of mixed origins, why they were of different sizes, and why there was no obvious pattern to them. But, what kind of map was this? She could make out nothing that looked like rivers, mountains, or cities, though she supposed the symbols could be lakes or ponds. A chill raced up her spine as it came to her.

"These are islands," she murmured. "This is the Naeli Gulf, isn't it?" She knew there were said to be thousands of islands in the Gulf within a week's journey from Rontaia, most of them uninhabited, and many children's stories told of wild and mysterious adventures there.

Paoro's eyes shone in the dim light, and he nodded. "Cloti left clues, in some of her poetry, and it took me forever to puzzle them out. It came to me one day, as I was staring out at the river, thinking of how the water flows down from the mountains, forming tiny streams that merge one by one to form rivers, all of which flow into the Agra, then out into the wide sea." His eyes had a faraway look as if he were staring out into the ocean's endless horizon. "I remembered seeing a map of the islands on the wall of the university library, and something about it stuck in my mind. I went back to the library, though I had to pay for entry since I'm no longer a student or a teacher, which was galling, to say the least." He shook his head, and Patia remembered how he used to fall asleep in the library when he was a student, slumped over a pile of books.

"When I saw it again, my mind immediately made the connection to this text, and I sketched out a facsimile and brought it home to compare." He took the book from Patia, whose arms were growing tired from holding its weight, and flipped through the latter half of the book until he stopped on a page with a penciled map glued to it. She studied it for a moment, then he flipped back to the text, and she could see the similarities clearly, though it was not in any way a perfect match.

"The text has many more symbols," she said, and Paoro nodded vigorously.

"Yes, and they are much more accurate than the university map, which I suspect was made by someone with more artistic skill than actual knowledge of the Naeli Isles. I did some further research and found nautical maps that were more accurate, but there were still differences, so I had to go and see for myself." His eyes were ablaze, and the despair in his expression had given way to excitement. "I chartered a boat, using up most of my savings, to set sail for the island Cloti refers to several times in her poems. She calls it the Isle of a Thousand Worlds. I always thought it was a metaphor, but after studying the texts over and over, I found enough clues to determine it must be a real island, represented by this symbol here." He pointed to the Circle of Circles, the ancient sign for infinity.

"And you were right?"

Paoro nodded, his eyes wet and brimming.

"What did you find there?"

He closed the book, set it down on a sliver of clear space on his couch, and beckoned Patia toward the tank.

A rank, rotten-fish odor greeted her as she approached, and Paoro let out a faint chuckle at the expression she made as she covered her nose with her new silk scarf.

"The taste is worse if you can believe it." He picked up a small ladle and vial, swung the glass lid open, and filled the vial halfway with the murky greenish-brown water at the bottom of the tank. He held it so the Chemist lamp shone through it, swirled it around several times, then lifted it up to sniff it. His nostrils flared and his face wrinkled for a moment, then relaxed into a peaceful smile, rendered sinister by the purple shadows. He held it out to her.

"Don't drink it, please. Just smell."

Patia held it a few inches away and wafted with her hand, almost dropping the vial as the stench hit her nose, like rotting crab mixed with human shit. Paoro's hand clamped around hers, and he removed the vial carefully, breathing out a long sigh.

"What you are feeling is the merest hint of what the tincture can do, if ingested in the correct proportions by body weight."

"What do you mean, what I'm feeling?" Patia's voice echoed throughout the room in almost visual waves, and she had the sudden sense of being underwater, but she could breathe, like a fish.

"Now do you see?" Paoro's voice reached her a half-second after she saw his lips move. "Don't worry, it won't last more than a few minutes at this dose, but if you want to sit down…" He gestured toward the circular meditation rug with the candles, and Patia drifted over to it and melted onto a large cushion at the edge of the rug. Paoro was sitting next to her, but he was also standing next to her by the tank, holding up the vial, and he was walking toward the rug, sitting down cross-legged on the floor next to her.

"It's a hallucinogen," she managed, the words escaping like bubbles from a fish's mouth. The versions of Paoro and herself standing by the tank vanished, along with the moving Paoro, leaving only her and what she assumed was the real Paoro seated facing each other on the rug.

"It has that side effect, especially at first, but you should experience a clarity, shortly."

His final words rang clear, and the room came into such sharp focus it was overwhelming at first. Patia noticed the individual hairs on Paoro's wrist, the delicate movement of the murky water in the tank, the low hiss of the flame from the Chemist lamp. But there was something more than these minute physical details; it was as if she could feel Paoro studying her, not his eyes on her, but his thoughts, his awareness. When she turned her gaze to meet his, the feeling intensified, and she heard his voice, muted but still comprehensible, though his lips did not move.

"It's okay," the voice said. *"It won't last much longer. I just wanted you to see—"*

"Don't do that, don't talk like that, I don't want that. Please stop."

Patia's heartbeat was throbbing in her throat, and she scrambled to her feet as panic surged through her body.

"Okay, I'll stop." Paoro remained seated, holding up his hands, flashing a guilty but spacey smile. Patia had the strong urge to haul off and kick that smile off his face. "I just needed you to know what it is, what it can do. Why I need you."

Patia backed away from Paoro, who made no move to stand. Her vision and thoughts were becoming clear again, and her breath came steadily, though her heart still raced from the experience.

"You might need me, but I don't need this." She took a step around Paoro, keeping her distance as if he were a poisonous snake, and picked up her bag, which lay on the floor next to where she had sat.

He held up the vial, his eyes glassy in the shadows. "One whiff of this has the same effect as a vial of the highest-rated meditation tincture."

Patia paused. It might well be true, based on the effect she had felt, which was many times stronger than what she'd experienced from tasting her best tinctures. If the effect were the same as a tincture rated 10, it would be worth up to a hundred *lep*. And if this effect could be achieved through a stable tincture with controlled dosing, the value of the sludgy water in the tank would be in the millions. But there was no way Paoro could pull that off on his own; based on the mess he'd made with the sulfur powder on the table, it was clear his alchemical skills had only gotten worse since she'd last known him.

"You want me to help you distill it?"

Paoro shook his head, deep laughter welling up and filling the room. "It doesn't need to be distilled; only diluted. That's not the problem." He stared off at the tank, his eyes full of worry. "I think it's dying." He drifted toward the tank, and Patia followed as her curiosity and the obvious value of its contents overwhelmed her anger at Paoro. She tied her scarf around her nose as he lifted the tank lid, then moved to the side so she could get a closer look. Inside the tank was a pile of the kind of light, porous rocks often found by the seashore, with green moss coating the rocks closest to the water level. The green gave way to a thicker coating of light gray higher up on the rocks, whose texture resembled the pus from an infected wound.

"Not too close," Paoro said, edging his body between her and the tank, and she pulled back, her head light again, her vision transforming everything into a wavy, undulating version of reality, as she had felt before. She leaned against the edge of the couch, closing her eyes to chase away the unnerving instability of her surroundings. The nebulous, flowing darkness she saw behind her lids was much worse, so she opened her eyes and accepted the hand Paoro offered. He led her away from the tank, back to the cushion where she had sat before. She saw herself and Paoro walking across the room, then the vision dissipated, and her head cleared more quickly than the first time.

"Sorry, I forget how sensitive one is the first few times. But, you saw it, yes?"

Patia nodded, and a shiver ran up and down her spine, spreading out through her limbs so she had to shake them like a wet dog.

"I saw...some kind of ooze or slime, I guess. What is...is that...?"

Paoro blinked his acknowledgment. "I've tried to keep the environment as close as I can, but the river water isn't salty enough, and honestly I don't know if the Chemist lamp is helping, but I needed something to mimic the hotsilver in the cave."

Patia nodded; though she'd only ever seen it once, hotsilver gave off a faint purplish glow, and it was thought to cause illness or even death to anyone who spent too much time in its presence.

"How do you know it's dying?" It certainly didn't look healthy, but who knew what a sea-cave dwelling ooze was supposed to look like?

"It's shrinking, and growing thinner, as if it's losing whatever it is that holds it together. It keeps wanting to flow down into the water, and I am forever coaxing it back up with a long spoon."

"So why don't you just go back and get more? You know where it is, and you got it before."

Paoro closed his eyes, shaking his head gently. "It's too difficult of a journey for me in this state." He gestured limply at his gaunt frame, his tortured face. "And besides, it needs me. I may not be able to keep it alive forever, but if I go away it will die for sure. This might sound odd, but I feel...responsible for it. Besides, who could I trust to watch it? Do you know what they'd do if they had unfettered access to the Universal Tincture?" He finished his sentence in a whisper, and Patia shook her head.

"In theory," Paoro said in a low voice, "with the Universal Tincture, they could access the Caravan and the Thousand Worlds beyond from anywhere, with no cradle. Anyone on the continent could communicate with anyone else, without the intercession of a temple. In

138

time, it might render Endulai and its system of cradles and crossroads obsolete. The Caravan as we know it would cease to exist."

"I can't imagine it would be good for business," Patia said slowly, her brain struggling to grasp the practical implications of Paoro's words. "Even if they just use it as tincture, if the temple had its own high-quality supply, it could put half the alchemists in the city out of work overnight."

"Well I suppose that's one side effect, but they could also travel the Caravan and go wherever they wanted, uninvited and unseen. They could even travel beyond the Caravan, beyond this world, this time." Paoro's eyes grew wider and his voice sharper as he spoke. "What would happen if the gates to the Thousand Worlds were suddenly flung open, and anyone could travel anywhere, anytime? What if all people were in touch with each other, all the time? It would be chaos!" His voice rose, and Patia recoiled at his fetid breath.

"They don't know, do they?" Patia asked. "What this can do?" Paoro's eyes raised to hers, then closed as he shook his head.

"Not exactly, but they must suspect, or they wouldn't be funding me so lavishly. I made it into a tincture, trying to disguise the source and dilute it enough not to arouse suspicion, and it scored a ten. When I came back with more, they offered me double the usual rate, plus a room here, and anything I needed, for as long as I needed it. Their library contains copies of most of Cloti's known writings, copied from the original cylinder scrolls. I thought, perhaps, somewhere in there, or in the Thousand Worlds, I would find instructions on how to keep it alive." He raised his hands to his sides and let them fall.

"And you want me to go and get more, and bring it back, and do what with it?"

"I hypothesize," said Paoro, raising one finger as his face brightened with scholarly excitement, "that contact with a healthy organism would rejuvenate it, perhaps giving me time to figure out a better setup, with maybe some hotsilver, and some shielding in the tank, to keep the glow in, of course."

"And if you succeed, if you have a limitless supply of the Universal Tincture at your disposal, what then? You just said you didn't want to fling open those gates."

"No, I don't," he said, curling his finger back into his hand. "As I said, that would be chaos. But, with the right techniques, I expect one could figure out how to isolate the prime actors of the ooze and use them to make any number of specialty tinctures. Just think of the possibilities." He shot Patia a knowing glance, then turned back to stare into the tank for several breaths.

Patia's head was spinning with the implications; was he asking her to join him in his venture? She could ask for a sizeable chunk of the profits, and within a few months' time, she could make as much money as she had made in her entire career. And the idea of it, adapting the power of the ooze to make tinctures no one else would be capable of, was almost as intoxicating as the effects of the substance itself. Not only could she make meditation tinctures, but remedies for ailments of the mind, which the Endulians were sometimes able to treat with their philosophical techniques. If she could perfect and bottle that, she and Gero could be the sole purveyors of the first science-based medicines for mental illness, and the profits would be unimaginable.

"Fifty percent," she said, trying to calm the quaver in her voice.

Paoro turned around slowly, his eyes squinting with apparent puzzlement. "Fifty..." His eyebrows raised suddenly, and a smile grew on his face. "Fifty percent, fine, that sounds just fine. If you bring back a viable specimen, and *if* you can help me achieve a stable formulation." He held out his hand, and Patia let it hang in the air.

"A handshake's not going to cut it. I want this in writing."

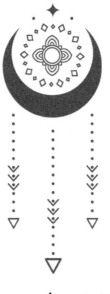

Twenty Eight

Gilea stepped into the bathroom, pulling the curtain shut behind her, and sat on the cold marble seat. As she relieved herself, she let the pent-up thoughts fill her mind, as Amini had taught her. There was no way to be certain Pleone wasn't listening in to her mind even here, but Amini had assured her Pleone tuned out bodily functions like eating and using the bathroom, so she should be safe for a few minutes.

Amini had instructed her to pursue deep meditation, using Cloti's script as a focal point whenever possible, in preparation for work with the deep tincture. Whenever she felt thoughts of Amini's plan creeping into her mind, she was to wall them off using the same techniques she used during meditation to hold back hunger, thirst, and the need to relieve herself, and whenever she ate or used the bathroom, she could allow the thoughts to surface for a short period. She assumed Amini had perfected this technique, but Gilea was still learning, and she was always afraid she'd let something slip. The next time she was face to face with Pleone, she seriously doubted she'd be able to keep up the façade, but she worked to keep these worries beneath the surface, hoping Pleone would have no reason to suspect her. After all, there were hundreds of minds in Endulai, and as powerful as Pleone was, she couldn't read all of them at once, could she?

Footsteps approached in the hallway, and Gilea cleared her throat as she stood up and rearranged her robes. She walled off her thoughts as best she could, bringing her focus to thoughts of Temi, which she had been keeping until she had time to savor them.

She returned to her chamber, closed the door, and lit a candle, holding her forehead over the flame until it heated the exact spot where Temi's paint had stuck when they had said goodbye. Though the paint had long disappeared, she could still feel its absence, and when she concentrated, it helped her conjure thoughts of Temi's face, painted yellow, and her hands, white as lilies, thin but strong. More images flashed through her mind, Temi's tender feet, the delicate hair on the back of her neck, her pale breasts smeared with the blue tint of the medic's balm. Gilea's heart warmed at the vision, and the warmth spread, bringing desire with it. She opened herself up to these feelings, this desire, which brought about a strange sense of incompletion. She had never shied away from her natural desires before, but with Temi, she had glimpsed something more, and she desperately wanted to recapture that feeling. The roots of her connection with Temi were woven throughout her heart and mind, deeper than any physical union she had ever experienced with any of her past lovers.

Within, as without. Affito's words echoed in her mind. *The mind is thought to originate in the body, but the body cannot contain the mind.*

She formed a heart with her hands and stared through it into the candle's flame, seeing in it the joy in Temi's eyes when they'd met in the Inkwell. She closed her eyes and summoned the feeling of connectedness they'd shared in the Living Waters, which had grown from the first timid tendrils of their mindshare to the full immersion as she'd sunk into the depths of Temi's mind. She returned to her own vision, as she lay at death's door in the Living Waters, of her and Temi walking together on the docks eating tri-fries, Temi ducking away from a swooping seagull into Gilea's arms. The scene always ended there, with a crumb of tri-fry on Temi's lips, Gilea wanting to kiss it off, a frozen moment of pure happiness. This time, her vision fused with the memory of the moment she only allowed herself to summon in rare, private occasions. The weight of the water suffocating her, her hands reaching out in vain for Temi's, her mind struggling to pierce the *sitri's* hold. The water rushing off her. Breath and light returning. Temi's eyes, bright and so full of relief she thought they might burst.

Temi's hands on her shoulders. On her cheeks. Temi's face moving in close. Her lips, cracked and rough but with such softness and warmth beneath, pressing against Gilea's for a fleeting moment, sending her world spinning out of control.

Gilea lay back on her bunk, pulling her robes aside, and let her hands glide across her bare skin as she replayed that kiss in her mind, felt Temi's hands gripping the back of her neck, their foreheads pressing together. She felt the shared space opening between them, Temi's mind probing hers, Temi's surprise at discovering Gilea's feelings for her. Gilea stretched her arms over her head, letting her mind guide her body, which flushed in response to the flurry of thoughts and sensations. Temi's hesitation as she opened up to let Gilea in, the catch in her breath as Gilea pushed past the surface, the joy as their thoughts and emotions mingled. Gilea's pleasure rose as she relived her exploration of Temi's consciousness, finding the bright golden threads that led away from her pain and sorrow to her happy place, her vision of Rontaia. Gilea's Rontaia intertwined with Temi's, the synergy of their shared imagination forming a city of such light and beauty it was almost impossible to look at. Gilea's breath grew short as she recalled the feeling of their minds interlacing like vines racing together toward the sky, and she felt an unbearable tension building within her even as her mind floated farther and farther away. Something snapped inside her, and she crashed back into her body, which pulsed with unexpected ecstasy. She pressed the back of her hand against her mouth to muffle the moan that rose unbidden from her throat as slowly diminishing waves of pleasure rolled through her.

She lay spent, staring at the ceiling, sweat chilling her body as a faint breeze crept in through the window. She pressed her eyes shut, feeling something more than the physical release, something deeper, tucked away in the hidden universe of her heart. A crackling energy raged deep inside her chest, like a ball of lightning locked in a cage of bone and flesh to which only Temi held the key.

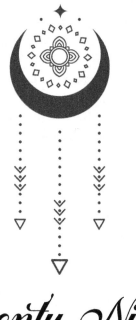

Twenty Nine

Patia watched Gero dozing at the table, his blue scarf poking out from beneath his collar, his quill jutting at an awkward angle above his ledger. Four jars of skin cream sat on the table, with a neatly penned P nestled inside the florid G of his insignia. She hadn't helped, and she wouldn't accept any of the profits, but her heart warmed to see their letters together. Gero stirred, blinking as he straightened his grip on his quill and dipped it in the inkwell. His eyes lit up as he saw her, and he left the quill in the ink.

"You're back," he croaked, eyeing her expectantly. She smiled and sat across from him, pouring a cup of water and drinking it in one long gulp. She coughed as the last drops made their way down the wrong pipe. A giggle compounded her cough, and it took her a moment to clear her throat.

"I see you finished the face cream."

"Yes, and I added the P to the insignia. I think it looks better this way, and it never hurts to freshen up the logo."

"*Idiot,*" she murmured, taking his hand. "I love it. But just so we're clear, the profits from the cream are all yours, no matter whose initials are on the lid. I didn't help, so I don't get paid."

Gero's smile faltered, but he kept the twinkle in his eye. "Of course. Best to keep the business side separate."

Patia raised his hand to her lips and kissed it, sucking on his knuckle for a moment. "It's the other side I'm interested in right now."

"Yes, yes, there will be time for that, but don't keep me in suspense any longer, woman! How did it go?" Gero squeezed her hand. His body was tense, his face stretched with anticipation.

"We cut a deal," she said. Gero pulled his hand back, scratching his knuckles with his other hand, an expectant look on his face. "It's complicated, but if we can make this happen, and I *know* we can, it will give us all the tincture-making work we can handle for the foreseeable future. We'll have something no one else has, and we will be rich beyond our wildest imagination."

"You mean making...the Universal Tincture?" Gero's voice dropped to a whisper, his eyes wide with awe.

"Not exactly. Like I said, it's complicated, and I can't tell you everything right now. You're going to have to trust me."

"I do, I do, I do," he said, almost singing the words. "Anything you want, whatever you need from me, I will be right here with you."

Patia bit her lip as her fingers crawled across the table to find his. "That's where it gets a bit more complicated." She brushed her fingertips over the back of his hands, screwing up her face against the shock of sudden tears that welled up and spilled out before she knew what was happening. She clutched his fingers in hers, angling her face down to wipe her tears on her shoulder.

"Complicated how?" Gero said in a hoarse voice, his eyes full and wet.

"I have to go away for a while. To...find something we need to make the tinctures. Something that can only be found in one place."

"Is it far?"

Patia nodded, unable to form words as her face burned with tears.

"Is it safe?"

Patia shrugged. Another hot tear rolled down her cheek.

"I can't go with you, can I?"

She shook her head, then buried her face in her hands as a sob racked her body, squeezing the breath out of her, and another before she could take a breath in. She gasped, then let out a moan, her embarrassment at Gero seeing her like this almost outweighing her sadness as she realized she would be leaving him all alone in this shack while she went off chasing a foolish dream.

"There he is again," Gero said, standing next to Patia as she sat on the dock watching the distant swimmer, whom she'd noticed a few times before. "In all the years I've lived here, I've hardly ever seen anyone swim in this river."

"For good reason." Patia thought about the waste hole in the floor of the shack, and the hundreds of alchemical shops, tanneries, and other industrial facilities along the river's edge.

"And yet he's been out here almost every day about this time. I suppose he must enjoy it."

"No telling what some people find pleasurable."

Gero leaned his shin against her back. "There are a few things that can be predicted..."

Patia craned her head up to smile at him as she reached behind her and ran her fingers up his thigh. He drew a sharp breath when she cupped his balls, awkwardly because of the angle, and gave them a gentle squeeze.

"You are an absolute demon," he managed with shortened breath.

Patia kept hold of him as she turned around and pulled herself up to stand with her other hand on his hip. She squeezed him a little tighter as she leaned in for a kiss, extra slowly, and by the time their lips finally met, his breath came in short huffs. She took her time with the kiss, leaning her hips closer to feel his growing hardness, pressing against it. She let go and reached around to grab both buttocks and pull him in roughly toward her as her lips and tongue devoured his mouth. She stopped abruptly, pulling her lips away as she reached behind his head and untied his silk scarf then took a half step back, whipping it through the air a few times. If she was going to leave him alone for several weeks, she wanted this to be a night neither of them would soon forget. She motioned him back with one hand as she swirled the scarf with the other, and he shuffled back toward the bed, as she directed. The back of his knees hit the bed, and he untied his robe at her gesture, his eyes wild with confusion and joy, his body not far behind.

She shed her robe and moved to the edge of the bed, where his feet were hanging off at an awkward angle. She picked up his feet and heaved them to the center of the bed, and he let out a little cry of pain, then laughed and said "It's okay, it's okay."

"Oh, it's not okay," she said, crawling onto the bed on all fours, hovering over him with the scarf loose around her neck. "But we're going to make it all better." She sat back straddling his legs, dropping the scarf onto his belly as she worked him over with both hands until he was as hard as he was going to get. She picked up the scarf and quickly trussed his balls tight and tied the ends around his cock, so he hopefully wouldn't lose what stiffness she'd been able to coax out of him. He let out a series of gasps, and he mouthed *What?* several times.

"We'll get back to that in a minute. But there's something I need from you first."

"Anything," he whispered.

"Good boy." She leaned close over him so their bodies were just touching, then ran her fingers through his beard, up over his lips, and around to the back of his head. She crawled forward, then raised up on her knees, still clutching the hair on the back of his head as she gazed straight down into his glassy eyes.

"Is this what you want?" She asked, rubbing the side of his head with her thumbs.

"Please, gods, yes," he moaned.

She smiled, maintaining eye contact with him as she lowered herself down onto his face. Her hips complained at the unaccustomed movement, and she shifted around until she found the right position, then sank down onto him. His tongue found her, and she closed her eyes as she slid slowly back and forth, imagining herself on the prow of a ship, cutting through the waves, as a shadowy island approached in the distance. The wind filled the sails, propelling the ship ever faster toward the island, where a bright purple light appeared. The light grew brighter as she moved atop Gero faster and faster, his hands clutching her hips, his mouth grasping at whatever part of her he could catch as she ground against his face. She froze in place as she came, her legs trembling as she struggled to maintain the exact right position and pressure. Pleasure flooded through her, and she felt a kind of aftershock of Paoro's tincture, the feeling of being in two places at once, here and not-here, herself and something beyond. A wet spurt hit her leg, and she giggled as she saw the release in Gero's eyes.

"All better now?" she said, slumping over sideways as her hips and knees suddenly burned with the exertion.

"I don't think I've ever been better in my whole life."

Gero hummed as he stirred the pot, bouncing lightly from one foot to the next as if he were dancing to some silent music. The smell of spicy, fishy *kurra* sauce filled the shack, and she eased in behind him, pressing against him as she wrapped her arms around his chest.

"Smells amazing! I didn't realize you were such a cook!"

"Well, I don't usually go all out just for me, but I had this *kurra* powder languishing on my shelf. We only got two crabs in the cage last night, but the flitters were thick in the tide pools this morning, so I added those."

"Are those bitterleaves?" Long strings of green floated in the bubbling orange sauce.

"They are! Some of the last of the season, and they're a bit tattered but they'll do. There's an inlet just upstream where they grow. I got a couple onions and some garlic from the veggie cart as well, and some flatbreads to go with it."

Patia pressed into his ass as she slid her hands inside his robe to pinch his nipples. "A girl could get used to this."

Gero stopped stirring as she toyed with him, then grabbed her wrists gently and turned around to face her, taking both hands in his.

"As could I." The twinkle in his eyes was tinged with sadness. "It makes me wonder, though, if what we have is so...something you could get used to, in your words, do you really have to go? Is there something out there that's better than what we have right here?"

Patia released his hands, turning away and clasping hers together as her face grew hot, regret and sadness mixing with a sudden burst of anger. She took a deep breath and turned back around.

"Gero, we've known each other for, what, two weeks?" He nodded, his eyes dropping as tears slid down his cheek into his beard. She stepped to him and took his hands again. "In that time I've come to see something I never thought was possible, never knew I needed. I need you, Gero, more than you know. But you're not the only thing I need." He pulled one hand away to wipe his face, which curved slightly toward a smile. "I've been pursuing my Works for my whole life, and I've never come this close to something...transcendent before. Not that what we have isn't transcendent, because it is. It truly is." She clutched his hands to her chest, wanting to kiss the tears from his face, but needing to keep a little space for the moment.

"I understand," he said, shaking his head a little. "I haven't felt this much excitement about my Works in a long time. What you know, what you can do...you are truly exceptional." Patia's heart filled with his words, and she felt tears rising up. She steeled her face against them; she needed to be strong, for Gero. "I just can't help thinking, and perhaps this is greedy of me, that we might have both."

"We can, Gero, and we *will.*" She clutched his fingers hard, feeling his strength as he grasped hers in equal measure. "I'm not going away for good. Just long enough to get what I need, what we need. Once we have that, we will have all the time in the world to pursue the higher Works together, Works most alchemists can only dream of."

"Make me a promise." His eyes had stilled, and their heat almost made Patia look away.

"I swear to you, on my book of Works and all the quicksilver in the South, I will return to you, and we will be together, always." Gero gave a slow blink, and Patia leaned forward and gave him a gentle kiss. "But first, I need to find a boat."

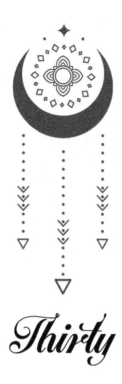

Thirty

Gilea's hands trembled as she sat on her bed and opened the letter, which she had clutched to her chest as she hurried through the dark hallways.

Dearest Gilea,

I miss you, and I think of you often.

I am very busy with production of the new pottery line, which features the swirls, the breathfins, the stickbirds, and even the emerald worm, though my skin crawls every time I paint its sinuous form onto a plate. Mother has secured placement in some of the biggest houses for the fall equinox, so the designs will be seen by all the painted faces in Anari, and in Tralum, where she has connections. She is difficult, judgmental, and exacting, but she knows her business, and we are poised for a breakthrough if all goes as planned, though it seldom does, does it? I apologize for boring you with such mundane details, but they occupy most of my time, and I thought you might like to know how I spend my days.

I can't imagine the life you must be leading at Endulai, but I try every day. I travel often in my memories to the Living Waters, to the connection we shared, the way you helped me see beneath the surface of my mind, and yours. I picture you probing the depths of your own mind, and others, and I imagine you must have made similar connections, if not deeper, in meditation with your fellow Endulian practitioners. I like to think what we had, what we have, is special, unique in all the world, for it truly is to me, and I hope it is to you as well.

People often speak of love, this mysterious, ineffable bond with another, and I have always wondered if I was deficient in some way because I do not feel these bonds in the way the poems and songs tell. This idea that there is only one person in all the Thousand Worlds for each one of us, and only in finding that twin soul can we find true happiness. But maybe happiness must be made, relationships forged by trials and shared experiences. Maybe there is not only one person for each of us, but we can form a deeper bond with one person by what we live through, how we cling together against the raging storms of life. And once we form that bond, nothing can tear it apart without our deciding to let it go. Maybe that is what love is, or what it should be.

I must stop myself from rambling and come to my point. Though I don't know if what I feel is the same as what our language calls it, I must speak in the common parlance and say it plainly.

I love you, Gilea.

I know you love me too. I felt it when we shared minds in the Living Waters, and in our brief visit in the Inkwell. I can tell what you feel is not the same. There is a fire in you that burns hot and fierce, while my feelings for you are like a thousand candles burning quietly. When I was inside your mind, I could feel you trying to restrain your fire through your mental discipline. Were you trying to shield me from its heat, or were you protecting yourself from getting burned because you knew I didn't feel the same way?

I may wear kid gloves, but I don't need to be handled with them. I know love means more to you than just an emotional connection, and though I don't feel

151

desire the same way you do, I am no prude, and I am aware that for most people, love and sex are often intertwined in mysterious ways. I don't know if I can give you what you need in that regard, but your absence has kindled new and surprising feelings in me, and I would like to explore this mystery with you, in time, if you can temper your fire with patience. It feels so strange saying all of this in a letter, but I suppose it would feel even stranger saying it in person.

I will be working my fingers to the bone in the coming days. Our production for the fall equinox will be complete by month's end, and it took surprisingly little effort to convince Mother of my plan to take a trip to Rontaia with samples, to look for a production facility if we can find the market there we hope for. Once our work here is complete, I will book passage on the first ship to Rontaia. I dearly hope you will join me. I will send word when I know the timing of my arrival.

I miss you, and I think of you often.

Temi

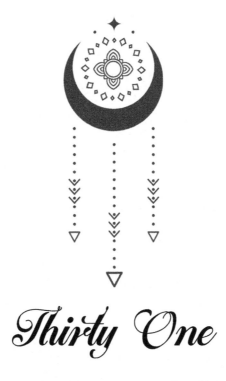

Thirty One

Patia lined the jars on the table, pre-measured and laid out in the order Gero would need them, with mystographic numbers written in chalk on the lids. She straightened a couple of jars that were a little out of line, her heart warming as she imagined Gero's smile when he saw the mise en place. He was late from his errand, and Patia needed something to do with her hands, so she rewrote the recipe, changing the order of the steps so he would have to read the third line first, then the sixth, the ninth, the twelfth, and the fifteenth before returning to the second, fifth, and so on. Gero would appreciate the extra note of caution; he treated every document as if it were in imminent danger of being stolen, his arcane secrets used for another's gain. She took the first copy to the edge of the dock, lit it, and held it above the water until she could feel the heat from the flames. She used it to light a half-smoked cheroot she had saved, then dropped the remnant of the paper into the river, which swallowed it with a brief hiss. She saw Vera cavorting with another otter in the fading beds of swayweed just past the dropoff. She let the thick smoke linger in her mouth, then trickle out the corners, dissipating in the warm, salty breeze. She had just tossed the butt into the river when Vera came swimming over, rolling onto her back and spinning in circles, her playful black eyes never leaving Patia's.

"I'm back," Gero called from the front doorway. Vera clambered up the ladder with remarkable speed, shaking her body and flinging water like a dog, then galloped into the shack, where she raced around Gero's ankles. "Just a moment, just a moment, you peckish little beast, let me see what's in the breadbox."

Patia moved to the doorway, leaning against the frame and watching Gero hobble to the table, open the box, and break off a piece of seabiscuit.

"Sit up, yes, that's it." He held out the piece and Vera balanced with her tail as she rose on her hind legs, gripping the biscuit between her teeth, then dropping to a hunched position as she audibly gnawed the rock-hard substance. "Good girl," Gero said, rubbing her rump with his sandal. "Good girl gets her treats."

"I'll be a good girl if it means I get treats," Patia said, stepping toward Gero, whose face lit up with a smile.

"Oh, I have a special treat for you, but only if you're very, very good." He patted his satchel, and Patia reached for it, but he swiveled sideways, keeping it just out of reach. "Later, when you've had a chance to prove you deserve it." The twinkle in his eyes was more mischievous than usual, and Patia closed the distance, slipping her fingers inside his robe and running them up toward his neck. She leaned into his crotch with her thigh, and he closed his eyes and blew out a tight stream of breath.

"You're putty in my hands," she whispered, nuzzling his beard as her fingers wrapped playfully around his neck. His hands found her hips, pulling her toward him as she angled his head down and laid her lips on his. Heat suffused her body and she leaned into him, a smile briefly interrupting the kiss as she felt him growing hard. She pulled her head back but kept pressure where it counted, and his eyes opened, soft, pleading, helpless. She released her fingers from his throat and pulled her body back, holding Gero's shoulders as he wobbled.

"Patia, I—" Gero closed his eyes for a moment, taking her wrists in his hands.

"You what?" she asked, her voice growing soft.

His fingers kneaded her wrists, and his eyes grew earnest, penetrating, and a little sad. "I've lived my whole life thinking it was an illusion, a fable told to keep people from seeing the ugly, naked truth.

154

A trick of bodily alchemy. I've said the words before, but I don't think I've ever truly meant them."

Patia pressed her forehead into Gero's, the warmth in her body coiling up inside her chest like a newly stoked fire.

"Say the words, Gero."

"Patia, I love you. I—" His voice broke as he gripped her shoulders, and he kissed her forehead, her nose, her lips. "I know it sounds ridiculous, a man like me, at this age, falling so completely for someone he's only just met, but—"

"I love you too, *idiot.*" She kissed him gently, her head growing light as the unaccustomed emotion spread through her. She had been with many men before and had been very fond of a few of them, but she had thought herself immune to this ridiculous societal notion.

A light nip on her ankle was followed by the caress of Vera's slick, wet fur as the creature wove between her legs and Gero's, chittering loudly. It was the first time Vera had gotten close enough to touch her.

"Who's a greedy little girl wants more treats?" Gero said, chucking Vera under the chin with his toe. He reached over and broke off another corner of the seabiscuit, holding it to Patia. "You want to try?"

Patia took the rough triangle and squatted, holding it out. Vera circled Gero's ankles a few times, then slunk over to her, rose up slowly, and took it between her teeth with surprising delicacy, then scurried back between Gero's feet to devour her prize, eyeing Patia every so often as she rotated and gnawed it.

"I spoke with Mani," Gero said in a light voice. "He suggested we ask around at the fishermen's docks. Says there're always a few boats available to charter."

"Even though I don't intend to do any fishing?"

"Well, I suppose you might want to eat something fresh while you're out, no? You don't seem overly fond of seabiscuits."

Patia did a mental inventory of her purse; she had a little over fifty *lep*, and she wondered if it would be enough.

"I'll pitch in if you're a little short," Gero said meekly. "Wouldn't want you going off on just any boat."

"A loan," Patia countered, touching his nose with her index finger. "*If* it comes to that, we'll put it in writing."

"If you insist."

There were over a hundred boats on the fishing docks, of all shapes and sizes. A few were actively loading gear or unloading fish, but most sat idle, and a fair number appeared unoccupied. Fisherfolk mended sails, sanded, varnished, painted, or otherwise maintained their boats in the still-hot sun. Others sat smoking, reading, or dozing on their boats, and none of them looked particularly open to conversation.

"Can't you just do this for me?" Patia pleaded, leaning her hip into Gero as they studied the activity on the docks.

"Your feminine wiles won't work on me this time," he said, bumping her hip away with his, then stumbling a bit. "But they just might work on some of these fishermen."

"Well, I don't know if I want to go on a boat with someone on whom my wiles would be effective." In truth, she was more than a little leery of the prospect of being stuck on a boat for several weeks with an unknown man, but she saw only a few women on the docks.

"You did mention something about having a wicked little knife. I'm sure you'd be able to take care of yourself if it came to that. But let's see if we can find someone who seems trustworthy."

Speaking with the fishermen was uncomfortable, as it wasn't the kind of bargain she was used to, and the small talk leading up to it was almost worse.

"Looking to charter a boat for a week or so," was what she settled on as her opening. The responses included a silent shake of the head, a few *Sorry, ma'ams*, some rough laughter, and a number of vague shrugs. She did get referred to several boats that might be available, and even talked to one fisherman for a few minutes until he heard her offer and waved her off.

"I'd make more than that running *falin* oil," he grumbled.

They made their way to the end of the last dock, where a boat sat with a ratty sail spread out across the deck, being sewed by a muscular nut-brown man with curly hair. A brownish mutt sat on the bow, eyeing Patia and Gero with keen eyes. The man raised up high on his knees, smiled, and waved, then his face quirked and he stood up all the way, his smile widening.

"Patia?" he said incredulously. He looked a bit familiar, but she never had been good with faces. His smile and his energy struck a chord, and it all came back to her. He was the guy in the canoe who'd paddled up along with the painted face after the swirls had stolen all her quicksilver. He'd sat on the dock and had a drink with her,

156

and his friend had seen her equipment and asked about her Works. She'd kind of liked him.

"Yes, but I don't recall your name. You were with that painted face scientist fellow, right?"

"Yes, Sylvan. The scientist, that is. I'm Leo."

"Leo, that's right. You were curious about the swirls. Did you ever find out what that was all about?"

Leo's face fell for a moment, then his smile flickered back to life. "We learned a few things, and I think Sylvan is still studying them." He paused, staring out at the river. "But, what brings you down to Rontaia?"

"It's a long story, but the thing is, right now I'm looking to charter a boat." She glanced down at the half-mended sail, the dried-out looking sides of the boat, the faded lettering. She didn't know much about sailing, but it didn't look like the most seaworthy on the dock.

"Really?" Leo stepped to the edge of the boat and leaped onto the dock without a second thought, landing with the grace of a cat. "Where are you looking to go?"

"An island out in the Naeli Gulf, maybe a week or two round trip, I hope."

"No shit? Which one?"

Patia worked her tongue inside her mouth. This man seemed as guileless as a child, but she wasn't ready to give up any secrets just yet.

"It's about four or five days out, from what I gather, if the weather is cooperative."

"This time of year's not usually too bad." Leo squinted as he looked west, studying the clouds, then down at his sail. "How soon do you need to leave?"

"Next day or two, I was hoping."

Leo nodded, clenching and unclenching his jaw. "I can have this boat ready in two days," he said, his smile blooming again.

"Are you sure?" Gero asked, eyeing the boat.

"Oh, no doubt, it's seaworthy now, but I need to finish this sail, check all the ropes, and finish pitching the hull. We can do it in two days, can't we, Max?"

A man had emerged from the hold, his pants wet to his knees, wearing blackened gloves. He eyed Patia and Gero uneasily, then shucked his gloves and called the dog over, squatting to rub its ears and head while he snuck furtive glances at them.

157

"Three would be better," the man muttered.

"Two is fine," Leo said, his smile genuine, almost infectious. "How much can you pay?" He asked the question with such disarming frankness that Patia responded immediately.

"Fifty *lep*," she said with what she hoped sounded like finality in her voice. Gero gave her side a gentle squeeze that felt reassuring. Leo cocked his head, blinking several times as he looked down at the dock, then smiled again as he reached out his hand.

"You know what? I'm planning to head out and do a little island-hopping myself, so we might as well join forces on this little adventure."

Patia looked to Gero, who blinked and nodded. She looked back at Leo, whose dark tan highlighted lean, powerful muscles, but his face had a childlike quality that made her immediately want to trust him.

"You've got yourself a passenger, Captain Leo."

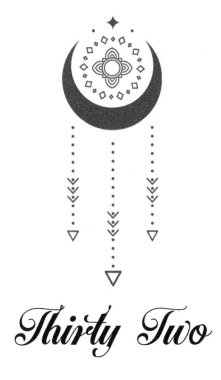

Thirty Two

"Today, I'll show you how to do crossroad support here at Endulai," Amini said, handing Gilea a vial of tincture. Nothing in her tone or facial expression betrayed her true purpose, and Gilea kept her mind calm as she uncorked the vial and drank it down. To her surprise, the deep tincture actually stung her throat less than the regular tinctures, but as she reclined in the cradle and the weighted blanket was laid over her, she felt herself falling out of her body long before the circlet was placed on her head. She drifted like a wind-blown leaf on the surface of a lake, and only realized she was in the tunnel of light when she was passing through the doorway. She landed in lotus position, her mind already serene and empty as if she'd been meditating for hours. She saw the cycles made by the other acolytes painted in the ether, a simple pattern of overlapping circles, and she flowed seamlessly into the cycle, adding her support to the others as if joining a dance she had known since before she was born.

She had trained extensively in the patterns, but this was the first time she had felt the tension, the weight of the crossroad, like a body being carried on a litter by four sturdy souls. Though only four were required, there were generally six acolytes at a time, a redundancy in case of unexpected fatigue. They worked in shifts of two or more hours, no more than once every other day, as Caravan support was especially draining. Amini had proposed a shorter run for her the first time, but as Gilea's mind joined the other acolytes in their cycles, she felt she could do this all day. She felt a tug from beneath and sank deep below as the surface of her mind maintained the connection with no effort on her part.

Amini's presence supported her like soft cushions on all sides. The upper levels of her mind cycled through the patterns, connected to the other minds performing similar cycles, which faded as the space around her expanded and her awareness was drawn to the depths below. Amini's support fell away and she was weightless, untethered, until after a time a gentle pressure surrounded her, holding her in place.

"You have retained the sitri's strength." Amini's mindvoice lilted with pleasant surprise. *"That will make things much easier."*

"How do you know of the sitri?"

"We meet every thirty-three mooncycles, in the pond outside the Annex. They choose who they communicate with carefully; they are more secretive even than we. I sensed an echo of it before when you first arrived, but I did not expect it to have taken hold so deeply."

"I was a conduit for one called Sage, in the Living Waters." Gilea had sworn not to share what she had learned, but Amini's familiarity clearly obviated this promise. *"They saved Temi, and me as well."*

"And what did you do for them in return?"

Gilea hesitated, unsure how to respond, how to explain what had happened. Had they saved the *sitri* from the Spreaders, or had they prevented a natural evolution in their society?

"No matter. We can speak of this later, once we have completed our mission. Open your mind's eye and look around."

At Amini's words, she suddenly saw bright patterns in the darkness like the moon and stars emerging from a passing cloud. Strands of coppery light flowed and twisted through the void, clustering together at various points, then spiraling off in different directions toward other clusters. It was bewildering at first, but with time she noticed the cords and clusters did not extend infinitely; they grew thinner, the clusters smaller, the farther they stretched from the center, until they stopped. Beyond the farthest clusters was only blackness.

"The Caravan," Gilea realized.

"The Caravan, and the Thousand Worlds. You see this large cluster nearest

160

us?"

"Is that Endulai?"

"Endulai is the center of the Caravan, the oldest active crossroad, but it was not always so, nor will it always be so. Look at the spaces between the clusters, and beyond. What do you see?"

Gilea strained her mind to pierce the darkness, and for an instant, she sensed something else, a texture to the void, but the glare of the coppery filaments and clusters was too strong, and the pressure surrounding her intensified. She loosened her mind, re-focusing on the bright lights.

"I...there's something there, but I can't make it out." Gilea suddenly felt spent, her mindvoice coming out like a drunk's slur.

"Relax, and think no more of it for now. You cannot delve too deeply on your first try. Fix that feeling in your mind, the sense that the void is not empty, but so full you cannot take it in. You can study this later, once you have rested, and when you are ready, we will try again. For now, we must re-surface, before the upper levels of your mind lose their focus and can no longer help support the crossroad. That is something Pleone might notice."

Gilea let the bright array of the Caravan fade, and she felt herself drawn up toward the cycles above, soothing in their simplicity, like the slowly circling water of the meditation pools. She fixed her mind on forgetting, and the coppery lights dissipated as she returned to the courtyard, in lotus position, surrounded by acolytes sitting in placid meditation. The cycles of her mind relaxed her fully, and she smiled as she felt the weight of the crossroad balanced in perfect harmony between her cycles and those of the others around her.

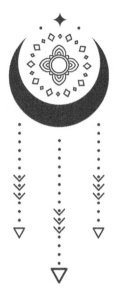

Thirty Three

Patia packed and repacked her bag while Gero was out getting "something special" for dinner. She hadn't come to Rontaia with much, and she didn't need all of that on the boat. She did have Paoro's containment vessel to carry, which was surprisingly heavy for its size, no bigger than a small muskmelon. A cage of brass wire protected a wide-mouthed flameglass globe with a lead-lined lid that screwed in tightly. The craftsmanship was impressive, and she tried to imagine how many of the coins donated to "the people" had been used to fund this endeavor. Patia wondered what Paoro had told them, how long he would be able to hold off their inquiries, when their patience would wear thin. That was his problem. Hers was finding the island and getting a sample back to Rontaia safe and sound.

Paoro had given her several glass capsules half-filled with a viscous light purple mixture sealed by a thin wax barrier. The mixture was made from the bodily fluids that made starfins glow. The other half looked empty, but she knew it contained some form of purified air. Once the capsules were shaken vigorously, the wax would break apart and the purified air would cause the liquid to glow purple, for up to two days before it faded. She was to drop one in with the ooze, in the hope that the purplish glow would keep it in decent shape until its return, when Paoro hoped to have completed his hotsilver setup to properly house it. He had given her four of the capsules in a padded wooden case, holding them just out of reach.

"You know how little I care for the coins of men, but these capsules are quite expensive, not to mention exceedingly difficult to acquire. And they could prove useful in our future endeavors. So please, use them sparingly."

She'd taken the box with gentle fingers and wrapped her scarf around it before tucking it in her purse, to be sure no harm would come to the capsules, which were the most precious and fascinating thing she'd ever had in her possession. She understood the chemistry of it, but how they got the fluids into a sealed glass capsule without boiling the efficacy out of them was a mystery, and to capture purified air in such a tiny vessel was a wonder beyond her comprehension. She hadn't been aware of anything this sophisticated when she'd lived here decades before. Though the talents of the Rontaian alchemists were dubious, the technological skills of their craftspeople were obviously superior.

She secured the vessel in its wooden crate and leaned her bag against it, though it was only mid-afternoon and she wasn't departing until the next morning. She was feeling irritable and out of sorts with the idea of this trip, the unknown sleeping arrangements, the odd man with Leo on the boat, the uncertainty of the entire venture. But her mind returned, as it often did, to that moment in Paoro's room, when the effects of the ooze had seemingly separated her mind from her body. If she could sample the water and experiment with a few isolating processes, she was sure she could find a way to extract its essence. Once she had that, she could make almost any tincture imaginable, bypassing multiple complicated and delicate procedures, and all that with minimal use of quicksilver. Paoro and the Rontaian Endulians might use it for their own metaphysical needs, but it was the infinite uses of its chemical properties that interested Patia the most. It would revolutionize alchemy and philosophical medicine, and she and Gero would be the only ones with the key to its exploitation. And if Paoro's use of the ooze ended up taking down the Caravan and Endulai with it, so much the better.

"All packed up and ready to go, I see." Gero stood in the doorway with a sack over his shoulder, a long loaf under his arm, and a jug of wine in his hand. His face held a wistful smile, and his blue scarf was twisted beneath the sack. His feet and legs were stained, as if he had washed mud off them, not very effectively.

"Not much to pack," she said, taking the loaf and the jug and giving him a quick peck on the lips.

"I expect not," he said, his eyes lingering on the crate. She had promised Paoro not to tell Gero what was in it, or exactly where she was going, and Gero had not asked, though the questions hung heavy in the air.

Patia laid the bread on the table and poured them each a vial of wine as Gero moved to the furnace, laid the sack gently on the floor, and started kindling the fire. As Patia approached with the wine, she noticed movement inside the sack, and a purple claw poked above the opening, followed by another. A spiky creature the size of her hand struggled onto the top, its antennae waving, then began crawling down the side of the bag, its legs sticking in the burlap.

"Mudcrawlers!" Patia said, her voice rising with childish delight. She hadn't eaten them since she'd lived in Rontaia, decades before. There were mudcrawlers in Guluch, but they were smaller and hardly worth the effort.

A long, brown shape streaked across the floor, and Vera snatched the creature off the bag and scampered off to a corner, dropping it and shaking her snout as the creature raised its claws in a defensive posture.

"You can have one, Vera, but that's all." Gero shook his finger at the otter, who angled this way and that, circling the creature, which rotated to match her movements. Patia handed Gero the vial, and they clinked and drank as they watched Vera toy with the mudcrawler for a while before pinning it from behind and cracking its shell with a precise bite to the back of the head.

"You harvested these yourself?" Patia asked, glancing down at his feet.

"Yes, with some difficulty, I should add, and a few good pinches." He held out his hand, which had several red welts on it. "But since it's our last night together for a while, I figured it was worth the effort."

Patia took Gero's hand and kissed the welts, softly at first, then licked and sucked them a bit. Gero winced, and she turned her eyes up to meet his and saw exactly the twinkle she was expecting. She worked her lips over his knuckles and along the sides of his hands, wet-kissing

164

the bones in his wrist and flicking her tongue across the tender under-side. Gero half-stifled a moan, cupping the back of her head with his free hand as she latched onto his wrist and sucked like a vampire, not letting go until she was sure she had left a mark. She let his wrist drop, and he drew a sharp breath as he examined the damage, a purplish oval on the light brown skin.

"When do I get my surprise?" she whispered.

"No dessert until you've had your dinner," he replied with a wry smile, rubbing his wrist and tilting his glass, swallowing a rather large gulp of wine as he sat down hard on the bench. "I don't suppose you'd mind filling the pot from the water barrel?"

Patia touched his arm, took the pot from atop the furnace, and filled it halfway from the spigot on the water barrel. It was a struggle to lift it back onto the furnace, but she managed, and when she turned around, she noticed Gero watching her. His wistful expression sparked a wave of heat in her face, and she busied herself checking on the mudcrawlers, blinking away tears that threatened to erupt out of nowhere.

"They're plenty lively," she said over her shoulder, closing the bag tight as Vera sidled over. "No more for you, greedy one!" Vera sulked over to Gero, rubbing against his ankles, and he hoisted himself to standing and fetched another piece of seabiscuit for her.

"Just one more bite and off you go," he said, pushing Vera away with his toe. She held the corner of biscuit in her teeth and slapped him with her tail as she scurried out the back door onto the dock, where she flopped down and started gnawing on her prize.

They sat across the table from each other, drinking wine and touching hands as they discussed the details of the tincture she had prepped for him. She had triple-distilled the seahops infusion, and given him instructions to distill it three more times before it would be ready for the next phase of the procedure. They had gone over it several times before, and Gero had asked numerous little questions, trying to poke a hole in her process, but in the end of course there were no flaws to be found, and by the time they had gone over the entire proce-dure, the water had boiled. Gero dumped the bag of mudcrawlers un-ceremoniously into the pot, knocking would-be escapees off the edge of the pot with a strainer, then clamped the lid tight. He refilled their vials and raised his in a toast.

"To the Thousand Worlds, without as within."

"Without as within," she murmured as if it were a time-honored ritual instead of something they'd made up on the spot. They drank, then Gero leaned over the table to kiss her. Their teeth clacked together as he lost his balance for a moment before catching himself with his hands on her shoulders. She laughed as she helped him up to standing, running her tongue over her teeth, which throbbed with the contact. She kissed him again, letting her tongue slip in and out of his mouth, nibbling and sucking his lips, smiling at the little moans he made. After a while, he pulled back, steadying himself against her as he swung his legs over the bench one at a time.

"They should be just about done," he said as he hobbled toward the furnace, a little unsteady with the wine. He lifted the lid, and his face lit up with pure joy. "Cut the bread and fill the wine, if you don't mind." He scooped the mudcrawlers, now bright red, into a sieve, which he shook, then dumped them into a bowl. He poured a generous portion of reddish powder over the steaming crustaceans, tossing them with the strainer until they were well coated. Patia put the sliced bread on the table next to the bowl, topped off their wine, and sat down, the smoky aroma of the spice mix setting her stomach growling.

They spoke little as they cracked and picked the mudcrawlers, dipping the fragrant white meat in the spice on the sides and bottom of the bowl. She made a mess of her first one, but the technique came back to her quickly, and they plowed through the crawlers in a matter of minutes, using the leftover bread to wipe every speck of spice and salt and mudcrawler juices from the bowl. She was pleasantly full, but she could have eaten a dozen more. Patia sucked each finger, in part to get the last essence of fishy spice, in part to cleanse the salt from the raw spots from handling the spiky shells. Gero did the same, and when they were finished, he brought over another bowl with two wet rags, fragrant with lemon and mint, and they wiped their hands and faces, tossing the rags back into the bowl. Patia refilled their vials, and they clinked and drank. She noticed Gero taking a smaller sip this time; he wasn't quite the drinker she was, and he was a little tipsy already.

"Thank you for a most delightful dinner," she said, raising her glass a little and taking a sip.

"Thank you for being here with me." Gero lifted his glass but set it down without drinking. He swung his legs over the bench with a slight groan and hobbled over to his desk, where he'd set his satchel earlier. He retrieved what looked like a scroll case, made of decorated

166

leather, with a fancy brass clasp that held it shut. As he lay it on the table, Patia could tell it was heavy, and a little wider and shorter than a typical scroll case. It had a small compartment with a tiny buckle and strap just above the clasp. He slid it across the table toward her, his mouth and eyes twitching with nervous excitement.

"Is this my surprise?" She hefted the case, which weighed about a pound, and fingered the brass clasp.

Gero nodded, covering his mouth with his fingers, which drummed nervously on his mustache. "I hope I haven't overstepped my bounds."

Patia undid the clasp and tried to pull the two halves apart, but they resisted.

"You have to twist it," Gero said, his fingers hanging in the air, trembling slightly.

She twisted the case open and pulled out a cylinder of black glass about nine inches long. One end was bulbed, with a slight curve, and the other end had a sturdy brass ring protruding next to a quartz square.

"Gero, is this an *olli*?" The one she carried in her bag was made of stone, and it had seen her through many a dry spell in Guluch when she was feeling too antisocial or busy to seek out a man to take care of her needs.

Gero nodded, covering his mouth with his hand, his eyes positively sparkling. "It's flameglass, so it won't break." Patia's heart warmed, and her loins stirred, but she kept a straight face as she slid her finger into the ring, which offered a steady grip, and let her thumb caress the quartz. It was smooth, perfectly flush with the surface, but it looked functional rather than purely decorative. The end of the cylinder it fit into was slightly wider than the other.

"Is this a button of some kind?"

Gero's hand moved from his mouth, his smile growing from nervous to excited.

"Yes, but it won't work unless you load it with one of the pellets here." He touched the small compartment on the case, and she opened it, revealing several round pellets like sparkly gray charcoal. "You unscrew the ring end and insert one of these pellets, and when you push the button, it vibrates, for up to a half-hour, I'm told."

Patia's body flushed with the thought, and she unscrewed the ring end, revealing a round chamber surrounded by silvery springs. She slipped one of the pellets into the chamber and screwed the cap back on, then lay the *olli* on the table between them, shifting in her seat as

167

her body seemed to anticipate the sensation. She reached out and took Gero's hands in hers, massaging his fingers, which were warm to the touch.

"I thought it might keep you company while you're gone. I hope it isn't—"

Patia squeezed his fingers tightly. "It's absolutely the most perfect gift anyone's ever given me." She pulled on his hands, using the leverage to stand and lean over the table, and he rose with her. She moved her face toward him, and his eyes fluttered shut as their mouths closed in. She hovered a moment, his mustache and beard tickling her face, their lips almost touching, then pressed into him, kissing him with sudden heat, her tongue flickering in and out of his mouth, her lips greedily devouring his. She pulled back, and Gero opened his eyes, which were glassy and hot.

"It must have cost a fortune," she said, sitting back down and picking up the *olli*, examining it from all angles. It was an exquisite piece of work, similar in quality to her alembic from the Silver Dock workshop.

"What else do I have to spend my money on? Besides, you said we were going to be rich once you bring back whatever it is you're sailing off to find."

"Thank you," she said, running her fingers over the bulbed end, whose shape would make it easier to hit her favorite spots. "But I'm afraid I can't take it with me." Gero's smile faltered for a moment, and Patia couldn't stop her smile from blooming. "Not until we run a full test of its performance." Gero's smile widened, and she handed it to him. "Hold this for me while I run off to the corner for a moment."

After she had relieved herself, she walked over and helped Gero to stand, then untied her robe and let it fall from her shoulders. She was sometimes self-conscious about her body, which time and gravity had changed more than she might have liked, but the heat in Gero's stare made her feel like the sexiest woman on the continent. She took the *olli* from him, turned, and sauntered to the bed.

"Be a dear and bring the red oil," she called over her shoulder.

She put Gero's ratty towel on the bed and sat down, propping the pillows so she could lean against the wall, and Gero returned, holding out the jar of oil with a timid smile.

"You put it on," she said, spreading her legs, the *olli* gleaming on the bed beside her. Gero sat down next to her, unscrewed the jar, and

168

set it on the bedside table. He dipped his fingers in, cupping his other hand beneath them, and swung his hands over, letting the red oil drip down onto her inner thighs and cunt, which warmed instantly as the oil flowed down. Gero locked eyes with her as he worked the oil from the outside in, his index and middle fingers gently teasing, circling over and around and barely inside but never touching her clit. His eyes were deep and earnest, but his gaze faltered as she grabbed his wrist and moved his fingers up and down.

Gero leaned in to kiss her, bracing one hand on her shoulder, kneading her muscles, while his fingers worked under her direction. She kissed him like a starved wolf at a fresh kill, moving his hand up and down with increasing speed, then she pulled back suddenly, pushing his hand to his lap.

"Move so you're facing me," she said, and Gero complied, sitting as close as he could, sliding his legs under hers. She leaned forward, took his fingers in both hands, and moved them to wrap around his cock, squeezing tightly, and he began pumping slowly up and down under her guidance as he grew harder and shorter of breath. His eyes moved down her body, then to the *olli*, which gleamed in the candle-light.

"Keep going just like that," she whispered, kissing him once more before leaning back against the pillows and picking up the heavy *olli*. The wine in her system softened the edges of the weird just enough that she gave in to it, sliding the cold, hard tip just inside her and moving it slowly up and down, side to side. She watched Gero, his eyes wide and wild and wet, pumping his cock slowly, reaching inside his robe with his other hand to rub his nipples, and she grabbed one of her breasts in response, pinching her nipple hard enough it almost hurt.

"Take your robe off," she said in a husky voice, sliding the *olli* inside her, a half-inch at a time. She pulled it out even more slowly, pressing the bulbed end up across the spot she liked, and she growled in her throat at the pleasure swelling inside her. The oil heightened her sensation, and she could feel the slick glass on each of a thousand different nerves, blooming with pleasure in rapid succession like a rock skipped across an endless pool. Gero was naked, holding onto one nipple as he stroked himself slowly, his eyes running from the *olli* up to her eyes, holding her gaze as they each worked themselves up in the slowest way possible, as if by common agreement.

169

"Slowly, now," she said in a quavering voice, "pump it as hard as it will go, then hold it in place and don't fucking move." She moved the *olli* up and down, sliding it along her clit, which throbbed with each pass of the bulbed end. Her thumb eased over the button as she watched Gero's valiant effort to bring himself to near-shiny hardness, his arm trembling a little as he held his cock tight. She savored the intense concentration on his face, the half-smile held rigid as he struggled to keep himself on the edge. She reached out with both feet, trapping his cock between them as she angled her legs wide, and Gero's hands gripped her calves. She pushed the bulbed end inside her, downward this time, moving it in slow circles until she found the spot she was looking for. She pressed down hard and held it in place, savoring the ineffable feeling of fullness. She squirmed with anticipation, and Gero's breath came in such short huffs she was worried he might have a heart attack.

"Be a dear and press the button for me," she said, locking eyes with him. His eyes went blank for a moment, then he gave a quick nod and leaned forward with some difficulty, given that she held his cock tightly between the soles of her feet. He wrapped his hands around hers, slid his thumb forward, and pressed the button.

"Mmmmhmmmm," Patia groaned as the vibration spread inside her like burning white sulfur, carried on nerve and bone and muscle, scorching everything in its path. She slid the *olli* deeper, forcing her breath in and out as the pressure coiled inside her, much faster and more intensely than she'd ever felt before. She clenched her teeth as she slid it out and pressed harder on Gero's cock with her feet as she spread her knees wide, hoping to slow her momentum, but as the *olli* glided in and out, up and around, the vibrations set off little bursts of pleasure that built and cascaded out of control. She pressed the shaft hard against her clit, and her hips bucked as the first wave of her orgasm ripped through her, quickly swallowed by another, and another, sending shivers down her trembling legs as her back arched uncontrollably. Gero gave a loud moan as her feet squeezed him ever tighter, and he exploded as she let go with her feet, pulling the *olli* out and falling back, gasping, onto the pillows.

Gero sat, hands on his knees, his chest heaving, his breath hoarse and ragged.

"Fuuuuuuuck," Patia managed in between aftershocks, sliding her legs to the outside of his, one of which was warm and sticky.

"Truer words," he said, finding her feet with his hands, cupping her soles gently. She shivered as one last wave of pleasure rippled through her.

"I don't care how much that thing cost," she sighed. "It was worth every *nomi*."

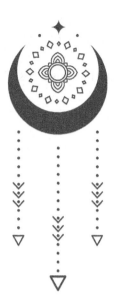

Thirty Four

Hey, Gil!

Aren't you proud of me for sending a message through the Ink-well? I know I can be a pretty cheap bastard, and the Endulian temple kind of creeps me out (no offense!), but I wanted to let you know I've finally got a boat rented and I'm setting out for a little scouting trip to find some sea caves for that roughabout we talk-ed about. I'm thinking a little after winter equinox if we want to recruit from Anari, but we could do one before the equinox if we work with the painted faces down here. Turns out there are more here than I thought! I really hope you'll join me—I know the last one turned out a little rough but it was pretty amazing too, right?

I convinced Max to join me on the raft downriver like I told you, and he's picked up sailing quicker than anything. He's so excited about the trip he can hardly sit still, and you know how Wolfie loves the sea. But the best part? I scored a paying passen-ger, not much but it helps, and what's wild is it's the alchemist we met near Guluch, the one who lost her quicksilver to the swirls.

How's that for a coincidence? I'm tempted to believe it's fate, but at any rate, we're setting out tomorrow and I'll check for messages when we get back.

I get it if you don't feel up for another trip right now, but let me know one way or another so I can find another minder if need be. I'd feel much safer with you in the boat, and I'm sure you'd feel much safer not being on it, but this one's going to sell out in a heartbeat, at premium prices, if I find the sea caves I keep hearing about. Tell Temi I said hi, and I look forward to hearing from you soon!

Leo

Gilea smiled and tucked Leo's message into her drawer. She wasn't sure if she would be ready to join him on another roughabout just yet, but she missed his boundless optimism, his ever-present smile, which she could almost see between the lines of his letter. As powerful as her experience at Endulai had been, working with Leo gave her a sense of freedom that was lacking in the surprisingly complex world of the holy city and the Caravan.

She stopped in the bathroom on her way to the council meeting to vent her thoughts and fears a little. Pleone had summoned everyone who worked with the Caravan, from the acolytes who attended the cradles to the highest masters, to a meeting, and the mood at Endulai had been tense since the announcement. Gilea hoped she could suppress her thoughts during the meeting, at least enough they would not stand out in the crowd.

She sat with Amini in the central courtyard, meditating by the fishpond, waiting for the meeting to begin. Amini shared what she called a trifle, a simple image passed from mind to mind. This one was a white butterfly, perched on a black flower, and every time its wings opened, they flashed a different color or pattern, which never seemed to repeat themselves. Gilea was glad of the distraction, and after a few cycles, she helped paint the butterfly's wings in fluid designs of her own devising, based on the patterns flashed by the *sitri* in the Living Waters. She felt Amini's smile at her attempts, which were crude by comparison, but it was a welcome distraction from the strain of the day's waiting.

The butterfly flitted away, and Gilea opened her eyes as her attention was drawn instinctively toward the central fountain. Pleone's motionless body was carried by four acolytes on a litter adorned with flowers, looking for all the world like a funeral bier. Affito stood by the fountain, eyes closed, a copper circlet on his head, and the already silent audience grew still as Pleone's litter was set down. Affito opened his eyes and raised his hands toward the audience, and Gilea found herself standing along with everyone else. The fountains suddenly went still, and doors to the courtyard, which she had only ever seen open, closed with synchronized *clunks*. Affito lowered his hands and opened his mouth to speak.

"In the Time Before, the ancients harnessed the powers of the mind, body, and earth to shrink the distance between peoples and bring their societies together as one." He spoke in a calm, level voice, no louder than a normal conversation, but his words rang clear throughout the courtyard. "The Caravan flourished for untold centuries, but as the civilization that created it crumbled, the knowledge of this mystical network fell out of memory. It took millennia to rediscover this knowledge and rebuild the Caravan, which has now been in continuous operation for over a hundred years." Affito paused, scanning the courtyard with his eyes, which seemed to glow with an otherworldly intensity. Gilea felt Pleone's energy emanating from him, and she breathed deeply to try to calm the terror building inside her.

"The Caravan works through a common agreement among all the Endulian temples on the continent, a delicate balance kept in place by our commitment to the sharing of knowledge and information, and by the hard work of our alchemists, smiths, acolytes, and masters alike. The sacred practices of Endulai, kept alive since the Time Before, help us maintain this balance, but recent events have shown that this hard work, *your* hard work, is in jeopardy."

Affito closed his eyes for a moment, and the silence that ensued was so tense Gilea felt her shields would break. Amini's hand touched her back, and she felt the sudden need to pee, which she suppressed with some difficulty.

"An unknown person, or persons, have been accessing the Caravan outside the formal channels. We do not know who, or how, or why, but they may be passing unseen, unnoticed, listening in on sensitive conversations of great political and economic import. If the security of information passed through the Caravan is compromised, the integrity of the Caravan will be shattered, and the system built and maintained over hundreds and thousands of years will fall into ruin again. Our very way of life will be threatened." Affito swayed, and sweat poured down his forehead as he continued with a slight tremor in his voice. As powerful as he was, the strain of channeling Pleone was taking its toll.

"Effective tomorrow at noon, the Caravan will be suspended for three days while we investigate the origin of these incursions."

Muted gasps swirled through the courtyard, echoing off the dome like the whisper of dead leaves skittering across stone. Gilea noticed a small commotion to her left as a group knelt around an acolyte who had passed out on the ground.

Need to pee. Need to pee. Gilea squeezed her mind around the thought so hard her whole body trembled.

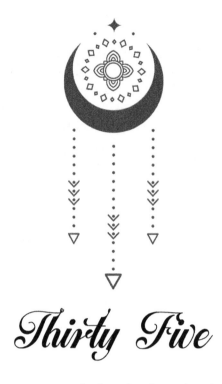

Thirty Five

Patia pushed Gero away gently, but firmly, as he clung to her on the dock. He held onto her forearms, as if for support, and his smiling face was streaked with tears.

"It's only going to be a couple of weeks, tops," she said, cupping his wet cheek with her hand. "And you'll be busy perfecting and selling that new meditation tincture anyway. You won't have time to miss me."

"I'll miss you stirring and measuring at my side. I'll miss your hips, the way you bump me with them on purpose as you brush past me. And your hands, always touching mine when you pass something off. In case you thought I didn't notice all those little things."

"You're definitely going to notice what I do with my hands and my hips when I get back. Better keep yourself in shape." She pulled away, and Gero laughed, holding onto her sleeve for a moment before letting go.

His eyes grew serious, though his mouth held onto his smile. "I hope you find what you're looking for, but it does neither of us any good if you put yourself in harm's way to get it."

She patted his arm, turning suddenly to hide the tears she had been so proud of keeping at bay until now. She wiped her eyes on her shoulder as she took Leo's offered hand and crossed the little gang-plank onto the boat, which had the name *Yprana* freshly painted on the back.

"You sure you don't want to come with us, Gero? The cabin sleeps four, and Wolfie doesn't take up much space." Leo held out his hand, and Gero waved him off.

"Thank you, but I leave such adventures to younger souls. I wish you fortuitous winds and forgiving waters."

"Don't you worry. I'll get her there and back in one piece. You have my word."

Gero stepped to the edge of the dock and reached out his hand. Leo stepped onto the gangplank and shook it. Patia turned and faced the river, watching the currents that flowed out into the sea.

Patia laid low on the aft deck as requested while Leo and Max worked the sails, and Sea Wolf sat nose to the deck, leaning against her leg, watching Leo's every move. The boat creaked and the sail flapped and the ropes stretched so tight she was sure they would snap, but every-thing held together and before long they were flying out of the river mouth, riding the current and the wind into the gulf. After a while, Leo had a few words with Max, then beckoned Patia to a sort of lec-tern set just above the captain's wheel, where a waxed map was affixed with sturdy brass clamps on four sides. A dotted line had been drawn with a red wax pencil, weaving through a field of islands to a red circle surrounding a small dot among a line of other dots jutting out from a larger island.

"I've been studying the map and talking to a few fishermen about the best way to get to this island here, which is called Oudi." His index finger pressed onto the larger island just outside the red circle. "Don't worry—I didn't tell them anything about your mission. They think we're delivering medicine."

"Who lives on Oudi?" Patia knew some of the larger islands in the gulf were inhabited, and many islanders lived and traded in Rontaia, giving the local dialect and food much of its flavor.

"One of the fishermen I spoke with called it Monument Island; apparently, it's been inhabited since ancient times, quite civilized from what I hear, and it's known for these great sculptures you can see from miles away. Not sure if the winds will take us close enough, but I'd love to catch a peek, and if we have any trouble at sea, it's good to know there's a place to get water and food near our destination."

Patia dearly hoped they didn't have any such detours on their trip. Though she didn't believe those who said some islanders were cannibals, she figured not all would be equally welcoming to strangers from the mainland.

Patia studied her Works book in the cramped sleeping quarters below deck as the sun reached its brightest, lying with the book next to the porthole to see by the reflected light. Now that she knew what the page of mysterious symbols was all about, she had decided to revisit the surrounding pages to see if she could garner any further clues. She'd studied them countless times, but the mystography they were written in was difficult to decipher, and she was sure she hadn't copied it perfectly in her haste decades ago. Mystography had never been her forte, nor reading in general for that matter. The complexities of substances and their chemical properties had always come easy for her, but she needed clean, precise language to make sense of a text. She wished she had Gero to help her puzzle it out; her eyes grew misty as she pictured him squinting through his reading glass and mumbling words into his beard, a smile slowly spreading across his face as his finger raised in the air.

No such smile grew on Patia's lips, and after an hour of poring, she had gleaned no more than what seemed like a bunch of pseudo-philosophical nonsense of the sort Paoro was always obsessed with. There was something about a library, she thought, or perhaps it was several libraries, and the word 'secret' kept circling back into the text, which was decidedly unhelpful, but nothing seemed to relate to her errand. She closed the book and returned above deck, deflecting Sea Wolf's probing nose as she held onto the guard rail and stared out into the open water before them. Max turned with his hand on one of the sail ropes to look at her, then quickly swiveled his head back around, as if embarrassed. He was a curious sort, and she hadn't heard him utter more than a few words to Leo and none to her. He had a lot more to say to Sea Wolf when he was not occupied with the mechanics of sailing, which Patia found as confusing as the most abstruse mystography.

Near dusk, as they approached the small island where they planned to anchor for the night, Leo shouted "Down sail!" He and Max loosened the lines and the sails fell as they coiled the rope on the deck with incredible speed. Sea Wolf stood at attention, cocking his head this way and that as he watched.

"Bait the pole, and I'll get the net," Leo called to Max as he wrapped one of the lines around a cleat.

Max opened a small hatch on the foredeck and pulled something that looked like dried fish out of a leather bag, then unhooked a long pole from under the rail with a spool of string attached. Sea Wolf ran over to Max, who boxed him out as he unraveled the spool and attached a piece of the dried fish to a hook.

"Not your turn," he said, and Sea Wolf sat back on his haunches, whining.

Patia noticed movement in the water all around them and looked over the edge to see hordes of small silvery-green fish swarming and flashing on the surface in a frenzy. The swarm extended for more than a hundred yards, and the boat was slowly cruising toward the edge of the disturbance. Max swung the pole over the side of the boat, then cried with delight as his pole bent slightly and he swung a small fish onto the deck. Sea Wolf barked at the flopping fish, and again, Max blocked him with his body.

"Don't get greedy, Wolfie," Max said, tapping the dog playfully on the snout, then proceeded to impale the fish on his hook and swing it back into the water. Leo tossed a net over the other side of the boat, and it spread out into a wide circle, then hit the water with a loud hiss. Leo's muscles bunched and stretched under his browned skin as he pulled the rope back, hand over hand, then finally hauled the net over the rail and tossed it onto the deck. Several dozen of the fish flipped in the net, and a couple of them flopped out on the deck. Leo dragged the net over to the hatch, emptying it with great haste, then kicked the fish that had escaped into the hole. He smiled at Patia, his chest heaving, as he arranged the net in his hands, then ran over and flung it over the side again, his broad back glistening with sweat. A sudden image flashed through her mind of Leo bearing down on her, his muscles taut, his smile wide, and she thought of her *olli*, hoping she'd have the privacy to use it before the trip was over.

"I got one! I got one!" Max cried, his rod bowed like a horseshoe, his face twisted with joy. Leo wrapped the cast net around a cleat and bounded across the deck to look over the edge, his ever-present smile growing even wider as he pointed into the water.

"Hot damn, Max, that's one hell of a thrasher! Hold on tight!"

"It's too heavy to haul up," Max said, leaning over the rail as the bowed rod moved side to side.

"Just hang on for a minute." Leo grabbed a net on a pole that was jagged on the end as if it had been broken off a longer pole. He tested the rail for a moment, and it wobbled, but he seemed satisfied and swung his lithe body over the edge, holding onto the rail with one hand as Sea Wolf barked and pushed his nose through the railing. Patia leaned over enough to see Leo dangling, net in hand, his feet propped on the hull as a sleek, silvery fish the size of a side of beef surfaced, thrashing, then dove again. Sweat beaded on Leo's tanned skin, and he lowered the net into the water. Max grunted, leaning over the edge with the rod, which bent and stretched as the fish dove, swimming this way and that.

"Nice and steady, Max. He's tiring." The fish surfaced again, thrashing with its tail, and Patia saw the hook fly out of its mouth just as Leo swung the net underneath it. The muscles in his arm bulged as he swung the heavy net against the boat, trapping the fish, which flapped against the boat in a staccato drumbeat for a few moments, then finally calmed. Leo continued smiling through his clenched jaw as he pulled himself partway up, still holding the net flush to the boat, every lean, ropy muscle in his body tensing with the effort. Patia's breath caught at this display of strength and agility, and she burned the image into her mind for later use. Max leaned over the rail, and Leo raised the net just enough so Max could grab it, and he hauled the huge fish onto the deck. Its body vibrated with a thousand urgent movements, and it skittered across the deck toward the edge of the boat. Max slipped as he scrambled after it, finally covering it with his body, and after a few more frantic movements, the fish went still.

Leo muscled his way over the railing, his face lit up with a wide, toothy smile as he heaved for breath, then knelt next to Max and slid his arm underneath him.

"I got him, Max. I got him." Max rolled over onto his back, blinking a smile up at Leo, who held the fish with his fingers in its gills.

"Nicely done, nicely done!" Leo thumped Max on the chest and held a hand out, which Max took and let Leo pull him up to standing. Leo arched his back, holding the fish up as high as he could, and let out a *Whoop!* into the darkening sky.

They ate seabiscuits and strips of raw thrasher, with a dusting of everyspice, while the smaller fish and the remainder of the thrasher were set to dry in a wooden box lit with a small *falin* oil lamp. The thrasher was rich with fat, and the flesh dissolved on Patia's tongue. Since leaving Guluch, she had eaten more fresh seafood than she ever had in her life, including when she'd lived in Rontaia years ago, and it was hard to imagine going back to the muddy stews and pasty porridge she was used to upriver. The water from the barrel was fresh enough but had an unpleasant resiny taste, which Patia imagined wouldn't improve as their trip wore on. After dinner Max brewed tea, which he served with a kind of silent reverence, watching as Patia held the steaming cup under her nose. It had a peppery odor, and when she drank it, her mouth and throat tingled long after she had swallowed.

"Good tea," she said, raising her cup. Max grinned, showing uneven, dirty teeth.

"I've been saving it for a special occasion. Brought it all the way downriver in this little tin box I have."

"It's the same tea you served us back at your place, isn't it?" Leo asked.

Max nodded, holding the cup under his nose and closing his eyes. "Zander said I could take half of it, so I did. Good tea to wash down fresh fish on a nice night like this."

Patia took another sip, staring up at the stars punctuating the darkening sky as the numbing taste lingered in her mouth. The Thousand Worlds were often represented as constellations of stars, and many texts had been written interpreting the myths behind the constellations as alchemical principles or formulas, but she had never put much stock in such flights of fancy. The workings of liquids, gases, and solids, their interactions with each other, required no metaphors to understand. Just careful study and practice, and the time and space to pursue the truth. But as the sky deepened and the stars popped out one by one, she couldn't help wondering if it was as some scholars said, that

181

each star was another world, and on each of those thousand worlds, someone was looking up at her star, imagining her world. Lodestone could attract iron from inches away, and the tinctures she made for the Caravan allowed communication across the continent. Might it not be possible that a tincture made from whatever was in that tank, whatever was on the island she was seeking, could put someone in contact with one of those other worlds?

The boat rocked in the waves, and Patia's eyes closed as she leaned back against the railing. She imagined a version of herself in some other world, just like hers but with just a hint more color. This other-worldly Patia might be sitting on a boat staring up into the sky just as she was, wondering if she was looking up at solids or liquids or gas, or if there was something else out there, invisible to the eye but accessible to the deepest reaches of the mind.

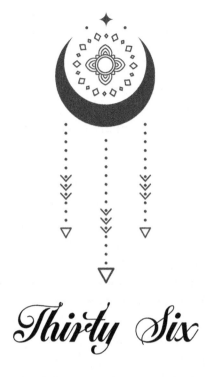

Thirty Six

Gilea clutched the vial of deep tincture, one of two Amini had slipped into her pocket in the chaos following the council meeting. She had tucked the other vial inside her pillow and hoped her suppression routine would keep its existence secret from Pleone.

"You will be assigned crossroad maintenance duty in the morning," Amini had mindspoken to her on their way out of the courtyard. *"All should be as before, and you should be able to do what is needed if you remember what we practiced."*

Gilea slipped the vial of tincture the acolyte gave her into her pocket and downed the deep tincture instead, feeling woozy as she eased into the cradle. She summoned and dismissed the need to pee, squeezing all other thoughts from her mind, as Amini had taught her. Before she realized what was happening, she was in the courtyard, in lotus position, the upper levels of her mind joining the others in the cycles that maintained the stability of the crossroad. The courtyard was alive with conversations, as visitors from crossroads across the continent hammered out last-minute details. Gilea slipped below the surface, sinking comfortably into the tangled copper web of the Caravan and the blackness surrounding it.

She followed the bright lines away from the largest cluster, which she knew was Endulai. In one direction, there were four more clusters close together, which had to be Guluch, Tralum, Freburr, and Anari, with a few smaller clusters here and there, connected by thinner tendrils. In the other directions, the clusters were dimmer and more spaced out, with a large cluster near the far end, which she felt must be Rontaia. A few very small clusters branched out from it, one of which glowed more brightly than the others as if it were alive with activity. She wondered what crossroad that was, so close to Rontaia, but she knew time was not on her side, so she focused all her energy on the lines leading to Rontaia. She traveled through the darkness parallel to those lines, using them as guides without traveling within them, and soon she approached the Rontaian cluster, which swarmed with an energy more chaotic than the others.

Gilea did not know how to approach or enter the crossroad without passing through the usual doorway, but as she stared at the cluster, she saw it was composed of glowing membranes like dozens of interconnected bubbles, each of them so thin as to be almost invisible. She steeled her mind and moved toward one of the membranes, passing through it like a hand through the water of a fountain. The temple room in Rontaia was abuzz with activity, dozens of heated conversations with the elaborate hand gestures common to speakers of the Rontai dialect. The figures were vague and hazy, like ghosts, and she drifted rather than walking among them, until she found Sali, in close consultation with two older women with grave expressions on their faces. Sali's gaze briefly shifted away from the women toward Gilea, then returned to the two women. He held up his hand to them as his head snapped back to Gilea. He looked at her, squinting, then said something to the women, who turned away, talking between themselves.

"Gilea? How—"

"There is little time. The Caravan—"

"I know. Come, we must speak privately. Follow me."

Gilea smiled as a halo of tiny flowers appeared above Sali's head. The halo rose up and widened into a large circle, and Gilea felt herself pulled into a blinding tunnel of light, like a miniature version of the Caravan tunnels. She soon emerged into a bare chamber, lit by a candelabra on a plain table flanked by two wooden chairs, not unlike Pleone's den. Sali sat in one of them, and Gilea eased down onto the other.

"Amini told me to expect you. We can talk here, but we haven't much time. Tell me what you know." His face was strained, and his voice carried an edge beneath its smooth surface. She hesitated for a moment, picturing her next conversation with Pleone, how she would hide what she'd said, if that was even possible. But Amini had assured her she could tell Sali everything, and that the future of Endulai, and of the Caravan itself, might depend on it.

"I guess you know Pleone has ordered the Caravan shut down at midday," she said. Sali closed his eyes and nodded. *"She said someone's been accessing the Caravan outside the normal channels, and that the security of information may be compromised. She told me before my last visit here that she thought the interloper was based in Rontaia. And when I was here before, and at the new mountain crossroad, I felt something, someone, you remember—"*

Sali nodded vigorously. *"Yes, and I'm sorry I couldn't tell you before, but it's true, sort of, and Amini said I could trust you, so I'm going to come clean. There is someone, an alchemist named Paoro, who has produced the Universal Tincture, which—do you know of it?"* Gilea nodded, though she still didn't fully understand how it would work. *"Yes, well, he can use the tincture, with no cradle, and no training, other than what he's managed on his own, to access the Caravan, and the Thousand Worlds beyond."* He shook his head, staring down into his hands for a moment.

"So that was who I felt before? This…Paoro, did you say? Here, and in the mountain crossroad?"

"He comes and goes as he pleases, and those of us with more extensive training can sense him. I was a little surprised that you could, no offense, being so new. But you're here using the deep tincture as if you've been at it all your life, doing almost the same thing Paoro does. I can see why Amini sent you. As you probably know, Pleone has cut us out of her deal with the Maer for sunstone, and they are new to the Caravan, thus very reclusive, and so far it seems they have only dealt with Endulai. Paoro went there to find out if what we heard was true, that they have a new source of sunstone, which we desperately need. Our supply is nearly exhausted, and we will soon be burning falin oil, which is not sustainable. We had hoped, with the Universal Tincture, we could find a way to operate without any fuel source at all, but…" He held his hands out to his sides and let them drop.

"Paoro must have a little left since he keeps visiting the Caravan, but he has been unable, or unwilling, to produce more of the tincture for us. He keeps telling us he needs a little more time, and a little more money, and so on. We have given him everything he has asked for, and more, and he has engaged another alchemist to help him, but we have no idea if or when he will be able to give us more supply. We

are at wit's end. *And now with the Caravan being closed, we fear...*"

"*Pleone will shut you out of the Caravan entirely,*" Gilea said slowly as the realization dawned on her. "*In retaliation for your shutting her out of your crossroad. That must be it.*"

"*We had no choice! She was mind-reading our acolytes, those who support our crossroad, and planting suggestions, making them find out things and tell her. I'm worried, now that you've come here, she might do the same to you. Her power is so great, even from across the continent, that I cannot be sure she has not mind-read me herself.*"

Gilea's head grew light as a terror seized her. She thought of Pleone's probing eyes, the ease with which she had sensed Gilea's every thought when they'd met in her den. The bathroom trick would not work in close quarters, or anywhere in Endulai if Pleone truly focused on reading her. Sali started to flicker, then fade, and Gilea strained to bring him back into focus.

"*The tincture is wearing off, and my control is slipping,*" she said, gasping for breath as the room began to spin. "*I will visit again if I can, or send a message through the Inkwell if it re-opens. Amini said you have a code, which...*"

Sali's hands reached across the table for hers, and she tried to grasp them but felt herself being pulled away like a fish hauled from the depths by a stout cord. She hurtled through the bright lights and infinite darkness, bouncing through her body in the courtyard, then back into the cradle, where she sat bolt upright, reaching for breath that would not come. The acolyte at the foot of the cradle hurried to support her, removing the circlet and rubbing her temples, and her breath returned in painful gasps. She felt the stares of the other acolytes, and she pressed her eyes closed and lay back in the cradle, tears streaming down her cheeks at the throbbing of her head and the pain that wracked her body like hot lightning. Amini's presence wrapped around her, dulling the pain, and she slipped into Amini's warmth as she fell out of consciousness.

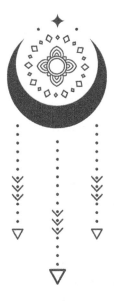

Thirty Seven

Patia rubbed Sea Wolf's ears absently as Leo and Max prepared to lower the little rowboat into the water. She watched the muscles in Leo's back stretch hard and relax soft, and she wished they would hurry up and get off the boat so she could have some alone time with her new *olli*.

"You sure you don't want to come with us?" Leo asked, smiling up at her as he stood up and drank from his waterskin, wiping a stray drop on his chin back into his mouth. "We'll only be gone an hour or so, just long enough to check out this cave I saw on my morning swim."

"I've got some work to do," she said, looking down at Sea Wolf, lest Leo catch the lie in her eyes.

"Suit yourself. Come on, Wolfie!" Leo slapped his knee, and the dog bounded across the deck and hopped into the boat, which Leo and Max lowered into the water with the dog inside. Leo held Max's hand and helped him down. Max moved slowly, awkwardly, and his face was pulled into a grimace as he let go of Leo's hand and took hold of the rope ladder on the side of the boat. Leo clambered over the edge of the boat like a tree rat, untying the dinghy and pushing off in one fluid motion.

"See you in an hour or two," he called, his hands already on the oars, his shoulders and chest flexing as he powered the dinghy away toward the island, which was little more than a heap of rocks jutting out of the water. Patia turned her back to them and removed the *olli's* leather case from the bag, blood rushing to her loins as she saw its black gleam. She unscrewed the end, inserted one of the little gray pellets with eager fingers, and screwed it on tight, careful not to push the button yet. She had three pellets left after this one, and she hoped to save one or two to use with Gero when she returned. She could almost feel the *olli's* vibration inside her just from the memory of it, hefting its weight in her hands, her mind humming with anticipation.

She lowered herself into the cabin once the rowboat had rounded the tip of the little island, quickly shrugged off her robe, and ran the *olli* over her body. The glass was cold and smooth, and it gave her goosebumps at first, then a warmth spread through her as she thought of Leo's muscles, his smile. A twinge of guilt slowed her momentum, but she shook it off. Gero had said he wouldn't be jealous no matter what, and this was her mind, her body, her fantasy to do with as she liked. She wished she had some of the red oil, as the salt air had left her dry. She stuck her fingers in her mouth a few times and wet herself with her saliva, and ran the tip of the *olli* up and down, up and down, until it suddenly slipped partway in. She lay back, pushing it in as slowly as she could, conjuring the images of Leo's chest, his arms, the tight coil of his muscles.

But just as she imagined him positioned above her, his image became blurry, his hard body replaced with Gero's soft smile and wispy hair, his eyes twinkling with the knowledge of what she wanted, what he was willing to do for her. She shook her head and tried to summon Leo again, but Gero's face would not be erased. She recalled the feel of his tongue flicking in and out, up and down, lapping and circling, until he found the right angle and rhythm and she bucked into him. Her thumb mashed the button and the *olli* came alive, jolting every nerve and pleasure center with its vibrations. As she moved it with increasingly frantic gestures, scenes from their previous lovemaking flashed through her mind, interspersed with things she'd plotted but had not yet had the time to enact. She wound herself up and down several times in just a few minutes before it all became too intense and she had to push the *olli* across her bedroll. She clutched her knees to her chest as waves of little tremors cycled through, diminishing each time until her body relaxed completely, vaguely buzzing, her sweaty limbs spent and limp. She closed her eyes and rolled over, clutching her pillow as if she were spooning Gero's scrawny little frame, pressing into his heat, smiling at the soft sound of his snoring.

Sea Wolf's barking woke her, and she scrambled to get everything sorted, hoping the flush in her face wouldn't give her away. She greeted the dinghy with a faint wave, watching as Leo kept two hands on Max to support him, then pushed his bottom as Max hefted his legs over the rail. Leo clambered over after, helped Max to his feet, and the two of them pulled up the dinghy on its rope and pulley system and secured it to the back of the boat.

"Get a little nap?" Leo asked, dusting his hands and kneeling to rub Sea Wolf's head and ears.

"I must have dozed off. Did you find the cave?"

"We did. It's got a nice swimming hole in it when the tide is low. The painted faces will eat it up."

Patia nodded as everything fell into place. Leo had hinted he was doing some exploration for a job, but he hadn't said what kind of job it was. But given that she'd last seen him with a painted face on the Agra near Guluch, it made sense. He was leading a roughabout to the islands and was looking for little adventures for his charges.

"Doesn't it wash the paint off? When they swim, I mean."

"Sometimes, sure. I guess that's half the fun. Gotta make it feel a little dangerous, otherwise what's the point?"

She wanted to ask him why the painted faces sought danger, why they didn't just stay in their comfortable enclaves, and so much more. But if she asked, that might give Leo an opening to ask more about her mission, and she was already having a hard enough time figuring out how much to say and how much to keep to herself. He hadn't asked anything beyond what she'd chosen to tell him, but the closer they got, the more he might need to know, and she was terrible at lying. He already knew she was an alchemist, and she'd told him she was seeking an ingredient for a tincture, which was technically true, and perhaps he didn't need to know any more than that. But would she feel comfortable going onto the island by herself, or would she have to ask him to accompany her? He seemed trustworthy, but she still wasn't sure it was a good idea for him to see what she'd come for.

"They were all right," Max said, glancing up to Leo for a moment before turning his eyes back down. Patia's brow furrowed, wondering what he was talking about. "The ones on your raft. They were nice, both of them, real, like. I always thought they'd seem fake."

"You're right, Max. They were all right. Patia, you met Sylvan, the doctor, when we came to get a look at the swirls, but I don't think you ever met Temi. Good people, I gotta say. Real good people." He squinted off toward the horizon, making a gesture in the air as if he were measuring the sun's angle. "But look, we need to pull up anchor and get a move on. The wind'll turn in about an hour, and we want to be clear of that archipelago before then."

He and Max set to work with rope and sail, and before long they were skating across clear water, pushed forward somehow despite the wind blowing almost crosswise. The science of sailing was as foreign to Patia as the most obscure mystography, and it appeared she had fallen in with a true scientist. She leaned against the rail, Sea Wolf lay his head in her lap, and they plowed forward into the wind and sun and endless water.

They sailed for two days with fair weather and favorable winds, anchoring off small unoccupied islands, eating dried fish, seabiscuits, and some kind of seaweed Leo had harvested on one of his morning swims. He was always gone before she awoke, and he would return soon after, his curly hair glistening with seawater, the lines in his face fixed in a permanent smile. Though she enjoyed watching his body move, her initial yearning for him quickly mellowed, and she appreciated him as a perfect creature of the sea, as if he had been made specifically to sail and swim. Even his hair flopped down over his brow enough to block the sun. Whatever little things went wrong, his smile never faltered for more than a moment before he had a solution, and set right to work, throwing himself body and soul into every task. Near midday on the third day as the boat plodded along on sluggish winds, Leo's smile leveled off as he stared at an indistinct cloud mass on the horizon.

"We're gonna get beat to hell by that storm if we keep sailing," he said, his jaw working a piece of dried fish sprinkled with his beloved

190

everyspice. "This boat's not big enough for the kind of seas we're likely to see. I'm going to veer a little off course, make for those three islands to the east, see if we can get a little protection anchoring between them. We might do well to go ashore for the night." He offered Patia a piece of the fish, which she took reluctantly, as it was hard to chew and even harder to keep the foul thing in her mouth long enough for it to soften. "Might want to get your stuff packed and ready to throw in the dinghy in the next little while."

As they approached the three islands, Patia saw numerous small boats clustered in a bay formed by a horseshoe of rocks that looked too even to be natural, though she couldn't imagine how so much stone could be moved and built up with primitive means. Leo dropped sail, and he and Max put out the long oars and made their way awkwardly toward the bay.

"Come on, Max, pull, dammit!" Leo called with some urgency in his voice. "Pull, or the current's gonna push us past it!" Max glanced over his shoulder, clenched his jaw, and pulled, his face dripping and his shirt drenched from the effort. "Patia, give Max some water please." She glanced at Leo, who jerked his head toward the waterskin he kept at the wheel, and she took it to Max, who looked up for a moment as if he were afraid of her. "Keep rowing, Max! Patia, just pour some into his mouth. Don't be shy!"

She managed, though she almost lost her balance and fell into Max's lap, and half the water she poured ran down his chin.

"Thanks," Max managed through clenched teeth, shaking his head when she tried to pour some more water in. She stood on the deck, watching as the boat narrowly passed into the harbor, slowing suddenly as they slipped out of the current.

"Max, stop for a second while I get us turned, then we're gonna make for the middle there. Hopefully, they won't mind us using their harbor for the night."

Patia could now see the boats more clearly, and they were more like the boats she was used to seeing in Rontaia than she had expected, but they were painted a luminous bright blue that matched the sky, or the sky when a storm wasn't bearing down anyway. Divers surfaced, and those on the boats lowered poles with hooks on them to pull wooden cages from the divers, with some kind of shellfish inside them. They dumped the contents and tossed the cages back into the water, and the divers disappeared beneath the surface again. Leo and

Max stopped rowing as they approached, and Leo scrambled up and dropped one anchor, then the other, and soon the boat held fast within fifty feet of the nearest of the smaller craft.

"*Komé Guiné,*" Leo called. It sounded like one of the island languages, and the greeting was vaguely familiar.

"*Spazoté,*" a woman on a nearby boat called back, looking from the boat to the harbor's edge as a well-muscled woman rowed the boat toward them. "You cut it pretty close there," she continued with an island accent.

"I hope you don't mind we weather the storm here. I'm Leo, and this is the *Yprana*. This here is my dog Sea Wolf, but you can call him Wolfie, my crewmate Max, and my passenger Patia."

"I'm Atha, and the *Yprana* is welcome to shelter here, along with Wolfie," at which point the dog cocked his head, "and the rest of you, of course," she added with a smirk that made Patia want to giggle.

"We really appreciate it. *Zapi.*" Leo pressed his hands together and touched them to his chest, and Atha repeated the gesture, her smirk growing beatific.

"I hope you'll join us for dinner and a dry bed. Even in the harbor, it would be a rough night to stay on the boat."

"We accept!" Leo glanced at Max, who nodded, looking anxious, then turned to Patia. The excitement in Leo's eyes was hard to deny, and the welcome had seemed genuine. She blinked her assent. The storm clouds had intensified, solidifying into a dense mass of dark gray, with an angry haze around the edges. Atha was right. This was no night to be stuck on a boat, especially one as rickety as the *Yprana*.

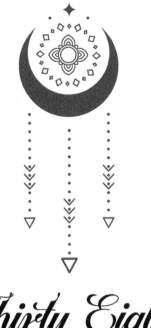

Thirty Eight

Gilea sat outside Pleone's room, visions of the *sitri*'s patterns playing over and over in her head. She had been studying them as she recovered from her latest bout with the deep tincture, and they brought a calm to her mind, helping her suppress other thoughts. As she watched the dots and circles appear and disappear, move and flow, she felt Sage's presence within her, helping her rebuild her mental strength. Amini had said her experience with the *sitri* had helped her with the deep tincture, so she hoped this technique would help protect her from Pleone's prying mind.

The guards opened the doors and stepped aside in unison, and Gilea entered the room, whose stillness was heightened by Pleone's immobile form on the bed. Gilea approached and sat in the bedside chair, her hand finding Pleone's under the covers, and she closed her eyes and found herself in Pleone's shadowy den. She sat across from Pleone, as before, with a teapot on the table, the same hints of hibiscus and fenugreek filling the space. Pleone's face wrinkled into a smile as she passed a cup of steaming tea to Gilea.

"*You've come a long way in such a short time,*" she said, her voice smooth and reassuring. "*Though it seems Amini's insistence that you were ready for regu-*

lar crossroad maintenance duties was premature."

"It went fine the first time, but I guess it took more out of me than I realized." The back of her mind was filled with the *sitri*'s watery patterns, undergirding her with a calm that suppressed intrusive thoughts.

"Your mind is more capable than most of those who maintain the crossroad. I sense something in you, a strength beyond your training, that almost feels like..." Pleone's head gave a little shake as she set down her cup, her thin lips forming a quiet smile. "I imagine you've met a few extraordinary minds in your travels along the Lonely Way. The universe tends to send us where we need to go, and now it has sent you to us, at a time when we need a fresh mind for a fresh start."

"You're going to restart the Caravan?"

"Well, of course! We can't have the spiritual and economic engine of the South shut down for all eternity. We've had our finest minds examining every tunnel and crossroad, and I've pinpointed the source of the incursions." She took a sip of tea, then sighed. "I've always had my suspicions, but now that they've been confirmed, we're going to re-activate the Caravan in two days, but the Rontaian crossroad will be suspended indefinitely until I am satisfied they have taken care of their problem."

Need to pee. Need to pee. Gilea squeezed her legs together, taking another sip of the tea, which was bitter on her tongue.

"But won't that...I mean, Rontaia is the second biggest city in the South. How will they..."

"I know you are from Rontaia, and I know your feelings for the place are strong, which is why you are here. Don't worry, it won't be forever, and I have a backup plan in place. There is an island crossroad only a few days' sail from Rontaia, and we're going to help expand the crossroad there to handle the backlog of business deals involving Rontaia until we can sort out the issues at the temple. I am sending you first thing tomorrow."

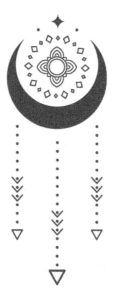

Thirty Nine

Patia sat to Leo's right, with Max to his left. Across the table sat Atha, dressed in a wrap dyed with streaks and swirls of blue and purple. Her hair was coiled in a spiral like a sleeping snake, wrapped in a wide silk ribbon of similar patterns. Her wife sat to her right, and their muscular son to her left. Both were dressed, like the other islanders, in wraps of elaborately dyed material, most with blue or purple predominant, but with splashes of other colors as well. Patia had seldom felt self-conscious about her apparel, but even those serving the table wore better than her dirty, salt-stained robe.

Leo chatted amiably with Atha and the others, and Max said nothing, gritting his teeth as if he was going to faint or vomit, or perhaps both. Patia followed along with the conversation, trying to make enough polite comments not to stand out, but she hadn't done this type of socialization in forever and she felt like a fish on a dock. Leo had asked about the shellfish they were collecting, and Atha spoke at length about the *voki,* which Patia knew as a luxury food for the rich in Rontaia, and whose shells apparently were used to make the blue and purple pigments they used to dye their clothes. She vaguely recalled some reference to their essence being used in meditation tinctures, but she had never seen it available for sale.

"So, do you trade with the mainland or what?" Leo asked, his mouth half full of a salad made of a crunchy, slightly bitter vegetable, mixed with herbs, dried garlic, and some kind of fruit juice.

"We do a lot of business with Rontaia, especially for dye for the *Noxi* outfits, and the essence, which the Endulians use in some of their tinctures." Patia perked up at the mention, and Atha turned a sharp eye to her. "Do you practice?"

Patia shook her head, taking a long sip of her wine, which was flowery and quite delicious, not unlike the lavender wine Gero was so fond of. Had Atha guessed she was an alchemist without her saying anything, just from her reaction to the word tincture?

"I've been to the temple in Rontaia," Atha said, closing her eyes for a moment. "It's quite peaceful, I found. I think about it sometimes." Her eyes grew soft as she took a sip of her wine, gazing off into the distance.

"Oh, the temple, yes, I've visited a few times," Patia said, her breath calming as she realized Atha had not been referring to her alchemy. "It's quite the peaceful place." She wasn't sure how many islanders practiced the Good Works, but then again, she hadn't been expecting them to speak perfect Southish, or be better dressed than the painted faces.

"Well, enough about me. Tell me, are you from Rontaia, then?"

"I lived there for a long time, but I've been in Guluch for the last thirty years. I just came down to Rontaia to visit some old friends." She felt comfortable saying it since it wasn't a lie, but a crushing feeling grew in her chest as she thought about how she would explain her presence on Leo's boat in the middle of the Naeli Gulf.

"I'm scouting out some sea caves for a trip for the painted faces," Leo said, "and Patia decided to tag along." Patia touched Leo with her elbow in thanks, though she doubted he noticed. He reached for a tray of steaming shells that had just been set down, picking up one of the shells with his bare hands and placing it on his plate. "We met in Guluch a while back."

"Well, if you're looking for sea caves, you should definitely check out the ones on Lavi, about two days' sail northeast of here. It's uninhabited, and it has a whole network of caves. They go on and on, and there are some hot springs in there as well. I can show you on a map."

"Thank you, Atha, that would be amazing! We're headed more or less in that direction."

Patia watched the muscular young man next to Atha pick up a long, curved fork and insert it into his shell. He twisted the shell slowly as he held his fork in place, and a fat, wrinkled blob slid out of the shell and onto the plate. He cut it with a knife, dipped it into an oily red sauce, then eased it into his mouth, seeming to swallow it without chewing. He smiled when he saw Patia watch him, his light brown eyes darting down to the shell on her plate.

"The trick is to find the thicker part, just behind the tongue. You can just reach it with your fork if you stick it in like this." He demonstrated with his curved fork, and Patia picked up the shell, which was almost too hot to touch, held it above the plate as he had done, and inserted the fork. "The first part you feel is the tongue, and if you put your fork in that, it'll tear off and you'll have a hell of a time getting the rest out."

She felt around with the fork, which stuck into something, but she had no idea if it was the right part, and she didn't want to make a fool of herself. Leo seemed to be having no problem, as he already had two shells on his plate and was chewing with abandon.

"Orfos, be a dear and help Patia get the first one out," said Atha's wife, whose name Patia couldn't remember. "It's harder than it looks," she said to Patia with a smile, "and we don't want you to go hungry."

Orfos leaned over the table, holding the shell in his smooth hands as he eased the fork in, turning it to face her so she could watch. The shellfish wiggled free and flopped onto her plate, sending a splash onto her hand, which she kissed off with a smile.

"Gods, I'm so, so sorry," Orfos said, covering his mouth with his hands.

"Not at all. Thank you." She picked up her knife and cut into the slippery flesh, dipped it, and let the spicy flavor of the sauce radiate through her as the unctuous mass slid down her throat. It was a bit like an oyster, but firmer. She quite liked it, and she quickly finished the one on her plate and reached for another. She felt all eyes watching her as she held the shell up, angled the fork in, poking around until she felt a firmer texture, and slid the meat onto her plate with surprising grace.

"You're a natural," Atha said. "I'm glad you like them." She raised her glass high above her head, and a dozen conversations quickly died down.

"Tonight we thank the seas for delivering our guests safely to our harbor, and we thank them for taking the time to part flesh from shell with us." A murmur ran through the group, then everyone drank, and the conversations slowly picked back up. Patia's head was light from the wine, which was stronger than its taste suggested, and she floated in and out of the conversation, letting her eyes wander over the crowd, taking in their colors and the lively conversations in their language. Her mind drifted to the detail about the essence being used for meditation tinctures.

She knew the temples had their own labs where they further processed the tinctures made by outside alchemists, adapting them to suit their needs. She wondered if the *voki* essence served a similar function to the catfish secretions, but her mind was a bit hazy and more than a little relaxed, and it was hard to concentrate. She looked at her glass, which was almost full, and it had only been refilled once. She shrugged, picked up her fork, and speared the last slippery bite of *voki*, then dipped it and closed her mouth around the fork. The sensation of pleasure at the taste warmed her chest, and as she half-chewed and swallowed it, something stirred in her mind, and she realized it must have been the shellfish more than the wine that had her feeling so good. It made sense, based on what she had just heard; as high as she was feeling, if this ingredient were sufficiently distilled and concentrated, it could be of great value in making tinctures.

After dinner, they listened to a long, almost musical poem in the local language, performed by a young man with crooked shoulders who spoke with an enchanting cadence. Though Patia could not understand any of the words, she listened, rapt, her eyes half-closed, and let herself be carried away by the sound into a state of supreme unconcern.

They left the next day with fresh water, food, and very warm wishes from Atha and the others. The storm had passed, leaving in its wake clear blue skies and steady winds, which Leo and Max used to great effect. They made up the time they had lost taking shelter from the storm, and by nightfall, they had anchored off one of the islands Leo had circled on his map, more than halfway to their destination. Leo swam ashore before dawn and returned with some fruits he had foraged, tied in a mesh sack slung over his shoulder. He whacked open the hard shells with a machete and scraped the pulp into a bowl, which he served along with the last of the nut pastries Atha had given them, which had gone stale but were still much nicer than seabiscuits.

Patia studied her Works book below deck while they sailed the next day, but if it contained any information she could use, it was buried too deeply in ancient mystography for her to discover. She checked the containment vessel again, making sure everything was in working order, then closed it back up and lay down on her bunk, feeling suddenly penned in. Though she often spent days at a time back in Guluch without leaving her shack, at least there she knew she could. Here she felt helpless, useless, at the whim of weather and tides and the goodwill and nautical skills of two men she hardly knew. Her heart twinged when she thought of Gero, stirring alone, humming one of his little tunes, but his humming would be a little less peppy, and he wouldn't be bouncing from foot to foot as he worked. She wondered if he was still wearing his blue scarf, or if he'd taken it off in favor of the old rag he'd worn before. She hoped he lay awake at night thinking of her, touching himself, as she dared not do, except in brief moments, given the close quarters. When she got back to Rontaia, he was going to have to put in some work to make up for lost time.

They sailed through clouds and light rain the next morning, but by late afternoon the sky had mostly cleared, and Leo steered the boat toward a rocky island dotted with scruffy stands of grass and scrub bushes. Large black birds with white heads circled the highest point on the island, swooping in to land on nests scattered across a wide gray cliff. Lavi, if Leo had followed Atha's directions correctly, which Patia suspected he had.

Leo and Max lowered the sails, tidied the ropes, and tossed out the anchors, and Leo unrolled a tarp to cover the aft deck to block the blinding sun. Three stools were spaced around a barrel, which served as a table. They shared a meal of dried fish and drier seabiscuits as the sun set, imbuing the island with a purplish glow.

"We're going to explore the caves in the morning, and it might take a little longer than last time. You should join us."

Patia eyed the rocky island warily. "It looks like pretty rough terrain for an old lady like me."

Lao slapped her knee, laughing through a mouthful of fish. "You're sprightlier than Max here. You'll do fine. Plus, there's supposed to be a sandy area on the other side where we can pull up the dinghy. Atha said they have hot springs, which should be amazing. Tell me you don't want to check that out."

Patia tucked a piece of the fish into her mouth and chewed on it a bit. On the one hand, it would be nice to have more alone time on the boat, but she had never been in a sea cave before. If she was going to retrieve her prize from the Isle of a Thousand Worlds, she might do well to get a taste of what she was in for.

"I wouldn't mind a hot bath, even if it's a salty one. If you think it's safe, I'm in."

Leo beamed at her, and even Max cracked a little smile.

"We'll have Wolfie there to protect us, won't we, boy?" He tousled the dog's head, feeding him a bit of fish, which Sea Wolf swallowed greedily, then flopped down on the deck, looking up at Leo with big, loving eyes.

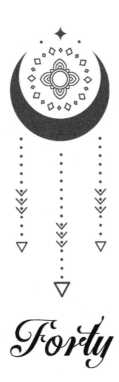

Forty

Gilea took the tincture the acolyte gave her and swallowed it without coating her tongue with honey first. She had learned how to drink it fast and wash down the remnants with her saliva, so the honey was no longer necessary. Her eyes closed before her head hit the cushion, and she summoned the *sitri* patterns as the circlet was laid on her head. She had a job to do, and she would do it, to the best of her abilities. She allowed herself to wonder why Pleone had chosen her, with her limited experience, but when she passed through the copper doorway, she heard the Rontai dialect all around her, and her heart warmed at the rich, full sounds and the rapid bursts of speech.

The Azure Island crossroad was laid out like a moonlit beach overlooking a small harbor, with gentle waves lapping at the shore. The details were hazy around the edges, as was common in the smaller crossroads, but the overall effect was pleasing. Wicker chairs and tables were scattered across the sand, with fragrant tapers on sticks casting a warm, mellow light over the proceedings. Islanders and Rontaians mingled, talked, laughed, and occasionally shouted, clustered around tables holding glasses of a delicate blue liquid.

"Gilea, so glad you could make it." The woman who spoke was per-

haps fifty, upright and beautiful, her reddish islander coloring glowing softly in the light from the tapers. *"I'm Atha."*

"Such a pleasure," Gilea said, pressing her hands to her chest in a bow, which Atha repeated.

"Well, as you can see, we're quite busy here, now that the Rontaian delegation has been cleared for entry. There are only eight of them, but they're so lively it seems like twenty."

Gilea summoned and suppressed the urge to pee, to distract Pleone if she was shadowing her closely enough to feel the strain in her mind.

"I hadn't realized...that is, I thought Rontaia was still under ban until this all gets sorted out."

"Oh, they are, but we recruited a handful to help us ramp up operations, and vetted them carefully, with Pleone's blessing, of course. They're here on the island in person, inspecting the crossroad, and having a bit of fun while they're at it, I might add. Come, you absolutely must try the voki. *Have you ever had it?"*

"No, it was all mussels and clams and fish for me when I lived in Rontaia. Only the painted faces could afford voki.*"*

"Well, it doesn't have the mind-altering effect in the crossroad, or at least we haven't figured out how to do that yet. But the taste is remarkably accurate."

"Sounds fantastic."

Gilea followed Atha toward an empty table, where they sat. Atha's hand drifted to the table, inches away from Gilea's, and Atha cast a sidelong smile at her, then summoned a burly young man with a subtle gesture of her chin.

He arrived with a tray of steaming shells, whose fragrance washed over Gilea, a bit like oysters, but with a musky undertone.

"Thank you, dear," said Atha, touching him familiarly on the arm. *"This is my son, Orfos, and this is Gilea, from Endulai."* She said the word as if it had magical properties, which Gilea supposed it would, to the inhabitants of a small island crossroad.

"Welcome to the Azure Isle," he said, laying a small plate and a long fork in front of each of them and placing four shells on the table. His face was tense with concentration; Gilea guessed he was fairly new to the Caravan, so maintaining his presence would be a struggle.

"Thank you," she said, pushing out a wave of reassurance to him. The lines in his face eased somewhat, and he flashed her a quiet smile before turning away.

"That was very kind of you," Atha said, laying her hand casually over

Gilea's. *"Orfos is new here, and he's never been the most assiduous at study, but with all the visitors we're going to be having, it's all hands on deck, I'm afraid."*

"I never realized there were island crossroads until recently," Gilea said, acutely aware of the soft warmth of Atha's touch, unsure if she should let it be or pull her hand away. *"I didn't know Endulian practices had spread beyond the mainland."*

Atha smiled wryly. *"Not all the islands practice, and even here some see it as a colonial influence. Though since our economy to this point has relied on providing voki to the painted faces, and their essence to Endulian temples, it seems pointless to insist on some kind of artificial separation. Besides, some of our traditional meditation techniques are so similar I can't help but wonder if they don't have a common source."*

"Everything is connected, if you dig far enough below the surface," Gilea mused. She slid her hand out from under Atha's and picked up the fork and the shell, which was hot to the touch. She found the dense muscle behind the *voki's* tongue and slid the creamy mass onto her plate. She wrestled it into her mouth and it exploded with briny goodness, with a delicate undertone like nothing she had ever tasted before.

"Wow, I can see why the painted faces go nuts for these."

"Right? And the psychological effect is like a mellow tincture, a bit on the fuzzy side, but quite relaxing. For all I know, there could be voki *essence in the tincture you took to get here."*

Gilea paused, trying to recall the taste and feel of the tincture, but she could not find any obvious connection. Those little vials had ingredients from across the continent, from the islands to the alchemy shops in Guluch to gods knew where else. The supply chain for the tinctures had to be almost as vast as the Caravan itself.

"I like your crossroad," Gilea said. *"They can be a bit stuffy sometimes."*

"Thank you," Atha said with a slight bow. *"We're still working on extending the visuals. We've never had more than three or four visitors at a time before, and we're still using* falin *oil, which..."* She sighed, and Gilea could feel her regret for the great sea beasts slaughtered for their oil. *"We're hoping our new partnership with Endulai will allow us to move on to a more efficient fuel."*

Gilea closed her eyes and nodded. *"Of course. An agreement regarding sunstone is being worked out as we speak."* It was all about the sunstone. Smaller crossroads could use *falin* oil, coal, or even wood, anything that burned, but it wasn't as reliable a power source and took a lot of labor. One sunstone could support a crossroad for a year or more. Gilea summoned the image of the sunstone she had seen at the Maer cross-

203

road and projected it before Atha, who touched her chest and gasped. Gilea focused her surface mind on the slowly spinning crystal, allowing her suppressed thoughts to bubble up below. Pleone was using her monopoly, bolstered now by her arrangement with the Maer, to dominate business across the continent, cutting off Rontaia and pressing the Azure Isle into service even as she orchestrated an uneven trade deal. She briefly wondered what Ujenn would think of this arrangement, then brought her focus back to the moment as Atha spoke.

"It's stunning, I..." Atha reached out her hand as if to touch the sunstone, though she must have known it wasn't real. *"I've only ever heard about it, but seeing it really takes your breath away."*

"I've never seen it in person, but I use the image in my practice sometimes. You can get lost in the facets."

"I will keep this image in my mind, and share it, with your permission of course."

"What is in my mind belongs to you."

"And mine to you," Atha said, leaning closer, looking up from the sunstone into Gilea's eyes, pushing out a subtle invitation like a whiff of perfume. Gilea must have given off a defensive vibe, since Atha leaned back, sipping her wine with mischievous eyes. *"I'm sorry, I've been too forward. It's just that we don't get many visitors as...entrancing as you."*

"Oh no, it's fine, you're fine, you're more than fine." Gilea shook her head as she took in Atha's defined arms and soft curves. *"It's just..."*

Atha waved her away with a smile, then leaned forward, a conspiratorial expression on her face. *"I understand. What's her name?"*

Gilea's heart fluttered, and she smiled hard to fight back the tears threatening to form.

"Her name is Temi."

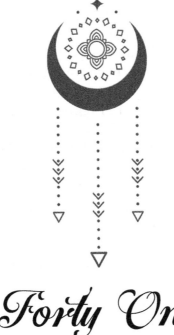

Forty One

Patia sat crammed in next to Max in the front of the dinghy, facing Leo, who powered the oars with an even bigger smile on his face than usual. Max held onto the gunwale, leaning away from Patia every time a wave pushed them closer together. She wasn't entirely comfortable touching this strange man either, but he seemed to physically recoil from contact, or most interactions, for that matter. She wanted to ask him something, to close the gap between them, as Leo had managed to do, but she couldn't think of anything to say that wouldn't sound stupid, so she turned and petted Sea Wolf, who was standing on the prow keeping watch, ears perked and muscles coiled for action.

"He's a good boat dog," she said.

Max glanced over at her for a moment, then turned and gave Sea Wolf a quick tap on the rump.

"He's the best boat dog," he said into his lap.

They circled the island, and as Leo had said, found a sandy patch of shore to pull the boat up to. Patia could see openings in the rock above sea level, and a few more farther down the shore, where it was too rocky to land. Sea Wolf waited for Leo to hop out before bounding onto the sand and scouting the perimeter of the rocky area surrounding the little beach, sniffing every rock and tide pool. Leo held out a hand to help Patia and Max down, then Max helped him pull the boat all the way up onto the sand.

"Not sure how much tidal change we'll see out here, but we best keep an eye out. What do you think, Wolfie? Is it safe here?"

Sea Wolf ran to Leo and shoved his muzzle in Leo's outstretched hand. Leo shook it, then picked up his pack from the dinghy and turned to study the island for a few moments.

"I'm going to climb up and check out that hole above, see if it connects to anything lower down. You two keep Wolfie company, would you?" Leo didn't wait for an answer. He walked to the edge of a large rock, climbed it like he was walking up stairs, and quickly made his way up to a ledge, behind which was an opening in the rock. He stared into the darkness for a moment, then turned and gave them a thumb's up.

"Looks good from here," he said. "Just give me a minute." He disappeared into the hole.

Sea Wolf barked once, and Max and Patia put their hands on him to soothe him at almost the same time.

"He'll be right back," Max said, though Patia couldn't tell whether he was talking to her or the dog. "He always comes right back."

"He seems like he knows what he's doing."

"He knows a lot," Max admitted. "He knows a lot about a lot, but he doesn't know everything."

"Nobody does, I guess."

They stood in silence watching the hole, with Sea Wolf leaning into Max's leg, doing the same thing. Patia studied the rocks, figuring she could climb up to where Leo had gone in easily enough, but she wondered if Max would be up to it, with his balance. They watched the hole for a while, then Patia got bored and started circling the edge of the beach like Sea Wolf had, looking down into several little tide pools, which had small red starfish and spiky orange urchins. As she was leaning down for a closer look, she heard a splash and the sound of air being blown out on the surface, and Leo appeared, swimming around the bend toward the boat. He emerged onto the beach a few moments later, stark naked, dripping wet, and with his biggest smile yet.

"You gotta see this. You can swim, right?"

Patia maintained fierce eye contact, though she could not erase the vision of his nakedness, his glistening muscles and water-shrunken cock, from her mind. As much as she admired his body, she didn't want to stare, though he probably wouldn't have noticed.

"Well, enough not to drown, but that's about it."

"Well, that's all you need! Look, you can either swim under there with me, it's only about ten feet, and I'll be there to pull you along. Or if you can climb, go up to that hole and make your way down from there. It's a little dicey in this one spot, but you'll be fine."

"I'll swim," Max said, turning his back and stripping off his shirt and pants, until he stood in nothing more than a pair of shapeless gray drawers, holding his hands awkwardly over his privates.

"Great. What do you say, Patia? Swim, climb, or just hang out on the beach for a few hours?"

She glanced up at the hole, thinking of what it might mean to climb down inside a dimly lit cave, then noticed the heat of the sun, which was growing stronger by the minute. She turned to Leo, forgetting that he was naked and re-seeing what she already could not un-see. She closed her eyes for a moment, then looked up at his face. His smile was the same as always, optimistic and carefree, and at that moment she wanted to channel his energy, the sense of freedom he exhaled with every breath. Who knew when she would have a chance to do something like this again? She was sixty years old and had never done anything like it before, and she didn't imagine her life with Gero would involve a lot of spelunking.

"Why the hell not?" she said, slipping out of her robe, feeling equal parts awkward and exhilarated. Leo hardly seemed to notice her nakedness, and Max strode ahead to wade into the water, turning his head away from Patia as he passed. Though clumsy on land, Max moved with surprising grace in the water and seemed to float and glide with the ease of a seal. Leo followed, standing ankle-deep in the water and holding out his hand to Patia, who waved it away.

"I can manage on my own, thank you very much."

"Sure thing! Just let me know if you need a hand. Wolfie, guard the boat." Sea Wolf gave a low whine and sat down, his tongue hanging low. Leo crouched and propelled himself into the water like a spear, twisting to come up in a fast crawl. He reached the half-submerged cave mouth in a few seconds, then treaded water as Patia dog-paddled over, with Max swimming just ahead, as if he were trying to stay close enough to help her if she got into any trouble. When she reached the edge, she hung onto a slippery rock, bobbing up and down until her feet found purchase on a ledge below the surface. Little waves smacked against the ceiling of the half-submerged entrance, and Patia could see that just inside, the tunnel disappeared below the water.

"Hold onto the left wall here," Leo said, treading water, "and keep one hand above you so you don't bang your head. You only have to go about ten feet before it opens up. Watch." He moved to the edge of the opening, braced one hand on the ceiling and the other on the wall, and slipped under, disappearing from sight. He returned about ten seconds later, shaking his head, flinging water from his curly hair like a dog. "I just went in there and back in that time, to show you it's not far. Patia, you want a hand?"

Her heartbeat grew fast and irregular as she watched the waves ride into the tunnel and ebb out. She shook her head, taking a few deep breaths, then maneuvered to the edge, where the underwater ledge ended.

"I'll be right in front of you. Just close your eyes and pull yourself forward, and I'll tap your arm when it's safe to surface." Leo's voice was enthusiastic and confident but gentle, and Patia could see how he'd be a good guide for the painted faces on their little journeys of discovery. She took another deep breath, closed her eyes, and slipped underwater. She pulled herself along with her left hand as her right hand found the ceiling, just as Leo had said, and was startled when a wave pushed her up so her head almost hit the top. She clenched her jaw and pulled herself forward faster, lungs burning, and she felt a tap on her shoulder and surfaced, gasping for breath as she treaded water.

"See? I told you it was a piece of cake! And look!" He gestured around, and Patia's eyes grew wide as she saw the cave, lit by multiple shafts of sunlight from holes in the rock above. It was about thirty feet in diameter, with a sandy edge on one side, and a watery channel leading off into the darkness on the other. The water glittered with reflected sunlight, casting little dancing moons onto the walls above.

Max surfaced, spraying like a breathfin, and his face lit up with a smile of childlike wonder.

"It's beautiful," he said, almost to himself.

"Right?" Leo answered. "The painted faces are going to eat it up!"

"If they aren't too scared to swim through that tunnel."

"They're usually pretty good swimmers, actually. And they can always climb in if they prefer. Speaking of which, I'm going to go get Wolfie out of the sun." Leo swam to the opposite side of the pool, clambered up to a slanted shaft about five feet out of the water, and disappeared into the darkness.

Patia's arms were growing tired from treading water, so she swam to the sandy edge, where she sat down, leaving her legs in the water but her torso above. She thought to cover her breasts for Max's sake, not that there was much to see, but he was busy staring at the dancing lights above. When he finally did look to her, his smile faltered only for a moment.

"Come on up if you want to sit. I won't bite."

Max made his way over to her, emerging to sit on the sand a few feet away, breathing heavily, his eyes glued to the walls and the water.

"I haven't seen anything this beautiful since..." he paused, his eyes growing distant. "Not for a long time."

"I have to admit it's well worth the dive." Patia paused as she heard Sea Wolf's little yip, and Leo coaxing him.

"Come on down boy, it's perfectly safe. You know I wouldn't steer you wrong." Leo appeared in the mouth of the shaft, facing away from them, still naked but with his pack in his hand. He turned, swinging the pack for a moment. "Hey, catch this, would you? I need to help Wolfie down." Max stood up, and Leo swung the pack several times, then hurled it across the cave, hitting Max in the chest. He fumbled but caught it just before it hit the water.

"Nice catch!" Leo called, then turned back to the shaft. "That's it, Wolfie, just a little farther." Sea Wolf's head appeared in the opening, staring down into the water for a moment, then looking up worriedly at Leo. "In you go," Leo said, wrapping his arms around the dog and launching back into the pool, where they landed with a splash. Sea Wolf surfaced, shook his head, and paddled over to where Max and Patia were sitting. He sniffed them both for a moment, then turned to Leo, who was still treading water, and swam back out to him. Leo held out his arms, and the dog swam up close, licking him on the face, and Patia barked a little laugh when she saw Leo lick the dog right back.

After a few minutes, Leo swam over to the sandy edge, standing with his crotch at Patia's eye level, then turning so his rounded, muscular ass was right in front of her face. She stood up, though with their proximity it did little to make her feel less awkward, but as usual, Leo didn't seem to notice. She liked that about him.

"See that tunnel over there?" he said over his shoulder. "I'm going to go explore down it, see where it goes. Atha said there were some chambers with hot springs in them. I don't know how far I'll be able to go without any light. I don't suppose you have any...anything on the ship that would stay lit underwater?"

Patia felt a giggle well up inside her, and she did a poor job of containing it. "I didn't bring my lab with me if that's what you mean. There are alchemical lights, made just for this purpose, but they're expensive, and I don't tend to carry that kind of thing on my person."

"How expensive?" Leo turned, his face twisted in genuine curiosity.

"I don't know, maybe ten *lep* or so? I haven't looked into it in a while."

"Could you make one? Back in your lab, I mean. Do you know how to do that?"

Patia shook her head. "It's not really in my wheelhouse. I might be able to figure it out, but..." Leo's face fell a bit, then quirked back into a smile.

"No, sure, of course, I get it. It's just, if I do come back here with the painted faces, I'm going to need some lights, and I'd rather get them from someone I trust than just buy them in the Chemist Market, you know?"

Patia's money sense tingled. She was sure between herself and Gero, they could figure out how to produce some glow vials and make a little profit, though she would be hard-pressed to charge Leo full price.

"I'd love to talk about that when we get back. We could probably do some business."

"Right on!" Leo took her hand and gave it a hearty shake. "Well anyhow, I'm going to see how far I can get. Can one of you go check on the boat, make sure the tide's not rising or anything?"

"I'll go," Max said, scooting down the sand, then pushing off toward the entrance. "Watch your head in those tunnels, Leo," he called.

Leo slapped his palm atop his head. "Always!" and dove into the water, reaching the other side in seconds. He turned and waved, then disappeared underwater. Max had already gone under, and Patia sat alone with Sea Wolf on the little sand shelf.

"Looks like it's just you and me," she said, scratching the dog behind the ears. He scooched beside her and put his wet paws over her hips, then lay his head in her lap as she continued scratching him. "Who would have imagined in all the Thousand Worlds I'd be sitting with a dog in a sea cave right now?"

Sea Wolf side-eyed her for a moment, then closed his eyes and settled in.

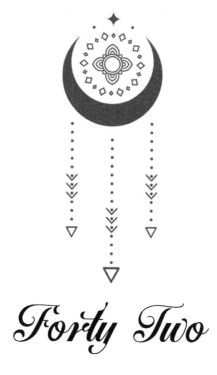

Forty Two

Gilea spent the day meditating, regaining her center after the taxing trip to the Azure Isle crossroad. She recalled the *sitri* forming an image of Endulai, with crisp lines and fine detail but with watery transparency, and she conjured this Endulai, staring into the candle's flame through the changing loops of her fingers as she worked her way through a series of hand moods. The Gilea in this Endulai was a ghostly figure, lacking substance, but the *sitri* layer maintained the tension of that surface image so she could sink below and process safely. Or so she hoped.

Amini had not been at breakfast, and another master had led the courtyard meditation that morning, with no explanation. Amini's presence was equally absent from her mind, and Gilea felt adrift without that anchor. Perhaps she had been sent away on mission, as Gilea had; surely there were many loose ends to be tied up before the Caravan could be restarted again. But Amini would have told Gilea, especially given all that was happening. It had to be something worse. If Pleone had sussed out Amini's plan, she might have taken action against her. Gilea wondered what kind of action she might take. Would Pleone use her considerable mental powers in violence against another master?

Gilea hoped not, but she certainly wouldn't be above putting Amini in forced seclusion, and she had the tools to do so with ease.

That evening, in the break between the ball sports and the evening pairings, Amini had still not shown herself, and Gilea slipped off to the bathroom to try to open their agreed-upon link.

"I'm glad we got the timing right." Amini's mind-voice was unsettled, almost panicked. *"I am confined to quarters, with guards maintaining a mind net to alert Pleone if I try to reach out."*

"Gods, I'm glad you're okay. I was worried Pleone might..."

Gilea felt Amini's indulgent smile from across the compound. *"She won't hurt me, or you. She may be many things, but that is not in her nature."*

"Then what?"

"She could shut us out of the Caravan. That seems to be her favorite weapon of late."

"I still have one vial of the deep tincture left. She can't shut me out."

"Choose your moment wisely. Come, we've talked too long. Same time tomorrow."

"Same time."

When she got back to the courtyard, Gilea was glad to find a friendly face, a woman named Doni, lingering by a fountain. They had shared minds a few times before during the pairings, and Doni had shown interest in sharing more than that, but she had never pushed. Her eyes lit up when Gilea approached, and Gilea pressed her palms together at her chest in greeting.

"I thought you'd paired off already," Doni said. "I was hoping..."

Gilea took her outstretched hands and tried to push out a wave of warmth, but an unexpected heat passed from her fingers into Doni's. An image flashed into her mind, of Doni pressing her naked body down on Gilea's, and she shooed it away, but not before Doni gave her fingers a gentle squeeze.

"Sorry," Gilea said, looking down to avoid Doni's eyes. "I didn't realize it would come out like that."

"You don't have to be sorry," Doni said, sliding her fingers up Gilea's forearms as she inched closer, the heat from their almost-touching bodies stirring Gilea with sudden urgency. She gripped Doni's arms, holding them in place, and breathed out slowly. The pairings, whether sexual in nature or not, were considered to be outside the realm of normal relationships, but Gilea's attachment to Temi had kept her from sharing more than a part of her mind with anyone.

213

"I'm not sure if I'm ready to—"

Doni stopped her with a gentle blink. "It's okay. You can just lie with me. Be with me." She turned, letting go with one hand and pulling Gilea along with the other. Her flowing robe gave just a hint of the shape of her hips, and Gilea smiled nervously as Doni led her to one of the wide hammocks under the arbor. She hoped Doni wouldn't misinterpret the pairing. They cozied up in the hammock, Gilea playing the big spoon as Doni nestled up tight, pulling Gilea's arm over her.

Gilea felt the pulse of Doni's invitation, and she opened her mind as much as she dared, sharing a portion of it with Doni, who caressed each thought and feeling Gilea had shared, offering her own in return. Though Doni had been at Endulai for much longer, she was still new at mindsharing, and Gilea had to guide her gently, shushing the physical urges until they passed through together into a calm, sleepy space full of warmth and peace. Their minds mirrored their bodies, Doni settling into Gilea's support, and it felt good to be needed like this, to be able to offer Doni the comfort she could not accept in return.

Gilea summoned the *sitri* circle, which started as a dot and grew outward, then echoed back to center. She felt Doni's mind growing in synch with hers, even her heartbeat, it seemed, governed by the movement of the watery rings. The rings' speed increased, pulsing like water under pressure, taking on a life of their own, pulling Gilea into their rhythm. Doni's body radiated heat like a coal furnace, and her mind swelled with their closeness, enveloping Gilea's consciousness, pressing to pass beneath the surface like wind-blown branches scratching at a window. Gilea's defenses flared as her thoughts flickered to Temi, and the growing bubble surrounding them sagged, settling like a shaken blanket as the space collapsed, leaving them connected, covered by a layer just thick enough to keep the world's chill at bay.

Gilea's mind began to form words, to apologize, to explain, but Doni wiggled in closer, pulling Gilea's arm under her belly, and let out a quiet "Shhhh." *It's okay,* she seemed to say with her body. *Just lie with me now. Just be with me.*

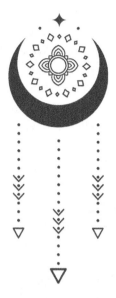

Forty Three

Patia ate an unsurprising lunch of seabiscuits and dried fish with Leo and Max in the cave. Leo rambled on and on about the hot springs, how big the chamber was, which he could apparently hear from the echoes, how it had built-in seats that seemed like they'd been carved somehow.

"They are absolutely going to be lining up for this one, I tell you. I might be able to get six on this one, at full price, when they hear about these caves. So we might need, maybe a dozen of those glow vials, or more. And they pay the expenses, so you don't have to give me a friend price."

Patia couldn't stop the smile from growing on her face. "Like I said, we'll work it out once we get back. I'm sure I can make it happen one way or another."

"You're gonna need a bigger boat," Max said, chewing with a strange sideways motion as if the fish hurt his teeth.

"Well if we get six signed up, we can rent a bigger one. If it's four, we can sleep above deck, under a tarp, while they sleep in the bunks. We'll work something out. I'm going to need a first mate, though." He elbowed Max, who shook his head.

"I gotta get back upriver, check in on Zander. He gets lonely all by himself I bet. He likes to think I need him but it's the other way."

"We could send him a message. We could even use the Inkwell. I bet they'd deliver it to him, for a few extra *nomi*."

Max wagged his finger at Leo. "No Inkwell, no way. It's bad luck to send one, and worse to receive. No, I need to check in on him in person. He needs me." He balled his hands together, wringing them slowly. "He needs me."

"All right," Leo said, clapping him on the shoulder, which made Max jump a little. "You still have time to change your mind."

"I'm not changing my mind."

"No, of course not. But you'd have time if you wanted to."

Patia brushed the sand from her fingers and stood up, using the rough wall for support. She had grown cold, and her hips were sore from sitting on the ground for so long.

"We better get you back in the sun," Leo said, glancing down at the goosebumps on her arm. "Wolfie, you ready for a little climb?" Sea Wolf snapped to attention, and Leo rewarded him with a head scratch, then picked up his pack. "All right, we'll see you on the other side."

He held the pack above his head and swam awkwardly across the cave with Sea Wolf at his side. When he reached the opposite wall, he hung the pack on a rock and boosted Sea Wolf up so he could just barely scramble over the edge of the opening and scamper up out of sight.

Patia followed Max, who stopped and looked her in the eye for a moment.

"I'll do just like Leo did, tap you on the arm when it's safe to come up," he said, then looked back toward the entrance. "If you want."

"Sounds perfect, Max. Lead the way."

Patia lay in her bunk, drowsy from the morning's exertions, and drifted in and out of sleep as they sailed. They were within a couple of days of their destination, and she tried to picture it in her mind as Paoro had described it: a tiny island no bigger than the dormitory at the Rontaian temple, near the tip of a string of similar islands, a heap of rock among dozens of others, scored with holes and crevices like bubble cheese. Beyond a narrow crevice would be a chamber filled with ghost-

216

ly purple light, and there she would find it, growing on the rocky walls with veins of hotsilver in them. She felt her mind detach, as it had done in Paoro's room, and she saw the chamber as if she were floating above it, but also standing in ankle-deep water, staring at its shiny wet surface, which seemed to pulse in time with her own heartbeat. Her fingers reached forward to touch it, and tendrils rose from it to greet them, like the tender ends of vines, unfurling to wrap around each finger. Veins of glowing purple streaked up her hands and arms, and she could feel her entire body transforming as the glow enveloped her, then her vision faded and the brightness of the sun pouring through the porthole ripped her from sleep.

They passed an uneventful evening moored off an island covered in dense bushes with bright pink flowers. Leo brought back a bouquet after his morning swim, sparing a bit of their drinking water to keep it fresh in a cup next to the wheel as they sailed the next day. By late afternoon they could just see Monument Island in the distance, and Leo's smile grew tense as dusk approached more quickly than the island.

"Dammit, I misjudged it," he said, straightening the flowers in the cup as he scratched his beard. "I really thought we were going to get close enough by nightfall to anchor off the island. The winds are going to change once the sun goes down and probably blow us off course. It'll be a pain in the ass getting us back around there. We might be able to drop sail and just drift, and hope to be able to push back up and circle around in the morning, but it's going to be close." He leaned over the map, studying it, his fingers moving this way and that, then he gazed out toward the island. "Unless..."

"We could tack hard to port," Max said into his hands, "see if we can make a little progress toward the shore, then drop sail once the wind shifts, and maybe we'll drift close enough to the tip of the island to find a reef we could anchor off of tonight before we get blown past it." Max spoke in a quiet, hopeful voice, glancing up at Leo briefly. Patia wished she had any idea what either of them was talking about.

"Maybe," Leo said, clapping Max on the shoulder. "It's worth a shot if you don't mind staying up half the night on lookout."

"I like it better at night, anyhow," Max said, his mouth twisting into a half-smile.

"All right then. Let's make the most of the wind we've got while we have it." He gave Patia a wink and a nod, then he and Max adjusted the sail, and the boat creaked as it leaned to the left but moved into the wind at an angle. Patia sat with Sea Wolf, watching the sun sink lower on the horizon, taking the day's heat with it and slowing the wind. They ate a quick meal of dried fish and seabiscuits, and it was all Patia could do to choke down a piece of each. Hopefully, Leo and Max could catch some fresh fish in the morning, as she didn't know how many more days of this she could take.

She slept fitfully, awoken by Leo and Max switching shifts on watch, her mind torn between the mystery of the island ahead and visions of Gero eating by himself at his little table by candlelight, feeding half his dinner to Vera, then crawling into bed alone, not humming. She tried to distract herself by thinking of all the things she'd do to him when she returned, the trick she had in mind with the *olli*, but her heartache tamped down her desire, and she spent the worst night's sleep she'd had since she left Guluch.

In the morning, she discovered the boat was anchored about a half-mile offshore, and Leo was nowhere to be seen. Max gave her a little wave as he sat tending a frayed rope end.

"You were right," she said, sipping her tea, which was hot but weak.

"I should have told him before we wouldn't make it by nightfall, but he wouldn't have listened anyhow."

"Well, maybe he'll listen to you next time. Is that his boat over there?" Patia pointed to a small rowboat floating, apparently anchored, with no one in it.

Max nodded. "He's diving for scuttles, where the reef is shallower. We're anchored on the far edge. If it weren't for the reef, we would have drifted past the island."

Patia's stomach growled at the thought of the rich, tender flesh of scuttles, which she had only tasted a couple of times when she was living in Rontaia. They were only in season there in the winter, and they were beyond her usual student budget. A circle appeared in the water next to the dinghy, and she saw a figure rise over the edge and drop something in. Her eyesight wasn't good enough to be sure, but its spiny outline certainly suggested scuttle.

"Leo does take care of his charges, doesn't he?" Patia took another sip of her tea, almost spitting it out it was so weak.

"He takes good care of everyone but himself," Max said, turning back to his rope.

Patia gazed out at the island, whose coastline was dominated by hulking black shapes, the famous stone monuments it was named after. It was hard to tell from this distance, but they had to be enormous, maybe a hundred feet tall, all in different shapes. Some of them looked to be human figures, while others might have been animals, and some were shaped like cubes, spheres, or triangles. It was hard to imagine how they could build so many, the person power required for such large structures. She wondered if they were all old, or if new ones were under construction even now. As she stood nibbling on half of a seabiscuit and drinking her now-cold tea, she watched Leo get back in the dinghy and row it back to the boat with powerful strokes. As he approached the boat, he stopped rowing for a moment and held up a large net with a half-dozen scuttles in it, twisting and snapping their claws in vain.

"I got some water on," Max said as Leo tossed the net over the rail, where it landed with a clack of shells. Leo hopped up on deck, his hair still wet from his dive, his body covered in sweat.

"Good. We need to boil these quick so we can move out as soon as the wind picks back up. We should be able to make our destination well before nightfall if all goes as planned." He nodded with his chin to a couple of fishing boats in a cove near where he had been diving. "Those fishermen were awfully curious about what we were doing here, and I figure the less they see of us, the better."

Patia wondered if Paoro had visited Monument Island, if he'd asked too many questions, tipped them off somehow to his errand. He never was one for subtlety.

Patia dumped the scuttles in the pot once it was boiling, careful to avoid their large but clumsy claws, then put a lid on it and snuffed out the flame as Leo and Max unfurled the sail and pointed the boat up the coast. The mast creaked as the tension of the sail ratcheted up, but everything held together. By midday, they'd gotten enough distance from the coast they could straighten up and sail more easily, and the boat no longer felt like it was being pulled apart. Leo gave Max a few instructions, then opened the pot, his eyes and smile growing wide as he looked inside and pulled out two scuttles, whose shells were now bright red from being boiled. He lay them down on his cutting bench, pulled out his knife, and went to work, dismantling the creatures in short order. He gestured Patia over to the bench, where the claws were cracked and the meat loosened from the tail, and a little bowl of everyspice sat to the side.

"You get two claws and two chunks of the tail meat," Leo said, slicing two lines in the tails, dividing each into three. "Have you ever eaten scuttles?"

"It's been a long time, but yes. Thank you so much, Leo. I don't think I could choke down another piece of dried fish at this point."

"Yeah, it does get a little old. If we weren't in such a hurry, I'd have us eating like painted faces every day. The sea always has something new on offer."

She opened a claw, which Leo had already cracked, and twisted it to pull out a fat lump of pearly white meat. She picked a few little bits of shell off it, dabbed it in the everyspice, and pulled the meat off the cartilage with her teeth, emitting a little moan as the taste flooded her mouth.

"So good, right?" Leo said, pulling off the smaller legs and chewing the little bits of meat off them. "You can't find them close to the mainland this time of year, but when I saw that reef, I just knew."

"Those fishermen you talked to, you said they were extra curious. What do you think that's about?"

Leo tossed one of the tiny legs overboard and pulled off another, studying it with furrowed brow.

"I asked them if it was okay if I hunted for scuttles, since I didn't want to infringe on their fishing territory, and they told me it was fine if I went farther out. Then they asked me what brought us out this way, and I told them the truth, or as much as I felt I could. That I was looking for sea caves for a pleasure cruise. Asked if they knew of any nearby. They gave each other a funny kind of look and shook their heads, then they started asking about the cruise, and why we wanted to take people into such dangerous places. It was weird, honestly."

"You think they might have sussed out what we're after?"

"Well, since I don't even know what that is, I kind of doubt it, but it was strange." He tossed another leg overboard and pulled off the last one. "Powerful strange."

Patia's stomach roiled with nerves, then piqued with hunger as her eyes fell on the succulent tail meat of the scuttle. They were so close to their destination, and the side-eyes of a few curious fishermen weren't going to get between her and the Thousand Worlds, nor ruin the taste of fresh scuttle. She scraped the meat from the shell with her fingernails, dipped it in the spice, and stuffed the whole delicious thing in her mouth.

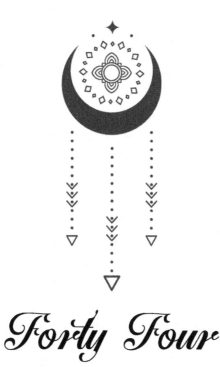

Forty Four

Gilea had to work to slow her eager steps so no one would notice her hurry as she made her way through the hallways toward the cradle room. A half-dozen acolytes and two masters stood in the semicircular entry room, waiting with varying degrees of impatience Gilea could feel through their veneer of calm. The Inkwell had been a casualty of the Caravan's closure, and there were a lot of backed-up messages to be sent now that it was finally re-opened. Gilea practiced her *sitri* patterns to distract herself from the thoughts of Temi threatening to consume her. She shifted her focus so that instead of seeing the patterns from the outside, as she had before, she now saw them from the inside. She pictured herself sheathed in evenly flowing water that swirled and flowed in all directions, like Sage in the fountain form she had first seen them in. She pictured the dots and circles Sage and the other *sitri* used to communicate, and the patterns began to take on meaning. It felt like progress, and it was oddly satisfying to see her thoughts from the inside looking out. She wondered if she could communicate this way, with sufficient time and practice.

When her turn came, she drank the tincture and lay back in the cradle, still warm from its previous occupant. She eased into a half-conscious state, seeing the patient acolyte at the foot of the cradle with part of her mind, and the cheerful operator with another. A book appeared in her lap, and a pen in her hand, and she wrote the message she had been crafting for the past several days.

Dearest Temi,

I miss you, and I think of you often.

Things are much busier at Endulai than you might expect. I've been places and seen things I never could have imagined, all without leaving the holy city. I wish I could tell you more, but that will have to wait until we meet again, which I look forward to more than words can express.

In your letter, you spoke of your hopes and your doubts, and I can put your mind at rest on one count at least: You will always be enough for me. I will wait for you or fly across the continent to you. Only say the word, and I will be there, in whatever way our hearts fit together. Be it candles or flames or the twinkling of distant stars, the light that connects us can pierce any darkness, bridge any distance. I have learned from my time here that the universe is in us, just as we are in it. The physical world we experience is but a hazy shadow cast by the body, which serves only to block the light emanating from deep inside. In your letter, you spoke of sex, and the role it often plays in love. While the pleasures of the flesh have been part of my past experiences, they are like paper lanterns compared to the sun that shines from your heart and mind, warming me to the core and coaxing life from the hidden seeds locked deep inside me.

No two people have the same experience, but in the common parlance and every language and dialect in all the Thousand Worlds,

I love you.

I can't wait to show you my Rontaia.

I miss you, and I think of you often.

Gilea

As she closed the book, the operator faded, and she returned to the cradle room. The acolyte offered her a cup of the orange blossom infusion, which she downed in one gulp and strode out of the room so the acolyte would not notice her tears.

Gilea sat bolt upright as Pleone's summons rang through her like the vibrations from a great silent bell. She summoned the thought *Need to*

pee, need to pee as she fumbled inside her pillow and found the last vial of deep tincture. She did have to pee, she discovered as she hurried toward the bathroom, where she downed the tincture as she released. She moved with steady speed through the hallways and stairs until she stood before Pleone's door, where the two guards nodded in acknowledgment. She smiled at them, feeling suddenly invincible as the tincture took effect; their powers of intimidation did not affect her in her current state. She breezed through the door and sat in the bedside chair, almost physically pulled by Pleone's call. She looked on the old woman's sunken, motionless face, ashen and dull against the shining copper of her circlet, and something like pity moved in her heart.

"Do not pity me," Pleone mindspoke as Gilea's hand found hers under the cover. *"I have lived longer than anyone expected, and have traveled farther and wider in my mind than I ever would have in my body. If I should fade into the Thousand Worlds, I would do so with an open heart."*

"Gods willing, you will not be called away so soon."

"This is not my time, Gilea. But come, join me where we can sit more comfortably."

Gilea squeezed Pleone's hand as they slid into Pleone's den, with a pot of steaming tea on the table between their chairs. Pleone's face twisted into a smile, which she half-covered with her hand as she observed Gilea.

"You've taken the deep tincture."

Gilea smiled and nodded, the answer flowing from her with guileless ease.

"I need it to see whoever is operating outside the Caravan. That is why you've summoned me so suddenly, isn't it?"

"Actually, no." Pleone poured twin cups of tea, sliding one toward Gilea. *"This is about Amini, whose absence you've no doubt noticed today."*

"I assumed she had self-segregated to meditate in her quarters." Gilea's mind suppressed the faint swell of intrusive thoughts, calming them without effort, thanks to the tincture's effect. *"She's been deep into some mystical diagrams of late."*

"Her dedication to her practice is always an inspiration. Even stuck in that bed every minute of the year, I still struggle to clear my mind enough to meditate properly some days."

"You are responsible for many souls. It would be surprising if you never struggled."

"Your wisdom, and more importantly, your control, have been impressing me

223

more and more of late. Your sitri skills have quickly made you our most reliable traveler, and you seem to see things that escape the notice of others."

"I had your help with that in Rontaia."

"The first time, yes." Pleone sipped her tea, furrowing her brow as she set the cup down with care. Gilea felt the panic trying to surface, but she tensed her mind and suppressed it.

"I don't catch your meaning."

"The first time, when I sent you, you used my gift to see more than you could with your own eyes. The second time, when you went on your own, you no longer needed my support." Sweat beaded on Gilea's forehead, and she felt her control slipping.

"What's the matter, dear?" Pleone leaned over the table, lowering her voice. "Do you need to pee?"

Gilea sank back as if gut-punched. Pleone's voice echoed distantly, and the light of the lamp refracted like sunlight through half-closed eyelashes. She felt the tincture's power waver, her walls buckling inward under the pressure of Pleone's pervasive energy. Just as she felt herself collapsing, her center was buoyed by a gently swelling force. She sat up, filled with radiant energy, and felt her face pull wide into a smile. She leaned toward Pleone, answering her in a low, calm voice.

"I'm done hiding from you, and I'm done with your games." Pleone pulled back, her eyebrows raising with mock admiration. "You don't control me anymore. You don't tell me what to do, or where to go, or what to say."

"Dear Gilea, no one is trying to control you. I'm trying to give you the tools to control yourself, to find your part in this great machinery. The Caravan needs you. I need you." She poured more tea into her cup, which was already almost full, and raised it slowly to take a sip. "We've found the culprit in Rontaia, but with the Universal Tincture, he can go anywhere he wants in the Caravan, and we can't stop him. So, we have to pressure the Rontaian temple to put a stop to it themselves. I see no other alternative." She paused, blinking, her cup in mid-air. "Do you?"

"Invite him in. Let me go to him, wherever he might be lurking, talk to him, and find out what he wants. Someone of such power we surely want on our side."

"Our side comes off a little disingenuous from someone who's been plotting with Amini to undermine me at every turn."

Pleone's words hit Gilea like a paper sword, bending at the point of contact, and she looked deep into Pleone's eyes, watching her confidence falter.

"Our side is the same: maintaining the Caravan so we can spread our practice *to all those willing to accept our teachings. The Caravan is supposed to be a place of learning, of sharing, of open hearts and minds, yet you seek to shut out the one place that is truly open. For all its flaws, the Rontaian temple does real good in the world, with actual people in need. And whom do we help here? Businesspeople arranging trade deals. Politicians seeking to exert influence over distance. The rich. The powerful. Is that what Endulai is about?"*

Pleone's eyes sank, the lines on her face tightening with frustration. She set down her cup and clasped her hands together in her lap.

"Nothing is free in this world, Gilea. To maintain this space, to provide food and clothing, tinctures, medicine, food for all the acolytes—it costs money. Without money, there is no Endulai. Without Endulai, our practice, our truth, would fade away, like the sun dipping below the mountains, and our light would become lost to the world. I appreciate your enthusiasm, your purity of spirit, but sometimes hard decisions have to be made, for the good of us all. My decision on Rontaia is not up for discussion."

"*You're right,*" said Gilea, setting her cup down and standing. "*Sometimes hard decisions do have to be made, which is why I'm going to Rontaia now, to lead them to the Maer crossroad so they can deal with each other directly.*"

"*You wouldn't dare,*" Pleone growled. *Amini,* she mindspoke with a menacing tone.

"*I will, and you won't try to stop me. And you won't touch a hair on Amini's head.*"

"*You think you can just—*"

"*See you on the other side.*"

Gilea closed her eyes and returned to Pleone's bedside, lifting the circlet off Pleone's head. She retrieved a thin band of lead from the pocket of her robe and pressed it along the inside rim of the circlet. She replaced it on Pleone's head, adjusting it so it looked natural, and stood up. Pleone's doctor, or one of the healers, would find the lead sooner or later, but not before Gilea enacted her plan. She leaned over and kissed Pleone's cold forehead, running her fingers over her cheek.

"I'm truly sorry," she said, then turned away and strode out the door.

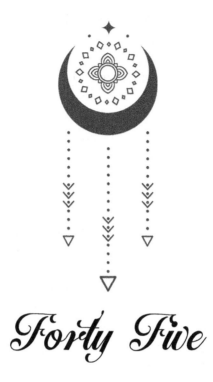

Forty Five

They cruised alongside the archipelago as if pushed by a steady hand, and Patia's nerves were vibrating with anticipation in tune with the humming of the sail lines. Leo and Max kept the boat on a straight course, and by dusk, they were anchored off the island just one short of their destination, less than an hour's sail the next day, according to Leo. They dined on scuttles and dried seaweed, each of them getting a whole scuttle to themselves, as it would spoil if they tried to keep it overnight. They sat on the deck after dinner, sipping tea and watching the sun melt into an endless puddle of deepening colors. As night brought the great curtain of the heavens down around her, a sense of calm settled into Patia's mind. She had come a long way from Guluch to Rontaia, and now out to this distant chain of rocky islands. She had the sense of certainty that came when she was about to add the last ingredient to a tincture she had measured and mixed carefully. Everything Paoro had told her so far had checked out, and the countless stars reflected in the slick black sea suggested a world of infinite promise or the promise of infinite worlds.

Leo's smile was more restrained than usual when he returned from his morning reconnaissance in the dinghy, sweaty and heaving for breath.

"There's no place to land the dinghy," he said between gulps of water, "and the shoreline's pretty rough, but I think I found a spot we could drop you at the edge of some tidal pools, and you can wade in. Shouldn't be more than waist-deep, I don't think."

"Did you see the opening we talked about?" Paoro had described it as a narrow crevice about ten feet above the water level on the north side of the island.

"I did," Leo said, frowning into his cup. When he turned his eyes up, the usual joy and confidence were missing. "I don't like the look of it, to be honest. It's a bit slippery and steep, especially lugging that box. I'm not sure how easy it will be."

"I don't need to lug the whole box," Patia reassured him. "I can fit what I need in my pack, and I can climb with that." She tried to project more calm than she felt, as she was not much of a climber, but if Paoro had made it up, so could she.

"If you decide you need a little help getting up there, I'll be ready."

"Good to know." She had promised Paoro on her Works not to let anyone else through the crevice. She had never broken such a promise, and she damned sure wasn't going to break it in what might be the most important moment in her life.

She sat in the front of the rowboat next to Max, who did not shy away from her as much as before. Sea Wolf faced forward but kept turning to give Patia concerned little glances as they approached the spit of rock, which seemed to thrum in her vision. The wind rose and the waves grew choppy as they rounded the north side of the island, and Leo had to redouble his efforts to keep them from being blown into the rocks. After some maneuvering, he steered the boat close in, and Max stood and used a long pole to stabilize them in the rocky shallows. Patia looked down into the clear water, which was alive with color. Orange anemones billowed with each passing wave as little purple and white striped fish darted in and out of their tentacles. Starfish and urchins dotted the rough bottom, and masses of light green tubelike structures flowed with the current. Patia could not tell if they were a plant or some kind of animal. She took a moment to check her pack, which contained the glass tank in its wiry cage, a waterskin, and some dried fish. She'd considered bringing her Works book, but she couldn't risk it getting wet, and she doubted she'd get anything more out of it on the island than she had poring over it for hours on the boat.

"I'll wave my yellow scarf from the crevice when I'm ready to be picked up," Patia said. "I might be a little while."

Leo nodded, squinting as he studied the crevice above. "We'll anchor just a little farther out, so we don't get pushed into shore."

"Mind your feet," Max said, pointing to one of the urchins. "You don't want to step on one of those."

"There's not much in this water I do want to step on, but thanks for the tip." Patia laid a hand on Max's shoulder, then took Leo's extended hand and backed over the edge of the boat. Her thin sandals cushioned the roughest edges of the rock, but it still hurt to stand on it. She held out both arms for balance and picked her way across the rocky bottom, careful to avoid stepping on the urchins and starfish, though there was no avoiding the slimy tubes that flopped against her legs. She waded, wincing with every painful step, until the water grew shallow, which made the rocks even more uncomfortable to walk on. Out of the water, she found a smoother rock to stand on, and she adjusted her pack as she stared up at the crevice, which looked like little more than a crack, but Paoro had assured her she would fit. She tightened the straps on her pack and her sandals as she studied the best way up the rocky face. There were plenty of things to hold onto, but the climb looked rough and unforgiving.

Her feet screamed with the pain of sharp points of rock, made only slightly more bearable by the soles of her sandals, and her hands grew raw and scraped as she pushed and stretched her way up. As her head reached the base of the crevice, whiffs of putrid air drifted out, and she turned away in disgust, wishing she had her hands free to tie her scarf around her face. She ignored the pain in her feet and the sharp edges of the rock digging into her palms and pulled and pushed herself up using every ounce of her strength. She knelt on the sharp rock, then rose to her feet, closing her nose and gripping tightly to the rock as the odor hit her. It was worse than the rotten, fishy smell of Paoro's tank; there was a deeper, more sinister putrescence beneath it, and she hastily tied her scarf around her mouth and nose, not that it would do much good. She turned and waved to Max and Leo, who were watching her from the anchored dinghy. They waved back, and Leo gave her two thumbs up. She turned toward the crevice, angled her body sideways, and squeezed through the opening.

It was dark in the crevice, but as she sidled through it, a faint light penetrated the darkness. The crevice widened quickly, ending in an oval-shaped opening, whose edges were lit with a purplish tint. She moved to the opening, her stomach lurching as the smell hit her full in the face, and when she looked down, her body was wracked with chills, and she was barely able to get the scarf out of the way before the morning's seabiscuit and dried fish came pouring out of her mouth, splashing off the wall and onto her feet. Below her was a chamber no wider than her shack back in Guluch, with faint glowing purple lines streaking up the opposite wall. The rocky floor beneath was puddled with water, and a large blanket of yellowish-white slime like what she had seen in Paoro's tank seemed to spill out from below the veins. In the puddles around the slime lay what must have been a dozen skeletons, mostly jumbled together bones, but one was still intact, and a handful of small crabs picked at the brownish-red bits still attached to the bones. Patia retched again, managing to avoid her feet this time. Tears stung her eyes, and her stomach roiled, tight and rotten, as she closed her eyes and nose and tried to breathe only through her mouth.

A familiar sensation of lightness filled her head, and she wrapped the scarf tighter around her face as a feeling of disconnectedness sank into her, and she into it. She had felt the same thing in Paoro's room when she'd sniffed the ooze, and she ground her teeth together, slapping herself on the face several times to slow the effect. She would not have much time, and though her limbs felt slow and clumsy, she backed down to her stomach and lowered her legs until they found purchase on the rocky wall below. It would have been a challenging climb in normal circumstances, but her head spun with stars and streaks of bright purple lightning. She felt her foot slip, and she could almost see her fingers losing their grip one by one as if time had slowed down. She fell, slow as a feather, and landed on her back with a tinkle of broken glass and an oddly warm sensation shooting through her back and elbow. The thick carpet of ooze cushioned her fall, and the pain she felt was a distant, dull throb, which quickly faded as her body and mind relaxed completely. The rocky walls and ceiling were highlighted in crisp purple lines, and the opening above filled with purple light, which slowly morphed into a fiery orange color. She rose from her body, floating up toward the opening, and saw a coppery tunnel streaking away from her, pulsing with rich, warm light. She drifted toward it, like a leaf toward a waterfall, and the orange light filled her mind as she was pulled into it. She felt no fear, no worry, only a deep sense of peace and connectedness as she slipped away into it, speeding far away from her battered body and the dank reality of the cave into a world of light, peace, and stillness.

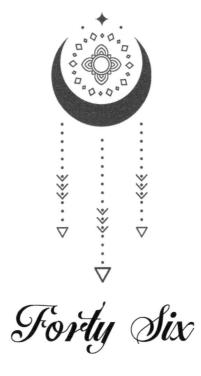

Forty Six

Gilea sat cross-legged by the pool, gazing down at the thinkfins circling, brushing against each other, and circling again. She sank into the rhythm of their cycle, focusing her energy on the brief moment of contact, with the ripples from their movement keeping her centered. She closed her eyes, but the cycle continued in her head. She opened her eyes each time the fish were about to touch, and each time what she saw with her eyes matched her mind's vision. After a time, she could no longer tell if her eyes were open or closed, and she knew it was time to leave her body behind.

She drifted outside of herself into her mind's darkness, skirting around the edges of the bright copper bubble of the Endulai crossroad, which was humming with activity. She followed the copper cords along the now-familiar path to Rontaia, but the cords were twisted away from the crossroad, racing out toward the Azure Isle and the other island crossroads. The Rontaian crossroad appeared as a faint bubble, and she could sense a small number of minds inside. She passed through the dim membrane into the temple, where three figures sat with eyes closed facing the Soulshape. They seemed unaware of her presence at first, then one of them opened his eyes and fixed her with a fearful look, which shaded toward hope as Sali recognized her.

"Come with me," she whispered.

He looked puzzled. *"We are cut off. How are you here? How can I—"*

"Share minds with me. I must show you something."

Sali glanced at the other seated figures, then closed his eyes in concentration. Gilea felt his consciousness brushing against hers, and she opened up and let him in.

"How are you here?"

"I have found a way around the Caravan, using a deep tincture. Do you have these?"

"We do, but they're very expensive and difficult to acquire."

"You will only need a few, but that is for later. I will take you for now. Are you ready?"

"Not really," Sali said shakily. *"But I have no choice but to trust you."*

"Good. This is going to feel strange, but stay with me and I will take you where you need to go."

Gilea felt Sali's mind snuggled tightly against hers, and they passed through the bubble into the infinite space beyond. She scanned the many glowing shapes in the darkness until she found the small, bright spot farthest from Rontaia, and they glided through the void, following no cord, like birds buoyed by ocean breezes. She looked behind her and saw a faint glowing trail in their wake, hoping it would not dissipate before Sali could get back. Sali's silence was filled with fear, tinged with wonder, as he took in the Thousand Worlds for what must have been the first time. As they approached, the bright spot grew bigger, its membranes thicker and brighter than those in any of the other crossroads. Gilea wondered for a moment if she could pass through it as easily as the others, but her hesitation vanished as a surge of strength bubbled up within her.

"Where are we going?"

"This is the Maer crossroad. I'm going to introduce you to Ujenn."

"You spoke of her before. She is…"

"Someone who can help you get what you need. Her appearance may come as a bit of a shock, so be prepared. I'm sure she will be delighted to meet you."

Before he could answer, she passed through the membrane, slowly, as if moving through honey, then emerged onto the rough stone parapet. Ujenn sat cross-legged, her eyes closed, with a pigeon cradled in her hands. She looked up, startled, at Gilea, then at Sali, but she regained her composure as she replaced the pigeon in the cage and pressed her hands together at her chest.

"Gilea, what a pleasant, yet unexpected surprise," Ujenn said with a slight bow.

"I do apologize for showing up unannounced, but the matter was urgent."

"No apologies necessary. You are welcome here anytime, as is your friend, who I believe has never had the pleasure of meeting a Maer before." She bowed to Sali with an indulgent smile, and he returned the bow, with a look of contrition.

"Gilea said your appearance might surprise me, but I hadn't expected you to be so...beautiful." He held his hand out toward Ujenn as he spoke, and Gilea smiled at his earnestness.

"This one can definitely stay," Ujenn said, winking at Gilea. *"I remember when I saw humans for the first time. They were...something."* Her eyes grew distant for a moment, then snapped back to Gilea, suddenly sharp and piercing. *"So, what is so urgent it brings you to our humble crossroad, with no invitation and no advance warning from Endulai?"*

"There have been some...changes at Endulai." Gilea paused, uncertain how much Ujenn could sense from her words, but at this point, it didn't matter. *"I've decided it's time to introduce you to the Rontaians, with Sali as their ambassador. If you accept, of course."*

Ujenn's eyebrows raised, and she turned to Sali, stroking her beard and twiddling with one of its many braids. *"If he comes with open mind and heart, we accept."*

"What is inside me is open to you," Sali said, closing his eyes and bowing more deeply.

"Come closer," Ujenn murmured, and Sali approached, kneeling before her, so their eyes were level. *"May I touch your face?"*

"Of course."

Ujenn's hairy fingers reached out and touched Sali's forehead, and they remained immobile for several seconds until she pulled her hands from his face and clasped them around his.

"Help me up," she said, and they stood together. *"I apologize for the precautions, but given the strange goings-on of late, I hope you'll understand."*

"Oh, absolutely," Sali said, staring at Ujenn, seemingly unaware of Gilea's presence.

"You have a beautiful mind, by the way. I look forward to getting to know you better as we discuss how to get you the brightstone you need." She glanced over to Gilea. *"That is why you brought him, yes?"*

"Rontaia and Endulai have had a falling-out, and I took it upon myself to

introduce you, as a way of bringing greater unity to the Caravan as a whole. I hope that wasn't presumptuous."

"It did occur to me that Pleone was dragging her feet a bit. I'm glad to hear things are taking a turn for the better, and we are pleased to make the acquaintance of friends of Endulai."

"Despite our differences, we all practice the same philosophy," Sali said with a bow.

Gilea felt a strange disturbance in the part of her still connected to her body. She turned to look back where they'd come in, but all she saw were the crumbling stone battlements and a dark mountain in the background. She narrowed her focus, and the battlements and mountain dimmed. She could see the lights of the Caravan and the other crossroads shining through. She could still make out the trail they had left on their way, faint though it was.

"Is something wrong?" Ujenn moved toward Gilea, who shook her head.

"Not exactly, but I need to go. Can you help Sali get home? There's a trail to follow if it doesn't dissipate too quickly. If you can get him through your barriers, he should be able to find his way back on his own."

"Gilea, I have no idea how we even got here, what—" Sali stopped as Gilea wrapped her hands around his head and pressed her forehead into his, pouring some of the energy of the deep tincture into his mind, hoping she'd left herself enough control to make it back herself.

Sali's eyes were wide with wonder as she let him go, and he nodded. *"I think I can find my way back, with a little help."*

"I can lower the barriers for him any time. I look forward to seeing you again soon, Gilea."

"Our paths will cross again." Gilea bowed to them, then turned to face the mountain again as Ujenn spoke behind her.

"Sali, before we get down to business, tell me a little bit about Rontaia. Is it true it's hot there all year round? That it never snows? I've always wondered…"

Ujenn's voice drifted off as Gilea pushed past the barrier and into the expanse of blackness, following her mind's disturbance back to her body at dizzying speed, like her first trip on the Caravan. Before she knew what was happening, she was passing through the bubble at Endulai, hurtling through walls and into the center courtyard where her body sat in lotus position. She felt the change in pressure too late, and she slammed into her body, which lurched forward, and she barely caught herself on the edge of the pool. Beneath her gaze, the thinkfins circled and shimmied together with an unusual cadence to their movements.

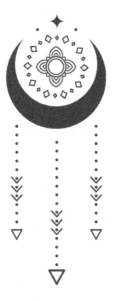

Forty Seven

Patia flew through the tunnel of coppery light, which was oddly silent, but she had the sensation of wind flowing over her, filling her, like the sail on the ship, moving her forward with inexorable force. The part of her mind that wondered what was happening and where she was going had sloughed off, and she moved skinless and shiny through this luminous space with a sense of calm that might have surprised her had she not grown so comfortable in her new reality. The light ahead grew brighter, almost blinding, and she passed through a kind of doorway of blazing orange-gold. Her mind lurched as feeling returned to her body: cold, especially on her feet, an icy wetness dappling her hands and face, though the cold felt distant, insubstantial somehow. She was standing, and her body swayed with the strange sensation, feeling almost ready to float off the ground, as if gravity had no hold over her. Her eyes were dazzled with tiny spots and flecks of white, pouring down from above, swirling in winds she could not feel. She looked down and saw a white powder covering the ground up to her ankles, and a childlike joy spread through her. It was snow, which she'd only seen a couple of times in her life, delicate flakes of frozen rain that floated down like tiny feathers and built up like sawdust on the ground.

Laughter sounded nearby, and she gazed through the snow and saw three women talking, with the reddish-brown skin common to islanders. One was enveloped in a hooded fur coat that reached down to the ground and pooled around her feet, and the other two wore fine leather coats, wool pants, boots, gloves, and felt hats.

"*I love what you've done with the place!*" said one of the women in the leather jackets, sticking out her tongue to catch a few snowflakes. "*When I heard about the snow I just had to come see for myself.*"

"*And look, there are mountains!*" the other cried, pointing at large peaks in the distance covered in white, though they looked false somehow, like an artist's rough sketch.

"*We're still working on those, but I'm so glad you like it!*" said the woman in the fur coat. "*Come, we've built a fire and a little shelter from the snow, and we have some boozy cinnamon tea. It's just delightful in this weather.*"

Patia felt her brow furrow as the woman spoke; maybe it was the snow, but she'd not noticed the woman's lips moving. She stepped forward through the swirling flakes, following the group as they walked to a rough wooden lean-to with benches around a roaring fire. The group sat, chatting as the hostess poured their tea, but Patia could only hear their voices faintly as though she were getting farther away instead of closer. She moved to the edge of the fire, whose heat she could not feel, and her vision grew light as if everything was obscured by a fine mist. The woman in the fur coat cocked her head, staring in Patia's direction for a moment, seeming to look right through her. She turned her head back to her guests, tilting her head back in laughter at something they'd said, and the mist grew thicker and brighter, until the shelter and the fire vanished and were replaced by a blinding light. A tunnel opened before her, filled with an orange glow, and it branched in several directions. She followed the brighter of the two and soon found herself hurtling through the coppery tunnel, with no more control or concern for her destination than a dandelion seed carried by the wind.

She was jolted back into her body, this time in more familiar surroundings: the Endulian temple in Rontaia, with three people seated, staring with serene faces at the strange fist-shaped sculpture in the center of the round chamber. It was warm here instead of cold, and everything felt more real, down to the odor of the beeswax candles and the bowls of fragrant dried flowers. Her consciousness flashed for a moment, and she suddenly found herself seated with her legs crossed, staring up at the sculpture, which seemed to pulse ever so slowly. Or was it her vision pulsing? She glanced around, and the walls, the shafts of light pouring into the high, round windows, the faces of those seated around her, everything moved and flowed, as if it were all made out of melting wax. Her stomach dropped, and her head felt miles above it, suspended on a long neck like the tubular plants she had seen in the tide pools. She smiled as a fire roared up from her stomach, along her long, wavy neck, and bright purple light poured from her mouth, flooding the chamber, illuminating the sculpture, which was visibly pulsing now, growing and shrinking like a frog puffing with air. She heard gasps, and heads turned in her direction, but as before everyone seemed to be looking through her, rather than at her. Her smile widened, and the room lit up with brilliant purple until she clapped both hands over her mouth, and the light went out, and all was darkness.

She was flying through the coppery tunnel again, and branches split off to one side and the other, above and below, but she was drawn inexorably down the thickest, brightest path. Her calm had eroded, replaced by a kind of fragmented panic as her mind unraveled like a knit sweater being pulled apart by mice. She felt faint, like she might sleep, or pass out, but her mind re-formed in a more nebulous, almost fluid state. She flowed down the tunnel now, bubbling and sloshing, until at last she poured through a hole of infinite light and landed with a splash in a pool of water she could feel but not see. She cruised the pool in a slow circle, solid again, but long and sinuous, her body wiggling to turn, then gliding straight. Though she could not see, she sensed another fish gliding toward her. Their bodies touched for a moment, splashing on the surface, then cruised away, repeating the circle, which was more of a figure eight, in an infinite loop. She swam, turned, drifted, brushed sides with the other fish, over and over, her body feeling every movement of the water, knowing where the walls and the surface and the bottom were, sensing the exact contours of the pool and the other fish without seeing, until she forgot about anything else other than the movement, the cycle, the brief moment of touch.

Then after one of countless passes, she was drawn to the surface, where she floated, her mouth gulping air she could not breathe, and her sight returned, as mist banished by the sun. A golden bronze face hovered over the water, rippled and wavy, and two hands slipped into the water so gently she could hardly feel the ripples they made. The hands curled upward, one in front of the other, and she glided into them, feeling their warmth, their strength, their gentleness. The face grew closer to the water, until two big brown eyes hovered just above the surface, staring down into the water. These eyes peered into hers, and she sucked in a huge gulp of air as the hands lifted her out of the water and cradled her. She felt herself expanding, her body re-forming, her mind flowing into it, and she lay, secure in the woman's arms, looking up into eyes wide with concern but strong with compassion. The figure spoke, but she could not hear the words, only the faint patter of a fountain and a sound like leaves blown by a breeze before an approaching storm.

"You are lost," came a voice in her mind. *"Tell me where you need to go."*

Patia's hands reached out to the arms of the figure crouched before her, grasping solid flesh and tight muscles. *Help me,* she tried to say, but her lips would not move. Her vision dimmed, then sharpened so she could see every painful detail, then dimmed again. *Help me,* she tried to say again, but the words dissolved in her mind before they ever reached her lips.

"Let go," the voice said as the figure's hands pressed against her temples. *"Let me in. I can help."*

She struggled to respond, to reach across the space between them, but no words came. She blinked as her vision dimmed again, and the darkness wrapped her in its silent wings and tucked her far away from the world.

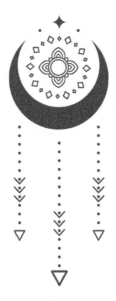

Forty Eight

Gilea held the fish-turned-woman, who had gone limp in her arms. Her mind radiated uncontrolled power like Gilea had never felt before, as if she had drunk a gallon of deep tincture and was dissolving into the Thousand Worlds. Gilea pressed the woman to her chest, wrapping her arms tightly around the woman's small body as she steeled her mind against the waves of confusion and panic emanating from the woman's mind. She summoned the *sitri* patterns, sending watery rings out from her center and back again, drawing closer with each pulse, until the rings tightened around them both, and she felt the woman's mind settle against hers.

"What is your name?" Gilea asked.

"Patia." Gilea felt the woman's surprise as the word passed into her mind.

"I'm Gilea. I'm going to help you find your way back to where you came from." She pushed out a calming vibe, though she sensed it had little effect.

"I don't know…I'm so lost…I don't know…"

"It's okay. Just think back to where this all began, and I will take us there."

Patia's jumbled thoughts rushed over Gilea. Swimming as a fish in a pool. Soaring through copper tunnels and infinite space. The Rontaian temple. A snowy campfire. A dark cave with a purplish glow. Patia's mind pulsed with the memory of the cave, and Gilea felt her way through the chaotic memories, finding the faint thread that connected them all. She followed the thread through a thousand twists and knots and curves and long, straight stretches until at last, she saw it. A rift in the blackness, as if a jagged knife had sliced into the fabric of the Thousand Worlds, with hot purplish-white light screaming out of the opening. She clutched Patia tighter as they burst through the fissure, through a short tunnel, and into a cave, where a body lay half-submerged in a puddle of frothy slime. A handful of skeletons were strewn about the cave, most bleached white, but one was covered in tiny red crabs picking away at the remaining fleshy bits. The patch of wall behind the puddle was the source of the purplish glow, which emanated from streaks of purple veining up the cave wall.

"Hotsilver," Patia whispered, looking up at Gilea with soft, bleary eyes before turning to stare at the immobile body, whose arms and legs were obscured by the slime, and only the toes and a few fingertips poking through the foam proved they were still attached. *"Hey, that's me!"* Patia rolled her head up toward Gilea, and Gilea lowered Patia's feet to the ground, keeping one arm around her back and under her armpit so she wouldn't slump down to the cave floor.

"How did you get here?"

"On a boat…with captain Leo."

"Wait, Leo?" Gilea burst out, her voice echoing off the cave walls. *"Curly hair, likes to be naked, smiles all the time?"* Patia nodded, flashing a loopy grin.

"I like it when he's naked. So pretty…"

Gilea's laughter lifted the weight of the tension surrounding her, and she felt light, airy, as if she might float away.

"Be that as it may, if Leo brought you here, where is he?" Gilea's words felt hollow as they escaped her lips, and she strained her mind to re-focus. Whatever had sent Patia flying across the Thousand Worlds was affecting her too.

"Outside in a little boat, but there's a big boat too, and a dog. Wolfie's a good dog."

"He is at that." Gilea smiled, thinking of Leo's dog, who had accompanied them on their last half-dozen roughabouts. *"Well, we need to get you up off the floor and out of this cave before that slime swallows you the*

rest of the way. Are you ready to give it a—" Gilea's words stopped, or the sound of them did. A great silence descended on the cave, erasing the dripping and sloshing of water, the click-click of the crabs' claws, the distant roar of waves. Gilea held Patia tight as the image of Patia's body lying in the slime began shrinking, floating away into the distance. The purple veins of hotsilver grew brighter, and Gilea had to shield her eyes against the glow, like the first rays of morning sun blasting over the horizon. The blaze faded, and when Gilea peeked out from behind her hand, she saw a very different cave from the one she had stood in seconds before.

Gilea saw the scene as if looking through a thin mist. The hotsilver was the same, and the general shape of the cave, but there was no Patia, no puddle of pus-colored slime, and no skeletons. A lone figure moved through the water with careful steps, holding a metal box. As the figure approached the hotsilver, it lit up her hairy face with its eerie purple glow, and Gilea could see she was like Ujenn, a Maer. She spent some time fiddling with a complex mechanism on the box, then she opened it and pulled out a glass globe the size of an apple, half-filled with an oozy substance that resembled the slime they had seen in the cave before. She held the globe in her hands, closing her eyes and murmuring some words, then lifted the globe and hurled it against the wall, where it smashed, leaving a splat of the ooze dripping down among the glowing purplish veins of hotsilver. She stood staring at the ooze for a long moment, then she cocked her head, as if she were hearing a faint sound, and turned toward Gilea and Patia, peering into the darkness around them. Her eyes grew wide as they locked on Gilea's, and the surprised expression on her face slowly melted into a curious smile.

"You are from the Time to Come. You are…human?"

"We are human, but I don't know when we are." Gilea studied the box in the woman's hands; it was made of shining bronze, covered in fine designs the likes of which she had never seen.

"Then it is true. Our downfall was inevitable, I suppose." She approached, and Patia clung to Gilea, who tried to push calming vibes into her. *"I am Cloti."* She bowed with hands pressed to her chest, and Gilea's mind swam as she tried to wrap it around the idea that this philosopher from thousands of years ago was standing before her, covered in hair from head to toe.

"I am Gilea, and this is Patia."

"You're…Cloti?" Patia's hold on Gilea loosened, and she stared at

243

Cloti with wide, wild eyes. *"I have seen your texts. Without, as within."*

Cloti blinked softly. *"And within as without. If you are here, it means you have deciphered my map. You must be quite the scholar."*

"I am no scholar." Patia shook her head. *"But I know some who are wiser than I."*

"And yet, without you, all their wisdom would have brought them no closer to the truth." She reached out and put her hairy hand on Patia's arm. Patia flinched only a little. *"The world needs doers. Don't sell yourself short."*

"Yes, ma'am." Patia slid her fingers between Cloti's and squeezed. The hotsilver flashed, and Cloti's eyes crinkled.

"I have to go. Or rather, you do." She looked from Patia to Gilea, then back to Patia, flashing a wistful glance. *"Back to your time. You've come to retrieve it, yes?"*

"Yes, but…" Patia let go of Cloti's hand and stared down at her nails. *"I'm not sure I want to anymore."*

"You're not sure what it will do to your world. If it's ready for what the earth milk can offer."

"It's not." The words flowed out of Gilea unbidden. Though the limitations and privilege of the Caravan chafed at her, there was a lot of work to be done before society would be ready for everyone to be fully connected at all times. *"Not yet."* She turned to Patia, whose head sank in a sigh, and she shook her head.

"That assessment is up to you." Cloti's eyes were deep with compassion and concern. *"If you do not retrieve it, take steps to ensure the secret is preserved and hidden. The time may yet be right before long. Let me give you something that might help."* She raised her hairy hand to Patia's forehead, closed her eyes, and Patia gripped Gilea's arm as her body straightened, almost vibrating with the effort, then went slack as Cloti lowered her hand.

"Thank you." Patia's thought was no more than a whisper as the hotsilver flickered again, and Cloti seemed to fade a little, becoming almost transparent. She smiled at them with her eyes, and Gilea felt a pang of sadness emanating from her, of deep loss, mixed with a faint but unmistakable feeling of hope. Cloti turned away, and they watched her fading form wade away through the water and begin to climb up the rocky wall toward the tunnel where they had come in.

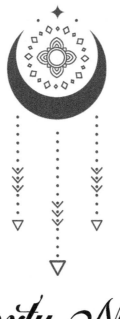

Forty Nine

Patia watched Cloti struggle up the slippery rocks, stopping at the top to catch her breath. She turned her hairy face toward them, put one hand on her heart, then disappeared into the crevice.

"*Was it really her?*" Patia whispered.

"*A memory of her,*" Gilea answered. "*An echo.*"

Patia stared at the dark crevice for a moment, then turned to study the blob of delicate pus-colored ooze, which seemed to throb as it flowed outward so its edges touched the shining purple veins of hot-silver. She felt suddenly drained, and the mere act of standing took all the energy she had and more.

"*I think I'd better lie down now,*" she said, holding onto Gilea for support. Gilea blinked her agreement, holding Patia with strong arms and lowering her to the wet floor of the cave. The water chilled her back, but the glow of the hotsilver warmed her mind, which grew fuzzy, as with one cup too much wine.

"*It's okay. I'm right here,*" Gilea said, crouching beside her, holding her hand as the edges of Patia's consciousness grew bright and dark at the same time. She closed her eyes, feeling Gilea's fingers gripping hers, her steady voice saying "*I'll be right here with you. Just follow the thread that leads to what holds you most in the world, and you'll find your way back.*"

Patia smiled as she felt Gero's hand, wrinkled but strong, holding hers, his bearded face hovering over her. She let out a long breath, staring up into his deep brown eyes, which gleamed with concern and compassion, and something warmer, deeper. She latched onto that gleam, which widened into a perfect circle of blazing copper as his pupils grew wider and wider, enveloping the cave in their glossy blackness. She poured herself up into the circle, flowing through stars and moons that zipped past her ever faster until her mind stopped seeing them as points of light moving through space but as coppery threads that stretched and twisted and wound their way through the infinite darkness. The sensation of speed, of movement, stopped suddenly, and she studied the path of the illuminated threads. They clustered together like vines climbing each other, occasionally branching out to the side, or above or below, though she was no longer certain which way was which.

"Go to him," Gilea's voice rang in her head, and Patia felt herself drawn along a cluster of bright orange filaments that spiraled upward, she thought, toward a circle of glowing orange and purple woven together. A warmth filled her chest, and her heart fluttered, then began beating again, strong and loud, as she passed into the circle and exploded back into her body, which lay half-submerged in a blanket of foamy ooze.

She was alone in the cave. The back of her body was cold and wet, and pain flared in a dozen places, but she felt a strength flow through her, and she pushed her way up to sitting, lightheaded and short of breath. She pulled her hand from the ooze, which released it with an audible *schloop*, and twisted her body sideways to get to her knees.

She fought through screaming pain in her back, elbow, and countless other places, and her body shook as she rose to a slouch. Her head thrummed and her vision remained wavy, but she withstood the sensation as if she had become acclimated to the hallucinatory effect. She glanced down at her pack, which lay smushed and soggy in the imprint of where she had fallen, the ooze flowing slowly over it to reclaim the space. The containment vessel inside was no doubt smashed, and if she reached down to check, she worried she would not be able to get back up again. Her mission had failed. She would return empty-handed, and never touch the promised riches of the Universal Tincture. The Thousand Worlds would remain forever locked here in this cave.

And perhaps that was for the best.

As she stood, staring up at the faint light from the crevice above, her mind swirled with symbols and letters, colors and textures, and the image of the pages of her Works book came to her, the script illuminated against a starry darkness. The symbols rearranged themselves in her mind, locking together with a flash into a long string that made more sense than any mathematical or alchemical formula she had ever seen. She felt her mouth pulling wide, a smile that swallowed her head and enveloped her mind, making her new again. She closed her eyes, and the formula shone brightly, elegant, logical, and deceptively simple. This was the gift Cloti had given her when she'd touched her forehead. There was another way to the Thousand Worlds, and she and Gero would find it. If she could somehow haul her decrepit body up the slimy walls of the cave and back out into the world above.

Patia dragged herself through the narrow crevice, no longer able to stand, her body screaming at the rough surface of the rock, the myriad sharp pains that took her breath away with each movement. The light grew brighter, and tears ran down her cheeks as she wormed her way around the last turn and saw the soft tones of the late afternoon sun painted on the water. She heard barking, and she lifted her head enough to see the little rowboat, with Sea Wolf standing erect, pointing with his whole body. She untied her scarf with trembling fingers and waved it through the opening, smiling through her pain as Leo and Max waved back, then hurried to pull up the anchor and row toward her. She tried to stand again, but her strength was gone, and her mind dulled with the many trials she had endured. She half-listened to the splashes in the water, her name being called, the sound of exertion. At last Leo's face appeared over the edge of the crevice, his curly hair fluffed by the breeze, his wide smile falling as he saw her.

"Gods, Patia, what happened?"

"I fell, but I'm okay. I'll be okay," she whispered. "Help me get down?"

"Of course. Where's your pack? Did you find what you were looking for?"

Patia coughed a feeble laugh. "Don't worry about my pack. I've got what I need."

"Are you sure? I'd be happy to climb down and—"

"Leave it," Patia pleaded in a rough hiss.

Leo recoiled a bit, then nodded, his smile returning. He gripped the ledge with both hands and pulled himself up, crouching in the entrance next to Patia.

"Okay." He looked down, then back to Patia. "Okay, this is going to be a little interesting, but we'll figure it out. I think I can attach a rope to this rock here. Max!" he called down, cupping his hands around his mouth. "Untie the anchor rope and toss it up, would you?"

He turned back to Patia, studying her face and her body. "Did you break anything?"

"I don't know. Maybe," she murmured. "It doesn't matter. It doesn't..." she drifted away, her mind losing tension, its shape dissolving, slowly spreading like the ooze toward the hotsilver lines that streaked across the sea toward Gero.

Patia lay in her bunk for the first few days of the trip back, drifting in and out of consciousness as she struggled to find a position that hurt only one part of her battered body. Her back throbbed from where she'd landed on the containment vessel, though the backpack seemed to have prevented the glass from slicing her open. Her tailbone was badly bruised, but not broken, she thought, though the same could not be said for her elbow, which was swollen and stiff, and burned with pain at the slightest touch. Leo had fashioned a splint and sling to keep it from moving, and the pain when she lay still in the perfect position was only bearable in comparison to the jolts of agony when she tried to move. Sea Wolf had taken to sleeping next to her, staring into her eyes whenever she awoke, giving her nose a gentle lick. Leo brought her water, and some fresh fish he had caught, though she couldn't eat more than a couple of bites. He brought her a bucket to relieve herself and held her in place while she squatted on the edge of her bunk, tears of pain streaking down her face. His gentle strength and ever-present smile were a small comfort, and after a few days, he offered to help her above deck so she could get some fresh air.

Max waved when he saw her standing in an awkward slouch with Leo supporting her. She gave Max a smile and a little wave with her good hand, and he smiled as he turned his head down. Patia held onto

Leo's hard muscles and pushed herself up straighter, though she could not stand all the way up because of the pain in her tailbone.

"That elbow isn't getting any smaller," Leo said, looking down at the yellowish-purple skin stretched around the swollen joint. "But I think you'll be okay until we get back, then we can get you to a doctor."

"Just get me to Gero," she said, gripping his shoulder. "He'll take care of me."

After a couple more days, Patia was able to get in and out of her bunk by herself. She spent part of each day above deck, switching between standing and sitting on her pillow on a stool, as she could not bear any one position for too long. Her appetite returned, and the fish and crustaceans Leo brought back to the boat tasted finer than anything she had eaten in her life. Even the water from the resiny barrel had a sweetness that gave a lift to her soul.

When at last the outlines of Rontaia appeared on the horizon, Patia's heart swelled and her throat twinged as tears of relief seemed to rush up from a well deep inside her, and she had to hold onto the railing as sobs of joy wracked her body. It had been a very long time since anyplace felt like home, but as they passed through the strait into the mouth of the Agra, she knew she would never return to Guluch. Her mouth twisted into a wistful frown as she thought of the handmade alembic she would never see again, then she thought of Gero, puttering around his workshop with his blue scarf wrapped around his neck. Her smile stretched her face until it hurt, but she could not pull it back, and her heart was so full she thought it would burst. Leo and Max had dropped the sail and were rowing hard against the current, and each stroke of the oars sent a rush of blood roaring through her ears.

She shared an awkward goodbye with Max, who stayed at the dock with the boat, and accepted a thorough licking from Sea Wolf. Leo hired a cart to take her back to the artisan docks, and she leaned against him as they rode to quell the pain of the bumpy ride. She promised that Gero would cover the cost of the cart, but Leo waved her off.

"Consider this a down payment for the glow tubes you're going to make for me."

He helped her down from the cart, along with the box, which she

249

had filled with her few remaining effects now that the containment vessel and her pack were gone. He smacked the side of the cart, which clopped off back toward the docks. He held the box with one hand as he took her arm with the other, but she shook him off gently.

"I've got it from here." She took the box, her back tweaking as she adjusted her stance to bear the weight. "Thank you, Leo. For everything."

"Hey, no worries. I found the spot for my next roughabout, and I guess you found whatever it was you were looking for." He cocked his head, his smile growing curious, then he shook his head. "Anyways, I'll come find you before long and we'll work out the details. Good luck with your elbow!"

Patia leaned in and kissed his cheek, and Leo kissed her back, then turned and walked down the dock with a bounce in his step.

Patia took a deep breath and hobbled across the warped boards to Gero's door.

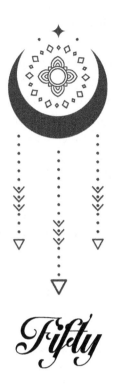

Fifty

Gilea sat beside Amini, with Affito on the other side. All the masters were seated in lotus position in a semicircle around them in the courtyard. Dark clouds threatened overhead, but the afternoon sun set them ablaze with vibrant yellow light. The wind whipping in through the dome swirled around the courtyard, flushing out the day's warmth and replacing it with a cool whiff of autumn. The vibe of the crowd was similarly refreshed with the absence of Pleone's invisible gaze. Gilea wondered how long it would take the healers to figure out the lead trick. Or perhaps they already had, and had decided things were better without Pleone in charge. Gilea certainly hadn't intended to take her out of commission permanently, and she would make sure to rectify the situation once everything was settled.

"As I'm sure you all know, our Overmother Pleone has withdrawn within herself, and for how long, we do not know." Amini's mindvoice was filled with gravitas, but not sadness. *"But it is our responsibility to act in the best interests of Endulai during her absence, as stated in the charter, so the Caravan can function smoothly, for the benefit of all."* She paused, and Gilea felt the assurance of her words spread through the assembled masters. The shunning of Rontaia had created an invisible rift, but few supported

it outright; most were merely cowed by fear of Pleone's mind and her authority.

"Gilea has taken the initiative, with my blessing, to bring Rontaia back into the fold, and their crossroad will be reopened by dawn tomorrow." Sighs of relief whispered through the courtyard, barely audible above the burbling of the fountains and the swirling wind, which now scattered a few raindrops onto those assembled. Gilea's jaw unclenched as she felt the masters' approval, and Amini squeezed her hand gently.

"There will be much work to do to repair the Caravan, not to mention the frazzled relationship with our southern colleagues, but that work has already begun, and I am confident we will be up to the task. The Caravan is meant to be for all. Our practice is meant to be spread to all those who will listen. We have grown too isolated in recent years, but that is about to change. If you all consent to this new direction."

A low hum vibrated Gilea's chest, as almost in unison the masters began releasing the sacred breath, and she joined the thirty-odd voices drifting toward the exact same pitch. They hummed as one and held the note until their breath failed. Silence rang throughout the courtyard, louder than the wind and thunder in the distance.

"It is decided." Affito's gravelly voice surfaced among the silence. "Tomorrow, we tighten the links that bind us to each other, and to all those who open their mind to the word and the way."

Hands pressed to foreheads, eyes opened, and the sun once again flashed golden among the dark shadows of the clouds.

Gilea stood with Amini on the dock, her bag at her feet, her heart in the sky. The boat rowed toward them so slowly it seemed like it was going backward, and Gilea's chest constricted with every stroke. She felt a slight tremor in her mind, and she tried to latch onto it, but it dissipated before she could grab hold. She closed her eyes and waited, and when it came again, she was ready. She coiled her thoughts around it, and its delicate vibration found its way into her heart, then bounced back again. She followed in its wake, clinging to it like a child holding a kite string in a windstorm. When it pulled taut, she inched her way along the tenuous connection until she was sucked in and bathed in the soft light of Temi's mind. She could not see Temi, or hear her words, but the warmth that flowed over her left no doubt. As they clung to

252

each other, it seemed the boat was pulled along by their connection, and by the time it had been maneuvered aside the dock, Gilea's heart beat in time with Temi's. The crush of disembarking passengers was like the fluttering of leaves in the wind, and the world went still as Temi stepped off the gangplank and turned toward Gilea, lifting the veil off her yellow-painted face.

In Gilea's meditation practice, she worked hard to block out all extraneous thoughts to focus on the moment at hand, but never before had she achieved such complete unawareness of her surroundings. They each took a few steps, and in the blink of an eye they were in each other's arms, teary cheeks pressed together, heat flowing between them. Temi pulled back, lifting the veil that had fallen down over Gilea's head, and stared into Gilea's eyes, biting her lip as tears flowed freely.

"I'd really like to kiss you now," Gilea heard herself say, and Temi's lips were on hers, their hands on each other's necks, for too brief a moment. Temi pulled back, dabbing her tears with her handkerchief as she let out a shaky giggle.

"I can't believe I'm here, with you, it's..." Temi let her forehead fall onto Gilea's, and a tendril of emotion slipped through into Gilea's mind. "I've pictured it so many times, but I never believed I would actually make it, that you would be here waiting for me. It feels like a dream." She leaned her head away, wiping her nose with her handkerchief.

"It's good to see you too." Gilea picked up her bag, nodding with her chin at Captain Olin, who stood on the front deck and responded by raising her cheroot. "Let me drop this off and we'll walk around a bit, stretch our legs, and be back before Olin leaves us high and dry."

"I got us a private room," Temi said, jerking the bag from Gilea's hands and turning toward the boat. "Or as private as you can get on a boat this size. Olin tried to give us the captain's quarters, but that didn't really seem fair. Still, we have a curtain! Come on, I'll show you to our quarters and we can have that little walk." She winked over her shoulder as she hurried back toward the boat, leaning hard to one side against the weight of the bag. Gilea grinned and turned to Amini, who stood a little way off, smiling beatifically.

"Be sure to reach out when you get to Rontaia," Amini said, lifting a finger in the air as she spoke. Gilea pressed her hands together at her forehead, bowing in time with Amini, then turned and hurried across the gangplank after Temi.

The southern winds were not favorable for most of the trip, so they floated and rowed more often than they sailed, making use of the wind when it turned in their favor. They spent their days above deck, sitting in connected silence much of the time. Temi joined Gilea in some meditation exercises, showing surprising ease with the gestures and terminology. At night they slept side by side, their arms and feet intertwined, and though they shared no further physical intimacy, their bond was stronger and more immediate than anything Gilea had experienced during the pairings at Endulai.

"Have you been practicing?" Gilea asked one day after a seated meditation, and she could almost see Temi's blush through her paint.

"I wanted to surprise you. I've been visiting the temple in Anari, against my mother's wishes, of course, and I find it makes a lot of sense to me, though I'm still very new to the whole thing." She picked at her fingernails, and when she looked up, her eyes showed excitement, and perhaps a little fear. "I was wondering…" She touched her forehead with two fingers, then reached them out to touch Gilea's, sending a hot shiver into her core. "Do you think we could try, like we did…"

Gilea brought Temi's fingers to her lips and kissed them, nodding softly.

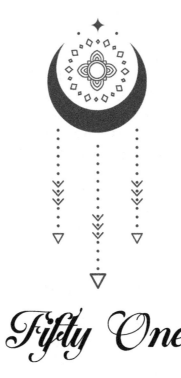

Fifty One

Patia watched Gero sleep, curled awkwardly on his side and snoring softly with every inhale. His fingers clutched the ends of his blue scarf, now wrinkled and sweat-stained, and the hair on his ears glowed in the light reflected off the river. Something moved near his feet, and a furry, brown mass uncoiled, stretching with a shiver. Vera leapt off the bed and bounded across the floor to rub Patia's ankles. Gero's eyes blinked open, and he rolled onto his back, stretching sideways.

"Vera, you scamp, are you trying to get into the biscuit tin again while I'm sleeping?"

Vera raced back to the bed, leapt up, and pounced on Gero's chest, squeaking and chittering.

"All right, all right, I'll get you a treat, just let me—"

Gero's mouth hung open and his eyes grew wide as he turned to see Patia standing there.

"Gods, Patia! You're back!" He struggled up to sit, then stood, wincing for a moment before breaking into a smile as he hobbled across the floor to Patia, who was doing everything in her power just to remain standing. He reached out to embrace her, then his eyes fell on her sling, and he took her face in his hands and planted a kiss on her forehead, then another on her cheek, and finally one on her lips. Patia kissed him back and leaned heavily on his shoulder as Vera danced in a circle around them both.

"What happened to you? Are you all right? Come, sit! I'll make you some tea! Oh, gods, it's so good to see you again!"

"I'm fine, but I wouldn't hate a dram of that chestnut whiskey if you've got any left," Patia said as Gero helped her across the room. She gripped his hand as she lowered herself to sit on the bed, which was still warm and redolent of his scent. "Well, not quite fine exactly," she said, wincing. "My elbow is broken, but I'll live."

"I'll fetch a doctor right away," he said, his fingers gently pulling away the sling to study the part of her elbow revealed beneath the cloth.

"No need to hurry. Except maybe with that whiskey?" She touched Gero's face, looking into his big, wet eyes, and pulled him in by his beard for a kiss.

"Of course, and I have some soma for the pain if you'd like."

"Gods, yes!" Patia laughed. "Whiskey first, then soma. Then we talk."

Gero pulled away, his hand hovering in the air near her face, then turned and splashed some whiskey into a vial. He sat next to her on the bed as she drank, his fingers kneading his robe. Patia downed the last drops of whiskey and handed him the cup, which he set on the floor. She found his fingers with her good hand and squeezed them, leaning her head sideways against his.

"Gods, I've missed you so much, and Vera has too, haven't you, girl?" Vera sat on the floor in front of them, and she raised her head as her name was spoken, then tucked it between her legs and started licking her fur.

"I've missed you too."

They sat in silence, holding hands, for some time.

"Did you...did you find what you were looking for?" Gero asked, at last, turning to face her.

"Yes," she said slowly, "but I couldn't bring it back. Not exactly."

"Not exactly?" Gero cocked his head, his eyes glinting with eager curiosity.

"I mean, no, I didn't bring it back, but...I think I figured out something almost as good."

"I see," Gero said, looking down, then back up, his eyes lit up with

256

excitement. "Oh! I finished the tincture, and it's just about had time to set. I think it's going to be a nine! Even the raw tincture had me seeing stars."

Patia squeezed his hand.

"Be a dear and fetch me that soma, and maybe a doctor. We'll talk business later."

The pain in her elbow had returned with a vengeance when Patia woke from her soma nap. She heard Gero talking in a low voice with a doctor in the doorway, and tried to sit up, but her elbow told her to stay put. The doctor, a woman half Patia's age with ruddy tan skin and short-cropped hair, set down a heavy bag and pulled up a stool by the bed.

"Gero tells me you've broken your elbow. Mind if I have a look?" Her fingers were already untying the sling and loosening the bandages holding the splint in place, which she did gently enough Patia did not cry out at the pain. She prodded the swollen area, which Patia thought had shrunk in the past day, though her fingers felt like daggers poking her skin.

"I've seen worse," the doctor said, reattaching the bandages and retying the sling. "It's a fracture, and the bones seem to be in the right place. Whoever made that splint knew what they were doing. Looks like it's not infected, though I'm going to recommend some *nasci* tea twice a day for a week, just in case." She reached into her bag and pulled out a tin, which she set on the bed. "Other than that, as long as you keep that splint tight, and don't do anything too strenuous, it should heal on its own within a month or so." She clasped her hands in her lap, studying Patia for a moment, her brows knitted with concern. She turned her head to Gero.

"Would you mind giving us some privacy for a moment?" Her tone was gentle but firm, and Gero gave a little bow and slipped through the curtain. The doctor watched as he walked a few steps away, then turned back to Patia.

"Looks like you had some fall there. Want to tell me what happened?"

Patia smiled, tapping the doctor's knee with her good hand. "I know what you think, but it's nothing like that. Gero's as sweet as they come, and besides, I could take him. I fell, is all. I was...spelunking."

The doctor raised one eyebrow. "Not many caves right around here, that I know of."

Patia waved her off. "In the islands. Sea caves. I slipped and fell, and landed on my tailbone, which still hurts, but it's getting better."

"Sea caves?" The doctor's face softened into a smirk. "Well, I guess you wouldn't make that up. I hope you don't mind, I just..." She pursed her lips. "I always like to ask, just to be safe."

"As well you should, and thank you, but I can take care of myself."

The doctor's smirk widened to a smile. "I bet you can at that, but you're going to need some help in the next week or two. You think Gero will take care of you?"

"Oh yes, he's an absolute doll. He'll wait on me hand and foot."

"Well, aren't you lucky?" The doctor stood up, turning toward the door and calling, "You can come back in now."

Gero ducked through the curtains, his eyes expectant.

"She doesn't think you hurt me, and she says you have to wait on me hand and foot for a month."

Gero smiled, his eyes shining, and nodded vigorously. "Hand and foot, for as long as it takes, my dear. Is there anything else I need to know about, besides the tea and the splint?" he asked the doctor.

She shook her head. "You know where to find me if anything gets worse. In the meantime..." she glanced down at Patia and gave her a wink before turning back to Gero. "Hand and foot."

Patia let Gero tend to her every need, and within a few days she was able to do most things by herself, though Gero seemed to enjoy helping her, and who was she to deny him this pleasure? He did not ask about what she'd learned on her journey, and she didn't speak of it right away, but he flashed curious glances when he saw her finally open her Works book. She flipped to the page containing Cloti's map, and she imagined the strange hairy woman sketching the figures in some dusty library in the Time Before, surrounded by books, scrolls, and all manner of alchemical equipment. She turned to the previous page, where she'd copied the ancient mystography from Master Helo's book, and as her eyes drifted over the symbols, she was surprised to find she understood some of what was written. She closed her eyes and saw the formula she'd seen in her ooze-induced haze, and when she looked at the book again, she noticed the page was written in the same script, which suddenly came clear as if she were reading Southish. A cackle erupted from her mouth, which she covered with her hand as Gero turned toward her, his eyebrows raised with anticipation. She motioned him over to the table, and he stood next to her, crouching to see the book, which she positioned between them.

"You've discovered something?"

Patia tapped her finger on the page and a dizzying feeling surged within her as if she were once again under the spell of the ooze. Her finger hovered over the first line, and she heard herself saying the words in Southish, without pause or hesitation.

It is said that the mind is a world of its own, but this is only partly true. It is linked by delicate tendrils and hempen rope and copper cables to a thousand other minds in a thousand different worlds, just as each star is but a small part of a greater galaxy. We see the constellations in the night sky as light seeping through pinholes in dark paper, and we interpret them as shapes that tell us stories, and this helps us smile as we fall asleep. But these flat shapes are illusions, flecks of a light so bright we cannot look directly into it, filtered by a blackness we perceive as a void. The underlying light and darkness, and every shade of the planets between, are not flat, or spherical, but infinite, if we can only learn how to see without looking.

So it is with the self. We do not exist as discrete individuals, alone and separate from all others. We are parts of a greater whole, which we do not have the natural faculties to perceive. To know the true shapes of things beyond our imagining, we must let go of our fear and sink deep inside ourselves, to the dark places between our thoughts and memories, our pain and our sorrow. It is in these liminal spaces that we find the ultimate connections to all beings and all worlds.

To find the Thousand Worlds, we must seek within as without, and in so doing we will see the universe reflected inside us, and ourselves shining down from the heavens.

She felt Gero's hand on her shoulder, and she reached up to grasp it.

"You can read Cloti's script?" he asked in an awed whisper, sitting on the bench next to her, his hand sliding down to her forearm.

"I guess I can, now." She shrugged her good shoulder, squeezing Gero's hand tightly.

"And you learned this...on your journey?" She nodded, biting her lip. "How?" His eyes were wide with amazement, staring into hers like he was gazing upon some great treasure. Her heart swelled, and she ran her hand up his arm, over his shoulder, and around the back of his neck.

"I don't think I can explain it, but...when I followed Paoro's instructions, it took me to a place with...connections, to the past, and to other places, I'm still not sure how, but Gero, I..." She squeezed his neck and pulled his head toward his. "I visited the Thousand Worlds, and I think I know, or I can figure out, how to access them again, with your help." She glanced over at the furnace, the alembic, the aludel, and all his other equipment. "Do you know where we can get some *voki* essence?"

"Yes, it costs more than gold, but it can be acquired, with the proper connections."

"That will help. I've got a lot to sort out," she said, gently tapping her head. "But it's all in here."

"You mean...the Universal Tincture?" he whispered.

Patia blinked. "The key to the Thousand Worlds."

Gero gripped her arm and closed his eyes as he pulled in close to seal his lips against hers.

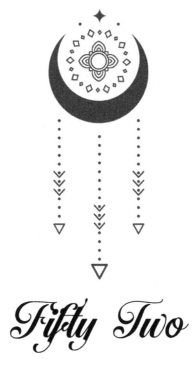

Fifty Two

Gilea pulled the curtain tight, not that it mattered since the elderly brother and sister on the other side were fast asleep and snoring. Temi lay propped on her elbow, her pale, unpainted face glowing in the warm light of the candle so it almost looked like she was wearing pastel yellow paint. Her hair was down, and miniature candle flames danced in her eyes, which probed Gilea's, sending her heart fluttering. Gilea edged onto the bed, sliding her fingers gently through Temi's, and closed her eyes to slow the warmth spreading through her limbs.

"I'm sure you must have shared minds with lots of people at Endulai," Temi said, squeezing Gilea's fingers gently between hers. "Not that I mind, it's just…I've only shared with you, so I worry it won't be the same, it—"

"It's never the same, no matter how many—and it's never been anything like what we shared when we—" Temi's smile stopped her lips, and her chest grew tight as her heart expanded, threatening to burst through its fragile shell. She thought of Doni, the moments they'd shared at pairing, the warmth and comfort they had found together, and guilt flooded over her.

"It's okay, I'm not jealous." Temi slipped her fingers out of Gilea's and ran them up her arm, resting her hand on the back of Gilea's neck. "I mean, maybe a little, but I don't expect…I can't be everything to you, and I don't want to be. But I do hope to be something." She pulled Gilea down, closing her eyes and leaning in with her forehead, ghostly white even in the shadows, now that Gilea's body was blocking the candlelight. Gilea slid her hand behind Temi's slender neck, brushing a few stray hairs out of place so her fingers wrapped around her delicate skin.

"You're as close to everything as I dare to dream," Gilea whispered. She closed her eyes as their foreheads touched, and she saw a flash, which faded into a gentle darkness. She felt Temi pushing out tentatively with her mind, and she relaxed all her defenses, letting Temi flow into her like dye squirted into water, billowing, spreading, losing density, tinting Gilea with her color. As their minds commingled, Gilea felt her thoughts softening in places and tightening in others. Where she expected control, she found flexibility, and where she feared she would lose her grip, stability.

As Temi's thoughts permeated her all the way, she saw her own face, jaws clenched with purpose, eyes full of dark fire. She saw beauty she had never glimpsed in a mirror, rich bronze skin shadowed by the dim light, long cheekbones, and full lips. Strong arms and shoulders, wrapping, embracing, pulling tight. Safety. Forbearance. Certainty. Deep, soothing calm. Her tears pulled her back, and as she tried to blink them away, she saw Temi's eyes staring into hers, inches away, felt the sweat on the back of Temi's neck, her heartbeat pulsing against Gilea's fingers. She took a long, slow breath in, then closed her eyes and breathed out, letting her mind flow into Temi's, swirling around like a wave filling a tidal pool to overflowing. She floated in Temi's thoughts, some velvety as seaweed, others prickly as urchins. She drifted between and among them until at last, she settled into a mass like soft tentacles, which curled delicately around her, squeezing her gently, holding her in place even as she swayed in the soft currents.

Gilea could not have said if they slept that night, but she rolled onto her back the next morning with a groggy smile. Temi snuggled up against her shoulder, tucking her arm and leg into the warmth between them. Gilea's smile widened, then she felt her face relax, and her body followed, drifting off with Temi into a shared sleep, heedless of the thumping on the deck above and the dull sloshing of the waves against the hull.

Gilea held Temi's hand as they walked along the docks, the cry of seagulls and the smell of fresh tri-fries stirring up old feelings that mixed with the new to form a dizzying emotional landscape. She walked as in a strangely familiar dream, one she had cycled through over and over but which faded from her mind each time. Temi jerked her arm this way and that, pointing and laughing with delight, and Gilea let herself be pulled toward a tri-fry cart. She held up two fingers to the vendor, who nodded and laid two triangles of dough into a pot of oil, which foamed and spattered angrily at the intrusion. By the time Gilea had paid and exchanged pleasantries, the tri-fries were done, and she and Temi had to let go of each other's hands to pass the piping hot pastries from one hand to another as they cooled.

Temi closed her teeth around a corner, then spit out the steaming nub into her glove with a squeak.

"Gods, that's hot! I've never burned my tongue so badly. I'm going to have a canker sore for days."

"The trick is, you crack it with your teeth, but you leave your mouth open just enough for the steam to escape before you crunch down. Like so." Gilea demonstrated, wincing as the hot steam shot across the roof of her mouth, then chomping once it had cooled just a hair. Bursts of cinnamon and honey exploded in her mouth, and she let out a satisfied "Mmm…"

"You make it look so easy." Temi held her tri-fry as if worried it might bite her, then turned another corner toward her mouth and grabbed it with her teeth, cracking it off sideways.

"Hot," she mumbled as she held the corner between her teeth for a moment, then closed her lips around it. Gilea could hear the crunch, and the little sound Temi made in her throat as she chewed sent Gilea's skin buzzing. "But, like, so good. I've had tri-fries in Anari, but—"

"No, no, and no." Gilea waved her tri-fry at Temi. "Not in Anari, not in Guluch, not at Endulai. Especially not at Endulai; they can't fry food for shit. But no, the only place you can eat a tri-fry is in Rontaia, and they always taste better on the docks."

"The air is so nice here," Temi said, holding her tri-fry up for inspection, turning the third corner toward her face. A streak of black and gray and white flashed in, and Temi shrieked and fell into Gilea's arms as a huge seagull flapped off with her entire tri-fry, pursued by a quickly growing crowd of competitors.

Gilea looked down at Temi's face, which was frozen in shock, and they both started to giggle at the exact same time. Gilea reached down with her hand to brush a crumb of tri-fry off Temi's cheek. Time seemed to stop for an instant. The sounds and smells of the busy docks vanished, and the scene was shrouded in an eerie blankness, ghostly figures frozen in mid-step, drained of all color. Only Temi's yellow-painted face and her hazel eyes stood out against the moment's dimness. The sparkle in Temi's eyes sent shockwaves through Gilea's consciousness, and she flashed back to her near-death experience in the Living Waters when Sage had healed her punctured heart. She had lived this exact moment before, down to the shape of the crumb, Temi's cheeks bulging with laughter, her eyes overflowing with joy.

Sound and sensation returned in a flash, and Temi's laughter subsided as she stared up at Gilea.

"Isn't this the part where you kiss me?"

"Is it? I never seem to know." Gilea's arm trembled, but not from holding Temi's weight.

"Idiot," Temi said, closing her eyes and angling her green-painted lips toward Gilea. Gilea pulled Temi's face up halfway, sinking the rest of the way to meet her. Their lips pressed together, and the noise of the docks faded again, drowned out by the sound of blood rushing in her ears as her heart sent wave after wave coursing through her body. She clutched Temi tight to her chest, moving her lips to lay tiny kisses on Temi's. Desire rose from her body, but her mind exuded a more powerful tincture, summoning flashes of their earlier moments of connection, the comfort of wrapping around Temi's vision of Rontaia, the crumbling of her walls as Temi explored every fold and crevice of her mind.

Temi's sharp intake of breath snapped Gilea back to the moment, and she stared into Temi's wide, shiny eyes until Temi sighed contentedly and used Gilea's shoulder for leverage to pull herself back to standing.

"I would very much like to repeat that experience, in a more private venue, if such can be found." Temi did a poor job of keeping a straight face, and Gilea felt her own smile cramping the muscles in her cheeks.

"I will find us a place." Gilea offered her half-smushed tri-fry, and

Temi took it, glaring at the seagulls perched on a nearby market stall, then tore off a large strip with her teeth.

"We'll have to get some more of these, you know."

"We will. But let's get you out of this sun for a bit before we go off in search of the perfect tri-fry. There's no hurry. We've got all the time in the world."

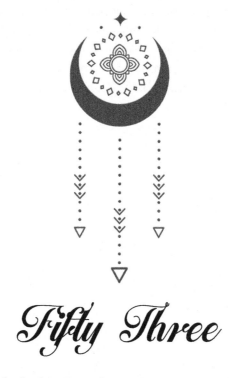

Fifty Three

Patia rested on the bed as Gero finished cleaning up his workspace and arranging the ingredients for the next day's work. Their first attempt at the Universal Tincture had been a failure, though they had been able to salvage a mid-grade meditation tincture out of it, which Patia hoped would earn a six rating from the Endulian buyers, despite its unusually thick texture. She and Gero had gone over the steps a dozen times, trying to figure out what they'd done wrong, until they realized she'd copied two of the early steps out of order, which had thrown the whole thing off. Patia ground her teeth each night thinking about her stupid mistake, which Gero had brushed off as a minor one that anyone could have made, but Patia wasn't buying it. In the first week, she had been in too much pain to think straight, but by now her elbow was mostly healed, and the pain in her tailbone only hurt if she sat for too long. It had been simple carelessness on her part, nothing more. They had another batch of skin cream to make before they could try again, but she would make damned sure not to repeat her mistake the next time around. There was little room for error, as they still had to pay Gero's rent, and earn money to reimburse the Endulian temple for Paoro's shattered containment vessel. Patia had even gotten Gero to agree to give Paoro a third of their profits from their first successful batch of the Universal Tincture, though there was no telling how long that would take. And once they'd mastered the formula, there was the small matter of deciding what to do with it. She knew the world wasn't ready for such a seismic shift, but if they could harness this power, they could achieve feats other alchemists could only dream of, and they would have riches beyond her imagining.

As Gero puttered, he kept sneaking glances in her direction, and she recognized the glint of desire in his eyes. She had taken care of his needs on a couple of occasions in the past several weeks, stroking him off awkwardly, as her right arm had still been bound in a sling, but he had accepted her caresses almost with regret. He wanted her to dominate him, needed it, and there was only so much she could do with one good arm and a bruised tailbone. She wasn't entirely sure if she was up to the task, but she hadn't had anything other than her *olli* for pleasure, and she longed for the heat of Gero's body, and of his desire. When he finished cleaning up and using the waste hole, to which he'd added a little privacy in her absence by hanging a ratty curtain, he washed his hands and brought a tray over to the bedside table, with his blue scarf draped over an assortment of objects, one of which was about the size and shape of the *olli*. Patia sat up, her heart and body stirring at the mischievous look in his eye.

"What's with the subterfuge?" she asked, reaching toward the scarf, but he brushed her hand away.

"There's no subterfuge," he said with an oddly serious tone. "But I will need you to close your eyes for a moment."

Patia pressed her eyes shut, struggling to keep a smile from blooming on her face. She felt Gero sit on the edge of the bed, lean in close, and tie the scarf around her head, covering her eyes.

"I thought you said there was no—"

"There isn't," he cut her off. "I'm going to tell you exactly what I'm doing, and when I'm doing it. And when I'm done, you're going to understand just how much I've missed you."

Patia's heart thudded in her chest, and she heard the blood rushing in her ears, felt it throbbing through her loins.

"First, I'm going to kiss you." His hands grasped her cheeks, and she felt his body heat as he leaned in, then his lips met hers. He kissed her gently at first, and she felt his hands slide down to her neck, under her robe to her shoulders and down to her breasts, which he kneaded as he took first her upper lip, then her lower, into his mouth, licking and sucking. Desire flooded her body, and she found his leg with her hand, which she slid toward his lap until he caught her wrist and placed it back on the bed. He pulled back from the kiss, and she heard him breathe heavily through his nose.

"Tonight is not about my pleasure," he said, untying her robe and pulling it apart, leaving her body tingling in the cool night air. "It's about yours, because as you've no doubt learned by now, that is all I desire." His fingers touched her outer thigh, sliding down to her knee, then crossed over to her inner thigh with a touch so light it was almost ticklish. He ran his fingers between her legs, letting the backsides of his knuckles brush across her cunt, then raking his fingertips through her pubic hair and back down, splitting so they squeezed her from both sides but did not delve within. She moaned and angled up into his hand, only to feel it melt away into the air.

"So eager," he said, his voice deep and indulgent. "So impatient. You will have your fill of pleasure tonight, but I will not be hurried." She heard the sound of two vials being unstoppered. "Before we go any further, I have a special tincture prepared for you." He placed a vial in her hand, and she raised it to her nose, sniffing.

"Soma, and seahops," she said, then sniffed again. "Lemon, and possibly eucalyptus? And is that—"

"Drink," he said, and she obeyed, downing the contents of the vial, which tasted like a meditation tincture mixed with lemon mint and sea hops. It burned her throat a little, and she coughed as she handed the vial back to him. Her head immediately grew light, and a pleasant buzz flowed over her skin.

"What is it?" she asked, her voice sounding echoey and far away. She heard the sound of a jar being unscrewed.

"It is meant to slow the passage of time even as it brings us closer together."

"I didn't think we could get any—" She gasped as his fingers slid over her cunt, coating it with an oil that could only be Rapture. His fingers inched up and down, exploring every fold and crevice, bringing a sense of languorous fullness. She angled into his touch, forcing his fingers just barely inside her, her body begging him to keep going. His fingers stilled as his thumb ran up under her clit, pressing from beneath and holding in place, and the pressure mounted, radiating outward until her whole body throbbed with budding pleasure. His thumb released, flooding her with desperation, and she gripped his thigh, digging her nails into his flesh.

"Please," she whimpered.

"Patience," he said in a soft voice, and she heard a series of metallic clicks, the sound of the *olli* being opened and loaded. Her heart drummed in her chest, and she could feel the blood coursing through her as the cold glass was leaned against her cunt.

"I'm going to push the button now." Another click, and the *olli*'s vibration shot through her, amplified by the oil and the tincture, and she was so close her breath grew short, even before the bulbed tip began moving, in wide circles at first, narrowing with each stroke until it stopped just above her clit. The tip pressed down, and she cried out as the vibrations ricocheted through her, bringing a staccato orgasm that caught her utterly by surprise. Her breath came in ragged gasps as the *olli* slid up and down, setting every one of a million nerves on fire.

"I'm going to fuck you with this *olli* now," Gero said, and Patia fumbled for him, surprisingly hard beneath his robe, and he did not stop her this time. She slid her hand into his robe, found his cock, and squeezed him tight as he slid the tip inside her, moving its curved shape so it rubbed back and forth against the spot she liked, in exactly the rhythm she would have used. She cried out again as another orgasm pulsed through her, and the *olli* slid out, then back in, faster and faster, and she tried to pump his cock in rhythm with the *olli*'s strokes but soon lost track as the vibration and the movement and the Rapture and whatever was in the tincture had her swimming in a sea of ecstasy. Gero's lips pressed against hers, and the movement of the *olli* slowed, pressing down with the tip as Gero held the vibrating shaft against her clit, sending waves of pleasure echoing through her. She bucked her hips, fucking the *olli* as he held it firmly in place until her whole body shook, and the last of her breath poured out in an animalistic groan.

She collapsed onto the bed, closing her trembling knees around his arm. He pulled the *olli* out so slowly it felt like it was a mile long, and her breath returned with a gasp. Her chest heaved, but her hand still held him firm. He had said tonight was about her pleasure, but she could feel his need rolling off him in waves, and she flashed a wicked smile as she reached down with her injured arm and gently took the *olli* from him, still feeling the vibrations reverberating inside her.

She turned partway onto her side so she could maneuver the *olli* without too much pain and touched it to the head of his cock, sliding her tongue in and out of his lips as he gasped for breath. She slid her good hand down and clenched his balls tightly, feeling his rush of pain and pleasure, his complete acquiescence to her every desire. She ran the *olli* up and down his length, which bobbed and pulsed, harder than she had ever felt him before. She hadn't seen or heard him applying the gray cream, but there was no way he was this hard on his own. She squeezed his balls and released, again and again, sometimes so tight he gave a little shout, other times so gently he moaned. Amazingly, he hadn't come yet; it must have been the effects of the tincture. She let go for long enough to maneuver the *olli* along the length of his cock, stretching the fingers of her good hand to hold it in place.

He made a sound like a wounded animal, whining with its last breath, filling her heart with delight. She clenched with all her might to keep the slippery glass tight against him as he bucked and squirmed. She tickled the underside of his balls with her other hand, and she felt his legs tremble as his whine rose to a shout. His hips bucked, and she grabbed his balls, though her elbow tweaked as she did so, and squeezed them tight, holding him firmly in place with both hands. She felt his hot mess squirt onto her stomach and legs, and she squeezed harder, and he gave another shout and came again. She slowly loosened her grip, moving the *olli* to the side, and pressed the button to stop the vibrations.

Gero reached up and untied the scarf, and their eyes met in the dim light of the candle. She pulled him in for a kiss, slow and soft, and he lay down on the bed next to her, running his hands gently over her hip.

"I see how much you missed me," she said between kisses.

"It's going to take several weeks at least to express the full extent," he replied.

"I get a sense." She kissed his nose, his forehead, both cheeks, then his lips again. "I missed you too, and you're right. We do have a lot of lost time to make up for."

Gero pulled back, his eyes deep and a little wistful, and brushed her hair out of her eyes. "How much time do you think we have?"

Patia propped herself up on her good elbow, running her fingers through his beard and cupping his cheek.

"I've spent the last sixty years believing what we have was impossible, a story told to keep people in line. But I've lived a fuller life since I've met you than I did in all those years by myself. I don't care how

270

much time we have left. I only care about spending every minute of it with you."

"Patia, are you going soft on me?"

She ran her hand along his hip, raking her fingernails down his thigh and running them lightly over the sticky head of his cock, which moved ever so slightly beneath her touch.

"I was going to ask you the same question." She leaned forward and kissed him, hard and wet, as her fingers slid over his cock and gave a little squeeze. Gero's moan sounded as much like pain as pleasure.

"Patia, I don't think—"

She grabbed him tight, and his eyes grew wide as he stiffened beneath her touch.

"You said this tincture makes time slow down. Let's see if we can make it stop altogether."

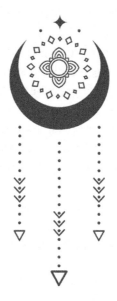

Fifty Four

"I can't believe it's still here," Gilea said as she touched Temi gently on the back and pointed. Leo's message had told her to meet him here at noon, and she'd been delighted at his choice. The clam shack with the cooling dome had been serving clams and iced beer on the space between the passenger docks and the cargo docks since before she was born, though she had only been there once, when Wulif had taken her and her mother. She had been too small to remember much except for the slimy texture of the clams.

"You know I've never eaten clams," Temi said, "but if they're anything like mussels, I'm excited to give them a try."

"You're going to love them. Hey, I think I see—"

"Leo!" Temi called, slipping from Gilea's touch and pounding across the boards toward a man with an unmistakable mop of curly hair seated at a barrel table next to an older couple. Gilea dashed to catch up, arriving just as Leo picked Temi up and swung her around, her feet almost hitting a man with gray hair and beard and a wry, amused smile on his lips.

Leo released Temi gently, turning to Gilea with open arms and a smile that was wide and wild even by his standards. Leo was a big hugger, and Gilea was not, but she threw herself into his embrace without hesitation, sinking into his comforting strength beneath his powerful body odor.

"Gil, so glad to see you! I was worried you'd decide to stay in Endulai forever and become one of those masters who just sit staring at a wall for days on end."

"I did my share of sitting and staring, but I'm ready to get out into the world again and mix it up." She pulled back, and Leo kept one hand on her shoulder for a moment, then released her and turned toward the couple seated at the table. They were both dark-skinned, in their sixties, though the man had to be close to seventy, with a scraggly gray beard jutting out above a dingy blue silk scarf. The woman was slight, with sharp eyes and a wary smile, and there was something incredibly familiar about her.

"Gilea, Temi, meet my friends Gero and Patia," Leo said. The couple nodded as their names were spoken, and Gilea pressed her hands together at her chest in greeting, sharing a knowing smile with Patia.

"Leo tells me we just missed meeting each other near Guluch," Gilea said to Patia, struggling to keep her voice level.

"He told me that too," Patia said with a hint of a smile, "though I wasn't in much shape to be meeting anyone at that moment, after what those damned swirls did to me."

"I think you landed all right, though," Gero said, sliding gnarled fingers over her shoulders.

"Idiot," she murmured, leaning her head in to touch his.

"They're going to make us some glow tubes for our sea cave roughabout," Leo said, his face stretched wide in a smile. "I've got it all mapped out. It's going to be amazing! Come on, pull up a stool and we'll get you some clams and a couple of iced beers. You'll absolutely die, they're so delicious!"

They sat nursing the dregs of their beers, empty clam shells overflowing from the bucket in the center of the table. The lively conversation, led by Leo's frenetic, tipsy attempts to engage with everyone, had subsided for a moment when the waiter arrived with five more glasses of iced beer, dappled with condensation.

Leo raised his beer, his eyes glassy from the alcohol and his smile more carefree than Gilea had seen in a long time.

"Here's to the salt air, to friends old and new, to travels past and journeys to come."

Patia's eyes twinkled as she opened her mouth to speak. Glasses hung in the air, inches apart, and all eyes turned to hers.

"To the Thousand Worlds."

Everyone clinked and drank, and Gilea closed her eyes as the cold, fizzy beer tingled down her throat. Temi leaned into her shoulder, and the buzz from the alcohol mingled with the fuzzy warmth of her heart. She floated in this moment, feeling Temi's mind cozying up to hers, and the Thousand Worlds had never seemed so far away, or so close.

Acknowledgments

This book is the product of the work of dozens of people besides myself, without whose help it never would have taken the form it now has.

My wife **Sarah,** whose patience and support buoys me on stormy seas;

My critique partner **Beth Blaufuss,** who helped me rethink the mess of a first draft, and guided and encouraged me as I worked it into its final form;

My incredible beta reader and supporter, **Susan Hancock,** who helped give me the confidence to write an older main character who was unabashedly sexual, and gave me gentle suggestions to improve her presentation;

My authenticity reader **Arina Nabais,** who helped me refine Gilea and Temi's relationship. Wherever I may have erred, it is through my own fault, not theirs;

My Shadow Spark colleague **Erika McCorkle,** who gave me excellent suggestions on a few key passages in the text;

My writer colleague **Marian L. Thorpe,** who was kind enough to help answer some questions to improve my depiction of Patia;

My cover artist, **Karkki,** whose art never ceases to inspire me;

My cover designer and editor, the inimitable **Jessica Moon** of Shadow Spark Publishing, who helped make my vision a reality and helped me avoid some major pitfalls;

My editor and formatter **Mandy Russell** of Shadow Spark Publishing, who pushed me to find the truth of the characters and their story, and designed the interior, among many other things;

My interior artist **Kriti Khare,** who drew the ethereal alchemical design on the first page of the book;

My artist **Elena Tarsius**, who drew the pages of fascinating alchemical symbols near the middle of the book;

The members of the Smutty Seven: **Krystle**, **Fiona**, **Angela**, **Connor**, **Thomas**, **Alistair**, and **Sara**, who gave me crucial feedback on some of the explicit scenes in the book;

My writer colleagues at Shadow Spark Publishing, a vibrant community of creatives who helped in countless ways throughout the process;

The book bloggers who were kind and generous enough to give this odd little book a shot, and who make the bookish world run;

And as always, the brilliant, glittering hordes of the #amwriting-fantasy community on Twitter. You are my people, and you never fail to inspire me.

Also By
Dan Fitzgerald

The Maer Cycle Trilogy:
Hollow Road
The Archive
The Place Below

The Weirdwater Confluence:
The Living Waters
The Isle of a Thousand Words (coming January 2022)

Dan Fitzgerald is the fantasy author of the Maer Cycle trilogy (character-driven low-magic fantasy) and the Weirdwater Confluence duology (sword-free fantasy with unusual love stories).

He lives in Washington, DC with his wife, twin boys, and two cats. When not writing he might be found doing yoga, gardening, cooking, or listening to French music.

Find out more about Dan and his books at
http://www.danfitzwrites.com,

or look him up on Twitter or Instagram, under the name danfitzwrites.

Kriti 2

Made in the USA
Middletown, DE
03 February 2022